Dedication

To Joy Lucille – my joyful light-bearer.

Author's Note

During the tempestuous years between 1800-1820 or the more specific "Regency" years of 1811 to 1820, it was common for the upper classes, especially the men, to drink various forms of alcohol as part of their daily life. A glass of port wine was often savored by the men after the evening meal. French brandy was considered superior and highly coveted even though England was at war with France. In these stories my characters do at times drink, and sometimes even to excess with serious consequences for their overindulgence. This is not in any way a recommendation on the part of the author or Pelican Book Group to advocate the drinking of alcohol or to abuse any substance. Laudanum is an opiate that was often prescribed medicinally (although many did become addicted to the drug). The use of these in the story are merely an attempt to use this period in history and its notorious excesses as a backdrop where appropriate.

The Captain's Conquest

Susan M. Baganz

The Captain's Conquest
COPYRIGHT 2018 by Susan M. Baganz

Contact Information: titleadmin@pelicanbookgroup.com

Scripture quotations, unless otherwise indicated are taken from the King James translation, public domain.

Cover Art by *Nicola Martinez*

Prism is a division of Pelican Ventures, LLC
www.pelicanbookgroup.com PO Box 1738 *Aztec, NM * 87410

White Rose Publishing Circle and Rosebud logo is a trademark of Pelican Ventures, LLC

Publishing History
Prism Edition, 2018
Electronic Edition ISBN 978-1-5223-9795-3
Paperback Edition ISBN 978-1-5223-9797-7
Published in the United States of America

BOOKS BY SUSAN M. BAGANZ

Black Diamond Regency Romantic Suspenses

The Baron's Blunder (Prequel) novella
The Virtuous Viscount (Book 1)
Lord Phillip's Folly (Book 2)
Sir Michael's Mayhem (Book 3)
Lord Harrow's Heart (Book 4)
The Captain's Conquest (Book 5)

Orchard Hill Contemporary Romances

Pesto & Potholes
Salsa & Speed Bumps
Feta & Freeways
Root Beer & Roadblocks
Bratwurst & Bridges
Truffles & Traffic

Historical Christmas Novellas

Fragile Blessings
Gabriel's Gift

Short Story Compilation

Little Bits O' Love

Lord, guide my heart to go where You lead.
~Miss Lucille Cameron

Victory:
νίκος nikŏs nee'-kos;
a conquest, i.e. (by implication) triumph; —victory

*But thanks be to God, which giveth us the victory
through our Lord Jesus Christ.
1 Cor. 15:57 (KJV)*

1

Spring 1814
Northern Scotland

Jared Allendale screamed as the whip flailed against his back. His once pristine uniform had been filleted and he was certain the red fibers melded with his blood.

"Tell us what you know," the Frenchie asked in stilted English. The stench of the cretin's brandy and fish-laced breath made Jared's stomach roil in protest. Half-starved, there was nothing to cast up.

"I would die before giving you what you want," he responded through gritted teeth. His head throbbed with weariness. *Kill me already. Please. Let me die rather than endure this.* He would never give Napoleon's lackeys the satisfaction of begging for his own death. He would also never give them the information they wanted on Wellington's troop movements and plans. England would beat the Little Emperor, of that he was certain.

Jared bit back a smile at the memory of his last mission where he'd infiltrated French lines. He came within a hairsbreadth of assassinating the tyrannical ruler, who marched hundreds daily to their deaths. Captured before he could accomplish his goal, he now suffered for his cocky foolishness and temporary feelings of invincibility. The whip cracked within an inch of his face. Jared grudgingly admitted his torturer was good at what he did.

"Speak, you English dog," the man growled in fury as he raised his arm again. The whip found its mark in the tender exposed skin on Jared's buttocks.

Captain Allendale screamed again and his bloodied wrists struggled against the rope that restrained him as he knees buckled. The tree he was tied to was rough, and abraded his face and torso as each lash of the leather slammed him into it. He lost count of how many lashes he'd endured.

Hadn't Paul been whipped? Jesus had. If only Jared were dying for this faith. Loyalty to mad King George and his fat, spendthrift son, the Regent, didn't seem as noble a cause. Alas, one didn't get to choose just what one would be tortured and likely killed for. In spite of its figurehead, Jared loved his English homeland. His course was set.

He longed to tell his brother not to worry over his eternal home. Jared forsook his debauchery to embrace the faith of his parents. He didn't fear death for he would see the former Lord and Lady Remington in heaven. *Oh, Dad, would you have been proud of me?*

The light of a torch came close to his face, the heat causing beads of sweat to multiply even in the coolness of the night. They never tortured him during the day except to come and poke, slap, or even haul off and punch him.

"Tell us or we will slowly bake you alive."

Of course, they couldn't throw him on a pyre and send him home in a box of ashes, they needed to hold the torch close to his backside. He screamed and pushed himself into the rough bark of the tree as if he could escape through it.

Soft fingers touched his face as a sweet, feminine voice cooed, "It wull be a'richt, mah loue." The scent of heather assailed him. Was this a new form of torture? The lyrical voice continued to whisper, "may loue, yer safe, na yin wull harm ye noo."

My love? Had they entrapped a Scottish lass to torture him? Soft lips touched his brow as the fingers tickled and tantalized in their exploration of his face. How did he come to be laying on his backside? He moaned. At least he no longer suffered the lashes and the burning. Lips found his and the sweet kiss aroused a new kind of pain. Her hands trailed down to his chest and healed his aches with their very touch. *What kind of game was this?*

Jared grabbed the woman's arms and flipped her under him. He touched her face and kissed her with all the agony and longing pent up inside. Her hands went around him, caressing his back. His torn jacket was gone.

She whimpered underneath him. He pulled back and opened his eyes to the most mystical woman he had ever encountered. Ethereal blue eyes sparkled at him in the moonlight. Her frizzy, white-blonde hair was like the finest gossamer strands of silk. And that smile as she gazed back at him, was heaven. Had an angel come to save him from his agony?

She pushed him away and he rolled to his side, allowing her freedom. She kissed him again. "Rest weel, mah loue."

He wanted more, but in a flash of white, she disappeared into the fog.

~*~

Jared awoke with the morning dew in his hair and on his clothes. The evening's night terror ended differently than all his previous experiences. He sat and stoked the fire and wondered at the image his tortured brain conjured up. He shook his head. If only a woman could take away the memories that came in the night and the very real pain that accompanied him as he was transported to those days in France, only a few years past, where he had been tortured.

He never spoke of the horror of those days, but he lived them in his dreams. He shook his head. To save scaring most proprietors of inns, he often chose to camp as he traveled, so that only the wildlife was bothered by his nightly agony.

He pulled out some bread and cheese and broke his fast. Did the sun ever go down in Scotland? It was mid-June and he swore it was dark a little over two hours a day. In a way he was grateful, for the nightmares were held at bay by the light. He stretched and warmed himself by the fire. He pulled out his pocket watch. It was still quite early. He rubbed his thumb across the engraved surface of the timepiece and remembered his brother's face as he gave it to him the last Christmas he had been home. Marcus had married Josie, and Jared recovered from a broken collarbone that conveniently kept him home to partake of his brother's happiness.

He came to appreciate a different side to his brother during those months he'd been home to recover from his captivity and torture by the French.

His brother, the upstanding virtuous noble, was willing to sacrifice his reputation, and even his life, to protect Josie. Marcus survived.

Jared shook his head. He was an uncle now, and grateful that he was not next in line for the responsibilities that weighed on his brother's shoulders. He pocketed the watch, rose to his feet, and put out the fire. He was only a few miles from Inverness. He saddled his horse and mounted.

This was his final mission for the Duke of Wellington and the Prince Regent. He'd made it clear, he was done. His time of service was over. Leave it to Nosey to give him one last mission as his *coup de grace* for his years of service.

"Retrieve this package in Scotland and return it to London and you are free of any further obligations to the Crown, except to find a wife and bounce some babies on your knee." The Duke cackled at that. Jared's reputation as a womanizer resulted in bets at Brooks as to when he would fall to the parson's mousetrap. Most assumed it would be just that, a trap. They never envisioned the rascally soldier would ever want to settle down to home and hearth.

That was if he could find a woman who would not be put off by his scars. Not quite the thing to spring on her on their wedding night, so how did one go about determining if a potential bride would be repulsed by her husband? He shrugged. He had time to figure that out. While making love in the dark was a possibility, it was never his preference in his more debauched past. But since his scars, he never made an attempt to discover how a woman would react. Reclaiming his faith precluded that option.

In spite of that, marriage was his goal. He would endure the whirl of a season in London and find himself a sweet young bride and take her to his own modest manor house close to Rose Hill and live happily ever after. Marcus managed marriage, as did Phillip, Michael, and now Theodore. He envied them all their happiness, but not the torture that it took them to get there.

He hoped he would experience an easier time of it and still find a love he could cherish. His parents modeled something rare and beautiful, and with Marcus and their sister, Henrietta, married and raising kids, he got left behind. He wanted in.

All he needed to do was get the package and return it to London, to the War Office at Whitehall. Simple. Scotland wasn't a battle zone.

He grinned to himself as Rogue, his stallion, plodded his way through the underbrush. He came far to reach the Highlands and his journey had been uncomfortable at best. He was half-way home once he got this bundle in his arms. He guided his mount down into the valley where the town was nestled. First things first. He desperately needed a bath, and a hot breakfast before he tackled his mission.

His hat sat on his head and a trickle of sweat already made its way down the side of his face as the summer sun warmed up the terrain south of Inverness. It was possible he would locate his package today.

He rode through the woods that ran along the eastern edge of River Ness, the sound of the trickling waters giving him guidance even as he traveled a road out of sight. At noon, he sat along the river as his horse drank. He enjoyed the repast the proprietor's wife kindly made up for him. He grinned. One more day and he could begin his journey back to London and home. As he leaned against the tree and watched the little circles appear in the water, he longed for his fishing pole. He would have plenty of days to enjoy that again. Maybe with his nephew, since his brother was never good at catching anything.

Jared barked out a laugh that startled his horse.

Rogue gave him a strange glance before he resumed his munching of the grass nearby. Marcus was good at almost everything he did. Jared at least was good at fishing and had been a good soldier. Retirement tantalized him with heady promises.

Get the package.

Return it to London.

Find a bride.

Return home.

Finally, these dreams were within his grasp.

He remounted and continued his journey south. Silently he cursed Wellington for making him take on this final mission. When he went in to resign he'd expected there would be no issue. Who refused a resignation and gave a fresh assignment? Apparently, Old Hawknose did. Jared respected the man but wasn't too pleased with the task. Having never been to Scotland, though, he found the scenery breathtaking. At least he wasn't riding past the bodies of the dead and dying. Noises like that haunted him as well. Would he forever be struggling with these unwanted souvenirs of war?

He stopped along the river. He was warm and close to his goal. He stripped his clothes and dove in to bathe in the sundrenched but cold waters. He emerged and had put on a fresh pair of pants when he spied her.

It was the fairy sprite from his dreams.

2

The sun shone on her and she appeared every inch the angel from the night before. Her blue eyes were wide as she gazed at him.

"You…" He could barely utter a word.

A pretty pink color suffused her cheeks and Jared remembered his undressed state. He grabbed his shirt, turned to put it on, and tucked it into his trousers. He followed it hastily with his waistcoat and jacket. His feet remained bare. Jared's heart raced. *Last night wasn't a dream? How?* He faced her. "Who are you?" he gasped.

The vision, who wore a rose-colored dress trimmed in silver, glided towards him, stopping within inches. If he reached out, he could touch her.

"A'm Lucille."

He tipped his head and nodded, waiting. When she said nothing further he pulled his head back. "Captain Jared Allendale, at your service, Miss Lucille."

"A'm a lady, Nae a lassie, but ye kin ca' me Lucy, if yi'll want. A' body else aroond 'ere does."

She reached out and touched his whiskered chin, a soft smile on her face. "Yer braw, A've ne'er seen th' lik'."

"I don't understand."

The angel frowned and then spoke with heavily accented English. "You're handsome. I've never met anyone like you."

Who was this? A Scottish lass or an English lady? "Thank you." Heat rose in his cheeks. Her hand dropped back to her side.

"Are you on a quest?" she asked in her melodic voice.

"I guess you could say that. What makes you think so?"

"Strangers come to the loch often. The monster is said only to show himself though if someone is about to die."

Jared pulled his fingers through his hair. "Monster?"

"This is Loch Ness. Surely you've heard of the monster."

"Fairy tales once upon a time, perhaps."

Her eyes grew big. "Nae, 'tis no fairy tale, m'lord."

"Captain."

Her beautiful eyes furrowed under the palest eyebrows he'd ever viewed. "Ah dinnae ken."

"I'm no lord. A plain mister who is a Captain in King George's army."

She smiled and nodded her understanding.

They stood and stared at one another. "Hae a guid day. Ah wish ye luck oan yer quest." She pulled a pink ribbon from her hair. Jared watched in fascination as the spiral locks tumbled around her pixie-shaped face. "'ere is a favor." She handed the ribbon to him.

"A favor?"

"Maidens gif knights a favor afore thay began thair quest tae bryng thaim luck. Ah gie ye mines."

He clasped the ribbon and in a whisper, she was gone.

Was this another dream?

~*~

Lucy slipped through the woods to her horse, threw herself on to his bare back and galloped toward home. She'd been struck dumb initially at the sight of that muscular yet scarred chest and back. She bit her lip. She had viewed much more than that! Nanny would be horrified if she learned about her journeys, much less the education she'd received, especially from an English laird. He may claim to not be a 'lord' but his very bearing spoke of the aristocracy.

She experienced visions of him for over a month in her dreams. She thought it was just her fanciful imaginings until she came upon him last night screaming in pain as he slept. Her heart urged her to offer comfort. She only intended to whisper and touch him, *but oh!* Her entire body grew warm, and not from the heat of a highland summer day. She hoped he would never tell of her nocturnal wanderings should he ever meet Nanny Tabor.

Since the dreams, she felt compelled to ride at night. With limited darkness anyway, there was not much opportunity. Her wraith-like appearance made her more conspicuous in the dark. White hair, skin, and horse? She might as well be a spirit. She shook her head at her silliness. God knew her heart was true and didn't fall into the superstitions of the people hereabouts. At her core, she was as British as the captain, in spite of her being raised here in the highlands, tucked away from society.

Her mother tried to raise a lady and taught her all the duties of a woman born to the peerage. It was not easy to do tucked away in their crofter's cottage on the

Aldourie estate. The Ivy Cottage was set apart from the grand house which provided privacy for Nanny Tabor, herself, and Mister Terrance McLaughly. With the passing of Lucy's mother two years hence, those lessons ceased. All Lucy understood was that this was a safe place from a real and palpable danger that lurked in her homeland.

Her brother, Damon, joined them for a time before he rebelled and ran back to father. A little over a year ago, Lucy received news that Damon died. That left her as the sole offspring of the Duke of Diamonte, not an enviable position to be in if her memories of her father proved to be true.

Her elderly Nanny and their man-of-all-work, Terrance, were her only real kin now, even though they were not related by blood. Their crofter's cottage beheld a view of the loch. The Camerons, who lived in the manse, helped provide for them out of a trust established by her mother. While they lived a simple life, Lucy was content with her basic needs met and the sense of safety.

She headed back toward the cottage, ran inside to grab her journal, and headed to the garden to sit in the shade under her favorite tree. She loved the peace and quiet of this space. To listen to the birds singing and the breeze rustling the leaves above. She pulled out the book and paged through her entries from a month past. She'd sketched the face she'd encountered in her dream. She gazed at it now and wished she could paint well. How would she capture the exact shade of his dunnock's egg blue eyes? Or hair the color of golden wheat? There was no way her pencil could ever convey the soft scratching of his whiskered face, or the tickle of those whiskers on her own cheek. She traced her own lips with her finger and remembered his kisses.

She groaned and leaned her head back. What was happening to her? At four and twenty she was quite on the shelf and had been content to be so if it meant her safety. So why this man, and why now? *God, what are You aboot?* A tremor of fear rattled her composure. She jumped to her feet and strode to the maze between their cottage and Aldourie. She ran into the entrance and jogged her way to the center where she collapsed in the man-made grotto there. It was her favorite place to pray.

~*~

Jared stood stock-still for some time after his fairy sprite disappeared. Was she for real? Part of him wanted to run after her and another wanted to strip and dive back into the cold loch. He glanced down at the ribbon in his hands. He lifted it to his nose. It was the scent from the night, heather. She was all that was lovely and pure.

She had seen him, scars and all. He must have shocked her and he assumed she was a maiden from her blush. But she had not turned away or shown horror at his scars. He gulped. If only...

No. He shook his head. He was not here for a dalliance. He was here to accomplish a mission. He found his stockings and boots and once he was packed up, he mounted Rogue and headed along the path, hoping to soon find what he sought.

It didn't take long to come upon Ivy Cottage. He dismounted and tied his horse to a branch where the stallion could graze. He strode to the front door and knocked.

A short stocky woman with reddish hair streaked with grey, answered. Her shrewd green eyes looked him up and down. He doffed his hat.

"I'm Captain Jared Allendale of the British Army. I've been commissioned by the Duke of Wellington to come here to retrieve a package and deliver it to London."

The woman's eyes grew large, her mouth dropped open, and a pudgy hand came to cover it. "Na! Is it time? Ah cannae hawp it." She stepped back and motioned for him to enter. "Dae ye hae th' code phrase?"

"A 'nighean mar a mathair." He had practiced this over and over and over to make sure he had the pronunciation correct. His success or failure depended on it. He had no clue why a phrase that meant "such a mother, such a daughter," was relevant to his mission, but it wasn't his job to question—only to do.

The woman nodded. "Dae ye hae papers?"

Jared smiled and shook his head. "Not without your code words first."

She nodded. "Chan urrainn do dhuine 'sambith seirbhis a dhéanamh do dhà mhaighstir."

Jared had memorized that phrase too so he would recognize it when he heard it. It was a quote right out of the New Testament, "no one can serve two masters." That one at least made more sense. His mission was for his king and his country, which he believed was a way to serve the sovereign King, Jesus.

He handed over the papers, which were written in English, Scots, and Gaelic.

She took them, scanned them over, and nodded. "I'll fetch Terrance. He'll get you what you want. It's not here right now."

"Kept in a safe place, I hope?" Jared raised one eyebrow.

"As safe as we could make it. I'm not sure…"

"Sure of what?"

"You'll see." She walked out the back door and yelled for the mysterious Terrance. She returned and offered Jared tea.

~*~

Terrance found her in the grotto. He was winded from traversing the maze at a faster pace than usual.

Lucy jumped to her feet and ran to his side. "Haes something ill happened?"

The older man bent at the waist, supporting his upper body with his hands on his knees. He put up one hand to indicate she should wait. When he stood, she led him to the bench in the grotto. "Tell me, please, Terrance. Ye hae me worried."

"Th' time haes come, lass."

"Fur whit?"

"Yer escort tae London tae tak' yer rightful steid thare."

"My rightful place is here with you and Nanny. Ah will nae gang."

"Aye, ye wull. Come alang."

Lucy rose and escorted her trusty retainer out of the maze and back to the cottage. She had no intention of leaving Aldourie. She wasn't sure how she could convince them to let her stay. Perhaps she could win her escort to her side?

She walked into the front drawing room, her hair still unbound. She pulled up short at the sight of her handsome stranger. "Ye?"

He was fully clothed with his cravat tied neatly. He stood when she entered, his eyes wide with shock. He turned to Nanna. "I came for a package. What kind of May-game are you playing here?"

Terrance stepped forward and handed a sealed document to Jared. "Open it, it wull explain a'."

Lucy found a chair and sat to watch this unusual tableau play out before her. Who was this man and why was he here? What kind of escort was he? He slit open the envelope and perused the document within. He shook his head and when he looked up his face wore a distinct frown. "I cannot do this unless you will travel with us, Miss Tabor."

"Na, Ah cannae gang. A'm tae auld fur sic a journey." Nanny shook her head.

Terrance spoke up. "We aye knew this day micht come. Yer tae tak' her alone. It wid be tae dangerous fur ony o' us tae come alang."

Lucy gaped to these servants she called family. "Whit? Urr ye saying ah hae tae lea wi' him?"

"I cannot escort a lone miss all the way to London without some kind of maid. Her reputation would be in tatters," Jared protested.

Lucy took umbrage at this and put on the aristocratic airs her mother taught her. "I am not so feeble that I will fall into your bed, Captain. My reputation is not a concern anyway, as I am not going anywhere, much less London."

Jared's face fell but he finally spoke in a soft voice. "I think this has been a shock to us all. Lady Penelope Diamonte, you possess a rightful place amongst the *ton* and a half-brother I believe you would enjoy meeting, as well as your nephew. All of whom will be delighted to make your acquaintance. I do not know all the whys and wherefores of your being here and my coming for you, but I have a duty to fulfill and if you are the 'package' I need to deliver, then I will do my utmost to see you there safely and with as much haste as we can manage."

Lucy put her hand to her chest. "You know my full name?"

Jared waved the paper and handed it to her.

She rose to take it and stood to read it. She'd never fainted before in her life—until now.

3

Jared caught her before she hit the ground.

Nanny jumped up and led him up the stairs to a bedroom where he set his sweet burden down. He stepped back as Nanny wafted smelling salts under the young woman's pert little nose. He shook his head. Seriously? He would have a few words to say to the Duke about this assignment to be sure.

Not only was this a woman he was to deliver, but the Black Diamond's daughter! While the Black Diamond had been banished to France because of his treasonous acts, there was no guarantee he would stay there or that his minions spread far and wide might still do his bidding.

He leaned against the wall and watched as Lady Penelope's eyes fluttered open.

It would have been safer to stay in France himself than take on this mission. *Lord, help me.*

The young woman sat up and let her legs hang off the bed. Her mussed up dress was pulled up to expose her dainty ankles and feet. Jared narrowed his eyes. She was barefoot and her feet were filthy. This was someone who would become a lady amongst the *beau monde*?

Jared pushed away from the wall. "I need to think. I'll return later."

No one barred his exit and there were no farewells. Understandable, given how he had unsettled all their lives. Correction, Wellington unsettled all their lives. Jared rode to the shore of the loch and sat down under a tree to watch the water.

Fishing, Jared. Remember fishing. You can go fishing at Rose Hill when this is over.

The cost to get there might be high. How was he to get this beautiful sprite to London? Head north to Inverness and catch a packet that would head south? He was tired of sailing. He'd rather go over land if possible but that was a long journey as well. If he could avoid staying at any posting houses he could avoid the appearances of having a mistress. While he loved a comfy bed and pillow, he feared upsetting people with his nightmares. While they didn't come every night, they came often enough. Jared leaned his head back to rest.

~*~

Lucy folded her arms across her chest as she examined her two faithful friends. Nanny and Terrence were the closest people to her, like doting grandparents. And now they wanted to foist her on an Englishman to travel with him? Even worse, he was attractive and something about him called to her heart. How could she spend time with him on that journey and not fall in love with this wounded warrior?

She'd heard his cries during the night. She'd viewed his scars in the light of day. This was a man who had suffered for a cause he believed in and he would get her to London or die trying. And where would that leave her? Alone and brokenhearted. She didn't think she could bear it.

She left the cottage, meandering down to the loch

to one of her favorite views, a rock that jutted out from under the trees. This was her home for as long as she could remember. She didn't understand why her mother ran, only that there was fear for her and her daughter's safety. Had the danger passed now? Why would she in any way be needed by the British government? She was naught but an English lady raised as a Highland miss. Her mother at least taught her proper English, but would she be able to stick to only that after these years speaking Scots and Gaelic only? She read that they spoke French in London as well. Her French was execrable.

She sighed as she looked out at the water that stretched farther to the left or right than she could see from her vantage point. She would miss this place and the people. This was home. *God, how am I to follow this man?*

She realized that God had been preparing her with the image she'd received a month ago. Was it possible to fall in love with him simply from the picture in her mind? The Captain fit every ideal that she'd dreamed of for a man.

She needed to face it. She was already half in love with him. There was no turning back from that now.

She heard his steps before she saw him.

"May I join you?"

She nodded and made a space on the rock for him.

"This is a beautiful area. In all my travels, I don't think I've ever seen the like." He gazed out at the loch and across to the cliffs on the opposite shore.

"Aye, it 'tis. I will miss it when I go."

"You'll come?"

"Yes." She glanced over at him and even in profile he was handsome. Would she regret this? "How will we travel? What is your plan to get us to London?"

"Rogue and I are tired of sailing. Would you mind traveling on horseback?"

"I would be grateful to take my mount. I'm a proficient rider, unless you expect me to ride sidesaddle, then we will have a problem."

Jared nodded. "I don't understood how women do that, to be honest. Perhaps as we get closer to London we can hire a carriage and arrive with more decorum that way. I would hate to compromise your reputation by any untoward appearance."

"That has never been anything I've needed to worry about here."

Jared pointed to her feet as she swung them off the edge of the rock. "Do you own shoes? Or at least riding boots?"

Lucy grinned. "We are not so backwards up here that I go barefoot all the time. Yes. I have shoes—and boots."

"Would you be able to depart tomorrow?"

Lucy leaned over and bumped his shoulder with her own. "Aye, I will be ready."

Jared nodded.

~*~

Jared was surprised she'd agreed to come. There was something refreshingly honest about her. She was petite in stature but obviously possessed a willfulness about her. She did not put on any airs like the misses he met in Portugal, Spain, France, or England. He sat with her as a boy and a girl. Almost as if they were…friends.

The thought jolted him. Michael and Katrina had

been friends and while they were now happily married, it had been a wild ride getting them to that point. He had never even considered being friends with a woman. But now, the idea had some tantalizing merits. He closed his eyes as the trees rustled, and he inhaled the scent that he associated with Penelope.

They sat in silence. It was a pleasant experience to do that with someone. He spent too many years alone. Slinking through woods, and past enemy lines, eavesdropping in a corner of a bar. Always alone. *Trust no one.* The only people he'd been able to talk to had been his brother, Marcus, his sister-in-law Josie, and their friends, Philip, Michael, and Theo. But even they didn't understand his deepest struggles and fears. Only Marcus was aware of the way he relived his days of torture in his dreams.

This young woman understood that, too.

"Penelope?"

"I'd prefer to be called Lucy. I've been Miss Lucille Cameron for as long as I can remember. Lady Penelope ceased to exist when my mother brought me Scotland."

"I think I understand. Lucy?"

"Hmmmm?"

"About last night…"

She turned a pretty shade of pink that matched her dress. "I often struggle to sleep so I wander and came across you." She turned to him as she pulled her knees up and hugged them to herself. He could still spy her little toes peeking out from under the hem. "You were in such agony, I thought only to help you in your distress. I didn't intend…"

"Did I hurt you?"

She shook her head and stared out onto the loch.

"I'm sorry. I didn't realize you were a real person

until you pushed me away. I thought you were a part of a new, wonderful dream."

"I'm glad I could bring you something good."

He gazed out to the loch.

Toward the middle of the water emerged a dark figure.

"Lucy, what is that?" He glanced at her. Her face had lost all color which gave her a ghostly appearance with her almost white hair. "Lucy? Are you all right?"

A lone tear escaped down her cheek. "'Tis the monster."

Jared looked out as the last of a large tail disappeared beneath the water. "Monster?"

"Legend has it someone will die."

"That's foolishness."

"You don't believe that God can give us foreshadowing of things to come?"

Jared shrugged. "Well, I believe He could, but I don't think He does."

She rose to her feet, her lips firmly closed, and her eyes the color of a sky before a storm. "Come with me."

He jumped to his feet and followed her. She took him past the crofter's cottage, into the gardens, and through a maze. She grabbed his hand as she dragged him right and left, left, right, and he lost count of the pattern. Soon they arrived at the center and a small grotto there. She let his hand go and entered. She picked up a book, paged through it, and handed it to him.

"Make sure to note the date."

He accepted the open book. Her eyes beseeched him to take her seriously. He glanced down and was shocked to see his own image in black and white.

"What…how?"

She walked away, turning her back to him as she pretended to inspect one of the bushes. "I had a dream and your image haunted me, so I drew your picture to get you out of my mind." She turned to face him. "Imagine my surprise to find you sleeping under a tree suffering terrible agonies." She walked around to stand behind him. She traced a finger down the back of his jacket. "Your scars taunt you from the past."

Jared's cravat was suddenly too tight, and he struggled to loosen it. Sweat trickled down his back, but he wanted to believe it was because of the heat of the summer day. Another part of his mind told him otherwise. He turned to face her and gazed at her face with those big blue eyes peering up at him.

Her hand came up to touch his face and he felt it to the bottom of his feet. What was this strange thing she did to him? He'd never experienced anything like it before. He dropped the book and gently clasped her arms. He searched her eyes and she gazed back at him unflinchingly. He bent his head to bring his lips to hers.

The moment their lips touched she melted against him and every nerve of his was set on fire. He broke off the kiss and stepped back abruptly. He caught her as she almost fell. He lifted her up, took her to the bench in the grotto, sat her down, and dropped to one knee in front of her. "Are you well?"

Her wide eyes gazed at him and she gently touched his face as she shook her head. "Who are you, Captain Jared Allendale? How do you come walking out of my dreams and into my life, my world? Not only will you remove me from all I know here, you make me wonder if I ever really understood myself."

Jared rose, collected her book, looked at the sketch again, and paged through other images she'd drawn. He let out his breath in a whoosh. She sketched what she probably thought was her brother, but the image was her half-brother, Sir Michael Tidley. There were more drawings of him as well, including one of him fishing at what appeared to be the pond at Rose Hill. How could she possibly…?

"Are you fey?"

"I don't know. I've never experienced this before the past month."

"You love Christ?"

Her eyes grew wide. "With all my heart and soul. I read my Bible daily and love to go to my rock to pray."

Jared paced. What was he to make of this unusual woman? Not that it mattered. They were stuck together until they reached London. Lucy's question echoed in his own mind. He wasn't quite so sure he knew who he was anymore either when he was with her.

4

Lucy slowly packed her saddle bags. They were limited by what they could take with them. She still wasn't quite sure what the future held. She recognized it would not be anything like what she had known up 'til now. The thought excited and terrified her. She was safe with Jared. There was something solid about him even though he'd obviously been deeply hurt in his past. *God, will You use me to help him heal and become whole?*

Lucy closed up the bag. She braided her out of control curls. She found a cap that she could tuck most of them into. She wore trousers under her skirts for more modesty on their journey.

She stepped out of her room and pulled up short at Jared standing in the doorway. What was it about him that took her breath away every time? How would she make it to London like this? If only he were ugly or she'd not seen that image of him a month ago. But perhaps she wouldn't be willing to trust him with her life. She suspected that their journey would not be without difficulty.

He nodded and stepped forward to grab her bags. "Have you eaten? If not, grab something so we can be on our way." He left the house to go place the bags on her horse.

She grabbed two scones and followed him out into the sunshine. She handed one to him.

"Thank you." He took a bite, reached into his

saddlebag, and pulled out a pistol. "Can you shoot?"

Lucy nodded her head and went back into the house. She emerged with her own pistol and a rifle. She attached the rifle to her saddle and slipped the pistol in the pocket of her skirt. She went back inside and returned with a small box of bullets and put that in her saddlebag as well. "Any other questions, Captain?"

He finished off his scone and grinned. "You are full of surprises, aren't you?"

She winked at him and launched herself on the back of her horse, Fiona. "So, are you planning on riding out today, or will you stand around?"

Nanny and Terrance stood on the front stoop to wave them off. Lucy had said her good byes earlier. She needed to leave and not look back or she would start crying. Her years at Ivy Cottage had been wonderful and no matter what happened from here on out, she would hold those memories as a precious treasure.

Jared mounted, and they took off on the path heading south. Lucy followed and noticed how well he sat a horse. He was a soldier through and through and whatever injuries he suffered in his past, it had not interfered in the delectable picture he painted when on the back of his stallion.

The going was slow with the shade of the forest about them as they traveled toward Loch Duntelchaig where they would set up camp for the evening. They took a short break at noon to let the horses graze while they ate and drank from the waterskins they'd filled back at the cottage. The rest of the day was quiet as they moved carefully through the woods. Neither were inclined to talk although Jared occasionally would ask how she fared.

She liked the fact that he didn't need entertainment. She was too used to being solitary to be forced to communicate non-stop. Some of the terrain was rocky and they needed to navigate around the tall hills and mountains common in the highlands. By evening they arrived at Loch Duntelclaig and set up camp. They would travel around the Loch on the morrow to continue their journey.

Lucy collected firewood as Jared skinned a rabbit he'd shot. They would eat fresh meat tonight. She returned to start the fire. She prodded it with a larger stick and went to fill their water skins from the loch. She returned to find Jared just putting the meat over the flames in a skillet he'd brought.

"Would you mind if I go clean up while this cooks?" Jared asked.

Lucy shook her head and he rose to head to the loch but went further along the shore and out of sight. She heard a splash and resisted the urge to go peek and perhaps see again his muscular form.

Heat rose in her cheeks and it wasn't from the warmth of the fire, but from her improper thoughts. When had she become so depraved? Sure, she'd been isolated and in many ways ignorant of men, but regardless. She read from her Bible about the sins of the flesh. And didn't Jesus say that even if you thought about it...?

But what had she actually thought about? God's beauty displayed in the male form. Was it wrong that clothed—or not—she found Jared to be a fine specimen of a man, scars and all? She shook her head. Four and twenty and so innocent for all of that. She hoped that her trip to London would not force her to be part of the 'season' her mother had spoken of. Balls, routes, concerts, picnics, and any other kinds of soirees terrified her.

And what about her father? Was he still alive? She was assured by the letter that he was not a threat to her anymore. Did that mean he had died? She hoped so. She barely remembered the man except that he had been cruel, and terrified her even as a little girl. She didn't understand as a child the things he spoke of at that time, but as she grew to adulthood, her mother had been more explicit in the dangers that were out there for a young lady. Dangers far more potent than her curiosity about what her escort looked like without his shirt on.

Or what his lips tasted like when awakening from the terrors of the night.

"How is the rabbit coming?"

Lucy almost dropped the pan into the fire. She hadn't even heard him approach. She checked the meat. "I think there's only a little bit of time left before we can eat."

"Would you like to go wash up while I tend to this?" Jared's hair was wet and combed back off his face. He was clean and fresh and she smelled of sweat and horse.

"Yes, thank you." She rose and sought the bend he'd come from. She stripped to her camisole, waded in, and washed herself. Goose pimples sprang up on her legs and arms and she shivered. Once she had washed the day's filth out, she dressed in clean clothes and brought her wet ones back to dry on a branch near the fire. There were going to be days where this would not be an option so she figured it was best to take care of it now.

~*~

Jared watched Lucy disappear out of sight and groaned. Just the sway of her hips was enough to push him over the edge. She was the perfect traveling companion, making no demands or unnecessary chatter. She kept up and was intelligent when he consulted with her about deviations in their path. He worried about her fair complexion, but she kept a wide brimmed hat on her head. Still her nose and cheeks were slightly pink, probably from the cooling air.

He pulled the meat from the fire and set it down to let it cool. He hoped tonight would be free of the night terrors. Although Lucy was already aware of them, he didn't want to scare her or have a repeat of that first night she'd come upon him. He wouldn't compromise his own conviction to abstain before marriage. Would his past debaucheries undermine his ability to stay pure now, when he was asleep?

He wondered if his brother, Marcus, had struggled. If he had, the 'virtuous viscount' never let on to Jared. The day after Marcus and Josie's wedding he had never seen his brother smile brighter or appear more relaxed and content. He wanted that for himself.

He was surprised out of his reverie by Lucy's return.

She draped her wet clothing over low hanging branches, not too far from his own. Her hair was wet and hung in squiggly strands down her back, almost to her waist. He hadn't realized it was that long given how tightly it curled when it was dry.

She turned and caught him looking at her like a moonstruck calf. He shook his head, gave her a lopsided grin, and said, "Supper's ready, my lady."

A frown marred her lovely features. "I'm not used to that. Miss Lucy or just Lucy, please, Captain." She came and sat nearby on a blanket she'd spread earlier. She bent her head, clasped her hands, and began to pray out loud, "Some hae meat and anna eat, and some wad eat that want it. But we hae meat and we can eat, sae let the Lord be thankit."

"Amen." He'd been shocked at her prayer. They never prayed out loud at meals in his home growing up.

They ate their food in silence and Jared took the pan to the river to wash up. When he returned, he found Lucy bundled up by the fire, laying on her side.

"Do you find it hard to sleep while the sun still shines?" he asked.

"Even though I've lived here for so long, it is still difficult. So are the longest darkest days of winter where there is little sun at all and it's so very cold."

"I can't imagine. Winters in England have been something I've anticipated. Not so much for the cold and snow, but for the comfort of being with family and friends during the holidays." He could imagine tasting the wassail bowl now.

"Will you be staying in England or returning to the war after this mission?"

"I will be resigning my commission. Wellington is aware of this. And Lucy? You are more than a mission to me." Her face grew pink as he settled down across the fire from her with his gun by his side. "Good night, Lucy."

"Guid nicht, Jared."

~*~

He was roughly jerked awake and spat at. They had blindfolded him as they often did and shoved him around and laughed as he fell. The whip cracked, and the men cackled in response as he flinched. *Don't react. Don't give them the satisfaction.* The less response he gave the sooner they would leave him to writhe in his pain and agony alone. His body didn't always correspond as he didn't know what form the next attack would take. A kick to his groin forced a groan from him. He heard at least one rib snap with the next kick to his back, he whimpered in pain. The whip cracked, and he screamed as it met with the already ripped and raw flesh on his back.

Then it happened. The soft cooing of a woman's voice. "Yer safe mah loue. Wake up 'n' come back tae me. Yer nae bein' hurt anymair."

His body relaxed at her touch and words. When her lips touched his, his heart rate sped up once again. He struggled to awaken because this was not a dream. He returned the kiss and as he pulled his head back her wide-eyed gaze looked down on him. No censure or condemnation resided there, only compassion.

"A' better?" She asked as she sat back on her heels.

Jared watched the embers of the fire behind him as they flickered across her face and frizzy hair. Her head tilted as he gazed up at her. It seemed his nightmares only happened in the two-hour time period where the sky was actually dark in the great glen they were traversing.

"Yes. I'm much better."

She smiled, jumped to her feet, and was soon on the other side of the fire, tucked in and with her back to him. He watched until her breathing slowed. He sat up and stoked the fire. It might be summer, but in the highlands, it still got chilly at night. He lay on his side and kept his eyes glued to the bewitching sprite asleep on the other side of the flames. She really needed to stop awakening him with kisses. They were almost more torture than his nightmares.

~*~

Lucy made the coffee to go with their breakfast of the left-over rabbit from the night before, which she also warmed. Jared began to stir. He stretched and rubbed his eyes and she smiled at the lovely picture he presented. He looked so lost and needy in the throes of his night terror, but he was a man filled with tightly wound strength. She sensed it when he broke off their kiss last night.

She thought he might flip her like he had a few nights past, but he awakened to reality much sooner this time. That was probably a good thing because it felt too right to be kissed by him. She didn't know if she would have the will to push him away.

"Coffee?"

"Yes." He accepted the cup as he sat up, his shirt partly open, exposing golden hairs on his chest.

She averted her eyes and heat crept up her neck.

He set his cup down. "I'm sorry, Luce. I'll be right back." In a flash, he disappeared into the woods.

When he returned, his shirt was tucked in, a cravat hastily tied, and he once again wore his waistcoat and coat. He looked more like the proper English gentleman except for his whiskers and mussed hair. He picked up his coffee, took a sip, looked across the rim, and gave her a cheeky grin.

The rogue! He knew he had discomfited her by his

dishabille. The next few weeks would be torture.

"Lucy?"

"Hmmm?"

"Would you please refrain from kissing me?"

Her mouth dropped open. "Oh, but, Ah wis ainlie trying tae ease yer suffering."

"I realize that, and I appreciate your gentle way of bringing me out of my nightmares. I enjoy your kisses. It's just, that, well, if we are to make it these next few weeks with your innocence intact, I think we need to put a ban on kissing."

Disappointment warred with delight. "Urr ye saying ye lik' mah kisses awfy much?"

She heard him bite back a chuckle. "Yes, Lucy, I am definitely saying that."

"Well, then, Ah wull huv a go tae refrain in th' future." She couldn't help but flash him a little smile and the twinkle in his eyes let her know that they were fine.

She served him his portion of their breakfast. Together they cleaned up the campsite and were soon back on their horses skirting to the north of Loch Dontelcleig.

The travel that day was uneventful, and Lucy proved her own prowess as a hunter by catching a ptarmigan. The small bird wasn't quite enough for a full meal, but she had some rolls that Nanny had given them and some cheese. In all it satisfied.

They sat by the fire and talked about their plan.

"This area is filled with mountains. I think we'd be best served to follow the rivers as much as we can." She braided her hair again as they settled in for the night in spite of the brightness of the summer sky.

"I agree. It may take us several days to Aviemore.

As long as we have water and food to eat, we should be fine. When we arrive, I'll get us a night in an inn where you can have a proper bath and meal and not sleep on a forest floor."

Lucy tilted her head, the fire once again between them. "A'm weel. This is a fin adventure."

"Fine? Until it storms, we suffer injury or one of us falls ill. If we were hiding from some threat, this wilderness is great protection, but we are not. We need to get you to London. Perhaps we should have traveled down to Fort William and caught a packet there."

"Thare ur dangers tae be hud at sea as weel 'n' i'm nae sure if ah wid git seasick or nae."

He shrugged. "You wouldn't know until you were at sea, but it is not a fun discovery."

"Ye hae experienced it?"

"No, but I've seen many who have."

Lucy poked at the fire with a stick. "It's juist as weel we travel thro' th' bens as best we kin."

"You can speak proper English, is it difficult for you to do so? I find it difficult to interpret your Gaelic."

"It has been a few years since I've even heard, much less spoken, English."

"You have a lovely Scottish accent that will make you an original. We will need to talk more so that by the time we reach London you will be more comfortable in speaking it."

"I can try."

Lucy was rewarded with a broad smile from the man across from her.

"Shall we get some rest?" Jared reclined and looked straight up at the stars. "It amazes me that my brother and friends look up at these same stars. The same space that is equal to us all in spite of the distance."

Lucy smiled as she stretched herself out under her blanket. The stars did twinkle even though the sun had not fully set and would not for several hours. "Will I get to meet your brother?"

"I hope so. Marcus is the best brother a lad could hope for. He's more of a friend."

"You miss him."

"Ay, lassie, that I do." Jared tried to mimic the Scottish brogue. The fire reflected in his eyes.

"At least you will get to see him again. My mother was all I had. She's been gone neigh on two years."

"My mother passed many years ago. I'm sorry for your loss. There is no one to replace a mother in your heart, but memories are precious friends."

Lucy smiled up at the stars. "The Bible doesn't give credence to the idea that she can watch over me, but I do trust that God sees and loves me as much or even more than she did."

"He does. Hard to understand, sometimes."

"Yes. Good night, Jared."

"Good night, my pixie girl."

Lucy rolled away from the fire with a smile on her face. He called her *his*. For the span of this trip, she belonged to someone and that felt really, really good.

5

Jared managed several nights in a row without the night terrors. They followed the river beds and had on many occasions fished for dinner. He longed to reach Aviemore so Lucy might have a few evenings of quality rest. She was pluck to the backbone and never complained, but he noticed the weariness in her eyes and the droop of her shoulders by day's end.

There was a rhythm they developed as they worked together with few words. He liked that about her most of all. She wasn't a chatterbox and didn't fill his ears with gossip or inane thoughts. Survival was the game here and he couldn't imagine any other woman of his acquaintance who would be able to make a trip like this. No, that wasn't completely true. Michael's bride, Katrina, who was also related to Jared, would have had the bottom to withstand this journey and endured much more before she was happily settled.

But who would marry Lady Penelope Diamonte? She was an heiress in her own right. He assumed that would be the case. Why else would she be asked to come back to London? She was, by rank, above his touch and he would never aspire to more than a contradance with such a lady.

Did she even know how to dance? Had her mother taught her any of the rules of society? He wondered what horrors the Duchess endured that caused her to run into hiding in Scotland. Was it possible the Duke knew where his daughter was all along?

Jared frowned. That was a possibility and given the evil the Duke was capable of, that could mean their journey could have more complications than he had hitherto anticipated.

"Why do you frown?" Lucy dropped to her knees by his side as he held the fish over the fire.

He looked at her, his little pixie, as he had taken to calling her. She didn't seem to mind the nickname. If she weren't fey, he would never have labeled her thus, but there was something otherworldly about his fairy sprite that intrigued him. Especially now with her wide blue eyes gazing at him, those pink lips exposing pearly teeth, and that pert little nose. How could he have come to adore such a face in so short a time?

He shook his head. "Unfruitful questions, since there are no answers."

She sat back on her heels. "Like what?"

He bit his lip and considered her. For all her petite stature she wasn't fragile and helpless. "Did your mother ever explain why she ran away from your father?"

Her gaze fell and she fidgeted with her fingers. "Not in specifics. As I grew she shared more of the evil he was involved in. I learned there are people who worship Satan, sometimes with more devotion and passion than those who claim to worship Jesus."

Jared nodded and appreciated her speaking in proper English even with her thick accent. "Yes. I've dealt with several of your father's minions and seen and heard some of the horrors they would inflict, especially on young women."

Lucy nodded. "He planned to take me for one of his ceremonies and my mother caught wind of it. He branded her. He is known as *the Black Diamond*."

Jared's eyebrows rose. She knew about that? "Yes, I'm aware. I've met your father and he is all you say and more."

"Then you understand why my mother fled. I was only six at the time when we escaped in the middle of the night. We assumed new identities for the trip and took a boat here. Terrance and Nanny traveled with us. My mother took all the money she could. It was sufficient to meet our needs and she worked taking in sewing to supplement our income. In spite of all that, I never wanted for anything."

"And she explained the nature of the horrors that would have occurred had you stayed?"

Lucy nodded, and a tear trickled down her cheek. "After my brother was born, my father subjected my mother to many abuses. She never explained any details."

"Probably not something you will want to share with suitors in London."

"It does nae shock ye?"

"I'm friends with the Duke's illegitimate son, Michael. He's the spitting image of your brother, by the way, so don't be startled by the resemblance when you meet him."

"I didn't know my brother as more than a wee boy. He was a few years older than me. We weren't close."

"You took on new identities."

"They won't make me change it, will they? Lady Penelope died when we left London. I became Miss Lucille Cameron when we came here. My mother has some distant relatives here and we imposed on their good nature and name."

"You would give up being the daughter of a duke? That would give you great entre to the *beau monde* and open the door to a wealth of eligible noblemen to court you."

"*Beau monde*? What is that?"

"The aristocracy, the upper ten thousand, that includes the families of dukes to barons and even knights."

Lucy stood and hugged herself. "Are you of their number?"

"My brother is a viscount, but as a second son, I have no title, only a modest income, and a small property. I would never look so high as to wed the daughter of a duke." He came to stand in front of her and placed a hand on her arm. "Why? Does being a noblewoman bother you?"

"I would rather stay Lucy Cameron."

Jared frowned. "I wish you could. I don't think you can deny your lineage or if society would let you."

"What do they have to say in the matter? I am a free agent and can choose my own destiny and path."

"Why did you choose to come with me? Surely you understood that coming to London means taking up your birthright and any inheritance that goes along with it."

Her big eyes searched his. "And what happens to you when we return? Do you drop me off at Whitehall, wave farewell, and go on your merry way?"

He gulped. That had initially been his plan, but now…? "I don't know, Lucy."

She pivoted on her heel and strode to the river's edge.

~*~

Lucy crossed her arms and stared at the rippling water. She wished it could wash away the despair that weighed on her heart. How could she explain why she came? She hadn't thought of what the end would be. Only that she was to be with this man. And that had been enough to sway her heart and mind to acquiesce to the plan to leave with him.

"Luce?"

He came up behind her. She sensed his presence even though he didn't touch her. There was a vibration between them, something that thrummed with energy, pulsed, and drew her to him. She swayed and he stepped closer, right behind her, and wrapped his arms around hers. His chin came to rest on her shoulder. His breath tickled her ear and she fought not to squirm.

"I won't abandon you, my pixie girl."

She swallowed and leaned into his strength. "I came because of you. God told me I was to go with you. I hope I did not hear Him wrong."

"It is right for you to be here with me," Jared spoke softly. "I promise not to abandon you until you're ready to send me away."

She closed her eyes and let that thought seep into her bones. His lips touched her neck. Shivers ran up her spine and back down. She let her own arms drop, turned around in the circle of his, and searched the face that had become so dear to her a month before she met him. His gaze locked with hers. She wondered if he could read her heart and how much she needed him. He bent his head and his lips met hers in the softest brush of heaven.

He released her and stepped back. "I'm sorry, Luce. I said no more kisses and I violated that."

"I didn't mind, Jared. I enjoy your kisses."

He gave her a crooked smile that made her heart do a jig. "That would be the problem. I enjoy yours as well, my pixie sprite." He sighed. "We should turn in. We have a long day and tomorrow I hope we might reach Aviemore. There you can have a warm bath and a soft bed."

She nodded and followed him back to the fire. She settled down and stared up at the sky, filled with stars, the moon, and still lit from the summer sun. She smiled to herself as she remembered Jared's words and kisses. He would not abandon her until she was ready.

What if she was never ready to let him go? The thought that her noble, albeit dubious, heritage, would preclude him from courting her, left her wanting to cry. Instead, she rolled over, and told God all about it in her prayers.

~*~

The next day was miserably damp. Jared was grateful for his cloak and hat although he was melting under the weight of its protection. Lucy had a cloak with a hood but she was still fairly wet and uncomfortable. Even though he suggested going up higher into the hills to find a cave or outcropping of some kind, she'd refused. She seemed in a funk and didn't say much of anything to him as they packed up their gear in the morning rain.

Even Rogue, as well as Lucy's mare, Fiona, seemed depressed. They took a short break for lunch and took off again.

Within a short time, Lucy screamed.

Jared turned his mount to see Fiona rear and toss

Lucy to the ground. An adder had come out of the rocks and hissed. The horse backed up, almost stepping on Lucy and the snake advanced. Jared pulled his pistol, took aim, and shot the head off the snake as it reared to strike.

~*~

Lucy closed her eyes and the sobs she choked back last night bubbled up to the surface. She turned to cast up what little she had eaten. The dead snake collapsed almost on her lap, and its blood was splatted on her coat and dress.

Jared was there in a flash and called to Fiona. The mare had trotted further back on the path. The horse returned and stood close by.

"Luce, are you hurt?"

The sobs wouldn't stop, and he pulled her into the warmth and strength of his embrace. He patted her head and whispered softly in her ear that she was safe and he was there.

Her sobs subsided. She hiccupped and pulled reluctantly away from his embrace. She instantly regretted it as the cold and damp caused her to shiver.

"Let's get you up." Jared helped her to her feet and made sure nothing was broken.

She was sure she would be sore later but was grateful that neither she nor the horse had suffered injury.

Jared and she remounted and continued down the path. As they rounded the bend they saw the city they sought. Aviemore. Jared gave a whoop and Lucy mustered a weak smile.

Within an hour, they walked into the door of the

posting inn, seeking shelter. She was surprised when Jared asked for two rooms. He was told only one was currently available. The proprietor viewed them with a suspicious gleam in his eye. She was sure she appeared quite disreputable.

"My wife and I have had a terrible journey. I'll take the one room and if you could have a bath brought up for her, I will pay extra for that."

"Urr ye sure she's yer guidwife?"

Jared looked to Lucy with one eyebrow raised.

"A'm his guidwife."

The man pushed the register before them.

Jared signed and Lucy followed his example. She was, according to the register, Mrs. Lucy Allendale.

She was led up to a small room with a bed.

Jared dropped off their luggage and said he would give her time to bathe by taking a pint down in the lobby, but to save him some water too. She blushed at the thought of him sharing her bathwater. How would this work? They weren't really married.

Lucy slipped into the warm water and did not waste much time, not knowing when Jared would return. She dressed in a long gown and was drying her hair by the fire when he returned.

"I'm afraid the water might be a mite cold."

Jared shrugged as he removed his coat and waistcoat. He sat across from her and pulled off his boots and his soaked socks.

"You're not…"

Jared grinned but shook his head. "Nae, my lady, I'll move the screen here. You don't need to see anything you don't want to, Mrs. Allendale." He slipped behind the screen and entered the water with a deep sigh.

She focused on the fire and getting her hair dry and untangled. It was a hopeless case, so she instead opted to braid it. By morning it would be dry.

"Jared?"

"Yes, my lovely wife?"

"Where will you sleep?"

"I'll throw my blanket on the floor near the fire. I'll not be bothering you any more than I have on the trail."

"Oh." Lucy grabbed a blanket from the bed and brought it over by the fire as well as one of the pillows. She crawled under the covers in bed before he emerged from behind the screen.

"Good night, my pixie wife."

"Guid nicht, mah braw guidman." She rolled over to her side and drifted to sleep vowing she would never again take for granted a good bed and a warm room.

Nor a man who would sacrifice so much of his own comfort to see to her own.

6

They spent two days in Aviemore.

Jared enjoyed walking through the small town with such a lovely lady on his arm. The villagers greeted them warmly after hearing Lucy's Scottish speech, so he spoke as little as possible. They visited the local church to sit and pray. A young minister stopped them on the way out.

"A'm vicar o' this parish. Ah hear tell this young lassie merrit 'n' Sassenach. Whit wur ye thinking, lassie? Weren't th' Scots blokes tae yer liking?"

"Both of my parents were English. Does love abide by borders?"

"Ah pray ye you don't have too much trouble. Many an Sassenach has traveled to Scotland to be married over th' anvil as it were."

"Over the anvil? You mean Gretna? I would never so dishonor my bride by engaging in that type of marriage. Besides, she is of age," Jared protested.

"Blessings on ye for a long happy marriage 'n' many bairns to bounce on your knee."

"Thank you." Jared hustled Lucy away. How could he have forgotten? His ruse of husband and wife would have served well in England, but they were in Scotland with Scottish laws and ways. How would Lucy take this news? She obviously was not aware of the traditions and customs either.

"Jared, is something the matter?"

"I'm afraid so, my pixie bride."

"You don't need to keep calling me your wife. There is no one to deceive at the moment."

Jared led her to the village green, sat her down on a bench next to him, and turned to her. He took her hands into his, raised them up, and kissed them both. "I have some disturbing news to tell you. Please forgive me."

"Forgive what, Jared? What have you done?"

"What I did was forget where I was. My lie to protect your reputation did far more than that, I'm afraid."

Her lovely eyes narrowed, and a wrinkle appeared between them above her sweet nose. "I don't understand what you are talking about."

"The vicar reminded me of a tradition in Scotland."

"The 'over the anvil' thing he mentioned? What was that about?"

"Many times, if a man wants to marry a young girl in England, but the parents refuse to give consent, they elope to Scotland. They cross the border at Gretna and can marry over the anvil. All that is required in Scotland for a marriage to be legally binding is for a man and a woman to declare they are husband and wife in front of a witness. Sometimes even a blacksmith will suffice, hence the term 'over the anvil'." He tipped his head forward and searched her eyes, willing her to connect the tradition to their own situation.

Her eyes grew wide and her mouth dropped open. "Oh, but Jared, that cannot be true. You…and I?"

"It's not pretend, Lucy. You *are* married to me. I'm sorry I wasn't able to get you a ring or a nice wedding befitting your title."

Lucy stood and paced back and forth.

Susan M. Baganz

"We're…married. In truth?"

Jared was unsure of what she might do. Would she rail at him for his error? Would she slap his face and lock him out of the room, forcing him to bed down in the stables with the horses?

Instead of anger, she turned and gave him the sweetest smile. "You don't need to sleep on the floor."

"Wait, Lucy, if you want at any point to escape this marriage, I need to sleep on the floor. We can petition for an annulment when we get to London. If we do it quietly enough…"

Lucy walked away.

Jared stood and waited for her.

She turned back to face him. "You would never want to be married to me?"

"I didn't say that. I would only want it to be by choice. Your choice. My choice."

"I could never be your choice, though, could I? You said it a few days hence, I am titled, and you are not. The thought of a marriage between us, had we met in London, would never be an option."

A weight of dread pulled Jared's heart to his toes. "That would be true."

"So, we cannot stay married."

"It would be in your best interests if we did not. Once you reach London, you will quickly forget all about me as you will have your choice of men with far more wealth, station, and without my scars."

"You think your scars would keep a woman from loving you?"

He turned away.

"Jared?"

"Let me take you back to the inn. We will continue our journey early on the morrow. I will sleep in the barn tonight. We can pretend we had a fight."

"We fought, but I would never force you to the barn."

"No, Luce, for all our sakes, I think the barn would be best."

Their walk back to the inn was accomplished in silence, each party absorbed in their own thoughts.

Jared ordered a dinner to be served in their room and departed, instructing Lucy to lock the door until he knocked in the morning.

Jared took a walk down the lane. He beat himself up for making such a grave, tactical error. His brother Marcus would insist he honor the bond. His heart struggled with the very idea of letting her go when they got to London. He'd never gotten along so well with anyone before. She enjoyed fishing and could skin a hare without casting up her accounts. Lucy was everything and more he could wish for in a wife.

But she was a duke's daughter. And not just any duke, the Duke of Diamonte, also known as the *Black Diamond*. The evil, treasonous man who now resided in France, and was considered, for all intents and purposes, dead. Not that the Duke need have any input into Lucy's life. She was of age.

Maybe that was why he needed to fetch her from Scotland. So she could take her rightful place in society. She probably possessed a trust fund and could live as she chose. She didn't need to select a husband, although why any man would not want her...

The very thought of any man marrying Lucille Cameron was like a kick in the gut. Or would she have to return to her name of Lady Penelope Diamonte? He couldn't think of her as Penelope.

Sleep eluded Jared as he wrestled with the truth of

the matter. He was in love with the daughter of an arch-enemy of Great Britain. Even apart from that, he was too far below her touch. And even if he weren't, he could not imagine saddling her with the scars in his mind or his body. He fought the urge to cry. What woman would want him?

With those depressing thoughts, he returned to the stable and found a corner in Rogue's stall. He curled up to sleep for the night.

~*~

Lucy bolted the door after her meal was brought to her. She sat down but lacked an appetite. She was Mrs. Allendale. She liked the sound of that. But Jared made it clear he didn't want to be married to her. She banked the fire and crawled into bed. She felt more alone than ever before in her life.

Would any man really love her? Was the vicar right? She may be English in her heritage, but she was by necessity, Scottish, and she could not cut off such a significant part of her existence to please any man, especially one that represented the aristocracy her father was a part of.

Why couldn't Jared love her? Was it her Scottish accent? Her lack of sophistication? It was difficult to act the proper English lady while traipsing through the highlands and camping along riverbanks, fishing, hunting, and working as a team to survive. Did that quell any possible ardor Jared could have for her? He requested no kissing. Was it because he found her kisses distasteful? She'd thought he enjoyed them.

But he called her his pixie sprite and now pixie bride. His eyes appeared warmer as if he really cared.

Was it all an act to placate her until he could dump her on the steps of Whitehall to fend for herself? Had she made the biggest mistake of her life when she'd entrusted herself to this man's care?

He would do everything to get her physically alive and well to London. She was less certain how well her heart would survive.

~*~

A knock sounded on her door in the early morning hours. She jumped out of bed and ran to the door, but remembered Jared's admonition to not unlock it. "Who is it?"

"Mrs. Allendale, your husband is on a rampage in the stable. Can you calm him?"

Lucy grabbed her cloak and shoved her bare feet in her boots, unlocked the door, and flew down the steps behind the proprietor of the inn. She entered the barn and found Jared holding a pitchfork and keeping two young stable boys at bay.

"Stay back. Don't come any closer. I know what kind of game you play." Jared's face was contorted in anger. His eyes were bloodshot and his jaw clenched tight.

Lucy wasn't sure what to do. It was one thing to kiss a man in the woods, but this was an entirely different situation. And now there was an audience. She turned to the proprietor. "He suffered horribly in the war. If you would all leave, I will take care of this."

"Are ye sure, lassie? What if he harms ye?"

"He's my husband and would nae seek to harm me. I'll be safe enough. 'Tis my own fault for banishing him here after our fight this evening."

The proprietor grinned. "Aye, spent many a night in the stables myself." He called off the boys and they left the barn.

Jared glared at her. "Who are you?"

"A friend."

"I'm a lone soldier and men do not have women for friends." In spite of his words he put down the pitchfork but still held the handle.

She took a step closer to him.

"Stay back."

"I don't think so, Jared."

"I don't want to hurt you."

"You can't hurt me more than you already have."

His eyes squinted as he frowned. She took another step. And another. And another. She was arm's length from him. "Will you give me the pitchfork?"

"Are you a fairy?"

"Do you believe in fairies?"

He shook his head and frowned.

"You call me your pixie sprite."

His eyes softened as he looked at her. "You look like one. Do you cause trouble?"

"Nae, I cause no trouble." She took one more step and reached up to touch his whiskered cheek. She held his gaze. "May I kiss you, Captain?"

He responded by putting his free arm around her and dropping his head. His lips found hers and she wondered if he had eaten as he tasted her as if he were starved. The pitchfork dropped. She pulled back and let her hand fall from his face to his chest. "Will you come back to our room for the night?"

He nodded, and she took his hand to lead him out of the stable. She walked past the proprietor and the stable hands with nary a word spoken. It was as if

Jared didn't even notice them. She led him up the stairs and once in the room she locked the door.

He spun her around, pulled her into his arms, and kissed her.

"Jared?" She managed to speak as she came up for air. "Come sit by the fire."

He followed, sat, and pulled her into his lap. His strong arms held her close as he rested his head on her chest. Lucy's earlier anger dissipated as she held him close and caressed his head, letting her hands enjoy his soft hair. He relaxed, and his grip loosened.

She struggled to rise and drag him down to the blankets on the floor. She covered him up, took off her cloak and boots, and slid back into the bed wondering what had happened to her brave soldier.

7

Jared awoke to the galloping of horses' hooves across his skull. He rolled on to his back and his hands touched the soft blanket. On one side the fire blazed, taking the early morning chill out of at least this side of the room. He turned his head the other way to find Lucy standing in front of a small mirror, braiding her hair. She was already dressed for travel.

He rose to lean on one elbow. "I don't feel well. Would it be acceptable to you if we spent one more night here?"

Lucy stopped her movements and dropped her arms. She came to sit on a chair near his pallet.

"Do you remember anything about last night?"

"No. Wait. Didn't I sleep in the stables? How did I arrive here?"

"You took exception to the stable hands and threatened them. I'm afraid that the landlord has requested, nae, insisted, on our departure today."

Jared fell back on the pillow which amplified the pounding in his head. "Did I hurt anybody?"

"Nae, they came to get your wife and I was able to get you to put down your pitchfork and join me here in our room."

"Oh, Luce, I'm sorry. I didn't—"

"Take advantage of me? No. You like me well, but fell back asleep before you could do any more beyond a few kisses."

Jared groaned. These night terrors were exactly

why he could never marry anyone, much less her. He was too dangerous. The realization stung. All his best laid plans were being obliterated on this trip. "I had better prepare for our departure."

Lucy frowned. There were dark circles under her eyes.

"Hey," he knelt before her, "are you unwell?"

She glanced at him but didn't smile. "All is as it should be. Shall I await you downstairs?"

"No." He rose, threw his things in his bag, and grabbed both his and hers as they departed the room.

Jared stopped at the desk on the way out and motioned for the proprietor's attention. "My wife tells me I was a bother last night. I apologize for any harm I may have done."

The proprietor shook his head. "A little lost sleep is all, and my boys may have lost an inch of growth, but 'twill be fine."

Jared placed a generous amount of coin on the desk. "For your hospitality to my wife and me, as well as for your troubles. I thank you."

"Best wishes to you both on your journey." With that his hand reached out to brush the coins into his open palm.

Their horses awaited them in the front of the inn, fully saddled. Jared added their bags. Both of them mounted. They followed a path that took them slightly north through the valley between some mountains until they could reach Braemar.

By mid-day, Jared was ready to quit. He stopped by the river's edge, bent alongside, and instead of drinking, dunked his head into the cold water. He pulled it up and let the water fling from his hair as he gasped for air.

Lucy dismounted and was splashed by his impromptu bath.

Jared lay back on the grass. "Lucy, I'm sorry I let you down."

Her eyes narrowed, and wrinkles appeared on her forehead. "How have you failed me?"

"I trapped you in an unwanted marriage, dragged you across country, and burdened you with my nightmares."

Lucy dropped by his side and with one hand pulled hair off his cheek. "How is your headache?"

"Would you be a sweetheart and shoot me now?" He closed his eyes and groaned.

"And where would I be? All alone in the wilderness with two horses. How am I to get to London if you are not leading the way?"

"No one would miss me," he murmured. He felt the sting of her hand on his cheek before he realized what was happening. He opened his eyes.

She rose to her feet and paced. "You infuriate me, Captain Allendale. Your morose display does not do you credit. You cajole and then insult. You are ill, and I am sorry for it, but it gives you no excuse to belittle the love some people have for you." She growled at him and stomped off into the woods.

He was still resting when she returned, dumped a pile of sticks in the clearing, and started a fire. She said not a word.

"Luce?"

She acted as if he wasn't even there. She prepared some fish she caught by herself, prayed, and ate at the fire. She never invited him over although she left some for him.

"Luce?"

He finally rose, went to the woods to relieve himself, and returned to eat. He was weak, and his head still pounded. His heart hurt as well. He was unclear about what had caused her tantrum. Her lack of chatter was now a chilling reality, rather than a comfort.

She hobbled the horses and lay down, turning her back against the fire.

"Luce? I'm sorry. I'm not even sure what I've done, but I suspect it is more than just a delay in our trip and me getting sick."

Silence met his words.

Her breathing slowed. How could she do that? Throw a fit, say nothing, and then fall asleep? He hoped he would rest tonight. The sooner they got to London the better.

~*~

More days of silence passed. She said not a word. At least not during the day. He had a suspicion she quieted his night terrors once or twice with soft words in her sweet Scottish brogue. He wanted so much more than that.

They finally reached their destination of Braemar.

~*~

Lucy was done. She was grateful for the bath, the warm food, and fresh baked bread. Oh, and tea! Blessed tea was a welcome treat. She would sleep well.

This night Jared arranged for two rooms, although he still proclaimed them husband and wife.

She climbed into the bed and savored the pillow.

She missed the stars above, but not the bugs that tried to crawl on her. She shivered at the thought. London seemed to be an ideal place to be if it meant comfort.

She had been comfortable at Aldourie. She missed her view of Loch Ness. She had been raised to not be superstitious, but she'd heard of instances where people had spied the monster and someone close to them died. She sat up suddenly, heart racing. Jared! Was Jared the one who would die?

Calm down, God is in control, not some silly monster that chooses to break the surface of the water on a given day with no clue who will be watching. Keep Jared safe, Lord. I need him—I love him.

The next morning shone bright and clear as they remounted to head to Blairgowrie, which would be their longest journey to date and would be spent largely in the mountain passes.

Jared tried to wheedle her into talking.

She finally reached her limit.

"Come on, Luce, I thought we were friends, at least. Talk to me." He leaned against a tree with his makeshift fishing pole.

"What do you want me to say?"

"Why are you angry? Doesn't the Bible say to not let the sun go down on your anger?"

"This time of year, the sun doesn't really go down at all." She wiggled her own pole.

Jared rolled his eyes and tipped his head back to rest against the tree bark. "Don't be difficult."

"Difficult?" She put her pole down. "You have no idea just how difficult I can be."

"Luce, it wasn't a challenge."

She clenched and unclenched her hands and then walked downstream a few paces. She stood there, looking up at the mountains where some wild goats grazed.

He pulled his pole out and followed her until he came right behind her. "Hey, my sweet pixie wife, can't we talk about this? The silence is killing me."

"Hmph! I thought that was what you wanted. To die single and alone."

"I never said that."

"You implied it. You offer me an annulment, refuse to be with me, and after all that you want me to shoot you because you had a headache. Where does that leave me?" She turned and faced him with tears streaming down her face. "What about what I want? I've given up everything to follow you. How do I even know you are not like my father?"

"Oh, sweetheart." He pulled her into his arms as she sobbed. "If there is one thing I do want, it's you. All of you. And you know how you can tell I'm not your father?" He pushed her back from his chest so he looked her in the eyes. "Because no matter how badly I desire you, and trust me, from that first night you kissed me, I desired you—I have not allowed myself the pleasures that are mine by rights as a husband."

"But why?"

"Because you didn't have a choice. I would never want a woman trapped into a marriage with me unless she desired that. I'm no prize. I am not worthy of being your husband—because of my lack of title, land, or lucrative finances. My pixie-bride, all I have to offer any woman is my scarred heart, body, and all the love I can muster."

"Yes."

He shook his head and tilted it as he gazed at her face and the smile there. "What?"

"Yes. If that's what you are offering, it is more than enough for this orphaned spinster who has no social airs, doesn't know how to dance, and has no desire to be in any way associated with the *Black Diamond* by birth or rank."

He shook his head, stepped back, and dropped his arms. "You can't mean that, Luce."

"Why not? How did I get that image of your face, complete with that little scar by your right ear, if God hadn't given that to me? How did it come about that a month, and several images later, you showed up on my doorstep? I'm sure the Duke of Wellington had a slew of other agents he could have sent to retrieve this "package", but no, he sent you. Could God orchestrate it all? Had He not revealed you to me in advance, I would never have been willing to go with you. I gave up everything to follow you."

"Are you fey? Have you become so much like the Scots you hold to their old Gaelic beliefs in premonitions, dreams, and other supernatural events?"

"Don't you believe God is capable of doing everything I said? Is He not sovereign over all? Doesn't He know our dreams and desires even before we do?"

Jared shook his head. "My pixie-girl, you would have me believe that our accidental marriage was preordained by God?"

Lucy put her hands on her hips and tilted her head. "Why don't you want to believe it?"

Jared turned toward the mountain and threw his head back, eyes closed. "Maybe because through all I've endured and the sins I've committed, while I know God loves, I struggle to believe He loves me. That He would give me a woman as beautiful and loving, whose very touch eases my darkest hours...well, it is hard for me to accept."

"You spoke highly of your brother and your mutual friends. Have they ever held your past against you?" Lucy's voice was soft as she touched his back with her hand.

"No. But Lucy, they don't know the details. I've lied, stolen money, virtue, and dreams. I murdered men and women. I've done everything that was asked of me for King and country, but it has blackened my soul."

"Don't you understand, Jared? Jesus scrubs the black away to reveal something fresh and new. It doesn't happen overnight. You cannot take this Scottish lassie and drop her in London at a ball and expect her to do well. It's a process. Day by day you speak to me and encourage me in all I will need when I get to town.

"God works the same way. He takes our blackened souls and starts to polish away until we come to look clean, fresh, and more like Jesus. Hasn't he already started that in you?"

Jared turned to face her. "I don't know, Luce. I'd like to believe that God saved me and hasn't left me trapped in my sin." He lifted a hand to caress her cheek. "I look at you and am reminded of all that is good and pure in this world and I fear my very presence in your life threatens that in yours."

"How so? As you said, you always treat me as a lady and even though you are legally my husband and I have even invited you to my bed, you refused because of a bigger picture in your mind. Is that so bad?"

"But I have times when I'm not myself. That pitchfork incident has never happened before that I'm aware of. I've tended to avoid sleeping in posting houses because of that. I'd prefer to experience my personal terror where it doesn't disturb anyone else."

"You've never hurt me. It's as if you knew, even before we met, that I would never harm you."

Jared shrugged and let his arm drop. "I can't trust myself. You proved it to me with the stable incident. I possessed no memory of it the next morning. I've had moments...I'm sorry, Luce, I can't talk about it."

She tilted her head. "Can't or won't? What is it you are afraid of?"

Jared shrugged.

"I'm not leaving you."

He gazed into her cerulean eyes. "Someday you will, Luce. Everyone does at some point."

8

Jared resume his fishing. Lucy hated to admit it, but he was right. At some point, everyone leaves. Her mother was gone, and Jared told her that her brother had been buried in her absence, but that he had been married and fathered a child who was now the reigning Duke.

Nanny and Terrance were old. At some point they would die, and she would have been alone at Ivy Cottage.

She had seen the monster in the Loch. A silly superstition but people died, and there was no time limit that she knew of for the 'curse' if there was one. *Foolishness*. She climbed up the mountain a ways and found an outcropping of rock where she could sit. She watched Jared. Had he fallen asleep while fishing? It wouldn't be the first time. She shook her head and couldn't help but smile. How would she ever convince him that she loved him and would never willingly leave?

A rustling alerted her to an animal nearby. While none would necessarily be dangerous, other than the adder, she was still cautious. She pulled out her pistol from her skirt pocket. Lucy rose to her feet and followed the sounds a few steps.

Something cried.

Lucy pushed through a bush to find a lamb. She looked around to see if there were any other sheep, but none could be seen or heard.

"Hi there, sweet thing," she cooed to the frightened animal. "It will be fine. I'm here to help you." She placed a hand on the soft, fuzzy head and the animal stilled. Lucy managed to loosen it from the brambles it had been trapped in. "There. You are free now. Go find your mamma."

Lucy picked her way back down the mountain until she came to the small shore by the river. She glanced up at the rocky terrain and couldn't see the little lamb. *God, thank You for that little glimpse of You and how You come and rescue me when I get stuck. Help me show Jared just how much You love him.*

She walked over to where Jared napped under the tree. His pole tugged, and she reached over to bring in the fish. It was a decent size and with the wild kale she would try to make a bit of a stew for them. She started to prepare the fish and the kale with some water from the stream and set it over the fire. She figured the aroma would soon awaken her soldier.

A soft *baaaa* came from behind her. She turned to discover the little lamb grazing near her. It would raise its head, bleat, and return to munching on the grass. His fluffy cream-colored fur contrasted with the black on his face. She smiled. He was sure a cute little animal. He came up to her and tried to nibble on her blouse. She reached forward with her other hand and was able to scratch him above his nose. Lucy grinned. "You poor little thing. You need to find your mother."

~*~

A delicious aroma dragged Jared to awareness. He shivered and rose to go sit closer to the fire as the evening chill settled over the valley. "What is that?"

A fuzzy dog nibbled on grass by Lucy.

"That is a lamb. A baby sheep. *Baaaa baaaaa.* Surely they have sheep in England."

"Well of course they do, but not wild sheep, at least I don't think we do. What is this one doing here?"

"I rescued the little guy from some brambles higher up in the mountain. He must have followed me here. He even lets me pet him."

"We'll need to find his mother if we can. I'd hate to leave it here alone when we move on."

"I couldn't find any other sheep. The goats that were on the other hill across the river have moved further up."

"Could sheep have done the same on this side?"

"Of course. But a lamb could wander quite far from his herd."

"Well, if we can't find its mother, we could cook up the mutton and eat it over the next day or so."

"You are not killing my lamb."

"*Your* lamb?"

"Yes, I've decided he is coming with us."

"You're taking a lamb to London?"

"I'm sure we'll find a wonderful home for him along the way, but we cannot leave him alone to die out here."

"And what would have happened if we had not come along when we did?"

"He would have died."

"So why do you think the outcome should be different?"

"Because we are here and can make it different."

"Just because we can doesn't mean we should."

"Just because you have a night terror doesn't mean I need to comfort you. Just because an adder threatened me, didn't mean you needed to shoot it. We are making a difference in our world wherever we go, whether we intend to or not. He comes with us."

Jared held out his bowl for her to put the food in, sat down on his side of the fire to eat, and watched the sheep and Lucy interact. It really was a cute little thing. "Fine, he can come with us, but if he wanders off, I am not searching for him."

"I'm probably a better hunter than you anyway." She handed Jared the empty dishes and sat back down, pulled out her journal and graphite, and began to write or sketch or some such thing.

He wasn't sure. He gave up, went to wash the dishes, and tidy up the campsite as they settled down for the night. When he sat back down on his blanket to finally go to sleep he looked across the fire to see Lucy on her side, facing him, with a lamb snuggled up in her arms, both asleep.

Jared lay back and stared up at the moon and stars in the partially lit night sky. *Lord, I don't get it. How could You love me? You know better than anyone all I have seen and done. Help me understand. More than anything I would love to be worthy of a lady like Lucy. She's all I would ever imagine for a wife. I don't understand this journey. Lead us, and please, keep her safe.*

The next day, Jared handed up the lamb to her on her horse. Fiona handled the additional baggage without complaint. Jared was grateful the animal did not slow them down. He was also surprised that Lucy was inclined to talk.

"What do you think I should name him?"

"He's not a pet, Luce. If you name him, you will get too attached and it will be harder to let him go."

"Maybe I won't be letting him go. I'll keep him."

"My pixie-bride, you already have so many strikes against you when you get to London. A pet lamb will not endear you to *beau monde*. You cannot afford any more things that will set you so far apart. Your accent hopefully will be considered unique. You will have no trouble with your appearance, for you are beautiful and not in any way the average English miss. You can't dance. If you don't claim your father's title and legacy, you will be hard pressed to find yourself a husband."

"In case you forgot, I've already acquired a husband. If I keep you none of that is an issue. We can go to your home in the country and our little lamb can grow big and strong there."

Jared rolled his eyes and tried to focus on the rocky path in front of him. They had climbed up higher into the hills. As cold as it got in the evening it got quite warm in the daytime. He'd already shed his greatcoat, hat, coat, waistcoat, and cravat. He felt bad for Lucy with her petticoats and camisole.

Why was she so hung up on making this marriage real? He feared he was falling in love with the sprite. If any woman could be more perfect for him, he couldn't imagine who it would be. He was already in trouble with Whitehall for the mess he made in marrying her. If he consummated the marriage, he might be in even more trouble. Why did they believe it was important for her to travel to London? She would have happily lived out her days near Aldourie and probably married some fine Scottish laird and had a cabin full of bairns to keep her busy.

Auk! He had already spent so much time in Scotland, he was starting to think Scots! He closed his eyes and cringed at the image of his lovely pixie wife embraced by another man. He had no face and yet everything inside of Jared revolted at the very idea. He might, when he was thinking clearly, see all the reasons why he should not claim her as his own, yet deep down inside, he wanted her desperately.

After dinner that evening, he glanced across the simmering embers of the fire and saw her face reflected in the glow. Her frizzy, almost white hair was unbound. Some of it rested on her shoulder. He longed to touch it and wrap it around his finger. To let his hands get buried deep in the mop of curls and inhale the scent of heather. He wasn't sure how she managed to keep that scent about her as they traveled. He could barely stand himself by day's end but Lucy...

He rubbed one hand over his eyes, pulling the eyelids shut. Why spend time obsessing over what would never be his? He rolled to his side, away from the fire, and stared out into the darkening world around him. That same darkness enfolded his soul.

~*~

The growl warned Lucy that something was amiss. She looked around in the dark and heard it again. The deep guttural sound sent shivers down her spine.

Scallywag slept sound by her side and Lucy smiled at the soft snore coming from the little lamb. She rose slowly and checked to make sure her gun was still in her pocket. She looked across the glowing embers of the fire and spied Jared struggling.

"No!" He ground out and the ferocity of the word alerted her to another nightmare.

She threw some sticks into the fire and nudged the flames to life with some dry brush. She moved around the fire to find Jared struggling and tangled up in his blankets. His hair was wet with sweat in spite of the cool evening air.

She knelt down by his side and started to coo at him in a soft voice. "Nae, my handsome soldier, ye are safe and weel then. Let me help you, mah loue." She reached to pull at the blanket and found that at some point, Jared removed his shirt. In the firelight, she could see the ugly red strips that lined his torso. She'd forgotten the sorrow of those marks. She reached forward to trace one with her finger, but his freed hand came to grab her wrist and hold it tight.

"You will not get the information you seek." His grip tightened on her wrist.

"Jared, you're hurting me. Please let me go."

"You'll not sweet talk me. I know your type." He pulled back with his other arm.

Lucy saw too late what he intended as he aimed it for her face. The impact threw her head back and tears came to her eyes, but he held her fast.

"Jared, please wake up. 'Tis Lucy, your pixie bride."

He laughed. "Nice try, but I am not married." He swung back with his fist and pulled hard on her wrist. After the crushing impact to her nose, he pushed her back and away from him.

Lucy couldn't keep the tears from falling as pain radiated in her nose and cheek. Her arm ached and her wrist hung limp. She curled up in the grass and whimpered. She shivered, not from the cold, but for the first time in their short acquaintance, she feared him.

He came to stand over her. His jaw and fists clenched. The muscles in his arms and chest were tight.

Even marred by scars, he was beautiful. His hair was mussed and golden whiskers outlined his jaw. He glared at her. "You bother me any more tonight, and worse will come to you." He strode over to grab a rope from his saddle and came back to her, pulled her arms behind her, and tied them. "That should keep you 'til morning." He strode back to his blanket by the fire, stretched out, and went back to sleep.

Lucy shivered in the dark, too far away from the fire on the cold hard ground instead of wrapped in her own blanket. She was unable to wipe away the blood that traveled down her cheek to drip into the grass and her wrist throbbed. Her neck began to send shooting pains down her arms as she lay at an awkward angle. The muscles rebelled against their recent abuse. Her head pounded. She drifted slowly into a welcome darkness.

~*~

Her sleep did not last long, the dawn lightened the sky.

Scallywag came to lie down beside her, giving her much needed warmth. The generosity and love of this little animal warmed her heart and renewed her tears. The way her body hurt didn't help. Her arms were numb, yet the throbbing in her wrist continued. She tried hard to keep the bond as loose as possible to avoid further pain. Her stomach growled, but she doubted she would be able to eat anything and keep it down.

Jared yawned and stretched. He flung off his blanket and pulled on his shirt. He looked across the fire to her empty bedroll. He jumped to his feet, scanned the area and finally turned to see her. "Luce?"

She couldn't help but recoil from him.

"What happened?" He reached to touch her cheek and she flinched. He pulled his hand back.

"Please untie me."

He loosened the knot and slid the rope off her arms.

Lucy brought her arm around and used that hand to push herself to an upright position. She brought her other arm around and checked out the black and blue wrist.

Jared reached for her.

"Do nae touch me." She shivered, struggled to her feet, and made her way to the woods to relieve herself. She returned to the fire and sat close, wrapping her blankets around her.

Scallywag chewed on grass nearby.

Jared sat on a log near her. "Lucy? Did I do this to you?"

She nodded but refused to look at him.

He groaned, rose to his feet, and stomped away with a towel. He went to the river and returned. "Let me at least try to make this better."

She watched him warily as he dabbed at her bloodied face.

"I'm afraid we'll have to wash your hair to get the blood out. Oh, Luce, I'm so sorry. Your wrist? Did I break it?"

"I don't know."

"May I?"

Lucy nodded.

He knelt before her and gently took her arm, resting it on his thigh. He probed with the lightest of touch.

She cried out from the pain.

Jared shook his head. "I'm sorrier than I could ever say, Luce. Surely now, you can see why I couldn't marry you. The sooner I can get you away from me the safer you will be." He reached for his cravat and the flattest branches he could find and bound her wrist to keep it immobile. "I'll hunt for some food. I do not think we will be traveling today."

"Nae, we need to move on."

"Rest while I fetch our breakfast, it will be a long day regardless of our plan."

She nodded, closed her eyes, and drifted into a restless sleep.

9

Jared shot a grouse, plucked it, and cooked it over the fire. He struggled to own the fact that he had assaulted his pixie bride. His knuckles ached though, giving testimony to the fact that the bruises on her face were put there by him. What was worse, was that she flinched at his touch, a touch she used to seek and encourage.

He tried to convince her that she did not want to be married to him, but now he regretted that she finally understood the most basic reason why.

It simply wasn't safe. Oh, maybe if he were locked in his own room at night with strict instructions to be left alone...but he remembered how his brother struggled with that when Marcus nursed him back to life.

His chest physically ached when he gazed upon Lucy's battered face. If she had any living male relatives, he deserved to be run through for his ill treatment of her. He shook his head. His friend and fellow spy, Sir Michael Tidley, was Lucy's half-brother. Michael was good with swords and pistols, but Jared would never defend himself in such a duel of honor, for in this instance he had no honor of his own to defend.

Jared knelt down by Lucy and roused her so she could eat. He let her rest and fed her. She eyed him warily, but he admitted he deserved it. *I'm sorry*, in no way mitigated the damage he had done to her body, heart, and their relationship. Irretrievably rent asunder and he could remember none of it. He washed up the dishes.

Lucy grabbed her things and went downstream to bathe in the cool waters.

He stirred up the fire so she could warm quicker. He made some coffee for her as well, in hopes that it would offer warmth and perk her up.

Lucy did return, followed by the little black-faced lamb, Scallywag.

Jared shook his head at the silliness of the animal, but in spite of his initial misgivings, he was now inclined to humor his pixie bride in any way possible. There was no way to sufficiently make amends, but he could at least try.

After they packed up, he helped Lucy mount and handed Scallywag up to her to ride across the front of her saddle.

"Are you sure, Lucy?"

She nodded, eyes straight ahead and jaw set. She motioned for him to lead the way along the river path.

Jared prayed. Luce was her normally taciturn self, but now a wall had been erected between them. As much as he struggled to keep the affectionate sprite at bay, now he found he would gladly trade the torture of stopping her kisses to this barrier.

~*~

Lucy spied the storm clouds before she heard the thunder. "Jared!" she yelled and trotted up alongside his stallion. "A storm. We need to seek shelter."

He looked up at the sky and nodded. "Do we have time to find a cave or outcropping of rock to hide under?"

She scanned the mountain above, in front, behind, and across from them. "Across the river there, just a little way up—a small cave."

"Can you handle fording the river on horseback?"

Lucy nodded and followed him through a shallower portion of the river to the opposite bank. Lightning now flashed across the sky and the air crackled.

Jared jumped down from his mount and assisted Lucy by taking Scallywag off first.

They led the animals up a narrow path to the tiny cave where there was enough room at the opening to fit the horses, the lamb and them, but with the way the rain started pelting down, it was marginally protective.

"We could move the horses closer to the entrance," Jared suggested.

"No, we'll sit tight here until it passes over, but it could be a long-winded storm."

"If you're not too afraid of me, we can sit close here, share a blanket, and some warmth."

Lucy stood by Fiona and glanced over to Jared. He awaited her answer. She considered her options. If she wanted to sit, she either had to cram herself into the narrower spot leading deeper into the mountain, or sit by Jared. She had thought all day about what happened last night. Her head and nose ached, and her wrist shot arrows of pain up her arm which left her in a chronic state of being on the edge of tears.

This was the man she sketched and prayed for. This was the man she had entrusted her entire life and future to as they traveled to London. She understood it was the demons inside that tortured him from his past and that Jared would never intentionally hurt her. Her

Susan M. Baganz

heart ached almost as much as her head for the agony he was going through.

"If I say I'm sorry again for what happened, will you sit by me then?"

Lucy gazed down and dropped to her knees beside him. With her one good hand, she reached out to touch Jared's whisker-hewn chin. "You would never intentionally hurt me, Jared. I don't know who you thought I was last night or who had betrayed you, but the person you raged at in the dark was not me. Yes, I got hurt and I was scared, but I forgive you." Lucy sat down by Jared's side.

He wrapped a blanket around them both. His arm wrapped around her shoulder to bring her close to him, and she nestled against the strength of his chest. Jared leaned against the wall of the cave.

From inside it looked as though they were behind a waterfall, the rain came down so fast and hard.

Lucy's eyelids grew heavy and dropped. The rhythm of the storm and the warmth of the man next to her lulled her into slumber.

~*~

When she awoke, it was dark out and the rain still came down, but not as fast.

Jared's head leaned against the wall, snoring lightly.

Scallywag was snuggled up by her feet, almost like a dog would do. His little head popped up to look at her, and he bleated to make her aware of his dissatisfaction with the way the rain was keeping him from dinner.

Lucy's stomach growled too, and she needed to

relieve herself. She sneaked further back behind the horses to take care of her business and returned to find Jared's eyes open.

"This has been a miserable trip, Luce. We should have sailed instead."

"We could have hit storms, you could have had nightmares, and we could have drowned or been set upon by pirates."

Jared smiled. "Point well taken. We're committed to this course anyway. We'll be stuck here tonight though."

Lucy sat back down. "Yes, so what keeps me safe if we cannot have space?"

"I've been pondering that all day. My brother learned to leave me be during my terrors. They don't happen every night, so I hope tonight will be free of that."

"Maybe we should pray about it."

Jared frowned. "I doubt God is concerned about my terrible dreams."

Lucy caressed his cheek with her good hand. "You couldn't be more wrong."

"Pray if you like."

Lucy left a light kiss on his cheek and grabbed one free hand while resting her broken wrist on her lap.

"God, You love Jared and are fully aware of these dark dreams that torment him. I ask, in the name of Jesus, that You would keep his mind free of these images and memories so he can rest and I can be safe. Thank You for Your protection and provision on our journey. Thank You for giving me a man to call my husband who lives and loves me as You do." She squeezed Jared's hand and let go. She rose to grab her bedroll and stretched it out. "I'm afraid we'll have to sleep side by side. There's no space for anything else and no way to build a fire in here, even if we had dry wood."

Jared went behind the horses to take care of his immediate needs and then returned. He brought his great coat and long cloak. "I suggest we use these as an extra layer of warmth."

Lucy put her coat on and lay down on her side so that her sore wrist could rest on the saddlebag Jared placed on the floor for her.

Jared dropped down on the hard ground behind her. He moved the blankets over both of them. He brought the length of his body up against hers to avoid being rained on. He draped one arm over her torso to pull her close and snug to his body. His head was behind hers and her ear was tickled by his breath before he whispered in her ear, "Sweet dreams, my pixie sprite."

"Sweet dreams, husband."

~*~

The night passed in peaceful slumber and in spite of the events of the previous evening, Lucy slept well, safe, and secure in Jared's arms. When he had awakened, he pulled her close to his body and kissed her neck. It tickled and created other new sensations as well. Lucy slid on to her back and he kept his arm wrapped around her. Their lips met.

As Jared pulled back to peer at her in the morning haze, he took in her bruises. "I'm so sorry that happened."

Lucy tried to give a smile but couldn't quite manage it. "It did. We can't erase it, Jared. I still love you."

Jared sat up. "Love? What do you know of love, sprite?"

She sat up as well, and wrapped her arms around her bent knees as she rested next to him against the damp cave wall. A shiver ran through her body. "A little, but never experienced it beyond my mother, Nanna, and Terrance. And now, you."

"I never said I loved you." His voice held a harsh edge to it.

"You didn't need to. Love speaks volumes in the words it doesn't say."

He stared at her with darkened blue eyes.

"You protect me, provide for me, are concerned for my welfare. You have never been anything but kind and considerate."

Jared shook his head. "Don't mistake duty for love. You are the daughter of a Duke, Lucy, or Penelope, whoever you are. I'm the second son of a Viscount, my brother now holds the title. I'm not in your class. I have no right to love you and already anticipate your brother calling me out for what has happened."

"A duel? What foolishness is this? First of all, he need never know what has happened. There is no point, and by the time we arrive in London the majority of my wounds will be healed. And no right to love? Who dictates to the heart where it may or may not seek love? Love is and love does, and you have loved in every action, whether you be a groom mucking out the stables, or a wealthy lord."

"I'm already in deep trouble for what has occurred on this journey. Let's not complicate it with talk of love."

"And how will society think I came to be in London since I traveled alone in your company and with your name?"

"We'll try to cover it up and get a quiet annulment. It was an accident that we even find ourselves husband and wife."

"An accidental marriage, and yet you act like it is equal to the plague—something to endure and be healed of."

"I'm sorry, Lucy. I wish I could give you what you want and tell you what you long to hear."

"No, you don't. You lie to me and to yourself and would lie to those in London. Whatever lies you tell to yourself, I know the truth and always will." She rose to her feet. "Excuse me." She exited into the cloud that blocked the cave entrance.

The rain had ended. A misty layer rested over the valley and obscured their view outside the cave since they had not managed to get very high up.

Lucy returned from taking care of her most urgent needs and Jared left to do the same. Scallywag grazed outside the cave as Lucy packed up their bedroll in anticipation of them moving on.

Jared returned. "The river has risen considerably, and I don't think we can safely cross to the other side again. There is not much of a path on this side and most of the bank is flooded."

Lucy watched the muscle in his jaw move as he clenched his teeth. Had she angered him by calling him a liar? Or was he concerned about the difficulty of their travel?

They looked out at the fog.

"Do you want to wait until we can see further?" Lucy offered.

"This journey has taken long enough. No, we'll head out, but I'll lead on foot. It will be slow, but the fog should lift in an hour or two and then we can reassess."

"Fair enough." Lucy mounted with Jared's assistance and they mutually agreed that at this pace, Scallywag could follow.

They set out into the chilled morning air.

A shiver went up her spine and she glanced around to see if anyone was there. She had a premonition that someone was, and whoever it was, was not a friend.

10

Jared's feet slipped on the muddy trail and he hoped the horses had better traction. They couldn't afford to lose a mount in these hills. Lucy's stomach grumbled as he threw her into the saddle, but she made no complaint. She had not lashed out at him for her injuries either.

He was grateful for no terrors last night. In such close quarters where could Lucy have gone to avoid his rage? Holding her close was like donning armor against the evil that threatened his mind and soul. Lucy was his light in the darkness and he dreaded the end of this journey when he would have to let her go. A part of his mind chided him for being willing to give her up. Not easily because it would never be easy to move on in life without Lucy. It would tear part of his heart out to walk away from her in London. In the short time he'd known her she had been everything and more.

She lacked all the accomplishments of a woman of the *ton*. How would she survive there? She would be a diamond of the first water wearing the pretty gowns and her hair done up. He smiled to think that even then some of her curls would likely escape. But would the *beau monde* treat her well once they heard her accent and realized she couldn't dance or even ply a fan? She may be long in the tooth by London standards, but in many ways she was as innocent as that silly lamb that followed her everywhere.

Who would be there to watch over her and protect her?

He suspected she would hate London.

If they truly were husband and wife, he could whisk her away to the country, prepare her well for a season, and show her off as the precious jewel she was.

The more rational part of his brain wanted to punch him in the nose for daring to even sniff at Lucy's skirts. He was a gentleman and a soldier, and he would do his duty. Emotions were not a part of any mission and he had forgotten that. Feelings got people killed. He could not afford to make that mistake. This was the most important mission of his life.

Jared's horse almost pushed him over as he came to the drop off of a high cliff. He looked around. How had they come to this pass? Did they have to go up or back, and then down, or risk the raging river? Jared cursed himself for his distraction.

Scallywag wandered up and around the drop off, finding a slight path that traveled steeply towards the river bank. If the lamb could make the trip down, perhaps they could as well.

He followed the animal.

They descended down beneath the cloud and found a small place to rest.

He helped Lucy off her saddle and she went to congratulate the lamb. Jared shook his head. He managed to bag a black grouse and prepared it for a mid-day meal, setting aside what they couldn't finish to eat a little later on the trail. "Lucy, we lost time yesterday. Can we push forward as long as we have light?"

His sprite looked up at him with those clear sapphire eyes and smiled. "Aye, 'twill be as you say."

Why couldn't she just get angry with him? She was too nice, too pure, too kind. He boosted her up onto the saddle and heard her loud exhale from the impact. She frowned at him. Good. Maybe she'd yell at him and affirm everything he already knew about himself.

He saddled up as they were on lower ground and they took off at a steady pace. Given the difficult terrain there were no gallops to be had, but they managed a decent trot at times.

As the sun was getting low, the temperature dropped.

Jared located a portion of the river that didn't look quite so dangerous. He took Scallywag up on Rogue with him and started across the river.

The current was stronger than anticipated and he was grateful he had tied a rope around Lucy's waist as well as his own. If one of them got knocked off…

He reached the shore and the rope went taut. He dismounted, set the lamb on the bank of the river and turned to watch Lucy's progress.

Fiona struggled against the water and did well until a large branch struck her broadside. The horse slipped and while she managed to regain her footing, the combination of the slippery saddle and the angle in which she slid caused Lucy to splash into the icy waters. She emerged and tried to stand. Fiona kept coming to the shore and Lucy held on to the saddle horn with her good hand, but she wasn't strong enough to withstand the rushing water.

Jared wrapped himself around a tree and grabbed the rope to pull Lucy ashore. He helped her up the bank and enfolded her in his arms.

She shivered and gasped for air after her dunking.

"If I'd known you wanted to bathe right away, we could have arranged it, Luce."

That got a smile out of her. The fear he didn't recognize at first began to dissipate and he couldn't resist placing a kiss on her slightly blue lips. All in the interest of restoring circulation and warming her up, of course.

Lucy returned the kiss and wrapped her arms around his neck to hold him closer.

Jared was the first to come back to his senses. He pulled back. Her cheeks and lips were both flushed with a healthy pink color. He couldn't hide his self-satisfied grin. He hugged her close. "Let me get a fire started so you can warm up. Get out of those wet clothes and put something dry on."

Lucy went to her saddlebag to get her stuff and went behind some trees to change.

Jared stood there for some time wishing...he shook his head to get images out of his mind that he had no right entertaining. He went about building the fire and warming up the meat they had not finished.

Lucy came out and hung her wet clothes on nearby branches to dry.

Jared had already unrolled her blankets.

She settled down across the fire and ate in silence.

"Are you well, my pixie bride?"

"Well enough. You had good foresight to use the rope. Thank you for pulling me to safety."

"Holding you in my arms was thanks enough. I hope you can sleep well."

"Jared?"

"Hmmm?"

"You seemed to sleep better when we, um, cozied up last night. Perhaps we should try that again?"

"I managed one night without ravishing you, but not for lack of desire. It is better for your virtue that we stay on opposite sides of the fire. Which also means that you let me battle my demons on my own should they arrive."

"Interesting choice of words, Captain."

"'Tis how it feels when the past rises up and forces me to relive it."

The corners of Lucy's lips drooped and she yawned. "I will honor your request, sir."

"Thanks, sprite, I would hate it should something bad happen again."

Lucy nodded to him and stretched out. She wrapped up in her blankets with her wounded arm elevated by the saddle bag. Her breathing slowed and the worry lines eased away from her forehead.

Jared was fascinated by the way her lashes fanned against her cheeks. The fire splashed light here and there in a constant changing watercolor painting that was mesmerizing to watch. He prayed he could be the man she thought he was. More than that, he prayed that tonight he would sleep peacefully.

~*~

Lucy struggled to consciousness at the sound of rustling. Someone or something was out there. She shivered and reached for her gun. She closed her eyes, prayed, opened them again, and waited for them to adjust to the dark. She heard the rustling again.

Something emerge from the brush and the eyes glowed golden. It crept towards Jared.

Lucy raised the pistol slowly and pulled the safety.

The being stopped for a moment, growled low and

deep, and took another step forward.

Lucy pulled the trigger. The report jolted her.

Whatever it was howled and dropped.

Lucy cocked the trigger back, rose to her feet. and came around the fire to the far side.

Jared stirred.

A large wildcat lay with a bullet hole between his eyes. No movement or breath.

She pocketed the pistol, and went back to Jared.

He struggled to sit and rubbed his eyes. "Luce?"

"We had a visitor."

He looked to the large animal who sprawled too close for comfort. "How…?"

Lucy bent to add kindling to the fire. Due to the moisture in the sticks it grew smoky. Lucy coughed and went back to her pallet and sleeping lamb. She reclined.

"You are fey, aren't you?"

"Not in the way of the Gaelic tradition. I have no supernatural powers except what God gives me in any given moment and then I am a vehicle for His work."

"Do you think He brought you into my life because I needed you to be a vehicle for His work in my heart?"

Lucy stared at the diamonds in the night sky as they twinkled above. "You probably know the answer to that if you asked the question."

She heard no response and turned her head.

Jared was sitting up and staring in to the fire.

"Does it bother you that He would go through such trouble for you?"

"It bothers me that he would put an innocent woman in danger for me. How do I reconcile a loving God with that?"

"I didn't balk for long at His leading to come with you, Jared. He paved the way to make me willing and I'm glad He did. I believe this adventure is doing a work deep inside of me."

"You think God brought me to you as well?"

"Maybe. God knew we needed each other to do the work He has called us to do, in each other."

"You've been beaten up, almost drowned, and saved me from a wildcat attack."

"You killed an adder for me. You also saved me from finding my security in safety and showed me that I have more to offer this world than drawings and dreams."

Jared shook his head. "I can't see that as enough of a benefit for what we've already been through and we are a long way from the end of our journey. I worry about my ability to keep you safe."

"Did it ever occur to you that it's not your job to keep me safe? It's God's. God was the one to awaken me to the danger and give me that shot. God was the one who led you to tie a rope around us both to ensure our safety. God was even with me after you attacked me. Jared, you had rage so deep I have no doubt that if I had been a real threat to you, you might have killed me. God stayed your hand."

Jared reclined on his back to look up at the stars. "I never knew when I was in Portugal, Spain, France, and even at our family's estate, Rose Hill, that someone like you was looking up at the same stars and that God was connecting the dots to bring us together."

Lucy smiled and closed her eyes.

~*~

A day later they reached Blairgowrie. Lucy was grateful for a hot bath and the opportunity to wash clothes. The hot meal of soup, fresh cooked bread, and a meat pie were like slices of heaven.

Jared had kept a respectful distance but playfully referred to her as 'sprite' or 'his pixie bride'.

She loved the way he said those words in his proper British accent. At the inn in Blairgowrie there was only one room available and she felt bad that he once again slept on the floor in deference to her. He even bought her a new dress and replaced her boots.

They started the journey to Perth on a more established road.

~*~

Tension rose within Jared as they headed south. He wasn't sure why, but now that they were done with traveling through the mountain paths, he feared there might be other, larger dangers that could await them. While the Duke of Diamonte had been banished, he did have minions all over England and he had no doubt that if they could interfere with Lucy's journey, they would.

That is, if they knew about it. He hoped they didn't.

11

Jared led the way through the door of the Rooster's Crow in Perth. He arranged for a hot bath for Lucy and left her to it while he sat in the public room with a pint of ale. He was surprised to see Lord Alfred Minter walk through the doors.

"Captain Allendale, what a pleasure to see you here. What brings you to this neck of the woods? Have the British decided to take over Scotland?"

Jared raised his mug. "Ferdie, one could say the same of you."

Lord Minter waved a hand in dismissal. "Same old story. Some ancient relative dies and leaves an inheritance of a pile of stone that is supposed to have some historical significance. In reality all it will do is suck me dry if I try to make it even modestly habitable. Because of that I've chosen to sell and came here to finalize the deal."

"Who would purchase a pile of rocks in the middle of Scotland?"

"Some dude called McAllister. He had the money, but I will admit he was creepy."

Jared traced his memory back. He'd overheard unsavory rumors about McAllister and a possible connection to the Black Diamond.

The hair on the back of Jared's head stood on end. One of Diamonte's minions was close. He needed to get Lucy out of here as quickly as possible.

He encouraged Alfie to join him for a few rounds

and when the young lord was asleep at the table, Jared rose and headed up to the room. He rapped three times and gave the lamb's name.

Lucy opened the door, gun in hand. She closed it behind him and turned the key in the lock.

"You bathed but have not dressed?" he asked.

"Something's amiss."

"What? What do you know?"

She pocketed her gun and went to sit down, but her right foot beat a tattoo on the wooden slats of the room. "Nothing. We need to leave. Go ahead and bathe, but then we must be gone."

Jared went behind the screen, stripped, and slipped into the lukewarm water.

"What kept you so long downstairs?"

"An acquaintance walked into the public room. He talked and I plied him with several pints of ale. He's asleep for the nonce, but you are right, we need to leave." He poured a pail of water over his head to rinse out the soap and stood to dry off and change. "I'm sorry that you don't get a soft bed tonight. Do you think Fiona can handle a few hours of riding?"

"She is a sturdy horse. It won't be a problem."

Jared dressed and repacked his saddle bag. He grabbed a roll off the tray and sipped some cool tea. Lucy methodically packed up the leftover food in a napkin to take with them. She threw her cloak on.

"I'm ready when you are."

"We need to exit out the back, Luce. I can't take you through the public room and risk you being seen by Lord Minter or anyone else. He recognized me and may have no idea who you are, but if I claim you as my wife to him, I can guarantee it will spread like wildfire through London within a week."

Lucy nodded.

Jared was proud to be with a woman who was not prone to hysterics and was active in resolving the issue, instead of fighting him over details or talking it to death.

They stole down the back stairs and managed to sneak into the stables, saddled their horses, and led Scallywag out. They walked into the woods and around the village at least a mile before mounting and galloping south.

The lamb rested across Jared's lap.

The path to Kinross was long and winding. After a few hours, they dismounted and moved into the woods until they found a clearing. They decided against a fire for the night and snuggled up close together for warmth as both fell into an exhausted slumber.

~*~

Jared awoke the next morning aware of the soft scent of heather and the tickle of hair against his face. He smiled. No matter how difficult things had been, this woman was game to tackle it with no missishness. He hugged Lucy tight.

She sighed and stretched.

What would it be like to wake up to this woman every day for the rest of his life? He had consistently seen her at her worse and she had seen him at his. He glanced at her bandaged wrist. It was like pouring a bucket of ice water over his ardor. There was no way. Lucy deserved far better than him when it came to a life-mate.

"Morning, Jared." Lucy managed to face him and

support herself on her elbow. She bent over and kissed his cheek. "Shall we go outwit my father's minions?"

"We don't even know for sure they are here." Jared rose to his knees facing her and bent forward to kiss her cute little nose. "But let's outfox them anyway." He helped her to her feet.

Together they packed up their bedding. They had a quick bite of what little food was left.

They took to the road but at any sign of a conveyance or traveler from any direction, they escaped into the woods. When they were surrounded by pastures, they gave the horses their heads and galloped.

They reached Kinross but avoided the main posting inn and stayed in one that was not as well kept.

Jared hated doing that, but figured it would be easier to get in and out. He really wanted Lucy to have the opportunity for a bath and a real bed, even if only for a few hours. He took care to order everything and sat downstairs with a pint of ale watching and listening as he had done so often through the years. He was disappointed and relieved to learn nothing that could in any way be alarming. He collected food he had purchased from the cook and took it up to the room.

Lucy was fully dressed in cleaner clothes and resting on the bed. He bent to give her a kiss and she gave a little smile, sighed, and never opened her eyes. He looked longingly at the bed. Twice now, for the sake of mutual warmth, they had shared body heat. Tonight, however, he had no such excuse, no matter how much he longed for the comfort of that mattress, pillow, and woman.

He changed his clothes quickly and stretched with

a blanket on the floor by the fire.

A few hours later a commotion was heard in the hallway. A body banged against their locked door.

Jared shot to his feet and readied his gun.

Lucy jumped up and did the same.

Loud questions were heard. A deep male voice, in French, looking for a Scots woman and Englishman traveling together.

Jared and Lucy looked at each other in alarm.

They heard the proprietor lie to the man and lure him down the stairs with the promise of some ale for his troubles.

Jared peeked out the door. The hallway was empty. The only way out of the first floor was down through the common room. He stepped back into the room and saw Lucy don her cloak.

Their eyes locked and time stood still. "Are you sure, Luce?"

She shook her head and went to throw open the window. "It's the only way."

Jared strode across the room, picked up their bags, and tossed them out the window, grateful their room was on the back side of the shoddy inn. He stepped out onto a smaller overhang and helped Lucy out. He balanced on the roof as Lucy poised to climb down a trellis. "Careful," he whispered.

She dropped the last few feet to the ground and grinned.

He came down beside her, grabbed the saddlebags.

Jared headed for the stables.

Lucy stayed hidden in the woods.

Jared went in to saddle up the horses and load the bags. He led them out with Scallywag following dutifully behind.

Once mounted, they traveled through the woods for many miles before they felt it was safe to take to the road. They traveled most of the night.

Jared decided to stop and helped a drooping Lucy off her horse. They set out their bedrolls and lay together for warmth. Jared found he didn't feel quite so bad that he was deprived of a soft mattress if the alternative was inhaling Lucy's heather scent and feeling her petite frame snuggled up to his. His only regret was that he didn't smell anywhere as good and he hoped she didn't mind too terribly.

~*~

Lucy didn't mind anything as long as Jared was close. He would always protect her or die trying and she would do anything to keep him from that fate. She took several deep breaths to slow her heartbeat down. As the fear and anxiety of their escape waned in the moonlight she grew so weary and fought to keep her seat. She was grateful he noticed, cared, and brought them here. Sleep came quickly.

At dawn, she turned in the circle of Jared's arm. He moved to his back and she cozied up alongside his length. She could feel his heart beating, steady, and strong. This was the third time they had, of necessity, slept so close together, and Jared did not have any nightmares. She wasn't sure if Jared was aware of that. He didn't have them every night, but she couldn't recall him having one since she'd been hit.

He kissed the top of her head and she leaned her face up to see if she could snag another on her lips. She smiled in satisfaction when he did kiss her again.

"Good morning, my pixie bride."

"Good morning, my handsome and noble husband."

His lazy smile faded. "I deserve neither of those compliments, but I thank you anyway."

They both rose to their feet and prepared for their journey.

At noon, they came upon a small thatched roof cottage with an older lady who called to them as they were passing by. "Come, you two weary travelers, come and break bread with me."

The woman's hair was pulled back in a cap, her dress was worn, and her shoulders hunched. She was probably lonely.

Lucy nodded to Jared who spoke for them both.

"We are grateful for your hospitality."

They dismounted and entered the tiny cottage to partake of cabbage soup and fresh baked bread.

Lucy thought it was divine.

Miss Angstrom, was a spinster who had cared for her mother up until her death, and was lonely. She stared at Lucy.

"Miss Angstrom, are you weel then?" Lucy asked, an edge of fear creeping up as she returned the woman's stare.

"You, my dear, are in some kind of trouble. This handsome man is assisting you. If we dye your hair, it will be harder for them to find you."

"We are not sure if we are in trouble or not, but we are being careful," Jared answered.

Lucy touched Jared's sleeve. "She is not a threat." Lucy turned to Miss Angstrom. "You have a suggestion for us?"

The older woman nodded her head and smiled. "I

can dye your hair a soft brown. Black would be too dramatic with your pale complexion."

"How would you do this?" Jared asked.

"With some herbs applied to her hair. They might tame some of that curl too. The entire process would take about an hour. Can you spare the time? I would like to help."

Lucy looked to Jared. "It would help me to not be so distinctive."

"How would they even know? You've been hidden away for years."

"My dad knew my hair color and the curl. He would have expected that would not change."

Jared glanced from one woman to the next and nodded his head. "Then let us proceed quickly. We have much ground to cover."

Jared was shooed to the small living area where he was invited to stretch out on the large divan as long as he removed his boots. He took her up on that offer and dozed.

Lucy allowed Miss Angstrom her way with the hair. The sweet lady hummed as she worked, and Lucy couldn't help but yawn and close her eyes. Miss Angstrom washed out the dye and combed through the snarls in Lucy's hair, then braided and put it up for her. She finally showed Lucy her reflection in the mirror.

Lucy gasped. She appeared so different with her hair a soft brown. Her bruise was more yellow.

Miss Angstrom applied some salve and something else to minimize the color.

"Miss Angstrom, have you ever thought to be a lady's maid? You work wonders with hair and I'm sure you would be a great asset to any woman of quality."

The older woman stood back and bit her lip. "Ah prayed fur God tae send me someone wi' a clear message o' His wull fur me."

"So, you would be willing to give up your little cottage for a life in service?"

"Aye, if 'twer for a lady like yourself. I would pack up instantly and go with you."

"Why?"

"Ah prayed, ye came 'n' brought up th' subject. It must be God's will, if ye'll have me.

Lucy rose from her chair and went to where Jared dozed. She bent down to give him a kiss by his ear and blew at it. He moved his shoulder to cut off her access and opened his eyes. She moved back and he opened his eyes wider and rubbed them as he sat up straight.

"Luce?"

"Aye, 'tis me, mah loue. I have acquired a lady's maid for myself."

Jared looked from Lucy to Miss Angstrom. "You want to become an abigail in London?"

Miss Angstrom nodded her head vigorously.

"Why?"

"Ah have nothing left 'ere 'n' a'm needin' employment."

Jared looked to Lucy. "How do we transport a maid and her belongings to London given our current circumstances?"

"Ah have a carriage, though it's not fancy. Ah have two fine horses tae pull it."

"May I see it?"

Miss Angstrom smiled and escorted them to the small stable where two sturdy horses raised their heads to appraise the visitors. The carriage was well-maintained and while not of quality of a Duke, nor even as nice as the one Jared's brother drove, it was better than most travel carriages he'd seen.

"This would do well. When could you be ready to depart? I am willing to pay you in full for the carriage and horses when we reach London."

"Do not worry aboot that. Ah could be ready within the hour."

"Luce?"

Lucy nodded and smiled. "I must know your first name though, as it is the fashion to prefer to just use a plain name for those in service."

Miss Angstrom bobbed a curtsy. "Aye, milady, I be Agnes."

"Well, Agnes, I believe I've acquired a lady's maid. Let us prepare for our journey."

Lucy packed up food and supplies in the kitchen and they transferred the saddlebags to the boot of the carriage along with Agnes's trunk.

Agnes also pulled out some dresses her mother used to wear as many could be made to fit Lucy and were brought along for the maid to alter.

~*~

Within the hour, the horses were harnessed and ready to go, with Rogue and Fiona tied on behind. Lucy wore a bonnet and a nice dress and looked so different, Jared was certain she wouldn't be identified as the Duke's daughter by any of that man's minions. If Jared tried, he could not have planned for a better disguise.

Agnes had even darkened his own hair color and as long as he shaved he would not be easily discovered.

He handed the women into the carriage leaving the cottage stripped of as much as they could manage to take that they thought could be useful. They would reach another town by evening and 'Miss Abernanthy', as Lucy would go by, would get a room with her maid. The 'coachman', Jared, would bed down in the stable. At least, that was his plan, he needed to discuss it with Lucy first.

Shy of town he pulled over and leaned in to talk to the women and lay out his plan.

Lucy would have none of it.

"No. You will sleep in my room as usual, for you are my husband. If you want us to be Mr. and Mrs. Allendale I would agree to that, but none other."

"Come on, Luce," he pleaded.

Lucy remained steadfast. "I'm sorry if I disappoint you, Jared, but remember your night terrors. I would hate to be evicted because my coachman tried to defend the stable with a pitchfork again."

Jared's blood chilled. "I don't know that it's safe for me to be with you either."

"I would feel safer with you there too in case our disguise doesn't work."

Jared sighed and nodded his head. "You win this round, my pixie bride." He tipped his hat, secured the door, and resumed with the horses. When had things spun out of control?

Then he remembered. His life had spun out of control the day he met the sprite who now sat inside the carriage. And He thanked God for disturbing his life with his accidental wife.

12

They pulled up to the inn later in the evening.

Jared assisted the ladies as they exited the carriage. He went in with Lucy on his arm and Agnes following. "A room for my wife and I, and another for her abigail, please." Jared slid a coin across the counter.

The stout innkeeper slid it in his pocket while having Jared sign the register.

The keys were given, a bath ordered, as well as a hot meal, and they left to go to the room.

Jared departed while Lucy bathed and returned later to use the last of the water. It was a relief to get the dirt from the road off his body.

They settled down as they usually did, Lucy in the bed and him on the floor across the room. "G'night, my pixie bride."

"Good night, my handsome husband."

~*~

Jared heard the heavy breathing before he saw the enemy but it was too late to escape their clutches. Pain radiated through his skull as he was struck. He dropped like a rock. He struggled to maintain consciousness so he could hear what they said as they trussed him up like a Christmas goose.

"Pat him down for identification."

Jared groaned at the indecent search. The sound earned him a kick to his groin. Tears escaped as he gritted his teeth to endure the onslaught. He was hauled to his feet but couldn't stand and could hardly see out of one eye. The foul-smelling animal in front of him growled and spoke to him in rapid gutter French that was too fast for him to understand.

"Je n'ai pas ce que vous voulez," Jared gasped. "I do not have what you want."

A sweet humming penetrated the dark and pain. His attackers disappeared, and a welcoming darkness wrapped around him.

~*~

Jared awoke the next morning, tangled in his blankets. He sat up.

Lucy stretched as she awoke, much like a cat would. She looked across the room and gave him a sweet smile.

"Did you sleep weel then, Jared?"

He frowned. He was as exhausted as a hangover, or the feeling he often had after a night terror. He shook his head. "I think not. Did I awaken you?"

Lucy was out of the bed and dainty feet peeked out from under her nightrail. She threw a robe on and came to kneel beside him. Her eyes were a cloudy blue. "I didn't know what to do. Someday, will you tell me all that happened to you? The way you reacted to what was happening physically almost made me wonder if demons were here to beat you up. I stayed away as you instructed. I prayed and hummed a song we used to sing at church. It worked. You relaxed and soon you were snoring again."

"I will have you know that Captains do not snore."

Lucy smiled. "Mine does, and it bothers me not a whit, mah loue." She kissed his lips and he growled as he returned it. She pulled away and danced across the room.

Jared's heart beat faster and every muscle poised to give chase and claim another kiss, or more. She slipped behind the screen to change and Jared fell back to the floor with his arm thrown over his eyes. He tried to concentrate on anything but the woman on the other end of the room.

She'd mentioned that she hummed a tune during his night terror and that doing so eased his fear and brought him out of the agony. Was that all he needed? Someone who could talk, sing, or hum him back from the edge? She once again lovingly gave of herself for him. He was grateful she had not tried to physically touch him, although given the nature of his dream, he doubted he would have been able to harm her, but he could never predict when they would come or what form they would take.

Lucy packed up her belongings.

He rose to finish his ablutions and to pack as well.

After a hasty breakfast, Jared loaded up the coach along with the lamb and two women. Rogue and Fiona were again tethered behind.

Jared took the bench seat and with a mild-mannered click of his tongue the two horses pulling the carriage lunged forward to cover the miles. It was with one saddlebag and a horse that he'd traveled north. He'd certainly acquired far more than that for the trip south. He was surprised by the smile that he couldn't shake.

His pixie bride was slowly being transformed on this journey from a backwoods Scottish peasant girl to the lady she was by birth. As good as that was for her, it would show her even more the disparity in their stations by the time they reached London. When they crossed the border, she would need to adopt her own real identity. And that would mean separate rooms and no acknowledgement of her as his wife.

The very thought depressed him. The one woman in all the world he could image sharing his life with was his for the taking. Now. But in a few weeks, she would be beyond his grasp. She would have given herself to him gladly and made the marriage real, but no, Jared had to be a gentleman. The old Captain Allendale would have taken everything she offered and more.

God, You promise to work all things together for good and I've made a mess of all this with my best intentions. Give me peace and wisdom as we head to London. Let me protect Lucy, even if it means from myself.

~*~

Lucy found the carriage to be stifling with the summer heat. If they opened the window they had dust blowing in. Scallywag slept at their feet and Agnes kept busy altering a dress for Lucy.

Jared was on the bench driving the horses. She missed riding with him even when they didn't talk. Now wood separated them, and she was afraid far more would get in the way of their marriage. She couldn't believe that, accidental though it was, it was not a mistake. She was content to wait it out, until Jared would finally acknowledge that God had brought them together.

He struggled with God's grace and mercy. She

was amazed last night that humming *Amazing Grace* could banish his demons. Could Jared really be under spiritual attack? Hearing the stories her mother told about her father's satanic activities, there was much The Black Diamond was capable of. As well as his cohorts, and Satan himself. Was her very existence that important to the balance of powers in the war between France and England? She had a lot to pray about, including whether God would allow her to keep Jared forever.

~*~

They pulled into Dunfermline and got their rooms for the night.

Lucy couldn't help but tease Jared with unexpected kisses. He looked so befuddled that it made her giggle. He had seen the world and been to war and yet there was such a purity to him in some ways that surprised her. She knew he had experienced horrors. Maybe someday he would share the horrific deeds with her and they could lose their hold on him.

The next day a few hours into their journey south, one of the horses dropped a shoe. Jared pulled the carriage over into a side road.

Lucy wasn't happy that he would ride Rogue ahead to Rosyth to get another carriage and someone to take care of the horse.

"You have the gun. Stay in the carriage and please, please be careful." Jared rode Rogue down the road.

The heat was even more unbearable in the carriage now that it wasn't moving. They had taken to traveling with the windows open in spite of the dust.

Lucy was certain that anyone who tried to accost

them would be immediately vanquished by her nasty odor. She could barely stand herself. She acknowledged, however, that Agnes smelled even worse. Their water supply was sufficient, but they rationed it as the day went on.

Scallywag begged to be let out, so the ladies left the carriage to stretch out and let the lamb graze. Both Lucy and her abigail removed their bonnets in a futile effort to cool off. Lucy stared up and down the road wondering at how little traveled it was. Was anyone near here? While she had become accustomed to sleeping outside, she doubted Agnes would be equally amenable to such a proposal. Her maid would certainly think it not worthy of a lady of her station.

Humph. Station? She hated the way her position already alienated Jared. She preferred their days on horseback, the snuggling in the cave, and the soft talks around the campfires at night.

Now Jared was distant and showed her the deference she was due. In the wilderness they'd been equals. He didn't treat her as dainty and incapable. Now, she couldn't open the carriage door or step outside of it without his hand there, in a glove no less, to assist her descent.

She missed the twinkle in his eyes and the smile of satisfaction after catching their dinner. Or the way dusk softened everything including the scars he bore on his neck and arms when he was free enough to roll up his sleeves.

Lucy was impatient for Jared to return. She knew naught how to continue this journey. She possessed little money of her own. Jared took care of everything and she would be vulnerable without him there.

Agnes sat under the shade of a tree to work on her

stitches.

Lucy was grateful for the older Scotswoman. It would be nice once they were in London, to have someone she could talk to in a language she was most comfortable with.

How much further would she be forced to change? She was determined that Captain Allendale would not get that annulment. She would not cooperate. She loved him too much to let him go. She wanted no other. She was so caught up in her musings that she failed to notice the dust stirring down the road or the sound of horses' hooves as they hit the dirt.

Soon three men drew up abreast the carriage and the central one dismounted.

He had reddish hair, the color of a fiery sunset. His beard was neatly trimmed, and he was dressed in a style that bespoke wealth. "M'lady, you seem to have fallen into difficulty. My friends and I would grant you assistance if you would allow."

The hairs on the back of her neck tickled and goose pimples appeared on her arms in spite of the heat of the day. "Sir, your kindness does you credit, but I fear we have not been introduced."

"Sir Langley. The man to my left is Mr. Cranston and to my right is Mr. Hennipen."

"My pleasure. I am Lady Allendale, and this is my maid. Our horse threw a shoe and my husband has ridden to town to get a blacksmith to help us."

"And he abandoned you here on the side of the road without protection?" Mr. Cranston frowned and one eyebrow raised.

"I didn't say that. I appreciate your offer of assistance, but we will be fine. You may continue your journey."

Sir Langley advanced on her.

Lucy held her ground but put her hand in her pocket to grasp the gun should she need it. The man stood before her all masculine strength and a cocky arrogance that immediately put her on her guard.

He lifted his left hand to touch her cheek. "I would be happy to engage in a little diversion before continuing my journey. He bent his head.

Lucy raised her knee to meet soft and tender flesh.

The man yelped, his face reddened to a darker shade than his hair, and he bent over swearing profusely.

The other two men dismounted quickly and advanced.

"I suggest you leave now, good sir," Lucy said through clenched teeth.

A blur of fuzzy cream and black threw himself in the same spot she had kicked, knocking Sir Langley onto his back. The lamb returned to Lucy's side and she could have sworn the animal sneered at the men before her.

The two who were still standing backed up.

"Get her! That lamb can't hurt you," Langley shouted as he tried to rise.

The other two men took a step forward.

Lucy pulled out her gun. "If you refuse to heed my requests, perhaps you will listen to this. I've trained hard to become a crack shot."

A bullet scattered dust at Langley's feet.

Lucy smiled at his startled expression.

Agnes stepped forward with the rifle, aiming it at his heart. "I'm a crack shot too."

The men hastily got on their horses and Langley shook his finger at her. "You will regret this. If you dare show your face in London, your reputation will be torn to shreds."

Lucy raised her gun, cocked the hammer back, and shot through his top hat.

Langley laughed. "Ha! You missed."

Lucy cocked the hammer back again.

Mr. Cranston had gone pale. "Langley, she didn't miss."

Langley took the hat off and stared at the neat hole right above the brim. A smidge lower and she could have scalped him.

"I suggest you leave us now, I promise not to shoot you in the back."

The men took off. Another bullet whizzed past Langley's horse's ear sending the horse into a panic and bolting down the road.

Lucy looked at Agnes and grinned. "You couldn't resist the temptation to put him in his place."

Agnes shrugged as she brought the barrel of the gun to point at the ground. "I doubt they'll forget you any time soon. Blonde or brunette, they will remember."

"I'm afraid you are correct, Agnes." Lucy grinned. "Ah, but what a memory I will have."

"'Twern't ye scared, m'lady?"

"My heart beat fast, but I was grateful for the diversion from our dreary day."

Agnes nodded and went to sit down.

Scallywag came to rest in the grass.

Lucy watched them both, put her gun away, and resumed her pacing. After feeling the heat on her face she put her bonnet back on. No use encouraging freckles or a tan. Lucy was almost ready to mount Fiona to travel to town when she spied a carriage coming from the south.

Jared was riding ahead on Rogue. Lines of fatigue were on his forehead and ruddy cheeks. He dismounted, gave her a kiss on the cheek, wrapped his arms around her and held her close.

Lucy wilted against his strength and soaked up the affection. When he set her from him and looked her over she felt warmer than ever. "Luce, are you well?"

She smiled and nodded. "I am, and you? Are you weel then?"

He nodded. "I brought a blacksmith." The man exited the carriage, tipped his hat to her, and went to work on the horse.

"I heard an amazing tale when I got to town. A man swore a witch put a hole in his hat. I thought for sure it was a bullet. Do you know anything about this?"

Lucy raised her chin. "What makes you think I had anything to do with that?"

"Mayhap because he also limped quite noticeably, and he attributed it to a large ram that protected the witch."

"Let's just say, I think he'll be giving me wide berth should we meet in London."

Jared grinned.

The blacksmith interrupted them to declare the horse fit for travel and departed with his fee.

Jared assisted the ladies back in the carriage, doffed his hat, and climbed on the perch to start them off again.

What other adventures might they yet have before London?

13

Jared grinned as he started south, retracing the path he'd already taken once. Lucy had routed a bounder and all his anxiety as he traveled, worried about how long he was gone, and what dangers might have befallen her, was for naught.

He was surprised at the overflow of emotion when he saw her standing there awaiting them. Her smile. He'd impulsively hugged her. A behavior that was beyond the pale in London. The thought depressed him. If she were his wife in reality he could skip London and go to his estate and make a nice life there for the two of them. He imagined the two of them teaching their kids how to fish and cook. He imagined that deciding to spend a night in the woods would not scandalize her.

Dreams. Nothing but foolish dreams. Since when did he become a lovesick schoolboy? Calf love? It had to be since she was too far above his touch even if she didn't believe it. But what did dreams hurt anyway?

Reality slapped him hard in the face. He understood the torture of dreams. He really couldn't add more to all that burdened him. Lucy was a job. Nothing more, and nothing less. She was a duty to be fulfilled and as with every other mission, he would walk away. This time for good. His only mission would be to set up a new life for himself. He already recognized that a wife would never fit into that equation. He'd be a doting uncle to Marcus's and

Josie's children and those of Phillip, Michael, and Theodore.

These thoughts depressed him, and his smile was as long gone as the sun when they finally pulled into the village of Rosyth and claimed their beds, his once again on the floor of his pseudo-wife's room.

~*~

He was alone in the dark and the stone floor was sticky with his own sweat. He had no strength to rise to the corner to relieve himself. He despised himself for doing it there. Dignity had long gone and only honor remained, but it was a poor companion on the cold painful nights waiting for his French demons to return. Vermin crawled on his skin and he had no strength to fight them off.

God, where are You? Will You abandon me here or are You, as You say in Your holy Word, with me even in the depths of the sea? Does that apply to this dank dungeon where I'm likely to die? I love You. You are my King and I want to die in a way that would honor You, God, my Father and Jesus, my Savior. Send me Your Holy Spirit to comfort me as You promised.

The cell door creaked and rattled, and the flickering light of a torch cast eerie shadows on the wall.

"English scum, are you ready to talk now?"

Jared remained still. They may have stripped him of his strength, his health, and even his dignity, but they would never strip him of his honor and faith. He was violated in the most heinous and shameful way possible and left trembling and bleeding, naked on the floor.

The cell door slammed shut and another piece of himself had been slain at the altar of the King of England. Now he understood, first hand, how a raped woman felt.

He wept. Deep sobs wracked his emaciated frame and every tear drained one more shred of hope he had of ever making it out of here alive.

Humming. He heard humming. He thought he was alone in the dark but there was a sweet woman's hum. It wrapped around him in the darkness of his pain and allowed him to rest.

~*~

Jared awoke and found his depression lifted. He smiled as he got the carriage ready and loaded the trunks with the help of a stable hand. He gave Agnes a lift into the carriage and turned to help Lucy.

Lucy tipped her perfectly coiffed head at him. She looked entirely like the lady she was. Her lips curled in a smile and there was a twinkle in her sapphire eyes. "How are you, Jared?"

"I am well." He frowned. "I did not disrupt your sleep last night?"

"As your wife, any disruption is an opportunity to pray and serve you." She reached up with a gloved hand to caress his cheek. "I can always rest in the carriage should I need to."

Jared took her hand, lifted it to his lips, placed a kiss there, and handed her up.

He took his seat and started the horses on the road to their next stop in Edinburgh. They finally arrived at the crossing at North Queensferry. Jared escorted the ladies into a private dining room for an early lunch while he arranged for their crossing. Afterward, he came and escorted the women, carriage, and horses to the Signal House until departure.

The ladies were seated on a bench to wait as other passengers gathered. He kept his expression neutral as he surveyed the milling people around them, mostly Scotsmen and women dressed in worn clothes but with ruddy and cheerful expressions. He generally found most Scottish people to be a friendly lot although he had no doubt that if he crossed them, they could be equally deadly.

Soon it was time for the crossing.

The ladies chose to stay in the carriage.

Jared stood by the horses' heads holding the leads. The day turned dark and grey and a storm erupted overhead drenching those who stood outside. Jared shivered as the cold drops of rain soaked his coat and waistcoat, and dripped off the top of his hat. He was grateful that although it was hot in the carriage, the women were at least dry. And armed.

A shot rang out.

A man yelped as he dropped out of the now open door of the carriage.

Jared ran to the man and lifted him up by his shirt. The man was bleeding from his upper arm and livid. His hair was plastered to his red face and foul language spewed from his mouth. At least Jared assumed it was foul since it was spoken in Gaelic. The man struggled against Jared's grip and tried to lash out at him but was forestalled by two other men, who dragged him away after berating and cuffing him with a couple of large fists.

Lucy appeared in the doorway as the rain continued to pour down. "He tried to force himself in here and made threatening comments."

Jared looked up at her fresh and innocent face. "You did well, Lucy. A wife worthy of any Captain."

"Good, since I'm married to one." She backed into the carriage with a wink to him as she closed the door.

Jared took a deep breath and went back to the horses' heads. They soon docked, and Jared was heartily grateful to be back on land. They drove past South Queensferry and on to Inverness. Jared wondered at the wisdom of going to such a big city but couldn't find any way around it. He traveled to the south edge of the city, pulled into The Quilted Kilt, and sought out the necessary rooms.

Jared collapsed into the chair by the fire.

The maid brought in the hot water and filled the tub.

Lucy paced as Agnes unpacked the items necessary for her mistress's comfort.

Jared reluctantly rose and went to the door to give Lucy her privacy. She met him at the door and clasped his arm. She rose on her tiptoes and in *sotto voce* said, "A true husband wouldn't need to leave, but could share this bath." A rosy blush came over her cheeks and he saw the invitation in her eyes.

Longing welled up within and he struggled to resist the temptation she offered. All his dreams never conjured up this. He gulped, lowered his head to hers, wrapped an arm around her waist, drew her close, and kissed her. He pulled away, gave her a slight bow, and left the room.

He entered the public room, asked for a scotch whiskey, and pounded the drink down reveling in the burn. He closed his eyes to hold back the tears and only saw his imaginings of what was taking place upstairs. He ordered a second and sipped that one as the locals mingled. He stood when he figured enough time had elapsed. He struggled to keep his feet under him and chuckled. It had been a long time since he had been this drunk. It was a potentially fatal thing to do in his line of work. He cursed himself. He was on the job and had just compromised his mission. He shook his head in an effort to see clearly but the dizziness only increased. He stumbled up the stairs and was let into the room.

His pixie bride was dressed in a nightrail that covered her to her toes. Her hair was unbound. Her eyes showed concern as she helped him to a chair. "Are you unwell?"

"Drunk."

She frowned, untied his cravat and removed his boots. She began to unbutton his waistcoat and he waved her off. "I...can do it myself." Did he slur? He fumbled with the buttons, removed his coat and waistcoat, and rose on shaky knees. He reached for his shirt to pull it over his head.

"Jared?"

"Hmmm?"

"Normally you do that behind the screen."

"You afraid to see my stripes? I'm done up like a tiger." He gave a growl and giggled like a schoolgirl.

She blushed as he pulled the shirt off. She came near and turned to trace one of the scars.

Senses he hoped would be deadened by the liquor sprang to life. He growled, turned to draw her into his arms, and kissed her.

She pulled back. "Jared?"

"I want you, my pixie bride."

She smiled and pulled him toward the bed. "I'm

yours. I belong only to you."

He drew her onto the bed with him, pulling her close for another mind-numbing kiss.

~*~

Lucy traced the strong chin and delighted in the freedom to play with his hair as he snored next to her. She snuggled into his arms and he pulled her close, seeming to need her even in his sleep. She smiled that at least she had that this night.

She was awake before him in the morning, and kissed him into consciousness.

His blue eyes fluttered open.

She kissed his lips and let it linger until he responded. She pulled back and smiled down at him. "Good morning, husband."

Jared startled and blinked rapidly.

Lucy laid her hand on his naked chest, feeling the hairs there that intrigued her so much.

"Lucy, I don't remember much of last night. Did we...did I...?"

"Consummate our marriage?" Her heart warmed. "No, Jared, much to my disappointment, you fell asleep with your kiss on my lips."

Jared visibly relaxed and closed his eyes. He threw one arm up over his forehead.

Lucy moved to rise but he caught her with his free hand. "I'm sorry, Luce."

"What are you apologizing for? For not making me your wife in truth or for giving into temptation when you had determined not to?"

Jared frowned. "Both. Luce, you are my light and my grace. I cannot imagine my life without you but you deserve better than me and I'm trying hard to treat you with honor, but…"

"But if your brother found you in bed with me he would insist we marry posthaste."

"Yes."

"So, what is the problem? We are already wed, and I have no desire for an annulment. Do you find me unattractive?"

Jared sighed. "You are perhaps the most beautiful woman I've ever met, inside and out, and I desire you more than you realize. Please don't torture me while I try to be honorable. I am but a man and can only be pushed so far, and I would be loath to have you attached to me only to regret it later."

"You assume I am too feeble to know my own mind?" Lucy sat back and jerked her hand out of his grasp.

"Luce, it's not you. The night I hit you in the midst of my nightmare proved to me that I am not fit to be a husband to any woman."

"You are a man with needs, you will seek to fill those elsewhere?"

"As a follower of Christ that option is not open to me."

"So, you will remain celibate the rest of your days?"

Jared's teeth clenched tight. He refused to answer her. She reached for a glass of water by the bed and tossed its contents in his face. He jerked upright and sputtered as drops of water dribbled down. His brows lowered. He glared at her.

"You don't want to be tempted. What about me? Everything about you tempts me and I'm a married virgin. In the eyes of any gently bred person—even if you never touch me—you have ruined me for any other man. None could compare to you for your courage, your integrity, or your devotion to your duty. I am far more than a duty, Jared. I'm not a package to be delivered to London. I. Am. Your. Wife."

She crossed over to the fire and hugged herself tight as the tears flowed and sobs wracked her body. She hadn't felt this level of grief since she buried her mother. The sense of abandonment was profound. If she did not have Jared, she had no one. She knew not her half-brother or her nephew and sister-in-law. They were strangers to her.

His touch made her jerk away. "Don't..."

"Luce..."

She shook her head and put her hands over her ears.

He came around to the front of her, now wearing a shirt that hung open at the collar exposing those intriguing hairs. He used a finger to force her face up to his and she reluctantly met his gaze. A handkerchief dabbed at the tears. He pulled her to his chest and held her close.

She lifted her hands from her ears and wrapped her arms around his neck.

The sound of a carriage and the shouts of people below in the courtyard stole his attention and he rushed to the window to glance out. "Luce, we need to make haste." He glanced over at her. "Would that we could make you appear like a boy."

"A boy?"

"Lord Winter is here. We've recently discovered that he is one of your father's henchmen and as evil as they come. I've never personally met him, but I have no doubt he is in pursuit of you—and me. If we could but disguise you."

He knocked on the adjoining door to call for Agnes. He explained the dire situation and the abigail left to discreetly see if she could find an outfit suitable for Lucy.

"A boy? You want to make me look like a boy?" She motioned to her chest.

"It won't be easy, and I hate to ask this, but how do you feel about your hair?"

"My hair?"

Dread pooled in her stomach as Jared stalked over to her. "Yes, I think we may need to cut your beautiful hair."

She sniffed and nodded. "Whatever it takes, Jared."

He frowned at her. "I'm sorry, Luce, but the one thing Lord Winter loves is beautiful young virgins, and he would not hesitate to use you abominably before he sacrificed you. He may try to make you believe he'll take you to your father but he wouldn't hesitate to use you as a pawn to gain the Duke's favor and resources. You would be tortured in the process."

She frowned. "How do you know this?"

"Lord Phillip's wife, Beth, was almost a victim of his. He is a bloodthirsty man."

14

Jared went to prepare the carriage.

Agnes worked to get Lucy to look like a boy. They agreed she would be Luke.

Nothing could have prepared him for the slight young man who came to stand before him and offered to hold the horses' heads while he loaded up the carriage and placed Scallywag inside.

"You too, Luke. Get in."

"I'd like to ride up on top with you for a while. I get tired of being cooped up in the carriage."

Jared caught himself from helping her up to the lofty perch on the carriage, but he needn't have worried. Lucy/Luke was as nimble as a goat. He sat down next to her and smiled. Thigh to thigh he would be close to her for part of their ride which was equal parts delight and torture. In spite of their argument this morning, Lucy was at peace with him for the nonce.

"I hate to say this, Luke, knowing how much trouble you had to go through, but you smell like a woman."

She wagged her eyebrows. "I guess I'll need to make sure no one else comes close enough to catch a whiff. Or do you suggest I roll in the dirt?"

"No, you'll get enough of that sitting up here. I'm sorry I made you do this."

She shrugged. "One more piece to our adventure."

"One step more in your path to scandalizing

society should this ever be made known."

"If I become a pariah, would you still want me?"

"I would always want you, no matter what society decrees."

"Oh, so if I'm ruined it's all right for you to love me, but not if I am a proper daughter of a Duke?"

Jared swallowed. "Something like that. But remember, it's not safe for any woman to be my wife. It is nothing against you as a woman…or a friend."

"Can you be friends with a woman and not want more?"

Jared shrugged. "I never tried."

"Well I tried to be friends with a man and found it will not do for me."

He jerked his face to hers.

She stared straight ahead. Her legs were slightly open just like a young stable boy and she gripped the side of the carriage for balance. Her shorn locks appeared appropriately boyish under the cap she wore.

He wondered where her curves went and was surprised at how well Agnes managed to hide them. He knew they were there and wished he were the one to unwrap them tonight. He shifted in his seat and growled as he urged the horses forward.

"Will you teach me to drive?"

~*~

She mourned the loss of her curly locks. They had cleaned them up and wrapped them in paper so as not to leave any clues in the room. With her dyed short hair, the hat, boots, and all the trappings of a young man, Lucy was shocked and pleased that she could physically pull it off. She'd witnessed the banked lust that simmered behind Jared's cool blue gaze this morning when she'd looked like a young woman. His surprise at her boyish appearance now was amusing.

Sitting on the bench was something she couldn't do as a woman, so she reveled in the freedom of being closer to Jared even now in the tedium of their journey. Asking him to teach her to drive was inspired and she relished him holding her hands as he taught her how to hold the reins and control the two old horses pulling the carriage.

She went over their argument and came up with no good answers for the barriers that stood between them and a happily-ever-after. She would gladly give up any title or claim to an inheritance if it meant she could have Jared forever. She was grateful for every day that she could look in his eyes, see his smile, or enjoy his kisses.

She was courting scandal all along this trip to London and she wondered at the larger purpose of it all. *God, what is this all about? Did you arrange this so I could find my one true love in Jared? Or am I a pawn in a larger battle going on?* She didn't think Jared had any more insight into it than she did. He had given no indication of it. Maybe he was also concerned about what would happen in London. If it came down to doing his duty and protecting her, where would his allegiance be? The thought sent an involuntary shiver down her spine.

"Are you well, Luke?"

She shrugged her shoulders. "As weel then as I can be given our circumstances."

"What would you wish was different? Wait...I'm not sure I really want you to answer that." He gave her a wry grin.

She mirrored his smile. "In an ideal world?"

"I guess."

"I would love to live in the country with the noblest man of my acquaintance and make love to him day and night and litter the countryside with our precocious offspring."

Red color surged into Jared's face as he shifted in his seat. Their thighs touched and it spread warmth through her.

"No balls and feasts in your honor? No visiting with royalty? No shopping expeditions and new bonnets and all the falderals that women are supposed to like?"

"I was never raised with those things. I could be polished to an aristocratic sheen enough to please those in London, I am sure. I have no desire to even try. I also have no desire to be fawned over or panted at by men because they think I'm pretty or they are after my inheritance."

Jared's left eyebrow quirked.

"If I cannot have what I desire, a small cottage on the Loch Ness will suit me fine."

His Adam's apple bobbed.

"You would return to Scotland?"

Lucy turned away, handing the reins off to him. She never imagined leaving her little cottage and the wild beauty of the Loch Ness or Aldourie Castle. She had friends there and had been safe and secure.

She did not possess the love of the man she adored. Without that, no place she would live would satisfy. A heavy cloak of darkness wrapped around her soul and the will to live seeped out. *What is the point, Lord, of going on if I have to do it alone? Or in a marriage with a man who doesn't understand or accept me as Jared does?*

"Luce?"

"It's Luke, remember? I think we need to stop soon. I suspect Scallywag is in need of a break."

Jared pulled over on a stretch of road and they dismounted.

Everyone saw to their own needs one at a time.

When it was time to depart, Lucy went to sit in the carriage with Agnes and the lamb.

She wished she were a man in some respects because right now she wanted to kick someone. Or punch them. Decidedly unladylike pursuits. She checked her gun as she glanced out the back window.

"What has ye all in a dither now, lass?" Agnes set her sewing down and wiped her brow with a kerchief.

"Men, this stupid war, and my stinking inheritance."

"By men, I assume you mean the handsome gent who is driving this carriage?"

Lucy nodded.

"Give him time, milady. Some men are a bit slow when it comes to love."

"You never married, did you Agnes?"

A pained look crossed the woman's countenance. "Nae. Never married but I 'twas once in love."

"What happened?"

"War."

"Oh. I am terribly sorry." Lucy reached over to touch the woman's hand.

"'Tis no matter now. Many years 'ave passed and yet I love 'im still."

"Was there an understanding?"

A sly smile transformed the older woman's face. "Aye, you could say that. He was my one and only love in many a way."

"Oh?" Lucy tilted her head to examine her abigail.

"Aye, he was a good lover and would have been a good husband and provider."

"I'm shocked, Agnes." Lucy put her hand to her flattened chest.

The older woman smiled. "Aye, gut memories to keep me warm on lonely nights, but I regret not once grabbing for what I desired."

"But it is not right outside of marriage."

"We were handfasted but had not made it public, so we were as pledged to one another as any man and wife would be. But we had not made a home together before the war called and he went."

"So, what do I do?"

"He's yer legal 'usband, aye?"

"Aye, that he is."

"Even if he weren't, he has compromised ye too much to nae do right by ye."

Something for her to think about. How did she get Jared to understand she was more than a duty, however, and to let go of his vain hope of an annulment?

~*~

Jared's throat was raw and all his energy evaporated in the heat. They hadn't made it to their destination and had a long way to go over many desolate miles. Fearing he would fall asleep at the reins he pulled over and almost fell off the bench to the ground. His legs failed to support him and he sank to his knees. He leaned over trying to catch his breath as a wave of dizziness overcame him. *No, I do not have time for this now. Please, Lord, no…*

The carriage door opened and Lucy was talking to him. He couldn't make out the words, and why was she dressed as a boy? "Your hair, pixie bride, where is your glorious hair?"

More words he couldn't understand as he was dragged to the coach.

~*~

When he awoke, he was in a comfortable bed in a cheery room with a small boy sitting near his bed.

He groaned as his had throbbed. "What happened?" he croaked.

The boy sat up and came to sit on the bed next to him. "What do you remember?"

He gazed at her to take in and make sense of the person before him. "Lucy?" He gave himself to the darkness.

~*~

"I think his fever broke." A sweet feminine voice penetrated the pit he was in. He had been sick? The last he remembered he had been… He tried to sit up and open his eyes. "I have to…"

"Rest, Captain Allendale. You must rest. You have been terribly ill."

He had known kittens with more strength than he now possessed. He tried to focus his eyes on the person speaking.

"Aye, 'tis me, Jared. Your pixie sprite."

"Luce?"

"Aye, call me Luke. The proprietor thinks I am

your servant or valet."

"How long?" he managed a scratchy whisper.

"About a week. I've lost track."

She reached an arm behind his upper back and helped him up while putting a glass of barley water to his lips. He drank but couldn't help grimace. She lowered him to his pillow and caressed his whiskered face.

"I'm not much good as a valet. I do not know the first thing about shaving a man."

Jared looked at her. Her hair was a shade lighter than the brown it had been. By the time they reached London she might be back to her almost white blonde hair. He mourned the loss of the long tresses she'd had.

"Jared?"

"Hmmm."

"A Sir Michael Tidley arrived yesterday asking for you. The proprietor stated you were here and ill and Sir Tidley claimed a friendship and asked to see you. I denied his request."

"Did you?" Jared smiled as he wondered how Sir Michael took to being turned down by this pipsqueak of a valet. "How did he take it?"

"He stared at me for the longest time, smiled, nodded, went to procure a room, and await your healing."

"Please send for him. He is a friend."

Lucy nodded, doffed her cap, and went in search of the knight.

Lucy led Michael into the room.

He sauntered over to the bed. "Jared. How do you fare?"

"Not well. I have been apprised of my illness only now, and of your presence. I am glad you are here. I could use your assistance."

"Whitehall sent me, stating I may have a vested interest in the outcome of your mission. Katrina sends her love. When I found out you were ill, I was tempted to come and wake you up by dumping some whiskey down your throat."

"That would only be fair given that I did that to you last we met, but I'm grateful you chose to restrain yourself." Jared smiled. "How is fatherhood?"

"Exhausting. While I'm glad that Katrina is a hands-on mother, Adam has a voracious appetite and only sleeps three or more hours at a time, and little Michaela is a terror." Michael yawned.

Jared couldn't hold back his grin. "You love it. I can tell. You and Katrina will have one wild tale to tell them when they get older."

"So…" Michael nodded over to Lucy, "do you want to introduce me to your lovely servant?"

Jared gulped. Michael was smart. Too smart to be fooled by a disguise. "Meet Lady Penelope Diamonte, who has gone by the name, Miss Lucille Cameron, became Lady Allendale a few weeks back, and is now my valet, Luke."

Michael's jaw dropped. "You're my sister?"

Lucy's eyes grew wide.

"Luce, it's all right, Michael is one of the good men. He's here because somehow Whitehall got wind of our need for assistance."

Lucy stepped forward and gave a slight nod of her head. "Nice to meet you, brother."

"Did you know Damon at all?"

"Only as a small child."

"Well, I'm apparently his spittin' image and look much like a shorter version of our father. You must take more after your mother."

Lucy frowned. "Shall I leave you two alone?"

"Where did you plan to go, Luce? Grab a pint in the common room downstairs?"

Lucy brought her head up and glared at him. "You have something against a good Scottish ale?"

Jared grinned. "Not if you bring me one as well."

"You are too sick for that."

"No, Mrs. Allendale." Michael glanced to Jared. "I will hear the story behind that." He turned back to Lucy. "It would be safer for you to remain here as a dedicated servant to your master. Winter is in town."

"Has he seen you?"

"No, but it has been a few years. The only difficulty will be my resemblance to my father. That is hard to hide."

"What if you wore a wig and dress?" Lucy inquired. "Agnes could get you some dresses."

"No. I will not do that. It raises too many complications for our travel. How soon do you think you will be well enough to resume your journey? Theo would allow us access to the Diamonte estate near Newcastle-under-Lyme. You could recover more strength there."

"I am too weak to drive the carriage." Jared moaned and yawned.

"I believe he needs more rest," Lucy offered.

"I can drive the carriage and you can tend to your husband inside."

"Not my wife."

"Excuse me? Jared, did you just say my little sister is not your wife when you introduced her as Mrs.?"

"It's a long story."

"All the best ones are."

"I'll get an annulment when we get to London." Jared was getting weaker.

"You compromised her reputation beyond repair so you cannot abandon her when you get to London. No. We will speak no more of this now, but listen well, Captain Allendale, she is not without family to defend her honor."

Jared slipped into darkness and dreamt of meeting his good friend on a hill with pistols at dawn.

15

Lucy could hardly believe her luck in having her half-brother come to assist her with Jared. Yes, she knew he was really there to help Jared with her, but he was on her side and the feeling that he would defend her warmed her heart to him. He took her to the other side of the room, turned to her, and whispered, "Lucy, that's what you prefer, am I correct?"

"Yes."

"Good. I want to assure you that I will stand by this marriage. You may continue to assist him as I know you already have. I'm across the hall should you need anything. We can try to depart on the morrow." He turned to leave.

"Michael?"

"Yes?" He looked at her.

"Do you know why Whitehall has sent two of their agents to get me? I was perfectly content in my obscurity in Scotland."

"Would you be content to return there now?"

Lucy looked to Jared who softly snored. She shook her head. "I would return if he refuses to honor the marriage, but I doubt contentment lies in any future without him."

Michael nodded and grinned. "You love him."

"Aye. Now if only he would love me."

"I don't think love is the issue, Lucy. Duty is getting in his way. Perhaps when this mission is accomplished he can move beyond that and into a future with you."

Lucy swallowed and nodded. "Thank you, big brother."

Michael grinned and left the room.

Lucy turned to keep vigil over her patient and pack for their journey.

~*~

The next morning, they managed to get Jared comfortable in the carriage and set out for Biggar. It would be a long journey and exhausting for everyone. After one stop, Lucy chose to ride atop with Michael.

"Jared tried to teach me to drive."

"You want the ribbons for a few miles?" He handed them over to her and she took them. She was changing in so many ways on this trip and not only in the way she dressed or the names she held. Changes were taking place deeper inside.

Michael leaned back and crossed his arms. "When did you realize you loved Jared?"

Heat rose in her cheeks. "It will sound odd, but I dreamt about him weeks before he arrived. I even sketched several pictures of him before I met him. I came across him at night in the throes of a nightmare and in an effort to calm him..."

"You kissed him?" Michael said the words softly and with no condemnation.

"Yes. I kissed him. I never expected to see him again. He overturned my entire life and took me from all I knew and yet, I love him."

"Why didn't you take a packet through the North Sea on down to Gillingham? You would have been there by now."

"Jared was reluctant to spend that much time on the water and no place to escape."

Michael sighed. "I cannot blame him. We have both sailed enough with this war and I prefer land."

"You served?"

"I'm retired now, but I was a spy, most often in London, but traveling back and forth across the channel."

"You have a child?"

Michael grinned. "Two, and a lovely wife, Katrina, a woman I could never begin to deserve."

"You must miss them."

"I do, although I have enjoyed sleeping through the night."

Lucy grinned.

"Has Jared continued to have nightmares?"

"Not every night."

"Violent?"

"Only once."

"Do tell."

"We were in the mountains and he had a particularly horrific one and was tangled in his blankets and struggling and I sought to help him."

"And?"

"I no longer physically go near him when they occur."

"Am I to assume he hit you?"

Tears came unbidden at the memory of that night. "He didn't realize it was me."

"The nights he has no nightmares, what has been different?"

Now Lucy was certain her face was ruddy. "We were sleeping together, holding each other."

"And how do you help him on the nights when he

is sleeping alone?"

"I pray and hum hymns softly. It calms him and he doesn't awaken in such a dark mood."

"You are good for him, Lucy. Now, as your brother, I need to ask. Have you consummated the marriage?"

Lucy shook her head and focused on the road.

"You want to change that fact though?"

She nodded but could not meet his gaze.

"Keep trying."

"He has been steadfast in his refusal as he thinks that will be the ticket to an annulment."

"You have time, Lucy, but I do not suspect it will be any easier on you both even if you get what you want."

She frowned. "No happily-ever-after for this girl. I'm small and appear like a ghost when my hair is normal. I speak with a Scottish brogue, have a pet lamb, and have never been in society. I already know I am beyond the pale in London."

"Being the duke's daughter and being married to a war hero like Jared will help people overlook your perceived shortcomings and regard you with favor. No one even need know about your unusual pet. You will probably set trends and soon everyone in London will be imitating your delightful accent."

"And I could curse at them in Gaelic knowing they would never interpret my meaning."

Michael laughed. "You might want to save that for your fights with your husband."

Lucy handed him the reins. "When you pull over, I will go rest inside and check on our patient, although I'm certain he is in good hands with Agnes."

"Never fear, Lucy, God hears and knows your

heart's desire."

"That doesn't mean I get what I want, Michael."

"I realize that, but He knows best and you can trust Him."

"Of that I am aware."

~*~

Jared missed Lucy during the morning, but she was back now and quiet. He wondered what conversation she had with Michael. Would he be facing pistols at dawn?

Lucy fell asleep leaning against him and he could smell her heather. He was grateful for her care while he was sick and wondered if he bothered her with any of his terrors. She had not spoken of any since the time he hit her, but he was certain she knew exactly when he had them. Now he was afraid he would start having dreams of another sort and feared he might act on those instead. He wrapped his arms around his sleeping wife and prayed for strength to endure this journey.

They pulled into the Rooster Crow Inn late in the evening.

Michael took care of the arrangements and helped Agnes and Jared from the coach.

Keeping up her role as a servant, Lucy helped get the baggage to the rooms and tended to Jared, making sure a hot bath was brought as well as nourishing food and a dark ale.

Lucy waited for Jared to take his bath and took hers while he ate. She spied the blankets he had on the floor and in a fury whipped them off the floor and back onto the bed.

"What are you doing?" Jared complained, but not with much energy.

"You are still sick and are sleeping in that bed." Lucy left some of her buttons on her gown undone. For days, she'd slept in her clothes to keep her secret but for tonight she wanted to be Mrs. Allendale in whatever capacity he would allow.

"And where will you sleep?" he asked warily.

"Jared, get into bed." She walked him over, tucked him in, and kissed his forehead much like her own mother used to do.

"Lucy, I don't deserve you." He rolled to his side and was soon asleep. Lucy went to finish off his ale and climbed under the covers to spoon with her husband as she had been doing for the past week. The only difference was her attire.

~*~

She was awakened by murmuring. Jared rolled over, sniffed her neck, planted delicious kisses there, and his hands roamed. Would tonight be the night she finally became his wife in truth?

~*~

Morning came. Lucy rose quickly, bound herself, dressed, and arranged for breakfast to be brought to the room.

Jared stretched and yawned and rolled over to look at her as she sat tucking her hair into her hat.

She was in a bad mood and wished for a way to expend the energy that thrummed in her veins. She was afraid the first man to cross her this morning would meet with a fist to his breadbasket. She hoped she could refrain from the more feminine slap, but right now she felt nothing like a lady. She went to the stable and instructed her saddle to be placed on Fiona.

When Michael arrived to help load the trunks he looked at her with the unspoken question.

"I'm riding my horse this morning. We both need the exercise."

"It's probably a moot point for your horse, that has been walking and trotting behind the carriage all this time. I'll assume that last night didn't go as you liked or you would never make this choice."

Lucy frowned. At first, she didn't understand but enlightenment dawned. Of course, she would have been too sore to ride her horse astride if… "I'm angry and hurt and frustrated and if I don't ride I might hurt someone."

"Would it help to punch me?" Michael asked.

Lucy bit her lip in an attempt to stave off the tears that threatened. She shook her head. "No, but if I change my mind, I'll let you now. Be warned, you rile me and I might give it to you."

Michael nodded and with one hand lifted her chin so she was forced to look him in the eye. "I understand." He went inside to get Jared and Agnes.

Lucy threw herself over her horse and they pranced around the courtyard.

~*~

She was angry with him, but he had no idea what he had done. Had he said something offensive in his sleep? Why would that bother her when hitting her in his sleep was forgivable?

Michael placed Scallywag into the carriage, and looked at Jared before he closed the door. He shook his head. "Jared, you must be the most addle-pated, bacon-brained person alive."

The door slammed, and Jared was more confused than ever. Somehow, he'd angered two people he cared very much about.

Agnes sat across from him with her needle and thread as she kept remaking dresses, if and when Lucy ever got to wear them again. She glanced at him and shook her head.

"What? What sin have I committed that has offended all of you?"

Agnes set down her sewing. "How did you sleep last night, Jared?"

He squirmed in his seat. "I had good dreams, I think."

"Hmmmm. I wonder why."

Jared shook his head and leaned back against the squabs so he could rest some more while he tried to think about what might have happened. The day promised to be long as they planned to pass through Coulter and make it to Abington by dark.

Scallywag had been a decent and relatively quiet companion. But today the lamb fidgeted and would put his front hooves on the seat to look out at Lucy as much as he was able. She rode up closer to the other horses than by the carriage itself.

He remembered Lucy in her lovely gown, her eyes large and the purest blue. She was like an angel as she forced him to bed and tucked him in. He fell asleep quickly and remembered being comforted, safe and warm throughout the night. He dreamed about holding Lucy and…

Had she crawled into bed with him? He remembered dreaming of her touch and at just the thought he longed for her. He tried to remember. Did he say anything? Did he…? No. She wouldn't be riding that horse if he had.

He fell into a troubled sleep.

~*~

A gunshot roused him from slumber and he reached for his weapon.

Agnes wisely pressed herself against the corner, out of range of the windows.

Jared looked out the back and saw nothing. The carriage slowed and he heard Michael yell. Jared reached up to open the small vent behind the bench seat that allowed a passenger to communicate to the driver when needed. He still couldn't make out what was going on.

Fiona was whinnying.

"Jared, we need you."

Jared came out of the carriage with his gun and was confronted by two men wearing masks.

A third red-haired man had lost his mask and was struggling with Lucy. She rammed her knee in a strategic location, and walloped him across the jaw, sending him to the ground.

Michael held his rifle aimed at the two men on the horses.

Jared stood by the carriage with the pistol.

"Stand down, men," Michael bellowed.

The men dropped their weapons, turned their horses, and ran the other way.

Michael fired a shot over their heads.

Both Jared and Michael aimed now at the man Lucy had wrestled to the ground and was now pummeling.

Michael jumped down and handed the reins to Jared as he ran to save the man from Lucy. "Luke, I think you've beaten him up enough to realize that he cannot take your horse." Michael pulled Lucy away from the man and aimed his rifle. "I suggest that if you want to avoid a hanging or a bullet you mount up and head out as fast as your friends did. And pray that we never see your mug again."

The man stumbled to his horse and struggled to mount as the animal danced away from him with every attempt. Half on and half off the man was almost dragged away until he gained his seat and urged the horse to a gallop.

Michael turned to Lucy. He shook his head. "Do you feel better now?"

She shook her head.

Michael surveyed her about any other injuries.

When she turned to lead Fiona back towards the carriage, Jared was shocked to see the bruise developing on her cheek and around her left eye that was swollen almost shut.

Michael went to tie the horse to the back with Rogue.

Lucy sank to her knees by the side of the road and cast up her accounts.

Jared was still holding the reins. After the anger of the morning he doubted Lucy would want anything to do with him now.

Agnes exited the carriage, went to Lucy, and pointed to a spot on her arm. Lucy shook her head but Agnes argued with her. Lucy removed her coat. Blood soaked through one sleeve near her shoulder.

"You were shot?" he bellowed.

Lucy turned to him. "And what if I was? You could go to London as a widower, collect my inheritance, and retire to your estate single and happy to be rid of your wife so easily." She stomped past him and entered the carriage in a huff with Agnes following.

Michael came to take the reins. "She's still spittin' mad so I would tread carefully for the sake of the family jewels." Michael smirked.

Jared gave him a shove in the shoulder before he entered the carriage and shut the door. Soon they were back on their way.

Lucy was spewing words he did not understand at a rapid pace and occasionally looked his way. Agnes ripped the sleeve off the shirt and bound it, occasionally responding in Gaelic.

He thought he had seen her angry before, but instead of relaxing after the fight, she was wound up. He kept his mouth shut more out of fear than anything else.

Her face turned pale and she slid to the floor of the carriage, which did not please Scallywag a whit.

16

Jared and Agnes lifted Lucy to his seat. He pulled her close. Her pulse was slow and steady. He laid her on her side on the bench with her head in his lap.

"You realize she'll not be any less angry when she comes to." Agnes resumed her sewing.

"I know."

Each breath caused a slow rise and fall of her shoulder. The black and blue deepened in color around her face.

He rubbed a smudge of dust off her pert little nose and then he played with her silky hair. Was there ever a woman more perfect for him than her?

If only her father was not the Duke of Diamonte— his archenemy.

Jared left a hand resting on her hip lest she roll off the bench and the other in her hair as he leaned back into the squabs and closed his eyes.

Lucy slept the rest of the way to Coulter and the men took turns guarding her as they escorted Agnes and sought refreshment. Water skins were filled and some food purchased for Lucy if she awakened later. The horses had a rest and some food and water, and they were on their way again.

Jared wondered at Lucy sleeping so long. "Are her injuries worse than we thought?"

Agnes shrugged. "The cut above her eye and that bruise were not made by a fist. A boot or the butt of a gun perhaps."

"She could have a concussion."

"That is a possibility. May I suggest that she become your wife again so when a doctor is called her secret is not questioned?"

"How can we do that?"

Agnes shook her head. "She is unconscious. I just finished one of her dresses here as well as mended one of her camisoles. We can change her here in the carriage."

Jared shook his head to clear it. "Now?" He gulped. "You want me to help?"

Agnes frowned. "For a married man, you are quite dense. Yes. Now. With her limp like this I could not do it on my own regardless, so either you help or I call for Sir Michael."

Jared shook his head and gulped. "Tell me what to do."

"Captain Allendale, before you get all flustered, realize that while you were sick no one else cared for you but her. *All* your needs. Now, as her husband, you can return the favor."

Jared nodded and proceeded to undress his unconscious wife.

~*~

When she was clothed and once again resting on his lap he marveled at the change with the lace and frills of a pretty dress. Even with her short hair, she was most definitely a woman. Not that he ever had any doubts.

He thought back to Agnes's comments. With all that they had gone through there was no escaping this marriage. He had too thoroughly compromised his wife even though he had refused her every push to consummate the union. He wondered at that. Would his accounting before the Duke of Wellington be any more severe for having done so? No one would believe him anyway once they saw her dainty beauty. She was his pixie bride full of light and laughter and she was the perfect partner for a man like him.

He leaned back and smiled as he contemplated the rest of their journey. He hoped it would be far more enjoyable now that he made up his mind.

He insisted on carrying his wife to their room and a doctor was called. He cared for her needs and his heart filled with tenderness as she rested so peacefully and innocent in his arms when he finally crawled into bed. He would wait. She would get better and they would come to an agreement about their marriage that would satisfy everyone. Well, except perhaps the Duke of Wellington. Did it matter?

He had to admit that it did. It mattered a lot. Why was his pride so wrapped up in a successful mission? Because he'd failed once? He never gave up the secrets, but the consequences of his failure continued to haunt him in the dark.

~*~

Lucy woke, reached for the edge of the bed, and retched. Her head pounded, her left eye didn't want to open all the way and it ached. Her arm burned. She dropped her head back to her pillow and rolled right into a solid wall of muscle.

"Good morning, my pixie bride." She glanced up to see Jared's perfect teeth, the straw-colored stubble on his jaw and chin, and those startlingly light blue eyes that glittered like jewels. Her skin tingled underneath his hand that rubbed her back and drew her closer into his embrace.

"What happened?"

"You were angry with me and took it out on a would-be horse thief." He pulled her closer.

She sighed into his embrace as she fell back asleep.

~*~

When she awoke later, she was alone in the bed.

Jared sat by the fire, elbows on his knees with his hands clasped in front of him. Would she ever not love this man?

"Water," she managed to gasp out through her dry mouth.

Jared brought her up from the pillow and helped her drink.

Hadn't she just spent days doing this for him?

"I need the chamber pot."

He pulled it out and helped her from the bed. "Can you manage? I'll go over here and promise not to watch."

She took care of herself, drank some more water, and collapsed back on the bed. Her stomach growled. "You can turn around now. Thank you."

He came to her side with a half-smile. "Anything for my pixie bride."

Anger stirred within her as the memories came flooding back. "Is Fiona weel then?"

"Yes, she was uninjured."

"How long have I been like this?"

"Two days. If the doctor clears you, we will travel again tomorrow to Lockerbie."

"That would be nice. Can I get something to eat?"

"I will see to it."

~*~

The next morning, they departed in the carriage at as early an hour as possible with a picnic lunch packed.

Jared insisted she rest on his lap and it felt so—intimate—to do so. She admitted it was comfortable as he would massage her back, or rest his hand on her hip as his other hand would play with her hair and massage her scalp. She was soon asleep.

Late that night she managed to walk on Jared's arm to their room and undress herself.

Jared came in later, stripped down to his unmentionables, and crawled into bed beside her. He snuggled her to his chest.

She rested one hand on his heart which beat steady underneath. She lifted her face up to his, caressed his cheek, and reached up to kiss his lips.

He returned the kiss and pulled away, kissed her nose and her forehead, and snuggled her close to himself once again.

She wanted...but she was still recovering from her fight and wasn't really ready now. For once she appreciated his restraint.

~*~

Jared was in agony. Even if this was all he could ever have of her he would strive to be content with that. If he held her in his arms every night...maybe he would be freed of his nightmares. She was like a shield that kept them at bay with her very touch. He feared he was fast losing his status as a gentleman, keeping his wife in limbo like this yet living in every way possible as her husband.

It also shocked him when he had seen the tattoo of a diamond on her shoulder. The duke branded his own daughter with his symbol in some twisted act of possession. In a weird way it made him want her more, to keep her, protect her, and make her smile.

Her injury allowed Lord Winter to get ahead of them on their journey south, as Michael went around talking late at night, visiting other posting houses and discreetly asking questions.

Jared suddenly realized that his friend was also now his brother-in-law.

They needed a real wedding. They were married but it didn't feel legal because they had not had the ceremony. Maybe if they could cross that hurdle his conscience would permit him to take Lucy as his true wife.

It was three more days before they reached Newcastle-under-Lyme.

Jared had been here once before, not six months hence, and realized he was more familiar with it than she was. He led her up the stairs.

The butler opened the door and exclaimed, "Lady Penelope, you have come at last!"

Lucy took in her childhood home.

"Does any of this look familiar?" he asked.

She shook her head. "None of it."

The housekeeper gave them a tour and a running dialogue of Penelope's childhood antics and stories about her beautiful mother. A portrait of their family hung in the drawing room and Lucy stared at it, only recognizing her mother. "Michael, were you not acknowledged?"

Her half-brother shook his head. "I only learned of the relationship recently. Our father knew about me but forbade my mother from speaking of it. She never married."

"We can stay here tonight if you wish it," Michael offered. "Theo and Valeria are not in residence. The property is now under Lord Harrow's administration until Dartanian comes of age. He is your nephew."

"No. No. I'm sorry, I know it costs money to stay at a posting inn but I cannot stay here." She ran out the front door and into the carriage where Jared found her sobbing.

"My pixie bride." He closed the door and pulled her into his arms.

She pulled back as her body shuddered with sobs. "I don't know why I'm crying. Why the place upset me so. I can't stay there. It's evil. If it were my home I would burn it to the ground."

Jared frowned. "You have no memory of your childhood here, so why...?"

"I don't know."

Jared held her close. "You do not ever have to return here again if you don't want to."

"Promise?"

"As long as it is within my power to do so, yes, I promise."

Lucy tilted her face up to receive his kiss and he poured his heart into it.

~*~

"There is still time," Lord Winter told his men. "We must grab her before it is too late. It would not do to kill Sir Tidley or Captain Allendale or we will have the entire British military on us like lice." He waved his hand. "Get her and do not fail this time. We cannot let our opportunity pass. She is mine."

17

Lucy reveled in the scent of sage and man as Jared carried her to their room that evening. He set her feet on the floor and she reached up to receive his kiss. She untied his cravat as he tried to unfasten the back of her dress. She purred and Jared chuckled, a sound that resonated deep in his chest. Maybe tonight...

~*~

The next morning Jared awoke her with a lingering kiss. She smiled. There would be no annulment. They had crossed that barrier between them in more ways than one. He had cared for her so gently and she looked forward to a lifetime of nights in his arms.

"We need to rise and be on our way, my pixie bride."

"I do love it when you call me that, but I have no special name for you."

He grinned at her. "Maybe in time you will."

They dressed and ate in their room. Lucy could not stop smiling. When they went down to the carriage, Michael turned to her. She winked at him and a broad smile crossed his features. He placed a kiss on her cheek and whispered in her ear, "I'm happy for the both of you."

Jared scowled at Michael.

Lucy playfully slapped his arm. "He's my

brother."

Michael slapped Jared's other arm. "I'm glad I don't need to shoot you. Now make sure you keep my sister happy."

A slow smile emerged on Jared's face and a tinge of pink as well.

Lucy ducked her head, entered the carriage, and reached for her husband's hand when he sat next to her. That touch alone made her wish they would reach their next stop as quickly as possible.

Agnes eyed them and nodded. "'bout time, ye got down ter business, Captain."

Jared's blue eyes twinkled as he looked at Lucy. "Yes, ma'am, 'bout time indeed."

~*~

Lucy held tight to Jared's hand. Her extra sensitive spirit warned her that danger was ahead. She had no proof, so would Jared and Michael take her seriously? She removed her sketchpad and a pencil from her bag and began to draw. She looked up to see Jared watching her intently.

"You are anxious, Luce. What's afoot?"

"Trouble."

"What kind of trouble?"

"You believe me?"

Jared smiled. "Sprite, you drew a detailed picture of me before you met me. I need no more convincing that you possess unusual gifts."

Lucy found comfort in his gaze and continued to sketch. She handed it to Jared when she was finished.

The frown deepened and lines appeared on his forehead. He opened the door to speak to Michael. The carriage slowed. Jared climbed out to talk to her brother.

Agnes remained silent.

Lucy studied her. "I'm glad you've been along on this journey."

"'Tis me pleasure, m'lady."

"I don't know when I will ever get used to that."

"Mayhap, never." The woman went back to her sewing and hummed a Gaelic tune as she did so.

The sound grated on Lucy's nerves, setting her on edge. When Jared opened the door to the carriage again, she jumped. "Oh! It's you."

"Sorry, we've had a change of plans and I hate to inconvenience you, my pixie bride, but I need your assistance."

Jared removed familiar items from a trunk and led Lucy into the woods. "Jared?"

"I'm sorry, but Michael and I feel that you and I would be safer on horseback and should travel a less direct path to Stratford in case your sketch is real."

"But if Michael is set upon, he will be alone." She changed into her young boy outfit and balled her dress and shoes up.

"He won't be alone." Jared handed her a pistol. "We'll be shadowing him but from a bit further ahead." He kissed her forehead. "This will not be comfortable for you and I apologize for that. If I had known, then last night..."

"Last night was an answer to this woman's dream, Jared. Don't spoil it with what-ifs. I'm sure I will survive this day in the saddle as long as I have you to comfort me later."

Jared grinned. "You can count on that." He turned to get the horses and they sneaked off through the trees.

Michael set forth without them.

"When did you suspect Agnes was in cahoots with Winter or your father?"

"I started to suspect when she so placidly accepted everything and listened intently, but rarely joined the conversation."

"Much like a good servant would."

"Aye, but she has been left to shift for herself too often and I cannot believe she was sewing all that time. She should have two trunks full of dresses for me if that were the case and yet she is still working on the same one she was a week ago."

"How astute. I knew there was a good reason I fell in love with you."

Lucy pulled her mare up and looked at him as Rogue danced around. "You do?"

"Do what?"

"Love me?"

He shifted in his saddle and color rose in his cheeks. "More than my own life." His steady blue eyes met hers.

"Well, let us pray it does not come to that, because I loved you from the first moment I kissed you in your dream."

"You are a silly wench. Impossible."

They were riding forward again. "What's so impossible? I mooned over your sketch for a month before I saw you in the flesh. I was ready to love you. You, on the other hand, had no notice of the nature of your quest and I believe would have refused it had you known."

"That is perhaps why Wellington is in charge and I am not. He played me well. I would have refused the task had I known the truth. I only hope he is accepting of our marriage for it cannot be undone now."

"No, and for that I am grateful." She winked at him and they continued on in silence, keeping a wide berth of the road and watching for any potential assailants.

It was two hours later as fatigue and soreness were beginning to take their toll on her muscles, when Jared pulled up short and stopped her. He pointed slightly ahead and right near the road. Jared put a finger to his lips. Lucy nodded.

There was a log across the road and the two men were waiting off to the side, armed and ready to attack. Their horses were fidgeting.

Fiona and Rogue remained silent.

Within minutes Michael drove up with the carriage and came to a halt at the log. He scanned the woods.

Lucy was sure he had seen them, but he gave no indication.

Michael got down to move the log. The men jumped up. One held a gun on Michael, who put his hands up. The other masked man went to the carriage and pulled Agnes out. She screamed and yelled at him that she wasn't the one they wanted. The man cuffed her with his fist and she silenced. He spoke words they could not hear and dragged her off, tied her hands, and threw her over the horse. The men galloped down the road.

Jared and Lucy waited a bit, then went to help Michael move the log. Soon Rogue and Fiona were tied behind the carriage and Jared and Lucy were alone inside.

Lucy leaned into the side of her husband as he

wrapped his arm around her. "You made me a believer, my pixie bride. Please let me see any more of those images you have. Even if they don't make sense to you."

"I will." She gave him a kiss and enjoyed a few more since they now had the carriage to themselves.

~*~

Jared held his wife close. Today could have ended much differently if God had not warned them through Lucy's gift. He wondered what other blessings were in store as he gave himself over to loving this woman.

They reached Stratford and checked into an inn with Lucy once again posing as a valet. Jared had as much fun taking off her cravat as she did his when it came time to sleep.

They left before the sun rose in the morning.

Lucy was once again the prim and proper Lady Allendale.

Jared was proud to have her on his arm but dreaded the upcoming interview at Whitehall once he delivered her there. Now though, he knew he would not be leaving her. He pulled her close in the carriage and kissed the top of her frizzy hair that was starting to lighten with every bath she took. He wrapped a curl around his finger and marveled at the softness of it. All of this woman was a wonder and delight.

He deserved none of it and he felt guilty for spoiling any opportunity for her to make a better match. He was selfish and while Michael seemed to think his actions honorable, he felt the opposite. The one thing he did appreciate was that thus far, when she was in his arms, the night terrors were held at bay. She made everything better and he only hoped he would prove worthy of her.

Lord Winter was a cohort of the Duke of Diamonte. Had the Black Diamond returned to England? Would he dare follow through on the plans he made when Lucy was all of six-years-old, to use her as a sacrifice? The diamond on her shoulder infuriated him. That man branded his child like he'd heard the cowboys in the colonies did to their cattle. He wondered if she even remembered it. Michael had cried when he shared the horror of watching Katrina branded with the same symbol. He had been unable to protect her or stop them and it took a long time for him to get past that.

He thought about Josie, his sister-in-law; Beth, Phillip's wife; and Valeria, Theo's bride, who was also Lucy's sister-in-law. Along with Katrina they were all women of hidden strengths. He admired them all and he felt as though somehow he had won the prize of the bunch. Lucy would be well-received by them. At the next stop, he would send a missive to Marcus to make him aware, as well as a note to the papers to announce their marriage. Just how do to that with her name having been changed posed a challenge. He'd think of something.

He would also ask Marcus if they could have a small family wedding when he returned home with his wife.

Wife. She relaxed against him. She wasn't asleep but just as when they were in the highlands, there was a comfortable silence between them. He had a wife. He needed to get her a ring when he got to London. He needed to write his man of affairs too, establishing provision for Lucy should anything happen to him.

Given the dangers ahead that would be his first priority tonight.

They arrived in Stratford and found a small inn off the beaten path that would hopefully keep them out of Winter's sights.

~*~

Lucy missed her abigail, but knowing she had been a spy leaving messages and possibly meeting with her father's men, angered her. She was stiff and sore from her ride, but grateful her husband was willing and able to fill the position of maid.

Michael had threatened to room with them for protection and Lucy bit her cheek to keep from laughing at the livid expression on her husband's face. Michael was a cheeky fellow and Lucy found she enjoyed his silly banter. He had proven he could be serious when it mattered, and she understood that he and Jared had history together that went back many years. There was trust on both sides. She was safe.

The next morning, they started out again. They debated keeping the carriage and paring down to just horses, but Jared wanted another day of recovery for her and she had to agree it would have been more than she could handle to have ridden all day. Tomorrow…

She sketched as they rode. Jared chose to drive for a while so Lucy could get to know her brother better. She learned more about his tumultuous road to the altar with Katrina and how he had married her when he had amnesia. He didn't learn until later that he had a half-brother who had looked just like him, but who had already passed away. It caused some difficulty, he reported, when he met his brother's widow. His nephew also looked a lot like him which made his wife suspect he had fathered a child of his own on the wrong side of the blanket. Misunderstandings were resolved, and they were all friends.

Michael told her silly stories of his time in London. Lucy asked how she could be a lady when her husband couldn't be a "lord" simply due to her birth. She didn't mind being married to a Captain as it was a title well-earned, whereas dukes did not have to do anything to earn their title but be born the next in line to inherit and have their predecessor die. All those things were outside the realm of their control.

"How will I be addressed in London?"

"Lady Allendale."

"Even though my husband has no title?"

Michael nodded. "Strange, isn't it? You get the honor of the appellation of lady because of an accident of your birth to a Duke and Duchess."

"I do not like it, Michael. I've always been a miss or a lass, and while I've tried to learn to act like a lady, I was not meant to be part of the *haute ton*."

"It's ridiculous. I only had entre to the *beau monde* because I was knighted by the Prince Regent for service I rendered to the Crown. Still, that leaves me a Sir, not a lord and my wife is a missus."

"Perhaps I can request that Jared and I escape to his home and avoid me even being introduced to all these strangers with their odd customs, food, and talk. Is English not even good enough for them to speak that they have to keep littering it with French? I thought we were at war with France."

"We are, yet society craves anything French. Fashion, idioms, and brandy if they can get it smuggled."

"So not all are supportive of the war?"

"Only as much as it can preserve their way of life. Most have no empathy for the wounded soldiers billeted home who lose their fiancées, jobs, or any kind of livelihood due to their sacrifice so that the *ton* can dance until dawn in freedom."

"Yet you have participated in these festivities."

"When it enabled me to do my work for the Crown, I did. I never bought into any illusion that they did anything more than humor me. None would have considered me a viable husband for their daughters even if I had a fortune to offer."

"But your father was a Duke."

"They didn't know that. My mother was landed gentry and never spoke his name to anyone, not even my shamed Grandfather. The weight of her keeping me instead of giving me to the foundling home was a huge sacrifice. I believe she really did love our father and mourned the lies he had told her to manipulate her into his bed."

"I'm sorry she endured that."

"Can I ask you something more personal?" Michael's voice had turned serious.

"I can always decline to answer, so yes, you may ask."

"Our father is an evil man."

Lucy nodded. "I am aware of that."

"He has a thing for diamonds and brands women he wants for his evil purposes, with a diamond on their shoulder. Did he perchance do that to you before your mother escaped with you?"

Lucy shrugged. "I can't see my back. I don't know."

Her brother looked at her with sad eyes. "Luce,

did he ever..."

"I was a virgin until a few nights ago."

The silence hung between them like a curtain, but Michael finally pushed through. "I want you to know, that your husband is the kind of man...he would have loved you anyway if..."

Lucy sniffed. "I believe you are right, Michael, but am grateful I didn't have that shame to bring to my bridal bed."

"The Duke may still be after you."

"Why?"

"Who understands the mind of a mad man? Winter obviously wants you and I have no doubt that it is for evil reasons. How he's connected to our father, I have no clue, but if he is after us, he is in deep, and we should be on our guard and praying."

"You know God then?"

"Yes, thanks to the faithful witness of my friend Marcus. He's your brother-in-law, by the way. You have a sister-in-law, Henrietta, who is a flibbertigibbet if I ever knew one. I adore her anyway."

"I appreciate knowing I will not be alone, that I have a ready-made family awaiting me in my new life as Jared's wife."

"If we can make it through the next few days alive, then yes, you have a wonderful new life awaiting you near Rose Hill."

"What do you mean, if?"

A shot rang out and the horses bolted.

18

A bullet whizzed past Jared's head from the side and the horses took off at a gallop, almost knocking him from his perch. He managed to hold on to the reins and steer.

The little door behind his seat opened. "Are you well?"

"The bullet missed but I cannot tell if we are being pursued."

"I'm on it."

Jared hoped Rogue and Fiona were ready for a good gallop. It would be easier on them since they weren't pulling a load. He tried to slow the horses, but they resisted. He heard the carriage door open and the sound of a gun being discharged. *Don't fall, Michael.* He heard the other door open as well. *What?*

Gunfire was discharged from both sides of the carriage. He glanced to the side and saw his intrepid bride holding on for dear life as she fired her gun. She slipped back inside before he could yell at her. Both doors slammed shut.

Michael spoke up from behind. "Got 'em. You can slow down now. We should probably check your mounts."

"Easier said..." Jared pulled on the reins, but it still took time before he could bring the horses to a walk and pull over.

He jumped down and opened the carriage door. He was about to scold his wife but stopped before a word escaped his mouth.

Lucy was bleeding and Michael had removed his cravat to staunch the blood. Her eyes were closed, and her face was even paler than normal.

"Is she...?"

"Very much alive. Just nicked her ear and it's bleeding copious amounts. Care to offer your cravat to the cause?"

Jared shook his head as he hastily untied his cravat and handed it to Michael. He moved to check the horses. They were lathered, but fine. He untied them and led them to the side of the road to get at the grass. He did the same to the other two and started to rub them down. Michael joined him. In short order they finished and leaned against the carriage.

"Lucy..."

"She's resting with a large pad against her head. She'll be right as rain in no time."

"The sooner we ditch the carriage and ride across country the better I will feel about this."

Michael nodded. "Tomorrow is soon enough. We left a pile of bodies for them to deal with first. We can only hope that deters them for a few hours at least." He took the lead horses to the front of the carriage and secured them. "Tie up Rogue and Fiona. You go sit with your bride and I'll get us to Stratford."

Jared nodded, tied up the horses, and jumped into the carriage.

Michael set off at a good pace designed to not tire the horses, given the run they already endured.

Jared leaned his head against the squabs to fight off the headache that threatened him. His sprite rested.

Her eyes opened and focused on him. "Hello."

"You saved yourself from a scold. I was all fired

up to come in here and let you know how dangerous your actions were and that you could have been hurt." Jared looked away from her. "You already proved my point."

"I am sorry I disappointed you. I'll never be the proper English maiden so resign yourself to that now."

"I don't want a proper English maiden. I want a Scottish sprite for my pixie bride. She would be the only woman for me." Jared fought tears. "When I saw all that blood…" He moved to sit next to her and raised a hand to caress her uninjured ear. "I was afraid I had lost you, and that would never do."

"Of course, it wouldn't, just as it would never do for you to act foolishly and risk your life for me." She reached up to touch his face and traced her thumb along his lower lip. She whispered, "See, I thought they might have hurt you and no one can do that and live to tell about it."

"They missed."

"I'm grateful."

"Tomorrow, do you think you could tolerate traveling cross country on horseback?"

"As a man or a woman?"

Jared grinned. "I've taken a shine to this young lad…"

Her eyebrows wiggled. "You have? My, oh, my, what other secrets do you have?"

"This is no secret." He bent his head and kissed her with all the love and fear and anguish of the past hour.

"I love you too," Lucy whispered back.

The next morning the carriage and two horses were sold in exchange for a showy gelding for Michael that looked as if he would keep up with Rogue and

Fiona.

"What's his name?"

"Cassiopia."

Lucy started to giggle.

Jared laughed out loud. "Sounds more like a girly horse."

"Apparently it was named by the owner's daughter." Michael had puffed out his chest.

"As long as he can keep up with us." Lucy, dressed as a boy, took off after Jared with Michael following behind.

The travel was slow as they stayed to lesser used lanes.

~*~

Lucy's ear ached and the cap she wore kept rubbing it. She was faring better on the horse than she expected, but that was because her husband had held her and not exercised his "husbandly rights" no matter how much she cajoled.

She was grateful now for his foresight and dedication to her comfort. He gave her a scold about putting herself in danger and she listened. She also determined, however, that her life meant little without Jared and if it came to it, she would step into harm's way if it meant saving his life. He had seen too much darkness in this world and she wished a life of light and grace for his future. How many more days or weeks before that would happen?

The trip was uneventful, and they spent the night at a small inn with Lucy once again pretending to be Luke, Jared's valet.

"Relax in your bath and I will return soon." Jared

kissed her forehead and left to share a pint of ale with Michael.

She soaked her aching muscles, dried off, dressed for bed, and fluffed her wet curls with her fingers by the fireplace. The window was open to let in the fresh summer air and keep the room from being stuffy. The curtains billowed from the breeze and Lucy smiled to herself at how content she was.

This trip and her accidental marriage had been a revelation. She fought back the fears of the future that threatened. A noise scraped behind her and she turned, expecting to see Jared.

A man dressed all in black pointed a revolver at her.

Her gun was behind him, on the bed. She was trapped with no one to help her.

"Yous come with me."

Lucy tilted her head and considered her opponent. "Where do you propose to take me?" If she could keep him talking long enough Jared would return.

"Yur da is wantin' ta meet cha."

"I have not seen my father for a long time. Last I heard he was banished to France and stripped of his title and lands. He doesn't sound like the kind of man I am inclined to want to meet."

The man growled. "Git oot the window."

"In my nightrail? Are you mad?" Lucy crossed her hands in front of her chest.

"I hadn't thought 'er dat." He dropped his arm a bit and scratched his head.

Good. Her father didn't hire the most intelligent of men.

"I'll tell you what. I will grab my robe and slippers and we can walk down the stairs to the front door. A lady cannot climb out a window. You must realize that."

"Dat'll be fine. Git on wit ye." He waved his gun at her to move.

She grabbed her robe and pulled on her boots. She would make a spectacle of herself and surprise the proprietor when she appeared as a woman, but she trusted that once this man was dispatched, that little problem would be easily taken care of.

"Could we stop for a pint before we depart? I've not had my dinner yet and that would at least tide me over until we arrive wherever my father is."

The buffoon scratched his head with the gun which made her wonder if it was really loaded or he was an idiot.

"Nah, we's gotta go, quick-like." He waved her to the door with the gun.

She moved to the door and unlocked it. She stepped out into the hallway and tried to speak loudly. "Where did you say my father is staying?"

"I didn't. Now keep quiet."

Lucy held her head up, tripped lightly down the stairs, and came to a stop in the public room. "Jared!"

The gun came up to her spine and the would-be kidnapper pushed her forward to the door.

A shot was fired.

Lucy fell forward to the ground and tried to catch herself with her hands. "Ow!"

The room erupted into shouts.

Lucy struggled to rise, stepping on her gown. A hand at her elbow pulled her to her feet.

"Are you injured?" Jared asked.

She shook her head.

The would-be kidnapper rolled on the floor. His

attempt to rise was stopped by Michael's fist. Blood was seeping from the man's shoulder and his gun was too far away.

Michael pulled the man to his feet. "Who hired you?"

The man was mute.

"He told me he was taking me to see my father."

Michael glared at the man. "Where is he?"

The man remained silent.

"Fine. You can tell the constable all about your attempted kidnapping." Michael called for a rope that was procured from the stable.

The man was tied to a supporting post in the room while one of the stable hands rode for the local law.

"Come, milady, and let us get you to your room." Jared escorted her away from the leers of the men in the pub. Once they entered the room he closed and latched the window and locked the door. He enfolded her in his arms. "I am grateful you were wise enough to bring him to where we could help you."

"He wasn't very sharp."

"I'm glad he wasn't successful." Jared leaned down to kiss her. They were interrupted by a knock on the door.

Jared went to open it.

Michael stepped in. "The constable is here and he would like to talk to you, Lucy."

"I guess I have some explaining to do?"

Michael nodded and gave her a wink. "That's my sister, outsmarting the criminals. I'm proud of you, Luce."

"Thank you."

Jared put an arm at her back and walked beside her down the narrow stairs as if to make his claim known to all and sundry. She felt conspicuous in her nightrail, robe, and boots. Michael led them to a private parlor and she recounted the night's events.

She was escorted back to her room and Jared once again locked the door. He stripped for bed and checked his gun in case there were any more unwanted visitors. He held her close and she felt safe, loved, and very much wanted.

The next morning dawned dark and grey. They met for breakfast in the private parlour, Lucy dressed as a valet again.

"Shall we set out? We are sure to get wet," Michael asked.

"I hate sitting here. It makes us too easy to find after last night's botched abduction. Someone is sure to try again." Jared shoveled in his breakfast.

Lucy tried to eat heartily as they might not be able to eat again until evening.

"We've traveled in rain before, Jared, and survived." Lucy didn't mind getting a little wet.

"My horse is untried with thunder." Michael chewed some more toast.

"I say we try. We are only two or three days ride from London. We are too close to lose heart now."

"Remember, Michael, even if we set out in a carriage, you would still get drenched."

Lucy sipped her tea and winked at her brother. It felt good to have a family to belong to.

"It's settled then. We leave as soon as we can make ready." Michael rose to leave.

"We are ready. We only need to grab our luggage and we can be off." Jared rose and assisted Lucy to her feet.

"Remember, Jared, I'm your servant. As much as I

love being treated like a lady, you will draw suspicion if people see you treating me like that."

Jared frowned and nodded. "I'll try to remember. It is hard to refrain from kissing you, no matter how you are dressed."

Lucy grinned, walked past him, and whispered, "Later."

"Promise?"

She nodded and headed up the stairs to get their bags.

~*~

The rain pelted them about an hour into their journey. They took to the main road as few would be traveling on this day.

Michael hoped the Black Diamond's minions would believe they had stayed put. He'd told the landlord to put it out that they were resting and playing cards in their room. It would not be long before their ruse was discovered.

They stopped mid-day to eat under the shade of the trees.

Scallywag leapt about to burn off energy before chewing on some grass.

Michael, Jared, and Lucy ate some damp bread and cheese and drank the water.

Lucy shivered as water sloshed in her boots. A bath tonight would be heaven. The heat of the summer day, along with the moisture, was creating a fog that made their journey spooky.

The fog made the going slower even as the rain stopped. The horses plodded along with their heads lowered.

Lucy's spirits sank as well. In two days, they might be in London and her life as she had known it, since meeting Jared, would drastically change. She was afraid it might not be for the better.

Jared dropped back to ride by her side. "Soon, Lucy. This will all be over soon. We'll have to get through Whitehall and then we can go to Rose Hill. My home is not far from there and needs a woman's touch."

Out of the fog emerged several horses. Large men were holding guns trained on Jared and herself.

Lucy looked behind her.

More men appeared with guns aimed at Michael.

"Ye'll want ta come wit us," snarled the man who must be their leader.

"And if we don't?" Jared asked.

"We shoot the men and take her anyway. Throw your guns down."

Grief and a glimmer of fear crossed Jared's features before his face was void of all emotion. He tossed his guns down. Michael frowned and followed suit.

Scallywag was across her saddle today and let out a baaaa of protest. One of the men cocked his gun and took aim.

Lucy bent over to shield the lamb.

Another man bellowed. "Leave her and the ball of wool alone. He can be dealt with later."

Lucy still had her gun tucked in her bag and a knife in one boot. Did Jared or Michael possess other weapons?

They were herded off the main road to a side one as quietly as a death march. Silence permeated the fog and gave her a chill.

Jared glanced at her with an eyebrow raised as if to ask if she was well.

Lucy pursed her lips and nodded. She was well, but scared. To get this far only to be stopped now seemed unjust. *God? Can You see what's happening? Help us, please!*

It seemed like hours before they reached a small house. They all dismounted.

Scallywag stayed close to Lucy.

Hands were tied behind their backs, and with Lucy in the middle, the captors marched them to the back of the house and in the door, leaving the lamb and horses unattended. A set of steps went down and they were prodded forward. Jared almost stumbled but caught himself. She prayed he was not beset with fears from his past captivity. The air grew cool as they descended.

Lucy felt safe sandwiched between Jared and Michael. They would do anything to protect her. Besides their love of her, she was also their mission, and these were men of honor.

They reached the bottom and continued on through a dark hallway. The men in front and behind had torches, but the three captives were left without.

Lucy had no doubts evil was planned, especially for her. If her father planned to sacrifice his daughter at age six, what would stop him from doing so now that she was an adult?

She smiled. If he hoped for a virgin sacrifice to satisfy his satanic god, he would be disappointed there. She would never regret that night or ever knowing Jared. He brought her adventure and had shown her strengths she didn't realize she possessed.

She had stepped away from everything she ever

knew to follow him. Even now, with the spectre of death possibly imminent, she had no regrets. She only hoped he would be spared any harm.

Michael was whispering prayers to Jesus. The guard behind Michael scolded him to be quiet even as he shoved her brother into her.

What would become of Scallywag? She never had a pet before, it would be a shame to be parted from one now. After all, the little lamb needed her. Didn't he?

Metal creaked ahead.

Jared was shoved to the dirt. The men grabbed her and shoved her in but she managed to stay standing. Michael followed.

The door slammed shut, a lock turned, and the men left, joking and laughing.

They were all alone. In the dark.

19

Jared spat dirt out of his mouth. His heartbeat accelerated, and his hands became clammy. His shoulders ached from the angle at which they had been tied behind him.

"Jared?"

Lucy's voice. She was here. She was safe. For now. He had a job to do. He mustn't forget. "I'm here," he croaked through the tightening in his throat.

She was by his side. "I need you to sit up."

"What are you thinking, Luce?" Michael stood off to the side. Thumps indicated he was testing the size of the room with his boot as he walked around its interior walls.

She whispered, "There is a knife in my right boot. If one of you could slide it out we could cut our bonds."

"Hopefully without lopping off a finger or two," Michael quipped.

Jared struggled to his knees. Lucy brought her boot between his legs and he was able to touch the top and lift out the knife. "Got it."

"Good. I'll take it from you and cut your ropes first." Lucy dropped to her knees behind him.

"Are you sure this is a good idea? Aren't ladies supposed to go first?" Jared whimpered, ashamed of the fear that terrorized him.

"You need to be free. Breathe deep."

He did as she bid. The knife was taken from his

grip. It touched his bound hands and the ropes.

She labored for a time, the only sound the friction of the knife against the rope and Michael's boot, still hitting the walls.

The rope loosened. He pulled, rolled his shoulders, and stretched them to ease the ache. "Good job, sprite." He turned to cut hers and stood to do Michael's.

When they were finished, Lucy hid the knife back in her boot.

Lucy stood by Jared and placed her hand on his forearm. He trembled. "You will be fine, Jared. I need you to be strong. We will get through this."

Michael stepped close. "The room is small. The walls are dirt. I can touch the ceiling and it is wood. My guess is we are under the cellar of some estate."

"So, what do we do now?" Lucy asked.

~*~

Lucy's words bounced around in Jared's mind.
What do we do?
What do we do?
What do we do?
Her touch brought him back from the brink of the madness he feared. How would he get through this without humiliating himself? She had no idea how his body had been tortured but his mind still bore gaping wounds.

"Will you give us what we want?"

"No." *Jared gritted his teeth in anticipation of the punishment to come. He despised these men. Not a very 'Christian' thing to do and he prayed for the ability to forgive but the pain continued and his heart shriveled up inside of him. Life no longer held any attraction. Better to die here, for his country, than to survive this having failed his mission.*

The most pathetic part was that he preferred his torture to the time laying in the dark, wondering and waiting for the next visit. At least they were in human form even if the Frogs lacked any decency.

Someone touched him in the dark and he recoiled.

"Jared?"

They never called him by his name. What new game was this?

"Allendale, its Michael, snap out of it."

Jared shook his head and felt a light hand. In spite of the dank, musty smell there was something new. Heather? Since when?

A humming by a woman. What was that? Then he heard it. A whisper. Jesus. Jesus, Jesus. He shook his head again.

Darkness. "Michael?"

"Here, Allendale."

A soft hand came up to touch his face, it sneaked behind his neck and pulled him down until his lips touched hers for a sweet kiss that grounded him firmly in reality. This was a different kind of torture and one he would gladly suffer.

"Thank you," he whispered in her ear. He pulled her into his full embrace and held her close. How God knew he needed this woman didn't surprise him. The fact that God orchestrated their meeting did.

"Are you weel then, mah loue?" Lucy whispered.

"I'm back. For now. Thanks to you." He planted a kiss on the top of her head and inhaled her scent which helped to drive the darkness out of his mind.

"Any time." She pulled back. "So, what do we do

now?"

"Anyone else have a weapon they didn't confiscate?" Michael queried.

Jared wished he could see his friend, but could guess that his expression was grim. "Nothing. Lucy, I didn't realize you'd taken to carrying a knife in your boot. Clever minx."

She gave a soft giggle. "Glad I can still surprise you. I have matches. If I had been wearing my skirts I might have been able to get away with a gun tucked in there, but not with these breeches."

Jared tapped her bottom, thankful he could tease her in the dark. He imagined her blush even though no one else could see it.

"No shenanigans over there, you two. I can still hear," Michael said with a tinge of humor.

"Any ideas, guys? You're the experts." Lucy left his embrace but held onto his hand. He needed her touch.

"Experts? You would trust men who have been captured time and again and whose only achievement is somehow escaping with our lives?" The humor was gone, and Jared's heart echoed the futility he heard in Michael's voice.

"There is nothing we can do at the moment, but rest and somehow be alert. The door is a gate so we can hear them coming and feel air flow and possible temperature changes." He turned to Lucy, walked to the door with her in tow, and then took a few steps to the side of the opening. He slid to the ground and dragged her down with him. "For now, we sit and wait. Michael, we are close to the door. Where do you feel would be opportune for you?"

"I'll find a spot. Don't worry about me. Keep your

bride warm." Michael followed that with a sound of a kiss.

"If you insist." Jared replied. He drew Lucy close to his body, wrapped his arm around her, and kissed her in a long and lingering embrace.

"You do have to come up for air sometime. I sure wish Katrina were here, though. Not a whole lot of privacy with a toddler and a baby demanding attention."

"Complaining, are you?"

"Not really, Jared. You just wait and see the wonderful things that await you two when we get past this."

"Waiting is the one thing we have no choice about. But we can choose to pray."

"Aye," Lucy whispered, "and we'd better be getting to it."

The fear and darkness evaporated within. Jared held Lucy close, sought God's help, and thanked Him for all He had already done for him. For them. He looked forward to a boring life as a farmer when this was over. That, along with being a husband and father. Life would definitely be worth experiencing with his pixie bride by his side.

Silence chilled him as it continued.

They listened.

A chill ran down his spine. He thought he was immune to the cold by now, but they were coming. He could hear their footsteps. Rage built like a small campfire where his fear fed it until it was a towering inferno. His skin warmed, almost burned from the heat. From the inside out it consumed him until he thought he would burst.

They entered and he exploded into a fireball of action, but lack of food and water left him weak, and soon he was flat on his stomach with a knee to his kidney, and retching from the punches they kept leveling at his head. The flame was doused as he slid into oblivion.

The humming. Someone was humming, but whom? He was the only one down here in this god-forsaken dungeon. His entire body shuddered in cold and pain, and every bruise was as if he was being pummeled all over again.

Soft, sweet melody hummed and was soon joined in by a male voice. Familiar? Friend or foe? The tension eased from his body and he let himself relax into the welcoming hum as it lured him home. Heaven was coming soon, wasn't it? He couldn't endure much longer. He hoped...

Steps were heard in the distance. Jared startled awake at the noise and it took a moment to remember where he was, in England, held captive with his wife and friend. Adrenaline started to flood his body. He jumped to his feet. "Michael? Luce?"

"Here," they both answered at once.

"Act passive so we can catch them off guard," Michael suggested in a whisper.

"Agreed," Lucy answered.

"Fine." Jared braced against the wall.

The torch flared and his head pounded. He shook it to clear his thinking. He closed his eyes against the brightness.

"Come along with ye. The master 'as requested an audience wit ye."

Instead of seeing a big British oaf, Jared saw a French captor. Something inside him snapped. He was tired of being a victim of their torture. He was not going down without a fight. Head down, Jared lunged forward and rammed into the giant, toppling him and the men behind him.

~*~

Michael grabbed for the torch and Lucy's hand. He pulled her out, and shoved the still stumbling men into the cell. It only took seconds to close and lock the door. They bolted after Jared as he ran with another torch down the tunnel they had originally come from.

They ran for some time.

Stitches in Lucy's side ached.

Michael slowed. "Are you ill?"

"I just need to catch my breath."

"Well, Jared is far ahead of us. It's as if the hounds of Hades were on his tail. We need to try to keep up if possible. He's not—"

"—himself. Yes, I know," she gasped for air, "but in this case, it...may have worked...in our...favor." Her breathing slowed and she stood up. "Let's go, but at a more moderate pace, these boots were not made for running, and are not precisely my size. I've got a lovely blister forming."

"Let us be off." Michael held her hand.

They took off at a slower pace.

While every step was painful, at least she could breathe.

They came to the end of the tunnel and climbed the stairs. Michael slowly opened the door to the cottage and entered. Once Lucy was inside they searched. No Jared. Michael had a grim set to his face. "Got that knife handy?"

Lucy leant over to pull it out. She handed it to her brother.

At the rear of the cottage Michael peeked outside and opened the door, with the knife held low. They stepped out and stood in the moonlight.

Their horses were there, but Jared's was gone. Michael picked up his gun and checked it. Still loaded. "Bumbling oafs," he muttered.

He handed her knife back.

Baaaa. Baaaa. A furry lamb emerged from the woods and ran to her. His black nose had blood on it.

"Did they hurt you, Scallywag? You poor thing."

Michael checked the horses. The saddles and bags looked untouched. He glanced at Lucy. "I think you need to put a dress on and look different as we head off."

"Why?"

"Because these idiots don't really know what you look like, and Jared isn't himself. He won't hurt a woman."

"Not true, Michael. He has hurt me before when he's been in this kind of state."

"Yet you married him?"

"That was quite by accident."

"You chose to stay married." He handed her a saddlebag.

"Yes, I did, Michael. Because I love him and he needs me."

"Being needed is a powerful thing, but it can also wear on you if it's not appreciated or reciprocated."

"I need him too. More than you know." Lucy stepped behind some bushes, unbound herself and threw on the dress. She pulled out a cape as the temperature had turned chilly. The rest she packed away in case it was needed again. She secured her bag and mounted, still wearing trousers under her dress for modesty and comfort since she rode astride.

Michael lifted the lamb to her and was quickly in his own saddle. "Well, shall we try to discover where your husband has disappeared to? Any clues?"

Lucy shook her head. "Your guess is as good as mine."

"The mission is to get you to Whitehall. We'll head south and hope to meet up with him."

"We're leaving him behind?"

"You are in too much danger out here, Luce. We need to get you to safety as quickly as possible. Don't worry, if I had been separated from you two, Jared would have done the same thing. Duty and completing his mission are paramount. Do you have your gun hidden?"

Lucy patted the weapon, now in her skirt pocket.

They took off through the woods.

Grateful for the moonlight, Lucy prayed that Jared would come to his senses soon and meet up with them.

20

Jared raced through the night until Rogue was lathered. He finally found a deep, wooded area to stop. He used grass and leaves to brush down his horse, even removing the saddle so the animal could rest and refresh.

Jared took a drink from his water skin and found some food in the saddlebag. He sat down at the base of a large oak tree and leaned against the rough bark. He closed his eyes and slowed his breathing.

He had escaped.

He had escaped.

He had escaped—alive!

His head pounded as if someone was knocking on a door trying to get his attention. Mentally he opened it and was shocked to remember that he had not been alone in the darkness of that prison cell. His wife and a friend had been there as well. In his madness, he had abandoned them to whatever fate was coming. He groaned as shame washed over him. Tears streamed down his face at his failure to be the husband and hero he wanted to be. He had no place serving his country. He belonged in Bedlam. Somewhere away from harming anyone else.

He tried to think about what might have happened after he tore out of there like the devil was on his heels.

Michael would look after Lucy and she was not incapable of defending herself.

The question was, had he given them enough opportunity to break free? Were they there or on their way to London? Michael would never chase after him but would seek to complete the mission.

He had only one choice. To return to figure out what had occurred. He rested for a few hours. Upon awakening, he saddled Rogue and headed back to the cottage, hoping he could remember the way he'd come.

Several hours later as the sun was midway in the morning sky, he found what he thought was the place. The trampling of horses' hooves was evident as well as their relieving of themselves. Had the captors removed the animals or had Michael and Lucy taken them? He checked the interior of the cottage and found the door to the tunnel left ajar, a torch on the floor. That could have been his and he could have left the door that way.

He lit the torch and descended the tunnel with all stealth. Not that the light would betray his presence. He stopped to listen. Men were cursing. He put the torch behind him and crept forward to make out their words.

"You idiot! How could you let them catch you off guard like that?"

"When the Black Diamond hears of this we're toast."

"Better to die here than face what he would do to us."

"Well, Lord Winter will not be pleased either."

"Will any of them even come to look for us? We've been gone longer than we should be."

"Don't know. Maybe. But if they do and find our prisoners gone, there will be hell to pay."

Jared grinned. They had escaped and imprisoned their captors. He went back in the tunnel and up the stairs to the cottage. He extinguished the torch and left it. Once outside he mounted Rogue but decided to see exactly where they had been hidden from the outside. He tied his horse out of sight, and then sneaked through the woods in the direction of the tunnel until he spied a manor house. One of Lord Winter's estates, if he was correct.

He back-tracked, mounted Rogue and headed for London. He had little hope he would catch up to Lucy and Michael, but at least he wouldn't be far behind. He only hoped that they would forgive him for his lapse of sanity.

Sure, it brought them freedom, but if Michael had not been there, he would have left his wife to the mercy of those brutes. There was no way she would have defeated them on her own. He shivered at the thought of what they would have done to her. *Lord, keep them safe.*

~*~

"What do you mean, they escaped?"

Four large men cowed before his greatness. He debated on their discipline. Did he let them get their revenge and try to recapture the redoubtable Captain Allendale, the lovely Lucy, and the enigmatic Sir Michael Tidley? Having all three in his possession would sweeten his future. He licked his teeth and smiled. He motioned to the man standing next to him.

"Thirty lashes each while I decide whether these men can be useful to me or not."

The men paraded out of the room, heads down. He grinned when he saw one with a tear tracing a line down his filthy cheek. Maybe he would watch the torture. It always made his day brighter when he did that. It would be even sweeter when he could have the escaped men watch him personally torture the delectable Lucy. She was his. Without her the promise of future status, wealth, and power would be denied.

He was not used to being denied and wasn't about to start now. He rose from his chair and followed the men down to the torture chamber. He might even wield the whip himself. It was satisfying work, why should his staff get all the fun?

~*~

Exhaustion flowed through Lucy. "Michael, I can't go on. We need to stop for a while or I will be falling off Fiona."

Michael frowned. "We can't have that happen." He led them deeper in to the woods to a shady glen by a creek bed. They dismounted and allowed the horses to drink.

Scallywag scampered about.

Lucy wrapped her cloak around her and dropped to the ground to sleep.

~*~

She awoke as the sun began to set. Her lamb was snuggled up next to her and the horses were sleeping on their feet nearby where Michael had tied them off.

Michael was resting but he was poised to act if the need arose, as evidenced when he opened his eyes and raised the pistol, before lowering it when he saw her. He closed his eyes and relaxed on the ground once more.

Lucy stretched, took care of her needs, and knelt by the creek to splash water in her face. She tried to fix her hair which was growing out and fell in her eyes. She wished for her cap she wore as a boy, since she could push the wild curls up and out of the way. Her bonnet had been crushed and had a distorted shape. It didn't hold the curls nearly as well.

The yawn Michael made startled her. Her brother struggled to rise out of his hard bed of dirt and leaves. One leaf stuck to his hair at an odd angle and she bit back a grin. "Morning, brother."

Michael blinked several times and then looked at her with a frown. "We slept the day away."

"True, but traveling at night has its advantages, doesn't it?"

"And its dangers." He brushed off his clothes.

Lucy reached up to pull the leaf out of his hair.

He stopped his movements. "Thank you."

They ate some bread and cheese and were soon on their way again with Scallywag on Michael's horse.

"Do you think Jared's all right?"

"I suspect so. What does your heart tell you?"

"Excuse me?"

"Jared said you are fey, that you know things a normal person wouldn't, that God reveals it to you. What does God tell you about Jared?"

"Sometimes I don't always know how much is wishful thinking and what is God's revelation to me. Drawings are unusual and not planned, those often are revelations unless I think they are just my imagination." She glanced at her brother, who raised an eyebrow.

"So, answer your own question, Lucy. You are husband and wife. Two become one. Is it possible that if something happened to the one the other would feel it?"

Lucy took a deep breath and closed her eyes, letting Fiona plod on without her direction. *Lord, is my husband weel, then?* She waited and peace wrapped around her, much like her mother's arms would after a nightmare. Lucy smiled. "I believe he is well."

"Good, then let us leave him in the good Lord's hands and get to London. We may reach it by mid-afternoon if we press on."

"And go straight to Whitehall like this?"

"Do you have a clean gown to dress in? A maid to put up your hair? I can arrange for a room and a bath, but beyond tha...wait. Katrina might have gowns that would fit you. I could put you up a hotel, go fetch some of her stuff, and bring it to you if you insist."

Michael was anxious to get her safe. "Michael, we'll go straight to Whitehall, as is. But what then? Who will keep me safe? Do you really think they will be fobbed off because the British Government is protecting me? I doubt even the Prince Regent and all his men could keep me from my father and Lord Winter if they wanted to get at me. How valuable am I in this war and why? I don't understand why I'm so important. I'm just a young woman from the Highlands of Scotland."

Michael smiled. "I adore your accent, by the way. Your mother did a wonderful job preparing you for this."

"You think she knew this day would come?"

"You'll see soon enough. While I believe some of your questions will be answered, I cannot figure out how you would be safe either unless we do away with your father—permanently."

Lucy wasn't sure how to respond to this. She didn't remember her father. She hadn't really had much interaction with him when she was a child and too much time had passed. Did she want him...dead? Wasn't murder wrong? But they had already killed, hadn't they? When their lives were threatened? Would her father really wish her harm if he came face to face with her? Could a man hate his offspring so much?

"Lucy?"

"Hmmm?"

"Our father ignored me until recently. He tried to kill me. He tortured me and Katrina and he almost—" Michael gulped and paled, "—raped her."

"Can anyone be that evil?"

"When they choose to follow Satan wholeheartedly, yes. He has chosen his god and his dabbling in the demonic has imbued him with supernatural powers. Don't think our God isn't greater. I believe that God has preserved us this far, but that doesn't mean God wouldn't allow painful circumstances to be used for His glory. Trust me when I say that until your father is well and truly dead, you, me, Jared, and this country are in mortal danger."

Dread filled her heart and her fingers trembled around the reins.

"The sooner we get this done and over, the sooner we can retire to boring, bucolic lives?"

Michael nodded. "Yes, although I doubt marriage will ever bore me—or you." He winked at her. "Let's pick up the pace."

Lucy nodded, and they rode in silence through the night, with the exception of occasional snores from the lamb.

~*~

It was mid-afternoon as Michael led Lucy through the streets of London. She yawned. Fatigue was besting her again, but they needed to finish Jared's mission. The town was noisy. She wondered if she would go deaf from the cacophony. And the stench! Rotten fish, smoke, and refuse combined to choke her.

The disparity between the wealthy and the poor was disturbing as well. Michael purposefully kept them away from the parts of town where they might encounter the upper ten-thousand, to protect her reputation. She didn't care much for that as she had no desire or intention of engaging with any who would raise their noses at the poverty around them and do nothing. She complained to Michael about it.

"Luce, there are men who are trying their best to rectify this, but it is not a problem one can throw money at. Many of those wealthy employ the poor and provide them with good wages, fair treatment, and a safe place to live. Not all are like that, though. Some, like Jared's brother, Viscount Remington, are working hard to change laws to benefit the poor. Don't be so harsh on your class. There are some wonderful people to be found in the midst of the thoughtless vain ones."

Lucy nodded and bowed her head, subdued and humbled. She judged far too quickly without knowing the facts. The truth of the matter was she knew little about the world outside her little cottage and the Loch Ness.

She gasped. The monster. She saw the monster and that would mean that someone—family—would die. She now had family. Husband. Father. Brother. Sister-in-law. Nephew and heir apparent. She put a hand over her mouth.

"What? What is wrong, Lucy?" Michael slowed down.

"We saw the Loch Ness Monster before we took off for London."

Michael smiled. "That sounds interesting. Why does that dismay you?"

"Rumor has it that when the Loch Ness Monster is seen, that someone from the Clan Cameron will die."

"You are a Diamonte so you are safe. Why would this superstition upset you so?"

"Because I have gone by the name Cameron. It could be me or anyone related to me. Even Jared."

"Humbug. Gaelic superstition. You can't believe a monster knows when death is coming to a person. Only God knows the future."

"That's what Jared said."

"Then listen to your husband. He's a man worthy of respect."

She nodded. On that, they agreed.

It was close to four of the clock when they arrived at the War Office at Whitehall.

Michael helped her down and left the lamb and horses in the care of a guard. They entered the arch and Michael led her around inside until they got to the office of Lord Hughes. Michael knocked on the heavy oak door. Lucy never heard the answer, but Michael peeked his head in, dragged her in, and shut the door.

"Lord Hughes, may I have the honor of presenting to you my sister, Lady Penelope Diamonte who now goes by the name Lucy Cameron."

Lucy gave a low curtsy, suddenly feeling embarrassed at her wild hair, filthy dress, and the fact that she wore breeches and boots underneath. She looked as far from a lady as anyone could. Unless one counted a lady of the night.

"My dear, may I compromise and call you Lady Cameron?"

"Lady Allendale would be more accurate, my lord, since Sir Tidley neglected to mention my marriage."

The man's face darkened. His eyebrows met in the middle with his scowl. "Captain Allendale married you?"

Heat rose in her cheeks. "Yes." She met his gaze. She had nothing to be ashamed of.

"That was not the assignment."

"It is a long story for another time."

"Where is your husband?"

Lucy glanced to Michael who answered the question. "We don't know. We expect him to arrive in London soon."

The man walked around his desk, sat down, and looked at the two of them. The silence hung heavier than the fog off the Thames.

Lucy shifted in her boots.

"My lord?" Michael stood next to her like the soldier he was, straight and tall with his hands behind his back.

"Sir Tidley. Go ahead."

"There have been several attempts made on Lady Allendale's life. What is the plan for keeping her safe?"

"You can leave her with me and I will see to her safety."

"With all due respect, I hesitate to leave her until her husband is here to see to her care."

There was a knock on the door.

"Enter," the General barked.

The door opened, and Jared stepped into the

room.

Lucy bit her lip as she waited for him to notice her.

Jared walked in and stood next to Michael. His hair was falling in his eyes and his face was haggard. His clothes were filthy and he obviously hadn't bathed in days. His scent reminded her of the nights in the Highlands. He had never looked more attractive to her than now.

Lord Hughes stood, placed his hands on the desk before him, and leaned forward. "What do you have to say for yourself, Captain Allendale?"

21

Jared wished he could have a private reunion with his wife, but he doubted Lord Hughes would be tolerant of his request. He had only been able to glance at her but even with her hair wild and her dress torn and filthy, he wanted her. To touch her, to hold her, to kiss her, know her peace beside him as he slept in the dark of the night when the nightmares came.

"Captain?" The man was fast losing his temper.

Jared had been on the receiving end of it before.

"Thank you for sending Sir Tidley to come and assist me on the mission. He has helped me protect Lady Allendale."

Lord Hughes tilted his head. "You do not deny the marriage."

"I do not deny or regret the marriage." Jared clenched his jaw and stared straight ahead. In his peripheral vision Michael winked at him. Cheeky rescuer. He owed him so much for protecting Lucy and completing the mission.

"That was not part of your assignment."

"No." Jared dug into his pocket and placed the sheaf of sealed papers on the General's desk. They were dirty and frayed at the edges. "You assigned me to bring you a 'package' and the instructions clearly stated that Miss Lucy Cameron was the package to be delivered along with these papers."

"How are the nightmares?"

Jared dropped his gaze. How had he known?

"Present and accounted for."

Lord Hughes looked to Lucy as Jared moved his gaze back to the front. "Lady Allendale, do you claim this man as your husband?"

Lucy looked the man in the eye and smiled. "I would have no other."

Relief flooded Jared's soul.

"You could not have selected a better man, in my opinion. My condolences on the death of your mother. I knew her during her come out and she was as beautiful and fair as you have grown."

"Thank you, my lord."

"Captain Allendale. May I extend your mission?"

"I told you I was done."

The older man sighed. "The alternative is to find some other men to provide a personal guard for Lady Allendale until we unravel all that has happened and come up with a plan. I realize you want to go home to Rose Hill and to your estate from there. I expect a written report on my desk before you leave, but you are hereby discharged from duty."

Jared frowned. "May I speak?"

"Yes."

Jared stepped forward. "Lucy is my wife and I will not abandon her. If staying with her means staying in service until she is safe and able to join me at home, I will stay."

"Remaining in service means the Duke could reassign you wherever he wants. If you chose to stay with your wife, that is your privilege but if you reject discharge you run a risk of not being able to be with her."

"My duty is completed to my country. My new duty and mission is to protect, provide, and love my wife."

"Well said, Allendale." Lord Hughes rose his hand to salute and Jared followed suit.

"It is done, then. Michael, you may return to Katrina and give her my love. Give her my thanks for lending you to this case."

Michael nodded to Lord Hughes. "It was my privilege to serve. I got to meet a sister I did not even know I had. To find her married to one of my dearest friends affords me great pleasure. I am honored to have been asked." Michael let his hand drop, then turned to Lucy to give her a hug and a kiss on the cheek. "Keep that slug in line and out of trouble, Lucy. I'll see you soon."

"Thank you, Michael." Her eyes watered.

A spark of jealousy welled up in Jared. But this was happily-married-Michael who was bestowing a chaste kiss on his sister's cheek. Jared wished he could slap his own face for his fanciful thoughts.

Michael turned and grabbed Jared's upper arm. "You are well, Jared?"

"Yes. Thank you for caring for my wife."

"We had a mission and we worked as a team. You got us out and free."

"That's not what really happened."

"It was the same result, Jared. Don't beat yourself up for something that turned out well."

"Will you be in London for a while?"

Michael glanced at Lucy. "As long as you and my sister have need of me. I'll be at our townhouse. If you need a place to stay, you are more than welcome. Lucy could borrow some of Katrina's dresses until you are able to take her shopping."

Jared nodded. "Thank you. We may take you up

on that offer. I forgot to ask. Do you still have Fidget?"

"No, ferrets don't live very long and now that I'm out of the spy business I have no need for one, much to my wife's delight." Michael turned and left, closing the door behind him.

Jared went to Lucy. "Are you well?"

"Now that you are here, yes." She reached out a hand to him.

He lifted it to his lips to bestow a kiss.

"A full report on my desk, Jared. Head to Michael's house and I will send men to come and stand guard." The general sat down. "Congratulations on your marriage, Allendale."

Jared couldn't help but give what he was sure was a goofy grin. "Thank you, Lord Hughes." He put his arm out and Lucy placed her hand on it. They left the building and found their way out to the horses and one little lamb bleating.

Scallawag ran up and nudged Lucy until she picked the creature up.

~*~

"Silly Scallywag." Lucy buried her head in the lamb's soft wool coat. Her heart was full of joy.

"Luce, I'm sorry. What I did was inexcusable. I abandoned you and Michael."

Lucy let her tears fall into the lamb's coat. She was too exhausted to even answer much less appease his guilty conscience.

"Luce, please forgive me?"

She couldn't hide it any more. "I'm so tired, Jared. Can we talk tomorrow?"

He frowned. He held the lamb while she mounted,

and handed the animal up to her. He climbed on his own weary horse and headed for the mews behind Michael's home.

Lucy tried to stay awake but slid off into Jared's arms once they reached the mews.

"Take care of the horses. Rub them down, extra oats. Keep this lamb secure as well. And you," he said to a stable boy, "bring those bags to the house."

"Aye, Captain."

Lucy couldn't even see the boy as sleep claimed her.

~*~

She awoke a little while later to find her fully clothed husband laying on top of the covers. He had only taken off his boots. She was snuggled under the blankets in her chemise. She raised herself up on one elbow. "Jared?"

His eyes flickered open a crack. "Hmmm?"

"Take off your clothes and join me under the covers." She leaned forward and began to undue his buttons.

"Don't start what you can't finish." His voice slurred with exhaustion.

"There's nothing to start right now, except to have you holding me as we sleep."

Jared pushed up, stripped to his underclothes, and sank under the covers. He pulled her close and within minutes they both slept.

Morning came and went. Lucy and Jared slept until mid-afternoon. Jared called for a bath for Lucy and food to be served in their room. Lucy enjoyed her bath and helped Jared with his. A maid had found some clothing from Katrina's closet that fit fairly well. The two sat eating and drinking a glass of wine.

"Is this an acceptable time to talk, Luce?"

"As good as any."

"Will you forgive me?"

"I already did."

"Then why the tears?"

Tear drops flowed unchecked and unbidden once again.

Jared pulled her from her chair into his lap and held her close as she sobbed. How did she begin to tell him of her fear for his safety? How abandoned she'd felt even though Michael was there? How her very soul was ripped asunder?

"I love you." She kissed him. "I missed you." She kissed him again. "I was worried about you." She kissed him with all the agony that was inside hoping that maybe, somehow, he would understand all that she could not put into words.

Jared returned the kisses. "When I realized what I'd done, I didn't believe I was worthy to live, to be your husband, to even be worthy of God's mercy."

"Love is not something you earn, Jared." She wiped away his tears. "May I suggest we get more rest and tomorrow morning you can start writing out your report."

Jared smiled. "Sleep? With you? You talked me into it."

~*~

Jared was on his back with Lucy snuggled up to him. How did he ever think he could live without her light and love? He couldn't sleep, although he should be resting well. He'd known many women over the years, but none since before he had been caught and tortured. None of them compared to his innocent pixie bride.

He slid out from under her. She mewled a protest and snuggled into his pillow. He covered her up. He threw on a borrowed robe and went to stir up the fire and throw more wood on. He sat at the desk and pulled out paper. Lighting a candle, he glanced at his wife. She still slept. Good. He began his report to Lord Hughes. Perhaps once that was delivered, he could get some clothes for his bride, select a wedding ring with her by his side, and plan to leave soon for Rose Hill. He looked forward to introducing his brother and friends to his lovely bride. He was tempted to flaunt her at a ball or two as well. He glanced at her again. She would protest such a plan he was sure. In time, surrounded by people she trusted, maybe when they were past this waiting, they could do just that.

He would waltz with her and all the men would envy him. The women who chased him knew not the burdens he brought to the marriage. He married a woman of beauty and courage. She never cowered from him or belittled him his illness. He poured himself a brandy before he picked up his pen to recount their adventure. Lord Hughes didn't have to know everything, but he did need to know some certain things.

A few hours later, his hand cramped. He put the pen away and closed up the ink. He dusted all the papers, folded and sealed them. He would deliver them in person. He yawned. In the meantime, he had a wife to keep warm and he was honor bound to take care of his duty and fulfill his new mission.

The next morning, he awoke and Lucy still slept. He shaved and dressed in clothes he had stored at Michael's for the few times he came back to London from overseas. He finished tying his cravat and left to go see Hughes with his report.

~*~

Jared left Whitehall, his ears ringing with the honest assessment of his mission. It was good he was done with this business. The tragic thing was that his mistakes could have cost Lucy her life and jeopardized the war.

He arrived home to find Michael sitting in his study. His friend looked up when Jared entered.

"Ah, red ears. I can only imagine the scold you received, friend. In my opinion, you did the best you could do, and no man would have cared for my sister with more respect and gentlemanly honor than you."

"I appreciate your commendation." Jared plopped down in a chair, extended his booted legs, and crossed them at the ankles. He let his head fall back and closed his eyes. "I wish this were over. I'm not under orders but I still have a wife to protect, and an unseen enemy."

"But we at least know the enemy's identity now. We had no clue who the Black Diamond was when he attacked Katrina and me."

"I wish I had never met the Black Diamond, Michael. I wish he had not tried all the things he has through his minions."

"I love onions but hate minions."

Jared jerked his head to Michael who flashed a dimple and raised an eyebrow. Jared laughed at the absurdity of his friend. "Thank you. I agree."

"What's next?" Michael inquired.

"I will take my lovely bride shopping. Did the hairdresser come to fix her up?"

The door opened, and Lucy walked in. "Mayhap you can see for yourself."

His wife walked in wearing a peach colored gown that gave her cheeks some color. Her curls had been trimmed and arranged in a fetching manner and was topped off by a perky bonnet.

Jared and Michael both rose to their feet. Michael whistled and Jared slugged him in the arm.

"Owe! What was that for?"

"Ogling my wife."

"Get used to it. She will attract every unattached man of the *ton* and a few of the attached ones as well."

Jared growled. "She is your sister."

"She is that, but she is also a woman and beautiful." Michael moved forward and gave Lucy a peck on the cheek. "You clean up well, sis. Have fun shopping with Mr. Grumpy Pants."

With a quick skip around her, he exited the room.

Lucy gazed at him with wide eyes. "You don't like?"

"I like very much. So much that I'm tempted to skip our shopping trip."

He watched as a becoming blush colored her cheeks. He'd been used to seeing her in peasant attire and as a boy, not the empire straight gowns that were in vogue.

Jared strode to Lucy, drew her close, and leaned in for a kiss. She returned it in full measure. He found his wife an apt and willing pupil.

She broke it up. "Do we have to shop? I am not

ready to be seen by the *beau monde* that you talk about."

"They are not like the Loch Ness Monster, sprite. They don't predict doom."

"But they can cause deep problems if the truth of my story would be known."

"We shall tell them I was in Scotland on business, met you, swept you off your feet, married you, and brought you back with me."

"That would be mostly true. But what about my relationship to the Duke of Diamonte?"

"What about him?"

"No one really knew about me, did they?"

"The Duke eschewed public gatherings. You may be safe from anyone knowing of the connection."

"But you are a Captain and I am Lady Allendale. If I had no relation to the Duke I would only be a Mrs. Allendale. Could we skip the title?"

Jared frowned. "I'm not sure that would be best, Luce."

"Why?"

"Because the truth always has a way of coming out and denying the relationship denies your relationship to your nephew as well. You haven't met him yet, but he is a great boy from what Michael has shared."

Lucy frowned.

"Come, we shall take our problems as they come. We cannot anticipate them all."

"Did you see Lord Hughes this morning?"

Jared nodded and kept his face passive.

"And?"

"He has my report, reviewed it, and we discussed my actions. I am no longer in his employ which is good. Had I not resigned I might have been decommissioned."

"But you served your nation well."

"Ah, but he dared to insinuate that my action, in marrying you, could be considered treason."

"What?" Lucy's eyes grew wide and her hand flew to her mouth.

"I have married the daughter of a known traitor, thereby aligning myself with his house."

"But...but I have no contact with him and do not agree with him."

"I explained that to his august personage. The fact remains, however, that my marriage to you alone would have compromised my service to the Crown had I wanted to stay."

"They wouldn't have trusted you."

Jared shook his head. His heart shriveled at the thought that his years of service and those days and weeks being tortured, never giving the enemy what they wanted would be cast aside and disregarded in light of this sweet woman who stood beside him. A woman whose reputation and physical well-being he had chosen to protect out of his duty to the Crown.

"It matters not, Luce. I'm done, and the opinions of others need not concern us, lest they take in their minds to restrain me from being involved in bringing down your father's empire in my efforts to protect you."

"How might they do that?"

"Isolate me until this battle is over."

"Isolate?"

"A little vacation to the Tower of London has been offered if they in any way think I have converted to your father's side."

"They would imprison you? But you could hang if

they decided you were guilty, and you have done nothing wrong!"

"Ah, but not in their eyes. The only thing I ever did right in my life was marrying you, Lucille Allendale. They disagree. But that is neither here nor there at present. We have our guards and eyes watching and our most pressing item on the agenda right now is to procure a new and fashionable wardrobe."

"Can you afford this, Jared?"

"Yes. My dearest wife, unbeknownst to me, there was a hefty dowry left for you by your father."

"We cannot accept it."

"It's yours and has now become ours due to our marriage. It is not something we can accept or reject. It is."

"Blood money. The money is why they think you have sold out."

"I have sufficient funds of my own to clothe my wife. Never fear. If you want to leave the funds untouched I will bow to your wishes."

"I'm so glad I married you." Lucy raised up on her tiptoes and kissed his cheek.

"Shall we go and break my bank?"

"If you insist." Lucy placed her hand on his arm as he walked her out to the waiting carriage. Pleasing his wife was a surprising delight to him.

22

"He's in London, my lord, with Lady Penelope. She styles herself as Lady Lucille Allendale."

"He has dared touch her? I needed her a virgin," he growled and the ineffectual minion standing in front of him cowered. It gave him pleasure. The Black Diamond templed his hands in front of his face, tapping his nose with them as his elbows rested on the mahogany desk in his study.

"They will not stay in London long. Have men sent to scout out Rose Hill and infiltrate themselves into Captain Allendale's estate as servants."

"Aye, my lord. It will be as you say." The man bowed and scraped his way out the door.

The Duke picked up a letter that had been received from the Little Emperor himself. Napoleon thought he deserved to rule France and more. The Black Diamond knew better. If anyone deserved to rule—it was him. His errant daughter was the key. Too many women had been branded and escaped, but he was not done and in the end, perhaps every one of them would be bowing before his throne in obeisance to his superior power. The thought made him smile.

He knew just how he would stir up trouble for Michael, his worthy opponent and by-blow, and for his friends, Remington, Westcombe, Harrow, and Allendale. It was time to end this, and them, once and for all. It hadn't been his original plan, but now that Penelope was mixed in with them, it had become a necessity. His master would be pleased and the Black Diamond anticipated some fun in the process. Fun, at least for him.

~*~

Dizziness threatened Lucy as she turned this way and that and pins flew right and left in the dresser's attempt to transform her into a lady of fashion. "Jared, is this necessary?"

Jared sat in a fragile looking chair and grinned. "I've been told women enjoy this sort of thing."

"Well, I, for one, do not." The dresser frowned. "No offense, Mrs. Bolton, I am certain your skills are unparalleled." The woman visibly relaxed and resumed her work. Lucy looked back at her husband. "Clothes are functional and nothing more."

"I disagree. You are my wife and it is your duty to please me. It pleases me to see you in pretty colors and looking the equal to any woman of the *ton*. You will have to be presented to them to appease curiosity, and I want to be proud of the gorgeous woman who will be by my side and dancing in my arms."

Jared whisked her around town for shoes, hats, and other folderol to make her a 'lady of fashion.' She wore a new gown of the smoothest cotton and a matching pelisse in a vibrant blue he said brought out the color in her eyes. Her rough warrior had become a gallant gentleman about town.

"This will be our last stop and then we can return home and you may rest."

Jared helped her down from the carriage and she found herself standing in front of a jewelry store. She glanced at him. "What could I have need of here?"

"A wedding ring, for starters."

Lucy smiled and allowed herself to be led into the august establishment of Holmes Jewelers.

Jared motioned for the clerk. "Curt, I've come to purchase a wedding ring for my wife. I would like to see something delicate with a sapphire the color of her eyes."

"Right away, Captain!" The spry clerk moved to another room and came back with a tray of sparkling gems. Lucy placed her hand on her chest. "Jared, this is too much."

"Nothing is too much for my bride. Consider this a bribe to put up with me for the rest of my miserable life."

"Your life with me is destined to be miserable?" Lucy tilted her head and raised an eyebrow as she asked.

Jared shook his head. "No. It would only be misery if you were not a part of it."

Lucy grinned and turned to the rings.

Jared picked up a delicate band with three perfectly matched sapphires and diamonds. He took her finger and slid it on. "With this ring, I thee wed."

Lucy stared in amazement at the ring. It sparkled and shone even in the dim light of the store. She looked up at Jared and smiled. "Thank you. It's beautiful."

Jared nodded and turned to the clerk to finalize the sale.

They turned to leave when a cheeky lad bumped into them right at the doorway.

Jared reached down to catch the youngster as he fell.

The boy looked at him with narrowed eyes.

"Whoa, son, I'll not harm you."

"Ca'tin Alndale?"

"Yes, my lad."

"I's bin try'n to catch ye all day." The young boy straightened his cap.

"Seems I caught you instead."

The boy grinned. "Aye, that ye did." He reached into his waistcoat, pulled out a piece of paper, and handed it to Jared. Jared gave the boy a coin. The young lad tipped his hat and scampered off to disappear into the crowded sidewalk.

"You knew him?"

"He's done work for me in the past. Come." Jared led her into the carriage and sat across from her to read his missive. She watched his jaw clench and eyes narrow.

"Jared? What is it?"

He looked up and smiled at her. "Nothing to be concerned about. We can go home now to rest. We have an invitation to a ball at Lord and Lady Simpson's home tonight."

"A ball? I do not know how to dance." Her palms began to sweat.

"All the better. I will claim the waltz and lead you through it and we can tell all the men that the Loch Ness Monster was not a very good dance master."

Lucy grinned. "Not if every time he showed his face, someone died."

"Does put a damper on any occasion."

"Indeed."

~*~

Jared escorted Lucy to their room and left her in

the hands of her new abigail, Moose. He laughed at the woman's name because she was a slight thing, but he had heard she was as stubborn as those odd creatures found in the northern part of the Americas called Canada.

It was hard to deny the plea he saw in his wife's eyes for his company. If he stayed she would not get any rest. It was nice to be desired though, and she was a tempting morsel that he was sure every buck in town would be rutting after.

He sought out Michael's study and opened the note again. Why had they not killed Diamonte when they'd encountered him last time? They had been too noble in allowing him to live, and now? Now the demons were surrounding him on every side and from within, and he feared he could not come out of this alive. He threw the letter in the fireplace and strode out the door. Time to visit his man of affairs and make sure Lucy was adequately provided for if something should happen to him.

~*~

Later that evening he chafed at the freshly pressed cravat. Michael had loaned him his valet to assist in fitting him out for the ball. He hadn't been to a London ball since Josie's come-out. He wished Marcus would be there. He missed his brother. He had written to appraise him of his marriage and to expect that they would have a real wedding with family shortly after they arrived at Rose Hill. Marcus wrote back expressing his delight.

Jared waited for Lucy in the drawing room. He turned when Michael entered.

"Nervous?"

Jared shook his head, and shrugged. "Perhaps a little."

"What worries you most? Let's see what the options are. Every man will want your wife. The women of the *ton* will be panting after you but ready to scratch Lucy's eyes out when they realize she won your hand. Or, perhaps, that one of our enemies will be there and all will go terribly awry."

Jared poured himself a brandy and went to sit down. "All of the above and then some."

"Much ado about nothing, as Shakespeare would say. Now if you asked Jesus, He would tell you He knows the beginning from the end."

"Michael…"

The cheeky spy waved him off. "No. Let me tell you what I think. I think you're in trouble. Whitehall is now suspecting you of espionage against the Crown, in other words, a double agent who has turned traitor."

"I had feared that would happen. It was the main reason I hoped to annul the marriage."

"But you fell in love with your wife, and what man wouldn't?"

"Michael, they might toss me in the tower if they believe they have enough evidence."

"But they don't and won't. There is no possibility of that because it is not true. No man has suffered more than you for the sake of King George and the people of this country."

"If it comes to it, see that I'm locked up in Bedlam, not the Tower, will you?"

"You are not mad, Jared. You are sane, and life will get better."

"I sure hope so."

Lucy walked through the door which had been left open. Jared set down his drink and rose to take a step towards her. The expression on her face was one of despair. Her eyes were dry but they didn't sparkle, and her lips were pursed.

She held up a hand to indicate she wanted him to stop. "I had not intended to eavesdrop but was waiting outside the door to hand my wrap to the butler before entering. It was enough time to overhear your words."

"Luce, I'm sure you haven't heard anything more than what I have said before."

"I didn't realize that an annulment would have freed you from suspicion of treason. How naïve I was. You had told me I would find someone more suitable. That you loved me too much to keep me. In reality, you loved yourself too much to willingly slip the matrimonial noose over your head. But I wouldn't leave it alone, would I?" She started to pace.

He glanced at Michael whose wide eyes and open mouth indicated his alarm. Jared shrugged and Michael returned the gesture. Great. No help from that quarter.

"Sprite—"

"Do not try to sweet talk me, Jared. I went searching for you after you had left to places unknown. I walked into Michael's study and saw a piece of paper singed, laying in the fireplace. I admit to a curiosity and picked it up." She looked at him. "It was the missive you received today."

Jared gulped.

Michael tilted his head. "What missive?"

"Shall I tell him? Wait. Let me share what I understand and you can tell me where I'm misinformed." She didn't wait for him. "The letter states that you are to bring me to a designated place and if you don't the word will spread like wildfire that you have betrayed everything everybody thought you believed in. Your reputation will be destroyed, your military record blackened, and you will end your days in the tower or worse, hanging on the gibbet with common criminals."

Jared stared at the floor with his hands clasped behind his back. He swallowed and it hurt. His blood pounded in his ears.

"Who was this from?" Michael asked.

"Does it matter?" Jared sat down. Even though Lucy still stood he couldn't stand for fear he would do such an unmanly thing as faint.

"Jared, I thought you were speaking in rhetorical terms, not that you really believed this could happen."

"It can, and it will."

"Why?" Michael asked.

"Because I will not sacrifice my wife for the sake of my name."

"A name I share. Your shame is my shame. That may not mean much to me now but if we have conceived, it could haunt your child his whole life."

Jared looked up and stars flickered behind is eyes. "Children?"

Michael chuckled. "You hadn't thought that far? It only takes one time, Jared, for you to become a father."

Jared hung his head with his elbows on his knees and hands clasped in front of him.

Lucy stood in front of him and crouched down, balancing on her toes. "I have another option."

Jared looked at her adorable face.

"I will be your bait. You lure these men with the reward of getting what they have wanted all along—

me. But because we know when and where, you can capture them and bring them to justice."

Jared shook his head. "It's too dangerous, Luce."

Michael jumped in. "I agree. You cannot do that."

"I can and I will." Lucy stood and took a step back. "Jared has been everything good and noble and I will not see his hard work and the pain he has endured end with him getting the death my father deserves."

"It's my fault he's free, Luce." Jared grabbed his drink and took a sip. The burn enlivened him as much as it relaxed the tense muscles in his shoulders.

"What do you mean?"

"I was the one who discovered his crimes, arranged for him to be deported, and the title shift to his grandson. I escorted him to the ship at the dock and we let it out that he had died."

"Why?"

"He's a peer of the realm and justice is different for them. I couldn't risk the Diamonte name being ruined for that little boy who is now the legal Duke. Our friend Theo is guardian over the estate and funds."

"It sounds like the Black Diamond might have an issue with more than you, Jared. Shouldn't we warn your friends as weel then?"

Jared took another sip. "I already sent missives to them all. They will receive them tomorrow, I suspect." Jared put the glass down again and came to stand in front of Lucy. "Do not ever doubt the depth of my love for you. I've been the least impressive husband to date, but if we can get through this I would love to introduce you to the bucolic life in the English countryside, where Scallywag can romp and our children can play."

"No monsters."

He hesitated. "I can't promise that. You know that."

She twitched a corner of her lips down. "I realize that. We cannot predict the future nor the victories that will be ours."

"Or defeats," Jared whispered.

"You've grown cynical, Jared. That's a side I hadn't seen in you before this mission," Michael stated.

Jared pivoted. "The world has been a brutal teacher, Michael, and in my mind the abuses are relived over and over again. I do not fear death. I know my future is secure and that final healing would be found once my spirit soars to meet our Lord."

"Sounds like a death wish. I know something of those."

Jared put his arm on his friend's shoulder. "Yes, I remember. I'm glad you lived to see the other side of that darkness."

"When I was stuck in it, I felt much like you do now."

"And how do you think I 'feel'?"

"Helpless, defeated, tired of the battle."

Jared nodded. "All that and more."

"We will accomplish little here tonight. I suggest we put on happier faces and attend this ball. It is a torture I would prefer to put behind me." Lucy strode toward the door and the men followed.

~*~

Jared led Lucy up the steps to the Simpson townhouse. The door opened, and they joined the crowd pushing through to gain entrance to the ballroom after being greeted by their hosts.

Jared kept a hand at Lucy's back. He looked down on his fey wife, his pixie bride. Would she enchant everyone she met here tonight just as she had him?

They reached the front of the line.

"Captain Allendale. We were delighted to hear you had returned, hale and whole."

"Lady Simpson, no one is gladder for that fact than I am. May I introduce my wife, Lady Lucy Allendale?"

"I saw you were bringing a guest but had no idea you had wed," the woman gushed. "Lady Allendale? Who were your parents?"

"My parents are deceased, my lady. I am the daughter of the Duke and Duchess of Diamonte."

Jared added, "We met in the Highlands of Scotland where she had been living and she swept me up in her magic."

Lady Simpson tittered and fluttered her fan. "I do so adore love stories, and to think we have the honor of revealing your marriage here. Congratulations to you both and I hope you enjoy your evening."

Jared shuffled Lucy toward the ballroom and along one wall.

Within minutes, Jared was surrounded by men. He fidgeted with his cravat which had shrunk in proportion to the number of people around him.

Lucy blushed, stayed glued to his side, and was gracious with every introduction and refusal to dance. Soon the men dispersed to more available prey and Jared found the air he had somehow been bereft of in their presence.

"Bad memories?" She looked up at him with eyes that saw too much.

"Yes. One of the reasons I generally avoid

occasions like this."

"We need not stay long." Lucy winked at him. Did that mean he was forgiven? She had been initially angry that he would not spare his reputation to save her life. As if there was even a choice in the matter. He hoped she wasn't plotting...no, no she wouldn't consider it. He shook his head and reached for two glasses of punch as a footman came past. He presented one to his pixie bride and for what would not be the last time, marveled that she had chosen him.

23

"We have him right where we want him, my lord." Lord Winter rubbed his hands together.

The Black Diamond leaned back in his chair. "He has to respond to the letter, first. When we have him, we have her. If we are fortunate enough we might even get my by-blow in the process. A three-for-one opportunity." He leaned forward and scowled at Winter. "No mistakes this time. This is your last opportunity to prove you are worthy to rule alongside me at the Pavilion after we have taken over the country. Napoleon will be coming soon, and I desire to give him a warm welcome."

"Your daughter?"

"I have my plans. They are none of your business at present. Do your job and you will be amply rewarded."

~*~

Lucy was aware of every breath and movement Jared took. The ball was too much for him. The men that surrounded him brought back some kind of memory. Her husband had obviously been a loner for much of the past few years. While she wasn't fond of the crowds, it was more because the noise, the smells, the myriad of unknown faces all swam around and overwhelmed her senses.

Jared's gaze was darting around the room. Their

back was near a wall and an exit was close by. He was gearing to flee any danger. The music started for the waltz and he looked into her eyes. "Will you do me the honor of this dance?"

She nodded and placed her hand on his arm as he led her to the floor. She had never danced before but leaning into the sway and movement of the three-quarter time came easily with him leading her. She looked up at him and he smiled.

"Are you enjoying your first ball, Lady Allendale?"

"I would enjoy it more if my husband could relax. We are in England. They will not attack you here."

"I wouldn't be too sure of that. The weapons of the *beau monde* may be subtle but just as lethal."

"You fear them?"

"In your words, aye."

"Relax, and smile at me so they believe it was a love match and not something else."

"Like an accident?"

"That will be a fun story to tell our children someday."

"You will make a great mother, Luce."

"You will be a splendid father, teaching your kids to play hooky from their studies to go fishing with you."

"Absolutely. It was what my father did and I didn't turn out too bad."

Lucy winked. "I think you turned out fine."

They twirled and swayed until the music ended and Jared escorted her off the floor. He found Michael and told him they were leaving. Michael opted to stay longer and asked Jared to have the carriage return to await his departure.

Lucy stepped into the carriage. Jared sat close to her and put an arm around her, pulling her close. She snuggled up into his embrace and rested there. His heart beat beneath her ear. Along with the clip clop of horses' hooves, and the sound of the carriage wheels, it provided a hypnotic background.

Darkness had fully descended and the gas lights had been lit.

They arrived at Michael's home and let themselves in as the butler had the night off.

Michael led Lucy into the drawing room and poured himself a glass of claret. "Would you like some?"

"Yes, please."

He poured her a glass. They sat together on the divan and sipped.

"How soon before we can go to this mystical Rose Hill you keep mentioning?"

"My brother's estate? Nothing mystical about it, it's home. We won't live there, but we will visit for a little before we hole up at my home, Pine Valley Manor."

"I can hardly wait. Do we need to attend any more balls?"

"No, tomorrow we do need to be here for all the visitors who will come to interrogate us. After that we should be free to depart."

"But what about the letter?"

A black cloud obscured Jared's features. "I'll take care of it. If anything would happen to me, you are well provided for."

"That is the least of my worries. Money is not why I married you. As far as I knew you had little which was why we slept outside so often."

"That was not for economy's sake, but to prevent me from disturbing other patrons with my nightmares."

"We found that I was your magic cure for keeping them managed or even at bay."

"And here I thought I was just getting a pixie bride." He nuzzled her neck and leaned over for a kiss.

"Mmmmm." Lucy sighed. "Shall we retire to a more private venue? I would hate to have my brother come in on us."

"We're married."

"He's my brother."

Jared rose and helped her up. They set their now empty wine glasses on the side table and walked up the stairs to their room. Jared, as was his habit, walked in first and checked out every space before motioning for Lucy to join him. He locked the door behind her.

"Now, sprite, where did we leave off?"

Lucy gave a sly grin as she sashayed around him to take off her shoes. He picked her up from behind, tossed her on the bed, and commenced with kissing her. She suspected she would not be getting much sleep tonight. That thought bothered her not a whit.

~*~

A sound jarred Jared to alertness. Slivers of moonlight peeked out from behind the drapes. He rose, threw a robe on, and stoked the fire. He glanced around the room. A letter had been slid underneath the door to the hallway. Jared grabbed his gun, ran to the door, and flung it open. He scanned up and down the hall but saw no sign of life.

He went back inside, set the gun down, and

picked up the letter. It was addressed to his wife. He itched to read it. He was a spy. He was used to intercepting mail and passing it on without anyone being the wiser for his viewing it. He set it down on the table. No. He would wait for her to open it. He paced around the room. Who had left it and why? That question would soon be answered when Lucy awakened. It had been an exhausting day and he wanted her to rest. Now if only he could sleep as well.

Jared crawled back in bed to wait.

~*~

A hand caressed his chest and he struggled to open his eyes. Hair tickled his shoulder and soon lips followed. He cracked an eyelid apart and saw the room bathed in early morning sunlight, and his fey wife paying him satisfactory attention.

The letter!

"Pardon me." He threw the covers back and and brought the envelope back to bed. He climbed in beside her, kissed her on the forehead, and presented the packet of paper. "This came for you in the middle of the night."

Her brows squished and her nose wrinkled. As much as he wanted her attention, he was more interested, at that moment, in the contents of the missive.

Lucy leaned back against her pillows and broke the plain, red wax seal. She scanned the interior of the letter. When she had finished, she dropped her hands to her lap and closed her eyes.

"Luce?"

She lifted up her hand towards him. "You might

as weel then read it. You are dying to anyway."

"Dying might be a tad exaggerated." He took the letter and opened it up.

Dearest Penelope,

I understand you have changed your name to Lucille. My little angel of light. The name suits you. You look so much like your mother. Regardless of what she may have told you, I loved her. I let her leave because it suited me to do so. But I have always regretted not knowing you and being a part of your life. I desire to rectify that.

If you but give me some kind of sign that you would welcome the opportunity to know me, your father, better, I would be honored.

You have grown into a lovely young woman. Lovelier and purer than even your mother was. My heart is incomplete until you have been restored to me, my lost diamond.

D.

"He wants to meet me," Lucy whispered.

"It's a trap." Jared folded the letter and set it on the bedside table.

"He crushes diamonds. Jared, he would crush me too. He cannot stand the light and it's not just me, but if he discovers I have a relationship with Christ, he will be furious. He won't be too pleased by my marriage to you, but it is interesting that he never mentioned you. He must know." She sat upright. "He knows we are here."

Jared nodded. "Yes, but that does not surprise me. We have not been in hiding since we came to London. If I wanted to hide you I could have and he would have never found you."

"Why didn't you?" She turned with narrowed eyes.

"Because you deserve better than that and the Crown did not feel it was necessary. You are still under their protection and I need to heed their dictates."

"Why? As long as what we do is not illegal, why should they care where we go or what we do?"

"Because they have a vested interest in seeing your father dead and keeping you alive and away from him."

"It makes no sense."

Jared drew her close and she rested her hand and her head on his chest. He closed his eyes and let out a sigh. This was contentment and joy, holding the woman he adored.

~*~

Lucy looked at herself in the mirror and didn't recognize this woman who stood there. Her soft ringlets framed her face and a strand of pearls graced her neck. The gown had a higher waist than she was accustomed to and made her small body appear taller. Jared appeared behind her in the reflection and kissed her neck. More skin was showing than she had ever exposed before, with the exception of last night.

"You look lovely, sprite."

She turned in his arms and wrapped her own around him. "I hardly recognize myself." She stood back to look him over.

Freshly shaved, and his hair fighting the styling by Michael's valet. His blue eyes glimmered. His cobalt superfine coat and the matching waistcoat gave him the look of a polished Corinthian-about-town. His trousers and freshly polished boots finished off the attire. She rose on her tiptoes to kiss his lips. "I'm the most blessed woman in London."

"'Tis true. This match was made in heaven." Jared returned her kiss, and pulled back. "We need to be ready to meet guests."

She nodded, put her hand on his arm to leave the room and they descended the stairs together.

Entering the drawing room, she was confronted with various vases of hothouse flowers. She wandered around to read the notes which gushed with flowery compliments to her. "It's as if they forgot I was married. Surely this is inappropriate." She looked to Jared who leaned against the mantle with a half-smile watching her.

Michael strode in wearing a green coat and a gold waistcoat littered with multiple colorful embroidered flowers. He winked at her and grinned. "Who gave you permission to turn my drawing room into a conservatory?" He strode over to her and planted a kiss on her cheek. "Good morning, dear sister."

He turned to Jared and a brief scowl crossed his features before he made them impassive. "You sent a missive to me saying we needed to talk."

"Someone got into the house last night and slid a note for Lucy under the door to our room."

Michael frowned and began to pace.

Lucy found a seat to watch them interact.

Jared folded his arms. "I thought Whitehall was protecting us? Or at least her."

"They promised they would. Lord Hughes seemed determined to keep her safe until we could get the Black Diamond."

"What will we do about it?"

Michael looked from Jared to Lucy and held her gaze. "How about another road trip?"

"What about the missive Jared received yesterday? If he doesn't comply then all his attempts to protect me will have been for naught."

"You will be alive. That is the most important thing," Jared defended himself.

"I have another idea." Lucy folded her hands in her lap as she sat up straight.

The men stared at her.

"What is your idea, sis?" Michael asked.

"Use me as bait to draw out the Black Diamond."

"Absolutel—"

They were interrupted by the butler announcing the first of many guests.

Lucy gave Michael a wink and he frowned back at her.

Jared gave her a sideways glance to let her know that this discussion was not over. He bent over the hand of a society matron, introduced Lucy, and spent the next two hours doing much the same thing. He also reminded the young bucks when their socially acceptable fifteen minutes were up.

By the time the last of the guests were gone and Lucy had consumed enough tea to qualify her for a whale, she excused herself and was able to flee to her room. After freshening up, she returned to find the room cleaned up by Michael's efficient staff, and her husband and brother locked in his study. Without her. Lucy sat and relaxed against the cushions of the chair. She closed her eyes only for a moment...

A sound alerted her to someone else in the room. She opened her eyes to find a tall man standing in front of her.

"Pardon the intrusion, Lady Penelope Diamonte, but I longed to meet you and knew of no other way."

Her heart beat erratically as she sat up straight. Why had she left her gun in her room? There was no knife anywhere either. Nowhere to put one with her shoes. "Who are you?" she croaked out.

His gloved hand went to cover his heart. "You crush me, my lady. Do you not recognize your own father?"

Lucy brought a hand up to cover her open mouth. "How? Why?" Her father? The world spun, and she clung to the edge of the chair with her free hand.

The tall man dropped to one knee. "I've been misunderstood and maligned and need help to prove I am not the traitor they say I am. I have done nothing but support the cause of England here and abroad. You had been safe in Scotland, but when I found out they wanted to bring you back here, I knew it was a lure to capture me. Believe me, sweet Penelope, I have missed you and long to be in your life."

Skepticism washed over her. Who was right? Jared and Michael, or this familiar stranger who stood before her? She struggled to avert her gaze away from his compelling eyes that bored into her very soul. She felt exposed, as if he could see every doubt. "What do you want of me?"

"Help me."

"I am no one, a mere spec in the greater war being waged around us. Lord Diamonte, I believe you will need to seek elsewhere for your salvation."

He barked a laugh. "Salvation. A term claimed by Christians about their ineffectual Jesus. I do not need salvation. I desire your help. We would become acquainted and be a family again. Wouldn't you like that? To have a family?"

Lucy tilted her head as she considered his words. "I have a family and have no need of the father who threatened me to the extent that my mother needed to flee with me."

A leather gloved hand rose with speed and she winced at the anticipated blow. Instead he smiled and in a low, guttural voice said, "You will change your mind in time. You are mine. You have always been mine."

"I belong to no one but Christ Jesus."

He sucked in his breath as if he had been punched in the gut. His teeth bared and gritted together. "We'll see just how powerful your Jesus is against my Lord Lucifer." He rose to his feet and slipped out the door.

Lucy rose to follow but found her limbs weak and the world turning curiously dark.

24

"Did you hear something?" Michael looked past Jared, who turned to glance at the locked door to the study.

"It was probably Lucy having a tantrum that we didn't include her in our discussion." Jared rose. "I suppose we should go join her." He strode to the door and noticed something on the floor. He bent down to pick it up. "I wonder who left this?"

Michael glanced at the letter addressed to them both.

"Are you armed?" Michael asked.

Jared nodded.

They opened the door with their weapons drawn and found the hallway empty with the exception of a chambermaid coming out of another room. She squealed and ran down the hall, dropping her supplies.

The men put their weapons away.

Michael shook his head. "I suppose I had better go assure her that we had no intention of killing her. Why don't you see to your wife and I will join you in a moment."

Jared nodded and wandered down the hallway, spying out every nook and cranny for evidence of the intruder. Where were the guards Lord Hughes promised? He would have to caution Lucy to arm herself.

He opened the drawing room and at first saw no

sign of his wife. Floral arrangements covered every available space. He came around to the main sitting area to find Lucy crumpled on the ground. By her side was a black rose.

He dropped to his knees, brushed the rose away, and placed his hand on her neck. Her pulse was slow but steady. He took a deep breath to slow down his own rapid heartbeat. "Lucy?" He rubbed her cheek. It was so pale. "Sprite, come on. Wake up. The floor is not the most comfortable place for a nap."

Her eyelids fluttered, opened, and she turned her head to gaze at him. "Jared?"

"Yes, my lovely pixie bride?" He scooped her up and sat with her in his lap, her head cradled against his shoulder. He took a whiff of her heather scent and wished they didn't have important things to discuss. They had not had much of a honeymoon and he longed for extended time to relax and enjoy married life.

Her hand rested on his chest. "My father..." She closed her eyes tight as if to block out an image.

"What is it, Lucy?" he whispered.

"He was here." She began to sob and he held her close as she soaked his coat.

Michael strode into the room. "What happened?"

Jared responded, "I found her on the floor with that," he pointed to the wicked flower, "next to her."

"I've checked everywhere and can find no sign of anyone entering or departing our premises."

"It's almost as if it's a ghost, if I believed in such things." Jared looked up at Michael.

"I've seen too much evil. I've come to believe that there are spirits that can manifest themselves in human form."

Jared raised his eyebrows.

"Remember Tristan?"

"Your valet who turned traitor?"

"I thought for sure he was dead, but he recovered and came after me again. It was unnerving to say the least to have my valet die twice, once in England and once in France."

"Has he stayed dead this time?"

"I suspect the wild animals took care to ensure there wasn't anything left to resurrect."

"I thought coming back from the dead was only something Jesus did?"

Michael shrugged. "He wasn't dead the first time, as I had thought. Still, Katrina had wounded him severely enough. He shouldn't have survived his injuries."

"So how?"

"The Bible talks about entertaining angels unawares. If angels can appear, why couldn't demons? The Bible also says we are at war against spiritual forces."

Lucy stopped sobbing. Jared dug into his pocket and pulled out a handkerchief. She blew her nose and wiped her now red and swollen eyes.

"You ready to tell us what happened?" Jared asked softly.

Michael sat on the nearest chair.

Lucy let out a shuddering sigh. "My father was here."

Jared glanced at Michael. "When?" Jared asked.

"While you were talking in private."

"What did he have to say?" Michael asked.

"Only that he was misunderstood and wanted to be my father in truth." She looked at Michael. "He said he was not a traitor and he needed my help to prove his innocence."

"He most certainly is a traitor, sprite," Jared responded. "I wish I had ended this when he caused Theo and Valeria all that trouble last year."

"You couldn't have. Doing so would have put you on the gibbet for murder, regardless of his crimes. One simply does not murder a peer of the realm."

"One banishes him to have him turn up again only to plague us."

"If you had died, I would never have met and married you," Lucy said.

"If I had killed your father there would never have been a need for you to be brought to London. You would have been able to live out your days in your beloved Scotland, overlooking the Loch Ness."

"I'm glad to have had this adventure by your side, Jared." She kissed his cheek.

"So, what do we do now?" Michael inquired.

"Read the letter he left?" Jared suggested.

"What's with the black rose?" Lucy pointed to the flower abandoned on the floor.

Michael crinkled his nose. He bent to pick up the rose and tossed it in the fireplace. The flames leapt to enfold it in their orange and yellow fingers, pulling it down into the wood and ashes.

"There's been another letter?" Lucy asked. She slipped off Jared's lap to sit by his side, her hands folded neatly in her lap, still holding the kerchief.

"Yes, another letter, delivered probably after your father left you," Jared answered.

Michael pulled the letter out of an interior coat pocket and tapped it against his hand. "I'm almost afraid to open it."

"He's taunting us, baiting us, while he gets ready to spring the trap."

"Open the letter," Lucy insisted.

Jared nodded to Michael who opened it. He perused the contents silently, swallowed hard, and looked up at Jared with stark fear in his eyes.

Jared held out his hands for the letter, which Michael handed off. He walked away to face the fire, leaning his arm on the mantel and his head on his arm, staring into the flames.

Jared started to read, fully aware that his wife was reading over his shoulder.

Sir Michael Tidley and Captain Jared Allendale,

I do not feel obligated to warn you, but my conscience could not be clear if I had not notified you that your families are in grave danger unless you cease and desist your pursuit of me. You will make it known that I am not a traitor and ensure I am welcomed back into the beau monde *with all the honor and glory due my exalted personage.*

Failure to do so will result in unfortunate circumstances that are beyond my control.

Start with returning my daughter to me.

   Lord Diamonte

Jared waited for his friend to turn around.

Minutes later the spy turned with steel in his gaze. "If he dares try to hurt Katrina again...Jared, we need to head to Rose Hill."

"We need a plan. I can't go rushing home. They may already have...we need to connect with Phillip and Theo too. They can help. If they see me leave town though, they will know I'm not championing his cause."

"We need to go to Whitehall with this."

"He'll be even more convinced I'm a traitor," Jared moaned.

"There's no way you can win this. You have to go. Every choice you make ends in your destruction. Even doing nothing risks everything for you."

"So, I will do what is right and trust God for the consequences." Jared sighed.

"Remember when Marcus had to face society with his alleged scandal?"

"He did that at my insistence and it broke his heart when Josie believed the gossips."

"And God vindicated him."

"That was the start of all this. Sir Bastion and Lord Widmore were the tip of the iceberg we've been chipping away at ever since. They went after my sister and Lord Percy first, but at least he was already aware of the dangers, having worked covertly for the War Office."

"I must come with you," Lucy said. "I will not be left here without you both beside me. It is too dangerous."

Michael nodded. "She needs to come and share what the Black Diamond has asked of her."

Jared rose to his feet. He went to the door and called for a maid to fetch Lucy's pelisse, reticule, and gun.

"Gun?"

"I want you armed at all times, sprite. It has become too dangerous even here and I do not know when or where we will be safe until he is dead." Jared watched the color drain from her face. "I'm sorry to speak so plainly."

"You don't know what it's like to grow up without

a father. He's offered me…"

Michael stepped forward. "I was denied his name or wealth. He's offered me power and prestige if I convert to his side. Don't be tempted by the lure of family. With him there is only death and destruction. I've seen it firsthand. Katrina has experienced it. Both Jared and I would spare you that if we could."

Lucy nodded. Jared helped her with her pelisse and she settled her gun in a hidden pocket in her dress.

Soon, they were off to Whitehall.

~*~

Lord Winter snickered. "You have them on the run now, Diamond."

Lord Diamonte nodded and gave a tight-lipped smile. The enemy was strong, and it would take all the powers at his disposal to defeat them. The battle looked secure and sure, but he had a niggling doubt that he quite possibly could be in over his head.

A footman came into the room. "A missive has arrived, my lord."

He lifted the paper from the silver platter and dismissed the servant. He eyed the missive and cracked the seal. He sighed. More demands from the Emperor. He wanted more money. But the Duke had no access to his funds at the moment until his name was cleared. And when it was? Now he grinned broadly. Then all hell would break loose.

25

The carriage bounced and jostled as it sped out of London. Lucy patted her chip bonnet down and secured the ties under her neck as they had come loose. Jared and Michael were riding with a contingent of military in plain clothes but all armed. She gritted her teeth at recalling the meeting with Lord Hughes.

He had been dismissive of their concerns and complaints. He warned that banished or not, the Duke was still protected by his exalted status and could not be murdered with impunity.

Michael and Jared hoped that brainstorming with their friends would help provide answers.

Jared was eager for her to have a real wedding which he said his brother and wife were preparing for them for shortly after their arrival.

A wedding. She was already married. She had the man she wanted. She didn't need any public display. It was important to Jared, however, and she would give him what he wanted since that was the case. It was a small thing in the scheme of all the intrigue that swirled around them.

When she set it all aside it was just her, a small Highlander girl, in love with a British soldier. The rest of the world didn't matter in the light of their love and friendship. Yet they would never know peace until this crisis with the Black Diamond was resolved once and for all.

They arrived at Rose Hill late in the day.

Jared opened the carriage door to help her alight. She touched the pavement with her half-boot and was immediately surrounded by a mass of people she didn't know.

"Calm down, everyone. Maybe we could go inside and freshen up and then I will introduce you all to my lovely bride," Jared said.

A dark-haired woman came forward with a big smile. "Welcome to Rose Hill. I'm Lady Remington. Let me escort you to your chamber where you can freshen up."

"Thank you." Lucy allowed herself to be led up the stairs and down a hallway to a suite of rooms that was sumptuous in its teal furnishings. She removed her bonnet and Moose helped her to change into a clean gown before descending the stairs where she found Jared awaiting her. He must have freshened up too. Did they have separate chambers or were they connected? She didn't want to sleep without him by her side.

"Lucy. How are you holding up? It has been a long day and we could do this tomorrow if you desire."

"No, but thank you. I am eager to meet these people who mean so much to you."

Jared beamed. He took her hand, placed it on his arm, and escorted her into the drawing room.

The room was crowded with people. Every head turned to look at her. She reminded herself that this was not as bad as a ball, where gossips waited for any sign of weakness to tear someone's reputation to shreds. No. These were all friendly faces. People Jared loved and admired. All people who at some time had an interaction with her father, the Black Diamond.

Jared took her first to a man about his same height, but with dark wavy hair and warm brown eyes. He was standing next to the woman she had met earlier.

"Lucy, this is my brother, Marcus and his wife Josie."

"I'm glad to meet you both." Lucy did a curtsy.

"No need to stand on formalities with us," Marcus said. "You're family now and it is a pleasure to meet the woman who finally won Jared's heart."

Josie smiled at her. "Welcome to the family and Rose Hill. We were thrilled when Jared wrote the news and we look forward to hearing about your adventures."

Jared raised an eyebrow. "What makes you think we had an adventure?"

Josie smiled and said nothing more.

Lucy met Lord Phillip Westcombe and Beth. Phillip was tall and blond and his lovely wife had the most beautiful red hair.

"We are glad to see Jared finally settling down," Phillip spoke. "He's the last of our group to do so. Never imagined he'd go to the Highlands of Scotland to find you."

"I never knew I needed to be found until he arrived," Lucy said.

Michael brought her to meet his wife, Katrina, a petite woman with brown hair, dark eyes, and a welcoming smile.

"Finally, someone I don't have to crane my neck to look up to," Katrina joked. "Welcome to the family. Michael tells me you are his half-sister." She whispered, "You have my condolences, but we can't pick our relatives, can we?" She winked.

"Hey!" Michael faked being indignant as he

goosed his wife, making her elicit the tiniest squeal.

"I'm glad to see my brother has more than met his match in you," Lucy riposted with a grin.

Jared turned her to the last couple in the room. "This is Lord Theodore Harrow and his wife, Valeria."

"*C'est un plaisir*, you look nothing like anyone else in the Diamonte family." Valeria spoke with a soft, accented voice.

Theo spoke, "Then that is our boon, isn't it?" His genial demeanor was more like that of a soft, stuffed animal. While not overweight, he was more solid than the other men and his face spoke of great gentleness.

"You are too kind, my lord. I take after my mother in my appearance. Or so I have been told."

"Having seen her portrait, I would agree," Valeria said.

"Valeria was once married to your brother, Damon, who died a few years back. You will get to meet your nephew, Dartanian, later," Theo piped in again.

Marcus spoke up, "Why don't we go in for a late supper and reconvene in the morning to discuss all that has occurred?"

"You will not exclude us, will you?" Josie asked with narrowed eyes.

"We know too well the consequences of that, don't we, gentlemen?" The men all murmured agreement. "We will all be present to hear them tell their story and figure out where we go from here."

Jared led Lucy to the door. "I, for one, am starved. Come, my pixie bride, let me escort you to the dining room."

Lucy allowed herself to be led and listened to the repartee of these four couples, all somehow linked to her and Jared and the situation with her father. After years of isolation in the wilderness, with no siblings, and the last two years without her mother, the whole evening was mutually overwhelming and comforting.

She belonged. These people were prepared to offer her friendship and maybe even love. She'd never had friends before Jared and Michael. She barely tasted any of the food although it all smelled divine. She sipped her wine and the muscles in her neck and shoulders relaxed. Jared was by her side. She was safe—for now.

She rose with the ladies after the repast to await the men, but pleaded exhaustion and was released to go to her room and prepare for bed. She made quick work and hoped Jared would not dally too long downstairs.

~*~

Jared watched his wife leave the room and missed her already.

"Love struck hard, didn't it?" Theo looked at him wide-eyed.

"Yes. I probably needed it to in order to get through my thick skull," Jared joked.

"Did you tell them how it came about?" Michael asked.

Jared rolled his eyes. "I hadn't necessarily planned on sharing that, but now you make it almost impossible after baiting me."

Michael raised his glass. "What are brothers-in-law for if not to embarrass you?"

"Come on, Jared. Last we had heard, you were going on your last mission. Next thing you're married and somehow the Duke of Diamonte is on your tail."

Marcus leaned back in his chair.

"I was bringing her back to London and in order to save her reputation we said we were husband and wife when we checked into an inn." Jared put up his hand. "And no, Marcus, I did not besmirch her honor, but did need to guard her. She was my mission."

"So why the marriage?" Theo asked.

"Oh, some law in Scotland that says if you declare you are husband and wife, you, in fact, are."

Phillip grinned. "Only you would accidentally get married."

"I got married and didn't even know it!" Michael claimed.

"You had amnesia as your excuse," Theo responded.

"Annulment?" Marcus asked.

"I'm surprised you would support that."

"She is kin to the Black Diamond. A dangerous liaison there."

"You surprise me, Marcus. Since when did safety come before honor? Don't you think I realized that? Fact is, I fell in love with her and she resented any implication that the marriage should not be real." Jared sipped his port.

"She seduced you?" Phillip asked.

Michael piped in, "I don't think he was too resistant, men. And I encouraged her."

Jared jerked his head up. His face and ears were hot. "You what?"

Michael shrugged. "My sister wanted you for a husband. She wanted a real marriage. She loved you. I encouraged her to pursue you. After all, it was not a sin. You were married!"

Jared closed his eyes and shook his head before

opening them again. "Conspired against by my wife and my friend."

"Well done, Michael." Phillip lifted his glass before taking a sip.

"Someone needed to do it. Marcus, were you aware your brother has a strong stubborn streak?"

Marcus chuckled. "Really? I would have never guessed."

Jared endured the ribbing and was encouraged to leave and not let his wife linger alone any longer. He rose and left the men. He took the stairs two at a time and strode down the hallway with all due haste.

He opened the door to the suite and saw the fire banked and his lovely bride resting in the bed. In spite of his honorable intentions to protect her from his own blackness, God had overridden him and joined him together with this lovely sprite. He did not regret it for a moment. He stripped and was soon in bed, reminding his wife of how much he loved her.

26

The next morning Lucy enjoyed breakfast in their room. Just her and Jared. Peaceful and quiet. No place to go.

"You do realize that you've not had any nightmares on any night we have slept together."

Jared lifted her hand and kissed it, his eyes never leaving hers. "I knew there was a good reason to marry you."

She slapped his hand away. "You realized no such thing. If you had, you would have been agreeable to the marriage much sooner."

"True. I am grateful for this beneficial side effect." He gave her a sly smile and her heart did a little dance.

"We need to meet with everyone this morning and figure out how to proceed."

"Do we need to? I hate involving these sweet people in our nightmare."

"They are involved. The last letter we got was a threat to them too. And some have had to deal with the Duke. Valeria, especially. She is Theo's wife. She lived under your father's roof while married to his son. She doesn't like to talk about those days."

"Fine. We will meet and talk."

"And plan our wedding. Would two days from now be sufficient time?"

"Two days to plan a wedding?"

"No. The wedding has been planned. I wanted to give you a few days rest before we did the ceremony. I would be happy enough to do it today."

"Two days are sufficient." Her husband brimmed with life and energy. The weight of the past few weeks was lifted now that he was here in his childhood home.

They left their suite to go downstairs where the rest of the family were gathered, visiting in various groups until the moment Lucy and Jared entered the room. All eyes turned to them and Lucy wasn't so sure about proceeding further.

Valeria brought Lucy to sit next to her and soon most were seated. Michael stood in front of the fireplace and Jared took his place behind Lucy.

"The ladies wanted to know—do you possess a tattoo or brand of a diamond on your shoulder?" Katrina asked.

"I cannot see my shoulder, so I wouldn't know." She glanced up at Jared.

His lips set in a firm line and he nodded his head. He moved a hand to her right shoulder and through her clothes traced where the brand was.

"Don't be embarrassed," Beth implored, "everyone here but Josie has been branded in some way or another with a diamond."

"If the men in this room had not acted to protect me, I'm sure I would have had one too, but it is not something I envy any of you for." Josie sat prim and proper in her chair, but her face was open and friendly.

"We have all in some way, interfered with the plans of your father. Initially, we only knew him as the Black Diamond. It wasn't until last year when we helped Valeria rescue her son from him, that we learned his true identity." Theo volunteered this information. He sat close to his wife. Her hand was in his, joining them together in an unusual display of affection.

"Is he really that bad? He said he wants to be my father. If I don't let him, he will ruin Jared's reputation."

"My reputation is probably in the process of being ruined at this very moment. He wants to brand me a traitor and Whitehall is amenable to agreeing with him. They are not certain I am as loyal as I claim."

Marcus moved forward. "They would doubt your integrity? After all you gave our nation? After the French tortured and almost killed you?" His voice was a growl.

"Ah, but Marcus, I married the daughter of a renowned traitor, whom I claimed to put on a ship to France."

"They don't even believe that?" Phillip asked.

"So, what do we do? He's threatened us all, hasn't he?" Katrina asked.

"First things first. Lucy and I will have our wedding in two days."

The women all started chattering at once and spirited Lucy out of the room. She looked back at Jared with narrowed eyes. The wedding was a ruse. She was sure he was plotting to work through this with the men alone and they had all just fallen for it. She wasn't allowed time to mull over the implications as the women began to discuss flowers, the dress, and the meal.

~*~

Jared went to shut the door behind the ladies and turned the key in the lock. "Well, now, gentlemen. Shall we get down to business?"

Michael shook his head. "Masterful, but you do realize we will all suffer for that later?"

"Worth the price, don't you think? As long as we can keep the women safe," Jared shot back.

"Provided they don't get a bee in their bonnet to do something of their own," Phillip mused.

"They wouldn't," Theo stated baldly.

The men all glanced at Theo shaking their heads.

"Katrina would be the ringleader. That girl has a penchant for trouble," Michael asserted. "I found that out firsthand."

"Lucy is an intrepid warrior in spite of her size and we've already argued about this. The glare she gave me as they left clued me into the fact that she was not fooled one whit." Jared rubbed the back of his neck. A headache threatened, and he wondered if he'd be sleeping on the floor in front of the fireplace tonight.

"So, what do we do? Is there any way we can be anything other than reactive? I hate waiting for the Black Diamond to attack, especially since that's what he expects of us." Michael paced in front of the fireplace.

"Lucy wanted to be bait," Jared offered. "I'm not agreeable to that option."

"We used Valeria as bait without her knowing it. She was less than pleased about the entire ordeal," Theo volunteered.

"Ah, but we got our man. Wolton is dead."

"How did you get away with that and not hang?" Jared asked.

"Self-defense, but we said he shot himself," Phillip offered.

"Putting himself in our crosshairs was suicide." Michael grinned.

"He did attack a lord of the realm, entirely justifiable," Theo added.

"So, can we do something similar with the Duke?" Jared asked.

"I thought you didn't want to put Lucy out there as bait?" Michael asked.

"Not alone. Perhaps if I were with her?" Jared offered.

"I think it would behoove us to seek God in this first. He may provide the answer we lack," Marcus added.

The men nodded. Michael sat. Heads bowed and Marcus prayed.

"God, we know that You are supreme over all kings and peers. You rule the nations and it is only by Your grace that ours has survived. You know the challenge we face with the Duke of Diamonte goes far beyond this war with France. It is a battle between You and Satan and we know we cannot win this battle unless we have come to You for strength, power, and wisdom in how we fight. As Joshua said, 'The battle is the Lord's' and we ask for You to lead and guide us. Protect our families in the midst of the battle. We worship and adore You, Jesus, and thank You for Your provision for our needs."

"Amen" was said in unison.

The men visited and caught up while waiting for inspiration to strike.

~*~

The ladies were holed up in a sitting room that Josie had designated as her space. They sat around the tea tray. The camaraderie they shared was amazing.

Josie finally shushed everyone. "Lucy, when did you fall in love with Jared?"

Lucy bit back a smile. "I loved him before I even met him."

"How could that be?" Katrina asked.

"God gave me repeated images, a vision if you will, of this man. I sketched them. When I saw him—I knew."

"You draw?" Valeria asked.

"Yes."

"Do you get visions of the future often?" Beth asked.

"No. I don't always understand which images will portend something. I would never call myself a prophet."

"Could we see your sketchbook?" Josie asked.

"If you'd like." Lucy rose to go to her room and collected her sketchbook. She held it close to her. Recent drawings puzzled her. She hadn't even shown them to Jared yet. Would the sketches provide clues to the danger they all faced? She came back to the room and handed the book to Josie as the others gathered around.

Josie gasped. "This is Jared in every detail. You say you did this without ever having met him?"

Lucy nodded. The heat rose in her face and she put her hands up to cover her cheeks.

"What else have you drawn?" Beth asked.

Josie flipped the pages until she came to a drawing that made all of them gasp as they looked from the page to her.

"How did you come to draw this?" Josie asked.

"The images come to me. Sometimes as I awaken in the morning. Sometimes as I sit quietly, praying or thinking about things."

Katrina stood up. "I'll go get the men. They need to see this. While they might be trying to come up with a plan without us, it is obvious that Lucy holds the key to a solution." With that the diminutive woman was gone.

Lucy raised her eyebrows. "How does that drawing help anyone?"

"Just wait, Lucy, and we'll make it clear." Valeria came to sit beside her, appropriated one of Lucy's hands and held it in her own. "God has given you a special gift. It is no accident that He brought you to Jared and here to Rose Hill."

Lucy couldn't find a word to say. She was exhausted by the amounts of conversation that swirled around the women as they chattered.

The men strode in.

"What has happened? Lucy, are you well?" Jared asked as he came to stand beside her.

She shrugged and shook her head. Was she well? Overwhelmed and confused maybe? A shiver shook her body and Jared noticed. He dropped to his knees in front of her and Valeria rose to go to Lord Harrow. Jared picked up her hand and held her gaze. "What happened?"

She gulped. "They asked to see my sketchbook and got excited about one of my more recent drawings. I have no idea why."

"Jared, you need to see this," Michael called him over. He handed the book to Jared. The other men stood around him to look on.

"Ladies, this woman drew a picture while we were traveling and showed it to us. We were able to stop, make adjustments, defeat our enemy and root out a traitor. She saved us all."

Lucy bit her lip. This wasn't about her. This was about God. He gave her the ability to draw and she couldn't help the images that she was compelled to put to paper. Like the several of Jared, she often had no premonition of their importance, only that she needed to draw them.

"This is what we had prayed for, gentlemen," Marcus announced. He turned to Lucy. "Well done, sister."

Lucy gazed up at Jared. His mouth was agape. "You never cease to amaze me, sprite."

"I don't understand." With all eyes on her and the energy thrumming through the room, her heart shook and her vision became strange, dark around the edges. She shivered as if someone dropped the temperature in the room. Her breathing grew rapid.

A soft voice in her ear and a gentle hand on her back pushed her down. "Head between your legs, it will pass." Lucy did as Josie bid her.

Jared was in front of her again, his hand caressed her cheek.

"I'm taking you to our room to rest."

"No. No," she tried to speak even though she was hyperventilating.

"Yes. We can discuss this later." Jared lifted her in his arms and carried her up the stairs. She leaned into the strength of his arms and savored the smell of sage. Peace. She was at peace in his arms. The tension inside her drained from her body.

Jared placed her on the bed, removed her shoes, and covered her up. She grabbed for his hand as he moved to leave. "Can you stay?"

He nodded. He slid onto the counterpane, pulled

her close, and held her as she drifted to sleep.

~*~

Jared waited until her breathing slowed and eased himself off the bed. He sat in a chair nearby to think about the revelations of the morning. Why had she not shared the drawing with him? Would he have even realized the significance of it? He was baffled by her almost-faint downstairs. She had managed a ball, so why would these people, predisposed to love her for his sake, overset her?

He left her and went downstairs to seek out the men. They were still with the women. All conversation stopped when he entered the room. He stood in the entryway and took in the tableau. For once he was not an outsider, even though Lucy was not currently by his side. It had been years since he had fit in anywhere. Rose Hill was home and while he had been gone on his missions, this was the place he had always dreamed of returning to.

"Can I look at the sketchbook again?"

Valeria handed it over to him. "She is gifted, Jared."

He nodded, took the book, and wandered to the far side of the room by the doors that overlooked the gardens. He flipped through the drawings of him, to the ones of Aulderic Castle, the Loch Ness Monster, the dead wildcat. Wait. Had she known of that before it happened? Had she been on alert for it? Did it even matter? She'd saved his life. The image of the log across the road and the men hiding, waiting to ambush them. She'd saved them all. She had not drawn the image of their capture and imprisonment. What would she have been able to draw? A totally black page?

He found another drawing, of him holding a baby. He blinked. Was she already with child? He was to be a father? He turned to stare.

Their gazes were all on him.

Marcus strode over to his side. "I suppose congratulations are in order?"

"I didn't know. I doubt she even knows. We've not been together long."

"It only takes once," Michael chided.

Jared growled at his friend. "She may not be with child yet. She's had images weeks before an event."

"That's different than nine months."

"What do you think of that other drawing?"

"I think our wedding is the bait my erstwhile father-in-law intends to use."

"Is there anything we can do to stop it?" Marcus asked.

"Lucy and I could remove to my estate and have the wedding later, or at some other location."

"We would only delay the inevitable," Michael offered.

"His threat is to all of us," Katrina volunteered.

Jared frowned as he gazed at the drawing of the Rose Hill Chapel. The drawing was detailed. The flames licking up the sides of the building and the doors barred shut indicated a terrifying death for them all.

27

Lucy stretched and with reluctance, opened her eyes. The curtains had been drawn and the fire glowed in the hearth. She was fully clothed but covered. What happened? She set her stocking feet on the cool floor. She patted her mouth as she yawned again. She walked to the window, pulling the drapery back to look outside.

Scallywag was frolicking in the yard with two small dogs. The sight made her giggle. She sobered. She had not been out to see her lamb since she'd arrived.

She checked the clock. How long had she rested? Looking in the mirror, she fixed her frizzy mop and pinched her cheeks. She slid on her shoes and prepared to leave the room only to find a letter in front of the door that had not been locked. She picked it up, went to sit by the fireplace, and cracked the red wax seal. The foolscap opened, and a familiar script covered the page.

Dearest Penelope,

You will always be my pretty Penny even though you go by a different name. I will make you a deal. I will spare your friends and even your husband, if you come to me alone. I long for an extended reunion with my beloved daughter.

D

He gave her no clues as to how she would even do this. Her life for the lives of nine people, one of whom was her much-loved husband who had already suffered so much. She blinked back the tears. Was there really any other choice? If she could only negotiate for Jared's reputation to be restored. She was not certain the threats to besmirch it had been followed through. She shoved the letter in her pocket next to her gun and left the room to find her husband or hosts.

The men were playing billiards while the women looked on. Only two men were competing, but the other three milled around throwing out encouragements or jeers. Jared was up against his brother and from what she could tell, they were evenly matched.

"Lucy, come join us over here," Katrina called out.

Jared's stick slipped as he glanced her way.

She mouthed 'sorry'. She went to join the women where a tea tray was set up.

"Are you better?" Valeria asked, her eyes radiating concern.

"I think so. I'm not sure what happened."

The women looked at each other and each had grins on their face.

"What?" Lucy asked.

"We saw one of your drawings and it made us wonder…" Beth volunteered.

"Wonder about what?" Lucy was confused.

Katrina brought the sketchbook to her and showed her the drawing of Jared holding an infant.

"So, Jared's holding a baby. I thought perhaps it was a niece or nephew."

"No man will gaze at a niece or nephew quite like that," Josie offered. "Especially Jared. He has little experience with infants and the last time he held one, terror would be a better way to have described the look on his face."

Lucy surveyed the picture again. Jared was a handsome man and she never tired of his face, on the page, or in person, awake, or asleep. They were correct. He looked besotted with this particular child. The child had frizzy hair... She gasped. She looked up at the women who stared at her with smiles on their faces.

She needed to think. When was the last time...? She closed her eyes. It was just before she'd met Jared and in the several weeks since. No. She was late. *But you've never been late before, Luce.* Stress and travel could have thrown her off, right? *Don't avoid it. Tired all the time, dizzy...* She swallowed hard. "Did Jared see this?"

The women all nodded.

"I don't think..."

"Doctor Miller will be here shortly, and he can examine you and make sure you are well. We have all been there. We couldn't be happier for you and Jared." Josie came across the small space, bent over, and gave Lucy a hug. "You are good for him. Don't ever doubt it. Even Marcus says he has never seen his brother so content."

Lucy closed up the sketchbook and hugged it to herself. Why did she let them look at it? "I'll put this back in my room." She escaped, hid the book, sneaked down the back stairs, and out through the rose garden to the stable yard where Scallywag was earlier.

She walked into the fenced-in area where the lamb was grazing with some of the horses. The little fellow scampered over and she bent down to hug him. "Hey, little guy. Are they treating you well here? I missed you."

The lamb bumped his head against her hand in an effort to get a scratch behind his ears. She complied, and the lamb closed his eyes in contentment. Fiona came over and blew on her shoulder to get her attention.

"Oh, I have neglected the both of you, haven't I?" She wrapped her arms around her horse and ran her hand along the mare's smooth neck, while clenching her mane on the other side.

"Lady Allendale?" A male voice called to her from the fence. She turned to face an attractive man who held a bag in one hand.

"Yes? And you are?"

"Doctor Bruce Miller. I was asked to come and check to see if you were well."

"Ah, yes. Of course." She kissed Fiona's nose and gave Scallywag a final hug before she exited the gate.

The doctor held it open for her and they walked side by side to the back of the house.

"Shall we go upstairs to get this taken care of? Then you can visit with the men before leaving?"

"I'm amenable to that plan, my lady. Do you know why they called?"

"I had a moment of panic and passed out. Because I drew a picture of Jared holding an infant, they believe I am with child."

"Is it possible?" Dr. Miller asked. They entered the suite and he examined her and asked her more questions. "It is too early to tell, my lady. If you have not, ahem, well, you know, within the next two weeks I would suggest it would be a likely circumstance."

"So, what do I do? I fainted."

"Are you under some stress? I don't understand the circumstances of your marriage to Captain Allendale, but marriage, moving to a new home, and meeting so many new people at one time can be overwhelming."

She nodded. He understood. "So, that is what it is?"

"Most likely. Don't worry. I'm sure the babies will come in time."

"I wasn't worried. I hadn't thought about that as a possibility yet."

The doctor nodded. "I suggest more rest and if you need time alone, take it. Not everyone thrives on being around a lot of people all the time."

"Thank you, Doctor." Lucy let him out as he said he could find his way to the men.

Lucy went to her wardrobe to don her new riding habit. She longed to be back on Fiona but regretted she would need to be the proper English lady and ride sidesaddle. She went down the back stairs again, amazed at how easily she had escaped notice once again. She entered the stable where Fiona had been returned to her stall. A stable boy saddled the horse and offered to join Lucy on her journey.

"I appreciate that, but you have work to do. I'll take my lamb Scallywag along."

The stable boy pointed out a scenic path and Lucy set out to explore. The only thing that would have made it even nicer, would have been Jared by her side. She assumed he would be disappointed right now to learn that there was a possibility that he would not be a father in the immediate future. She didn't think she could face his disappointment. As startled as she was at the thought of having a baby, she was equally dismayed at the possibility that it would not happen. How fickle could a heart be?

Until the issue with her father was resolved, she didn't want to complicate things by adding a baby into the mix. It was one thing to risk her own life, but to risk her child's?

She entered a shady wooded area and let her horse canter down the path. It led to a rise and at the top she found a beautiful view of the property. She traveled down the other side and soon found herself at a small lake. She dismounted and sat down by the water. Fiona grazed and the lamb came to drink and rest next to her. While she missed the beauty of the highlands, this area of the country had its own beauty.

God, what is it You want me to do? I can't see Jared arrested and tried for treason when he is the most loyal subject in the kingdom. The scars on his body are proof of his sacrifice for the cause of His King. How do I stop this?

What if it's not yours to stop?

The thought came suddenly. God was right. What made her think she needed to be the solution to every problem? Was it her stubborn Scottish upbringing that wanted to prove her worth by fixing this? It was her father who was at the root of the issue. How did she trust God though when the future was so murky with uncertainty and fear?

She was surprised when Katrina rode up and jumped from her mount. "I hope I'm not intruding?"

Lucy shrugged.

"Is this your lamb? I heard mention you picked it up along the way." Katrina petted the animal, scrunching her hands into the soft wooly coat.

"His name is Scallywag. We adopted each other. He's a pretty amazing animal and helped defend me once against an attacker."

"That must have been something to see. Michael used to own a smelly ferret. The animal once saved me from being attacked by your father."

"What could a ferret do?"

"He sprayed."

Lucy squinted.

"Ferrets have a horrendous odor when they spray. It took forever to get it out of my skin and hair and my clothes had to be burned. It was worth it to be freed from the kind of assault he'd threatened."

"I'm grateful lambs cannot do that."

"As much as that animal stank, he became devoted to me as much as he had been to Michael. I was sad when he finally died. Beth had a pet crow, he died saving her life. He ate food that was for her, but had been poisoned. She was heartbroken."

Lucy looked down at the little lamb as it napped, contented at her side. "I hope this little guy avoids any such fate. He's been a sweet companion."

"What is bothering you?"

"Why would anything be bothering me?" Lucy asked.

"Perhaps because you left us and never returned. The doctor came in and had a chat with Jared in private. When he came back he looked as if someone had taken away the sun."

"It is too early to tell if I'm with child."

"I'm sorry."

"I hadn't even planned on one yet."

"They don't go according to plan, Lucy. What about that drawing?"

"Some of my drawings come to me and I sketch them, but they don't always carry any emotion or hint that they are imminent."

"What about the chapel one?"

"It terrified me."

"Did you realize that chapel is the one you and

Jared are to be married in?"

Lucy gulped. "What?"

"It is identical to the chapel here at Rose Hill."

"I didn't know. We cannot marry there." Lucy shook her head. "I don't understand why it is so important for Jared to have this ceremony."

"You accidently found yourself married to him. Am I correct?"

Lucy nodded. "It did not take me long to decide that if I had a choice I would wed him. He was stuck on being honorable and providing me with a way out."

"He talked of an annulment?" Katrina gaped at her.

"Yes. He thought I could do better. That he wasn't worthy of me. He probably assumed that my attachment to him was out of necessity as he was my only hope for survival as we traveled."

"To hear him tell it, you have saved him many times."

Lucy shrugged. "That is unimportant. We are married. We do not need a ceremony to prove it."

"Why are you so set against this?"

Lucy sighed. "I would be wed without my mother. My father cannot be there for obvious reasons, nor would I want him. Jared will be surrounded by friends and family and I have...no one. I'm unused to crowds."

Katrina nodded. "You are not alone. We all welcome you into our family with open arms. We want to help you, encourage you, support you, and most of all, celebrate with you."

"I do not share your history. My family is intimately linked to a traitor."

"Valeria was married to your brother. Her son is

the heir and current "official" Duke of Diamonte. They have been more intimately connected with your father than you and suffered for it. Be grateful you were swept away by your mother. From what I have seen of your father's realm, it is filled with evil you may not have survived."

"The chapel is out. What are our other options? I'm not fond of the idea of a wedding, but if it is important to Jared, I would like to make him happy."

"You could get married at the local church in Didcot or hold the ceremony in one of the rooms in the house, even the ballroom if you wanted," Katrina suggested.

"Whatever Jared desires is fine. Let him make those decisions."

"You won't leave him standing alone at the altar?" Katrina asked.

"No. I would never do that to him." Lucy was horrified that Katrina even thought it was possible.

"Good. Shall we return and select a gown for you?"

Lucy nodded. The two women rose to their feet and brushed off the grass. Scallywag rose and stretched. "If you would hand him up, I'll carry him back on my horse."

The lamb secured, the two headed back toward the manor. At the top of the hill, Katrina pointed out where she and Michael lived with their family, and in the opposite direction she pointed to the general vicinity of where Jared's home was, obscured by the trees.

Crack!

The horses jumped and thrust forward. Lucy's hat fell off and a sting hit the top of her head. She had no time to think about the pain as she made every effort to keep her seat and not let the lamb fall as the horse galloped down the hill and toward the stables.

The horses were foaming and breathing hard as they skittered to a halt at the door to the stable. Stable hands rushed out and helped the lamb and ladies down from their mounts.

Katrina turned to Lucy and gasped.

"What? I lost my hat. I'm sure my hair is a mess." Lucy ripped off her gloves and reached up to pat at her curls only to meet moisture. Then the pain hit. She brought her hand down and looked at the red stain on her fingers.

Katrina led her to a bench. "Sit, before you faint. Your hair looks pink." She turned to call to a stablehand. "Ride to fetch Doctor Miller immediately."

"I was shot?" Lucy couldn't imagine.

"Perhaps it was a hunter?" Katrina offered.

Lucy tilted her head. "Don't placate me."

"Good. You have pluck. Just as I thought. Do you think you can walk? I can help you to your room and out of your habit before Jared even realizes you've been injured."

Lucy groaned. "That will be the end of my solo rides."

"You were with me. Remember? The shot might have been intended for me. We have all been threatened." Katrina had Lucy up on her feet and walking through the garden to the back door. "I think the Duke is a big bully who likes to terrorize people for fun."

"You don't think he's serious about doing harm?"

"Deadly serious. Make no mistake, the threats are not vain ones by any means. He likes to play with his victims before he pounces. Much like a cat and mouse. I should know. I've been his mouse before."

They were at the top of the stairs when Michael came toward them. "I was wondering where my lovely bride and sister...Lucy? What happened?"

"Help me get her to her room, Michael. Go intercept Bruce at the front door before Jared panics."

Michael took Lucy's other arm and she was grateful for the assistance. Her head was throbbing, and a full-blown megrim was taking over her head. "Please close the curtains," she said as they entered the room.

Katrina helped her to her bed.

Michael closed the drapes and then ran out of the room to meet Dr. Miller.

Lucy was in her nightrail and resting in bed.

The doctor cared for the gash in her scalp that had bled through the padding Katrina had been holding to the wound. Lucy kept still with her eyes closed, trying to shut out the pain. She groaned when Jared finally entered the room.

Everyone else left.

He knelt by her side and said not one word. He held her hand, kissed it, and bent his head over it.

Lucy drifted off.

28

Jared wept as Lucy slept. What happened? The doctor appeared two times in a day. His wife was pregnant, or possibly not, and now this. Someone shot at her. Her almost white curls were tinged pink.

With Josie's maid standing guard, he set himself to rights and joined his friends for dinner.

The room was somber as he entered. Tonight, as often in the past, he was alone, while his friends had their wives by their sides. The empty seat next to him screamed at him of his need for her in his life. What would he ever do without her?

Jared ate in silence as the conversation swirled around him. They kept away from what weighed on his heart. He glanced at Marcus and saw compassion and understanding in his eyes. He understood what it was like. Michael knew. Phillip lifted a glass in his direction and then sipped the wine. He too had faced the possibility of losing his bride. And Theo nodded when their eyes met. Every man here knew his pain and respected his need for privacy. They wouldn't rip open the barely stitched together wound on his soul, and he was grateful for that.

He skipped tea, went to their suite, and undressed for bed. He wanted to hold her close but was afraid he would make the pain worse. He rolled to his side and watched her breathe until his eyes drifted shut and sleep overcame him.

"Get up!" Hands gripped his hair and dragged him to

his feet. The pain seared through him as weakness overcame him and his limp legs refused to hold him in spite of his mental commands for them to obey.

A fist met his jaw as another man used him as a punching bag. Another hit his ribcage where more than one rib was already broken. Jared couldn't breathe.

"Tell us what you know."

A loose tooth wiggled after the next punch and blood flowed from his nose. One eye was swelling shut. The man let go of his hair and he collapsed to the ground. Once again, they did unspeakable things. Shameful things. Oh, God, please help me!

A soft humming was out of place in this darkness. The melodic "Jesus, Jesus, Jesus," broke through the pain he was enduring. A light. A bright light. The men were gone.

Jared jerked and his eyes shot open. The room was dark with the exception of a fire in the fireplace. He relaxed on a down pillow and a soft mattress. Not a dirt floor and stone walls. He could breathe. Lucy met his gaze with sadness.

"Did I disturb you?" he whispered.

"I love you, Jared. Try to rest now." Her eyes closed and her breathing slowed.

Jared took her hand and held it as he snuggled a little closer to her. He wondered how his pixie bride managed to infiltrate his nightmare, but he was grateful regardless. The next morning, he sneaked out of bed, dressed, and left a maid to watch over Lucy. He settled at the breakfast table.

Katrina walked in with Michael.

"How is Lucy this morning?" Katrina asked.

"Resting," Jared answered and sipped his coffee. "Thank you for being there for her yesterday."

"She is my sister-in-law and I hope will be a

friend. She is in desperate need of those. I could do no less." Katrina filled her plate and sat down next to Michael. "We talked about the wedding."

Jared perked up. "Yes?"

"She said we could have it here in the house. You get to choose everything you want. She wants you to be happy." Katrina sipped her coffee, set the cup down, and continued. "She loves you."

Jared grinned. "Heaven only knows why."

"Heaven and Lucy and the rest of us. You are a loveable man, Jared." Katrina looked to Michael. "Am I correct?"

"As always." Michael considered Jared. "You are not more flawed than the rest of us. Maybe more scarred, but not flawed. Grace and love cover much."

"I get that in abundance with her," Jared confessed.

"Can we discuss the details after we break our fast?" Katrina asked.

Jared nodded. "I need something to distract me."

Katrina smiled. "Good."

The next hour was spent discussing a room, flowers, and food he desired for their wedding.

"I am selfish. I have given no thought to what Lucy wants."

"She has given you all the decisions. She has not expressed any interest in participating in the planning."

Jared finished the plans and went back to his suite to sit with Lucy. He dismissed the maid and pulled up a chair close to the bed to watch and pray. The peace was interrupted when his sister-in-law, Josie, swept into the room.

Josie came to stand by Jared and put her hand on

his shoulder. "Were you aware that your brother kept watch over me?"

"He mentioned his scandalous behavior. I saw the painting you did."

"The 'Virtuous Viscount,' was a model of propriety even as he broke all the rules." She squeezed Jared's shoulder. "Your wife is as blessed in finding a man devoted to her."

"I need her, Josie. I need her so much it terrifies me."

"I understand. We will continue to pray for her healing and for this entire situation."

"Thank you, sis."

Josie kissed him on the top of his head. "Glad to help, Jared. We are delighted you found the right woman to wed." She left.

The quiet in the room weighed on him. "Hey, sprite," he whispered. "Remember when we traveled through the mountains of the Highlands and spent hours not saying a word to each other? I was never so comfortable being quiet as I was with you. Right now, I would rather you talk to me."

A soft, raspy voice answered. "What did you want to hear?"

Jared's head shot up.

His wife with the pink hair and blue eyes shining stared at him. "Are you in pain?"

"My megrim is gone, but I am weak and tired. I think I'll live to stand beside you on our wedding day. Did you make plans?"

"Yes. Katrina worked with me this morning."

"Good. When will we wed?"

"As soon as we can wash the pink out of your hair and you can stand on your own."

"My hair is pink?" Her eyes grew wide and Jared couldn't help but smile.

"It's a good color on you."

"Tease."

Jared nodded. "Anything to help."

~*~

A few days later, Jared stood in the morning room and awaited his bride. When Lucy came in, wearing a sapphire blue dress, her eyes sparkled like the ring on her finger. A flower wreath rested on her curls and she smiled at him as Michael led her to him. Reverend Martin spoke the vows and each repeated them. Jared's gaze never left his wife's face and hers never left his.

He regretted in that moment that they needed to wait to be alone. When they turned to face their friends, he saw the blush color her cheeks.

They all removed to the dining room for a feast that had been prepared. They sat and began to visit and enjoy the meal when the butler came to whisper in Lord Remington's ear.

Marcus's gaze darted to Jared and put him on alert.

"Pardon us. Jared, I think you need to come with me. Michael, I might need you too."

Jared rose and followed his brother and friend out of the room. They entered the study to find Nigel Neville there.

Marcus strode forward and greeted his guest. "Neville, what brings you to Rose Hill?"

The former Bow Street Runner held his hat in his hand and shifted the brim through his fingers so the headwear spun in a slow circle. "I've known you all too long not to warn you. I beg you will not expose me." His rapid, clipped speech betrayed his nervousness.

"What did you need to warn us of?"

"Guards are en route to come and arrest Captain Allendale on charges of treason."

Jared dropped his head. So much for a wedding night. It had come to this?

"You and I both know that my brother is a patriot of England. He was tortured for his country. Is Wellington aware of this?"

"I don't think so. Someone within the organization has initiated this. Even Lord Hughes was unable to stop it. He doesn't believe it is true."

"Where is Wellington?" Michael asked.

"Due in England any day."

Jared's head snapped up. "It's a trap."

"What do you mean?" Marcus asked.

"They mean to kill Wellington. The Duke of Diamonte is behind this. If they can distract the government with tales of treason, the government will be vulnerable." Jared rubbed his chin.

"So, the attack is from within and without?" Michael inquired.

Neville nodded. "I think you are right. And if they can separate you from his daughter, he might be able to nab her as well. He believes that sacrificing her is the key to his success."

Jared shuddered. "His own daughter? The man is sick."

Marcus and Michael both responded, "No. He's evil."

"We need a diversion so that I can get to Wellington and warn him." Jared crossed his arms.

"Why you? I could go," Michael volunteered.

"Sit down," Marcus ordered. "Let's think this through. The men coming here only know what they've been told. So, we need to respect them. However, I agree that Jared needs to flee. I'm thinking Michael should go with."

"Lucy will have a fit," Jared announced.

"Katrina can keep her company. It is best if we keep them in the dark though, lest they decide to take matters into their own hands," Michael said.

"Michael, you might be a wanted man as well, since you assisted Jared in bringing Lady Diamonte to London." Neville frowned.

"Wait. First of all, that was my assignment from Wellington himself. And second, she is now Lady Allendale. We married in Scotland and had a family ceremony not an hour past."

"Congratulations on your marriage, Captain. I suggest you leave immediately. I would go with you but should you be found with me in your presence it would indicate that I was privy to information I shouldn't have."

Jared raised an eyebrow. "Where will you go?"

"I'll not be endangering you. I will be heading north on a well-deserved vacation."

"Should you travel that far? What if we need you to help testify to Michael and Jared's patriotism?" Marcus chided.

"I'll not go far then. If you want, I can stay here and keep out of sight."

Nigel had worked hard to rise in the ranks at Bow Street and had become a valuable underground asset. "We can trust him."

"What will you tell Lucy?" Michael asked.

"I won't. I'll be leaving a note. Otherwise she may assume that her father absconded with me."

Marcus nodded. "Be off, and Godspeed."

Jared and Michael ran up the stairs. "I'll meet you out by the stables in a few minutes," Jared whispered.

Michael nodded and they parted.

Jared threw clothes in his saddlebag. He changed into less distinctive clothing and wrote a note for his bride. It broke his heart to leave her but having him taken into custody would be worse for everyone. At least with this option he had a chance of besting the real traitors. He only hoped Lucy would understand and stay safe here at Rose Hill.

He ran down the back steps and quickly had his horse saddled. Michael was right behind him as they rode off the property through some fields to another road instead of taking the main one, lest they meet any soldiers.

~*~

Lucy fidgeted with her food. Marcus, Michael, and Jared had all been gone too long. Something was wrong.

Katrina bit her lip indicating her anxiety was shared.

When Marcus came back in alone his expression was grim. His lips were a straight line and he avoided everyone's gaze.

"Marcus?" Josie asked.

"Hmmm?" Lord Remington glanced at his wife before turning away.

"Is there a problem?" Josie asked.

"There might be soon, but there is no need to

worry about it over this delicious meal." Marcus answered.

Josie's eyes narrowed.

When Marcus looked back there was a bleakness there that Lucy had only ever seen in Jared's face. Dread itched her stomach making eating undesirable. She set down her fork. She was the guest of honor. There was no way to graciously ask…

"Where are the other men?" Valeria inquired.

"I am not certain where they are," Marcus said.

Jared talked about his brother's integrity. The man refused to lie but could be tight-lipped when necessary. What occasioned it this time? She would not break through that wall. A hollowness pervaded her. Jared was gone. She was certain of it. She glanced across the table to Katrina who frowned.

Silence prevailed for the next few courses and Lucy could only feign her hunger. An uneasiness came upon the gathering.

When the dessert dishes had been cleared, Marcus looked at Lucy. "I'm terribly sorry this happened, we will be your family and you will always be welcome here."

Alarm was all-consuming now. "If you will excuse me." Lucy rose, left, and retired to their suite. She glanced around. It was much as she'd left it earlier. She saw the note resting on her pillow. She sat on the edge of the bed and broke the seal.

My Dearest Sprite,

I adore you and only the direst circumstances could drive me from your side. Especially today. Do not worry for me and stay safe. If all goes well, I will soon be returned to you and at that time, it is my fondest hope that we will be

able to go home.
    J

Lucy, dropped the note to her lap. Why have a wedding and abandon one's bride immediately afterwards? What was going on? He never even said goodbye.

The afternoon dragged on, lonely. Lucy sketched and showed it to Marcus who did not seem surprised at the image of soldiers coming down the drive.

"He was done. He resigned." She paused. "This will happen. That's why they disappeared."

Marcus spoke not a word but the pain evident in his eyes proved she was correct.

"What are we to do?"

"Wait here where you are safe," Marcus whispered.

"No place is safe as long as my father walks the earth." Lucy strode out of the room to find Katrina. She was reading in the library. Lucy closed the door sat next to the woman she felt closest to at Rose Hill. It was a novel experience to have a friend.

Katrina set her book down. "Did you learn anything new?"

"Only that this is why our men departed so suddenly."

Lucy showed the drawing to Katrina who gasped. "I'm so sorry, Lucy."

"I can only guess that my father set out the rumor of Jared being a traitor."

Katrina reached over to hug Lucy and Lucy wept on her shoulder. She sniffled and sat upright. "Thank you."

"Sometimes one has to have a good cry to see

things better and move on."

"I'm assuming you learned that first-hand."

Katrina nodded.

A commotion was heard outside and the ladies stood to glance out the window.

The image in Lucy's drawing was there in living color. Lucy tucked her sketchbook on a shelf and the two women went to the hallway to find Marcus, Theo, and Phillip talking with the Major who had come.

"We are here to arrest and take into custody Captain Jared Allendale and Sir Michael Tidley."

"For what cause?" Marcus asked.

"They are to face charges of treason."

"They are not in residence," Marcus held up a hand, "and I have no information on where they have gone."

The major smiled as he eyes narrowed. "We have instructions to interview their wives."

Lucy looked at Katrina. They strode forward.

Marcus stepped back to allow them to come next to him. "May I present, Lady Lucille Allendale and Mrs. Katrina Tidley."

The major gave an insulting bow. "I am under orders to take these two women under arrest for complicity to treason."

The guards moved around the men and seized the women.

"That is absurd!" Lord Harrow shouted. "Who would give such an inane order?"

"I don't know, someone at Whitehall down through the ranks to me."

"Men, it seems we have business in London, do we not?" Lord Westcombe asserted. He turned to the major. "You will rue the day you troubled these women."

"Maybe so, but I am under orders and must obey them. Come along, ladies."

Men on each side of the women clenched their upper arms to direct them out of the house, down the stairs, and into the carriage. They were tossed inside, landing on the floor and each other. The doors were locked behind them.

Lucy struggled to rise to be seated and helped Katrina up. Michael's wife brushed her skirt off and looked at Lucy. "They messed with the wrong ladies."

Lucy grinned. *Oh, yes, they certainly had.*

29

Jared and Michael made it to the coast and camped out while waiting for the anticipated docking of the ship bearing the Duke of Wellington. They had a makeshift tent where they tried to sleep as a storm moved in through the channel.

"It will be a rough crossing if he attempts it tonight."

"My last crossing was rough. Almost drowned." Michael stared out at the choppy waters as he twirled a twig between his fingers.

"I doubt the Duke will be traveling with smugglers." Jared nudged his friend.

"Some of those men were heroes in this war. All a front to transfer information and men like us."

"I know. I've met many who did not make it through for long."

Michael chuckled. "I almost got arrested by excise men one night. We gave them the slip, but it sure had my heart beating hard."

Jared chuckled. "We've both had our share of close calls over the years."

"Do you think we'll be able to enjoy the life we fought to preserve?"

"If we can live through this, Michael, I have every intention of spending the rest of my days in bucolic boredom with my wife and whatever children God sees fit to give us."

"Scratch the boredom part of that. You have Lucy

and want kids? You'll never be bored."

Jared had his knees bent and his arms resting on them, crossed. He buried his head in them. "I hope you are correct. That's if she ever forgives me for running off on our wedding day."

"A serious infraction, indeed, but she adores you and will get over it in time." Michael yawned. "Why don't we get some sleep? Will you disturb me during the night?"

"I don't know. Lucy is my cure and she's not here. Anything is possible. Just leave me alone and I'll get through it."

Michael nodded. "I'm sorry you had to go through what you did. And to now be accused of treason? It adds insult to injury."

Jared nodded. "'night, Michael."

"Good night."

~*~

The morning dawned with the world shrouded in fog and no sign of the Duke's boat. Jared and Michael waited, swapping war stories to pass the time. Jared was glad they avoided talking about their wives. The ache for Lucy went deep. His sleep had been troubled and filled with shame and horror. He awoke, and his soul felt as if it had bathed in manure.

Lord, please, wipe these wrongs done to me off my soul. I am Yours. Keep Lucy safe. Work these trials for Your good purpose.

Two days and nights passed. Jared remembered the days when he did this for a living. Michael too, had learned to be at peace being alone. Now Jared missed a fey sprite who brightened his world and brought the peace of God to his soul.

The moment came in the dark of the third foggy night. The boat docked off the rocks, a small dingy was lowered, and someone rowed in.

Jared and Michael were there to help the boat in.

"Captain Allendale? I thought you had retired. I heard you delivered that package as instructed," the Duke guffawed. "She tied the marital noose around your neck, did she?" He nudged Jared with his elbow, and then saw Michael. "Sir Tidley. I am singularly honored to have two of the very best, although retired, spies, here to greet me. What's afoot?"

The men sat down in the makeshift tent to brief the Duke on all that had happened. The man's expression was grave and his eyes like flint. "Shall we depart for London? Did you bring me a horse?"

Michael nodded and sprang up to fetch the horses while Jared ripped down their tent and packed up their saddlebags. They rode off in the night and reached London in the early hours of the morning.

The Duke took them to his home. "Come in and rest, we will see things clearer after some shut-eye and a good meal." He looked at Jared and Michael. "And maybe a bath and a shave would be in order as well."

The men agreed and sought their beds. Exhaustion kept the demons at bay. Later that morning after a bath, shave, and change of clothes fetched from Micheal's townhouse by a servant of the duke, they met in Wellington's study.

"Sit, gentlemen. The situation is more serious than you realized."

"We are wanted men," Jared stated baldly.

"Apparently, your wives were arrested and are at this moment in the tower."

Jared's heart sank to the heels of his boots.

Michael shot up from his chair and began to pace.

"They took our wives?" Jared gasped.

The Duke nodded. "The entire situation is suspicious. Michael, your wife has been a hero and patriot all along as was her father. Her service to the Crown has saved thousands of lives at great sacrifice to you both. Jared, your wife is innocent. She was hidden away and protected and has not had any contact with her father."

"That would be false. He has been in contact with her. He somehow contrived to visit her at one point. The treason accusations against me were to lure her in. But he would not have had her imprisoned, would he?"

"The Black Diamond is a dangerous fellow and not to be trifled with. I regret that your last mission has embroiled you further in the affairs of our nation when you have earned more than your share of solitude and peace."

"What I want right now, is my wife free of the tower," Michael ground out.

"Understood. First, we must have a wise plan. It is obvious that someone within Whitehall has been a double agent and under the Diamond's thumb."

"We can't go investigate, they will be watching for us," Jared mused.

"What if we went in costume to see the ladies?" Michael suggested.

Jared and the Duke stared at Michael, mouths agape.

"I am serious. Wigs and dresses and we could pass as ugly do-gooders who have come to relieve the suffering of the poor deluded women who have allowed their husbands to use them ill." Michael affected a higher tone and elevated his nose as he spoke.

"Is this a way to embarrass our wives or have payback for the times they have dressed in breeches?" Jared grinned. He was warming to the idea. At least he could see Lucy and ensure she was faring well, and possibly provide some comfort while they tried to plot a rescue effort.

The Duke of Wellington poured himself a dram of whiskey, slammed it, grimaced, and shook his head. "Do what you have to do to get information. I know nothing and if asked, have not seen hide nor hair of the both of you. Keep me informed."

Jared followed Michael out and they plotted where to get the outfits they would need. By the next morning, they were dressed in drab colors, with wigs and bonnets, money to get them past the guards, and items of comfort for their wives.

~*~

Lucy paced the stone floor as Katrina sat in a chair, deep in thought. The room was a far cry from Newgate, they were fed well, and even had a place to sleep. The room had cool walls and floor but was steamy from the late summer heat building up. The window would not open so there was no relief from that, although the scent of the Thames would only add to their discomfort she was sure.

It had been five days since soldiers had bound them and taken them to London against the wishes of Lord Remington, Lord Westcombe, and Lord Harrow. The men most likely followed and were seeking a way to free them. But where were their husbands? Were they even alive?

"Do not fret, Lucy. If I know our men, they will come for us soon enough."

"Before we are hung for crimes we did not commit? Oh, I wish I had stayed in Scotland."

"You do? And miss the adventures you had with Captain Allendale?"

"I would never regret meeting and marrying him. I am grateful to have become friends with my brother as well. But it is more important for them to defeat the Black Diamond than it would be for them to save us. They need to clear their names. We are but nothing."

Katrina shook her head, rose, and came to place a hand on Lucy's shoulder. "You surely cannot believe that tripe. Your father needs you for his human sacrifice to help him obtain the power he needs to overtake the Regent and rule this country."

"And what of you?"

"Me? He only wants me as a means to harm my husband—your brother—his son. He was probably shocked to discover I was still alive."

Lucy shook her head. "I have a hard time believing he is truly my father. I look nothing like him."

"Ah, but you have a sensitive spirit. Ultimately, this is a spiritual war, is it not? You are empowered by the Holy Spirit and he is empowered by Satan. Your father assumes your slight stature and faith make you weak. In reality you are far stronger than him because of the power that is within you."

"That does not make our victory certain."

Katrina frowned. "No, it does not. It does, however, mean that the outcome, for you and I, is a prize worth dying for and God may choose to use our deaths for His glory." Katrina smiled. "He may choose to use our lives too. We must think and act as if it is the latter He is interested in. The former is secure." Katrina gave a sly smile. "We must pray for guidance and to be on the alert for any advantage that may come our way."

"I am sure you are correct. I am grateful that God saw fit for us to be together in this trial."

"Shall we rejoice, then, in our sufferings, much like Paul and Silas did?" Katrina sat again and motioned for Lucy to do so as well.

"I doubt the prison cells will magically open and we will walk through unhindered."

"Stranger things have happened, Lucy."

"Let us sing and torture the poor guards with my lack of talent there."

Katrina grinned and began a hymn that Lucy soon joined in on as most of the songs were different from those she had learned in the Highlands.

Footsteps could be heard coming closer. Katrina nodded for them to continue and Lucy forced the air through her lips as anxiety tightened her back muscles. The steps came to stop at the door and a key scraped in the lock.

The door creaked as it was dragged open by the guard. "Ladies, you have two visitors. We are generous here and as they minister to your spiritual needs you will be granted half of the hour to visit." The guard bowed back and motioned. Lucy hated to pass judgment on anyone, but they were two of the ugliest women she'd ever seen.

The women came in and the door locked behind them.

Lucy stood still and in shock. Something about them...

"Oh!" cried Katrina launched herself at one woman, wrapped her arms around her, and they...they...

Lucy averted her eyes as they kissed.

The other woman had a silly grin on her face as she came to Lucy.

What kind of religion greeted each other like this? Greeting one another with a holy kiss was quite a different thing. She was sure of it.

"Sprite. You do not recognize me?" The woman spoke but it was not a feminine voice.

She gazed into blue eyes, saw that crooked grin, and knew. "Jared," she hissed, "what are you doing here? Are you trying to get yourself killed? If you do I will never forgive you."

Jared cocked an eyebrow. "As I would not be alive to notice, it seems a futile threat. Is Michael the only one to receive kisses from his bride?"

Lucy reached a hand up to touch his clean-shaven face. She pulled him down and gave him a kiss that certainly should have left no doubts about her desire for him, and her delight at seeing him.

When he came up for air, he hugged her close. "I was crushed to hear they had arrested you."

Lucy nodded. "They have cared for us weel then. I suppose they don't want skinny corpses hanging from the gibbet?"

"Do not even joke about that. Come, we have some work to do and little time to accomplish it."

Thirty minutes later, the guard returned. He found his prisoners on their knees, facing the window and murmuring earnest prayers in soft whispers. The missionary women nodded their thanks and were escorted out of the tower. Katrina gave the guard a tip as a reward for his service to them. They exited to the courtyard, crossed it, and reached a carriage left for them there. They sat inside and rode in silence to the mews behind Remington townhouse. They paid off the groom and entered in the back gate, through the gardens, and into a side door.

Without a word, they moved down the hallway to the study where Katrina knocked three times at the door. A solid male "Enter" was heard from within. Katrina opened the door and closed it. Once Lucy had entered, Katrina locked the door.

Three men jumped to their feet. "Who…?" Marcus asked as he took a step forward.

Katrina untied her bonnet, removed it, and pulled off her wig. She nodded to Lucy to do the same.

30

"Your foolish brother and my husband dressed in these clothes to come and help us escape from the tower." Katrina tossed the hat and wig down with a moue of disdain.

Lucy placed hers on top of Katrina's.

"Where are the men?" Marcus asked.

"Pretending to be us, up in the tower," Lucy offered. "It is a disguise that won't work for long unless they brought their razors with them."

"It will never work. They are taller than you and even in disguise could never pass for you both," Phillip offered. "I wish I could have seen them though."

Lucy raised an eyebrow. "They give women of faith a bad reputation. Not all are so ugly."

Theo struggled not to grin but lost the battle. "I'm sure they donned many disguises over the years but this…?" He shook his head.

"We need to rescue them. Are my children well?" Katrina had one hand on her hip as she tapped her toe.

"Josie, Beth, Valeria, and your nurse have been caring for the children at Rose Hill. Everyone was well last we saw them," Marcus stated.

"I miss them," she pouted.

"We'll need to visit with the Duke of Wellington," Lucy stated. "Well, not us," as she pointed between her and Katrina, "but one of you. I agree that we need to seek a way to rescue them."

"Did they bring stuff with them?" Marcus asked.

"The new wigs and dresses, since ours would never fit them. Beyond that, we never looked in the basket," Lucy offered.

"The basket!" Katrina ran to the door, unlocked it, and then tore down the hallway. Lucy watched her go and shrugged.

Marcus came to her and led her to a seat. "Can I order tea or something to eat?"

Lucy shook her head. "No. But I thank you. I do not think I could eat anything right now." She set her trembling fingers in her lap.

Marcus sat down beside her. "You know my brother loves you."

"That was never in question. Right now, though, I could seriously wound him." She clenched her hands into fists and brought one up.

Marcus chuckled. "I do not envy him when he does get out of the tower. If he is smart, he will stay there until you cool down."

Lucy frowned and raised a fist to him. "You would not be the first man for me to flatten."

Marcus raised both hands. "You would not hit an unarmed man."

"As both your arms are intact..." Lucy bit out.

Marcus rose and moved away.

Katrina ran back into the room and locked the door behind her. In her arms was the large basket the men had brought with them. Katrina sat it in front of Lucy and bent over to catch her breath.

They had not checked the contents of the basket.

She bent over and removed items from it. Gospel pamphlets, a prayer book, bandages? Lucy set them aside. At the bottom was a cloth that had covered the inside of the basket. She lifted the cloth up to find two letters. One for her and the other for Katrina. Lucy handed what she presumed was Michael's missive to her friend. She searched further. Finding nothing she repacked the basket and set it aside. She considered the note from Jared in her hands.

Katrina had ripped hers open and devoured the contents.

Lucy looked at the letter in her hands and blinked back the tears. What could he possibly have to say to her that she didn't already know? He loved her. She admired him for his daring rescue today. She feared for him as well. Especially if he were discovered.

Feet stood before her and she looked up.

Lord Harrow held his hand out. "Come, let me take you where you may be in private to read your letter."

Lucy rose. How had he known? He led her to another room with a pianoforte on one end. "Return when you are ready."

"Where else would I go?"

Theo pursed his lips and nodded his head as he pointed a finger at her. "Good point." He bowed and left the room, closing the door behind him.

Lucy touched the letter. This could be the last thing she might ever read from her husband if he did not survive. She finally broke the seal and carefully unfolded it, eager but also dreading the words that might lie within.

Dearest Pixie bride, my Lucy,

Terror gripped me when I heard of your capture. I pray you were not inopportuned by anyone. Both Michael and I regretted our departure as we never anticipated they would use you to get to us. Stand strong, Sprite. We will defeat this enemy or die trying. If it provides freedom for others, it will have been worth the price paid.

My one regret would be that I never showed you our estate. The place I had dreamed of making a home filled with peace, laughter, and love. None of these ever seemed within my reach until I met you.

Now do me a favor. Pray and draw. Perhaps the Lord will reveal to you a way to defeat your father and free us all from the burden of the charges that haunt us. I believe in you.

All my love, forever,
J

Lucy reread the letter and folded it neatly. She tucked it in her pocket and let the tears fall. *I love you, too, Jared. Please God, return him to me.*

A soft click alerted her to the door opening. She wiped her eyes and turned to see who intruded.

"Luce? I apologize for disturbing you. Are you well?" Katrina had gone no further than a step in the room.

Lucy motioned for her to come further.

Katrina sat next to Lucy. "It was a good letter?"

Lucy nodded. "I'm still going to kill him when this is over."

Katrina smiled. "Shall we string them up together? There's an ideal tree at Rose Hill."

"Not a hanging in the traditional sense. Can we hang them from their ankles and then tickle them to death?"

Katrina's smile grew wider. "So maybe enough blood will get to their brains?"

"I know they only sought to rescue and protect us, but at what cost?" Lucy fidgeted.

Katrina frowned. "Only God knows the future."

"Jared wants me to draw and pray. He believes God will show me the answer as I do so."

"You don't sound confident of that," Katrina said.

"It's an unknown and not a gift I can command. It is totally at the discretion of God whether He will reveal anything or not."

"But you know when it happens?"

"Some of the time, yes."

"I will send one of the servants out to get what you need. We will be staying here, out of sight. Michael suggested that since neither one of us is a stranger to breeches that we may want to be about the house dressed as men, just in case."

"What of the servants?"

"Loyal."

"This dress is far too big on me anyway. Could they have picked nicer colors? They have to be the ugliest I've ever seen," Lucy complained as she pulled at the dark, olive green cotton with dusky orange trim.

Katrina smiled and pulled at her drab brown dress. "I once wore something similar to this when I was undercover. My disguise worked so well, Michael did not recognize me."

"No!"

Katrina nodded. "Granted he had not seen me in a few years but I had always loved him. He did not recognize me until I got shot. I was dressed as a man and my secret was uncovered when they began to undress me. Phillip recognized me right away and was furious with Michael. Poor guy didn't know what hit him. I'll be glad to set this aside for breeches for a while."

"Much easier to ride astride in breeches than

sidesaddle." Lucy shuddered.

Katrina hugged Lucy. "I knew we would be great friends. No rides of any kind though until we have our men safe and our names cleared."

"Only if it's an emergency," Lucy offered.

Katrina smiled. "Oh, most definitely then."

The two women rose and went to seek clothing to change into.

~*~

Lucy had been drawing and praying and her hand cramped. She growled. "Nothing. I'm not getting anything."

"Give it time," Marcus offered. "Set it aside for now and come have supper. No visitors tonight so it is safe." He helped her up. "I suppose I have to allow you 'men' to stay for port after dinner?"

"I know it is a hardship, but I will acknowledge to a liking for the wine," Katrina said.

"Well, then you can hold your own with us." Marcus escorted her to the dining room, meeting up with Katrina, Phillip, and Theo.

The meal was punctuated by long stretches of silence. As the dessert plates were removed, Phillip complained, "It is not right that we sit here while Michael and Jared are in the Tower. We must do something."

"We are. We are waiting for God to reveal what we should do. We are waiting to see what Lord Wellesley, the Duke of Wellington, discovers and we are here waiting to see if Lucy's drawings reveal anything."

"I hate waiting," Phillip complained.

"Don't we all?" Theo countered. "Enjoy your wine. By that I mean the port, not your grumbling."

Phillip glared at Theo but did as he bid.

Lucy took a sip and savored the rich, full-bodied flavor of the wine. She had never had it before leaving her home in Scotland.

Soon she was on her way to her room, sketchbook under her arm. She was tired but dreaded sleep. Time was running out and she wanted to find any clue that would lead them to capturing the Black Diamond and clearing them all of false charges.

~*~

Jared stretched out on the hard cot. He made sure his blanket covered his boots which were not those of a dainty woman. They had thus far avoided contact with the guards by pretending to pray. It was not all pretend though. There was not much else to do other than worry. And pray.

Since no hue and cry had erupted after the women departed, he grew confident that Lucy and Katrina were safe with Marcus. Had the women found their notes? Would Lucy be able to unravel a plan to defeat her father?

Michael had been a taciturn roommate. He spent time gazing out the one small window. If his friend felt as trapped and hopeless as Jared did, contemplating an end to their lives was appropriate. If the Black Diamond had his way, there would be no trial. Neither Jared nor Michael were peers of the realm and even if they were...Jared shuddered to think of the courtyard where hangings of high profile criminals took place.

Soon he heard Michael snoring on the other side of

the small space. Jared yawned, closed his eyes, and prayed for sleep and a rescue.

He rested in the arms of his latest fount of information. He had not taken her virtue but had wooed her enough that she spilled her secrets. He wondered how valid they were. Somewhere in the night he was yanked from slumber and punched before he even opened his eyes.

She screamed. A gunshot. Silence.

He was dragged away. When he awoke, he was in the dark and stripped of all but his shirt and unmentionables. His toes were cold. His head ached. A one-way lantern shown in his face, blinding him. He couldn't see the voice that taunted and interrogated him. Was it the same one who beat him and did other things to him? His back ached from the ripped skin from the whip that had been applied. He had mistakenly put his shirt back on. He ripped it off shortly after as the blood dried to the cotton. It all bled again when he managed to work the shirt loose. Cold. So cold. He hadn't cried since he was a baby, had he?

Even in the faces of the dead corpses he had ridden through on his way to missions, he had been able to separate from and not react. Now those eyes haunted him. All the friends he'd lost and not had time to grieve combined with his agony. He was making up for it now.

"Jared?" A whisper. "Jared. Lucy needs you. Wake up."

Lucy? Who was that? He searched his mind until he found an image of a petite woman, small but strong, with a kiss that chased away demons. Yes. His Lucy. Thank God for his pixie bride. Maybe she would save him again.

~*~

"The Duke of Wellington has returned, it is said to contest charges against his favorite *aide-de-camp*." The scrubby child stood before the Black Diamond and showed no fear.

"And where is his favorite spy?"

"I dunno." The kid shrugged.

"I need better information than that if you expect to be paid. Off with you, now." The Duke flipped his hand.

The boy was dragged from the room, protesting his need for a crown.

"I'll crown you..." the Duke hissed to himself. At least he had the women. His son would always come to rescue his mousy bride. Would his despised son-in-law do as much for his daughter? Sure, she had grown into a stunning young woman, much like her mother. But he had plans for her. He grinned. She would be wishing for the noose after what he would do to her. Oh, he would have so much enjoyment and soon...he would be King. And his enemies? They would be quite dead.

31

Jared needs me.

Lucy tossed and turned and prayed that Jared would not have a night terror that would expose him to the guards as an imposter. She rose, lit a candle, took it over to the fireplace, and placed it on the table. The room was draped in shadow. She pushed the embers of the fire and threw some more kindling on. She was chilled more in spirit, but the shiver of fear was just as real. She grabbed a blanket, her sketchbook and pencils, and sat down. She curled her legs up and began to sketch. Drawing after drawing soon littered the floor and then finally—

She stared at the image before her and bit her lip. Would the Duke of Wellington go along with the ruse? Would the Duke of Diamonte fall into their trap?

She set it aside and yawned. Time was short. More than anything she wanted her husband beside her. She would do anything to make that happen. Anything.

~*~

Arthur Wellesley, also known as the Duke of Wellington, looked at the pixie who stood before him. He understood Jared was besotted with his bride, but the Duke's most trusted aide-de-camp had described this lady well. This woman was the key to resolving this mess.

"It is a pleasure to meet you. Lady Allendale, I

presume?"

"I am terribly sorry to interrupt your morning and disturb your staff, but it is important. I know we have never been introduced…" Lucy bobbed a curtsy.

The Duke smiled and held up a hand. "No apologies necessary. You are a highly-prized treasure and I'm surprised you managed to come here without some protection. There are many who would prefer to see you dead, I think."

Lucy shook her head. "Oh, not dead yet. They would prefer to torture me as part of a twisted, evil sacrifice that my father believes will gain him the throne of England."

The Duke raised his eyebrows. "Interesting. How do you know this?"

"My father is like a cat playing with a mouse. He enjoys creating terror in his victims before he finally pounces for the kill."

The young woman standing before him gazed at him with earnest and guileless blue eyes that reminded him of the waters in the south of Spain that shimmered in the sunlight. How had Jared ever managed to accomplish his task with this beauty beside him?

"Come and sit, my lady, and you can tell me what is so urgent. And if you can tell me why you are here instead of my top agent, that would be appreciated. Last I heard you were locked in the Tower for treason."

Arthur listened with fascination at the tale of her rescue and laughed at the impossible actions of Captain Allendale and Sir Tidley. "For two men bent on retiring, they have dug themselves deep into your battles."

Lucy blushed. "I am indebted to both of them, my lord. I would do anything to see them safe. Here is the letter my husband left me." She handed over the missive.

Wellesley scanned the script in Jared's unique scrawl. He looked up at the woman before him. "You have a gift?"

"Sometimes when I sketch I get images of something that will happen in the future. It was that way with Captain Allendale." She flipped her sketchbook to drawings of her husband and handed it to him. "I drew these in the weeks before he ever showed up at Loch Ness. When I saw him in the woods, before we were introduced, I already knew him. As if God intended him for me."

"From what your husband tells me, you are his perfect match."

"I'm glad he understands that. He fought it for some time."

"Allendale is stubborn but loyal."

"Of that I am well aware." She blushed.

"You have drawn something then? Am I to assume you are here because you have a plan?"

Lucy took the sketch book, flipped to the back, and showed him a page.

Arthur looked at the images in front of him. He shook his head. "You didn't show this to Lord Remington or even to Mrs. Tidley?"

Lucy pursed her lips and shook her head.

"Why?"

"They would deny me the right to follow through on this."

"And you think I would not do the same?"

"You want our men free as much as I do. You want the Black Diamond's reign of terror and treason to end."

"How do you know that this drawing is the key?"

Lucy took the sketch book and paged a few sheets back. "These images are only that. Images. With no depth or meaning. It's a feeling I get, as if the Holy Spirit nudges me and says 'this one.' Also, you recognized many of the faces in this drawing." She flipped back to her plan.

"Yes. And you have not been in society enough to have met most of these people." He regarded her as she stared back at him. "This is a dangerous business and I cannot guarantee you will not suffer as a result of this undertaking. There will be little I can do in such a plan to protect or keep you safe."

"I suffer now in a strange land, a strange town, and without my husband. He has served faithfully and does not deserve this treatment by his country."

"True. He does not. Nor do you." He released a heavy sigh. "I have little recourse but to agree to your mad scheme and pray that somehow, by God's grace, you survive. Your husband will have my head if anything bad happens to you."

"If I don't make the attempt, a noose will have my husband's head and I cannot bear to let that happen if there was some way I might stop it."

"You do not doubt he could escape the Tower? It has happened before."

"I cannot await that possibility."

"Fine. I will come for you at nine this evening. Do you have an appropriate gown? I do have my dignity and will not attend with you wearing those breeches, as lovely as they are."

Her face grew pink again.

"I will be dressed as befits my position in society." She rose to her feet and bobbed another curtsy to him.

"Thank you, my lord."

"The pleasure is all mine. Can you make it home safely?"

She winked at him. "You might be surprised at my talents, but I appreciate your concern." She spun on her heels and was out the door before he could utter another word.

Arthur grinned to himself. Today would be interesting indeed. Perhaps he would pay a visit to the 'ladies' in the Tower. This was a sight he wanted to see with his own eyes.

~*~

"Psssst!" Michael was looking uglier this morning and their attempts to shave with no mirror had been unfortunate. They both looked as if they had been slugging it out for a crust of bread.

Jared came to the barred window in the door. He looked out into the stone hallway. "What? I don't see anything."

"Exactly. There should have been a changing of the guards but a bell rang earlier. Maybe someone important has arrived? Anyway, they are gone, and…" Michael pulled on the bar as the door had no handle on this side. The heavy door began to move.

Jared rushed to help open it and stuck his hand in his dress pocket where he had a gun hidden. Both men looked down the hallway. Michael motioned for them to go left and Jared followed. Through twists and turns and staircases, and a few moments where they had to wait, they soon found themselves out a side door. No hue and cry had arisen yet, but they expected it at any time.

"Look!" Jared pointed to the street. "Lord Wellington must be near." The men scooted in an alley and shed their dresses and wigs, grateful they had kept at least a shirt, waistcoat, and trousers underneath. Anyone looking would be searching for women, not men. They crept around until they came to the carriage. Jared caught the groom's eye and held a finger to his lips. The groom nodded and grinned. Michael and Jared entered the carriage, lowered the blinds, and waited for the Duke to return.

"I can't believe we escaped the Tower," Michael said.

"I'm glad to be gone, but will be even happier to have our names cleared so we can show our heads without fear."

"Until the Black Diamond ceases to walk this earth, it won't matter."

"True."

The men waited in silence. After some time passed, the door opened and the Duke of Wellington took a step up and stopped.

"Well, what have we here? A pleasant surprise although you have denied me the opportunity to see you both dressed as women. I am disappointed, but you will make this up to me tonight." The Duke sat down, the door closed.

Jared had a sinking feeling that something was afoot, and that perhaps his wife was at the core of it. Jared opened his mouth to speak.

The Duke held up his hand. "No, do not speak. I'm sure it will be an entertaining tale, but not here or now."

They remained quiet and entered the Duke's home from the rear to avoid prying eyes from his neighbors.

The Duke brought them to his drawing room and offered them each a drink.

"How was the Tower, men?" He sat down and waited.

"Are the women safe?" Jared asked.

The Duke smiled. "Yes. Your ruse was successful, and I believe your wives are grateful and angry all in one."

Michael grinned. "Ah, but making up will be the sweeter for it."

Jared elbowed him in the ribs.

"Hey!"

"Has Lucy…?"

The Duke frowned. A lump formed in Jared's chest. "Your delightful wife visited me this morning. Alone. Wearing trousers. How anyone would ever think she could pass for a man must be blind. Delightful woman."

Jared opened his mouth.

"You are too impatient. Let me enjoy this moment where for once I know more than either of you." The Duke sipped his wine, closed his eyes, and savored it.

Jared grew antsy.

The Duke explained all that had happened and the plans for the evening.

Jared rose to his feet and paced. "We cannot let her engage in this foolishness. It is too dangerous."

"Have you had success in stopping your wife from doing what she sets out to do? If you do I want your secret." The Duke had a smug smile on his face as he watched Jared.

"You could have told her 'no,' couldn't you?"

"She would have engaged in the folly with or without me. I'm grateful she sought out my assistance.

Now with you two free, you can help."

"She didn't draw us in her drawing, did she?"

"At first, I didn't think she had, but when I glanced at it a second time I saw you both. I doubt she even realized she'd drawn you in." He went on to explain the drawing to Jared and Michael as they planned for the evening.

Jared's frustration and fear rose as they sought rooms to bathe, got a proper shave, and dressed for the evening. Once the borrowed valet left, he sank to his knees and bent his head in prayer.

Lord, I don't know how You will work this all out and it scares me. I wish I could say that I desire the safety of my country, but more than that I ask You would give me more years to know and love my pixie bride. If this drawing is truly from You, I know You have Your hand in the events that will take place and pray that somehow You will bring about Your perfect plan. You know the desire of my heart. More than anything I want to honor You with my actions tonight. Protect and guide us. Amen.

~*~

The Black Diamond rose from his bed and looked down with disdain at the woman resting there. She suited him for a time, but he had tired of her whining that she didn't like the games he wanted to play. They were too *rough* for her, she'd said.

The Duke smiled. He would show her what rough was really like. Tonight was a full moon and not just any full moon, but a harvest moon, which conveyed special blessings on those who worshipped on this night. His cohorts would have their fun and the sanctimonious lady of the night would find that her greater purpose was to satisfy the demands of the god they both served.

He chuckled as he walked away to get dressed. His daughter was locked in the Tower and her husband was still at large. He had no worries. Being King of England would be a sweet victory and one he meant to savor. Tonight, would be the beginning of the end of the Georgian empire.

He rubbed his hands together in glee. He could hardly wait. The only thing that would make it sweeter was if he could have his daughter to complete things tonight. He shrugged. If all else failed, he could retrieve her from the Tower. Hanging was too good for her. She was a traitor to her father and for that, she must be made to suffer.

32

Lucy couldn't eat. Her nerves were strung tight. She would snap if one more person asked her, "Are you sure this is a good idea?"

Katrina had not eagerly agreed to the scheme for tonight, but she would be there, as would Marcus, Phillip, and Theo. It didn't mean they approved or liked it.

"Jared will have my head if anything happens to you," Marcus had said to her earlier.

"Tell him I would do it with or without you." She handed Marcus a letter for Jared, 'just in case.'

She was armed, but more than anything it was the dress she wore that was her most potent weapon should she finally meet Prince George. As Regent, he could free the men and lift the cursed charges that hung over her and Katrina. If it did not work, however, there was much to lose. Her hand went to her throat, currently exposed along with more of her chest than was comfortable. *Use all your tools*, she told herself.

Before going down to dinner she sat on the ottoman by the fireplace and gazed into the flames. As they'd flickered and danced, it seemed much like the evil designs of her father seeking to destroy her and the entire nation. So much more was at stake than her neck.

Lord, rescue Jared and Michael. Keep them safe from harm and free them from the charges against them. Protect the King and Regent from the wiles of the evil that threatens and is only held at bay by Your will. Give me success tonight in the endeavor you have called me to. Guide me by Your Spirit and empower me by the same. For Your glory. Lord, if You decide this is my end, help Jared to cope and find love again. Thank You for these few short weeks as his wife. You have blessed me with adventure and love and I am grateful for these days You have given. I give myself now to Your keeping and trust You with my soul regardless of the outcome. Amen.

She rose and grabbed her wrap. With one final look in the mirror at her reflection she nodded to give herself courage. She could do this. She would do this. For God, for Jared, and for her country. She squared her shoulders and left the room.

Dinner started out quiet.

Katrina slammed her fork down and glared at Lucy. "I am not happy with this plan."

"You don't need to be. I'm not either, but it is what God provided so it is up to me to obey." Lucy continued to eat.

Marcus piped in. "Lucy is right. I'm not happy about this plan tonight, but we will all be there. We need to follow through and see what God might do."

"It is not a plan. It is a picture and a location. There is no 'plan' that you speak of and that is what concerns me. Who are we anticipating? Who will be there? What are the possible dangers?" Katrina scowled, picked up her fork, and resumed eating.

Theo cleared his throat and took a drink of wine. "We know the starting point and not the middle or end. We've had many situations like that but weren't always prepared for them. We are as prepared as possible. We know our enemy and that's more than we did in the past."

"Do you think he will show?" Phillip asked.

Lucy shrugged. "I'll not even try to guess. I anticipate the Regent being there and hope to plead my case with him."

"The Regent?" Katrina's eyes were wide. "Why didn't you say so earlier? I didn't see him in the drawing."

"You didn't look close enough. He was surrounded in the crowd."

Marcus shook his head. "That makes this mission doubly dangerous. The Regent has his own guards—"

"—and let us not borrow trouble before it arrives," Lucy announced. She took a sip of her own wine to help steady her nerves. "You have my letter for Jared?" She looked at Marcus.

He nodded and patted his inner pocket.

Phillip chuckled. "You are carrying it with you? Do you expect him to break out and join us tonight for a waltz with his bride?"

Theo chuckled. "I wouldn't put it past him. Wouldn't that make the evening fun?"

Marcus dug into the roast rabbit on his plate. "You sound just like Michael would at this point. He must have rubbed off on you over the years."

Theo shook his head. "No, just imagine the surprise when the two women thought to be in the Tower arrive. Even more so if the men show up separately. That will get the scandalmongers salivating, to be sure."

"Let us focus on getting through this." Katrina set her fork down and pushed the plate away. "I'm too anxious to eat any more." A footman came to clear her plate and she sipped her wine as she gazed at Lucy. "I'm sorry to give you such a hard time. I am worried about Michael. Could tonight push their execution to the forefront of the public eye?"

"I won't worry about that. I know what I have to do and intend to do it. I will not let the fear of all the imagined tragedies that could befall us keep me from what God has asked of me."

Katrina nodded. "I'm on your side. Forgive me for challenging you."

Lucy looked up to see the entreaty in Katrina's brown eyes. "Forgiven. I'm sorry I have not been more sensitive to your own loss. You have children who stand to lose a parent. I have no one beyond Jared to be concerned about. I've been selfish. I beg your forgiveness."

"Done." Katrina smiled.

Lucy responded with one of her own. She was anxious, and all the fears that had been expressed only scratched the surface of what was being tossed around in her mind like a hot coal. *Lord, purify me for this task.*

A footman entered. "Lord Wellington awaits Lady Allendale in the drawing room."

Lucy rose to her feet and motioned for the men to stay seated. "I will see you all there in a little while."

"God go with you," Marcus said as she exited the room.

~*~

Lucy entered the room where the Duke stood. "My lord, I am ready."

He took in her appearance and stepped forward to raise her hand to place a light kiss on the glove. "I feel as if I'm your real father and serving you up to the wolves."

"If I had to choose a father, you would be at the top of the list, my lord. Thank you for believing in me and letting me make decisions about my life."

"Your husband will be furious with you for this."

"If he is, it will mean he is alive. I will be grateful and take full responsibility for tonight."

"No, not full. Other players might be in this game and who knows what will happen then. You are ready?"

She nodded.

"Armed?"

She smiled. "And more than willing to use whatever weapons are at my disposal."

"A singular young woman. I can see why Captain Allendale fell in love with you."

"You mean other than my badgering him?"

"I doubt he minded being badgered by you."

"You'll have to ask him sometime. My goal is to have him alive and weel then enough to badger in the future."

The Duke held his arm out and she placed her hand on it as he escorted her to his closed carriage.

Once inside and the door closed, the figure that led men to victory on the battlefield gazed at her intently. "You are determined to see this through?"

"I am."

With a grim set to his mouth he scanned the scenery as it passed by.

Once at the townhouse ball they were slated to attend, the footman opened the door and let down the stair.

The Duke exited first and held his hand to assist her. "Ready, my lady?"

"Mrs. Allendale, if you please."

"So it shall be."

She placed her hand on his extended arm and together they regally ascended the stairs to the home of the Earl of Perkins who was celebrating the betrothal of the last of his five daughters.

Lucy was aware that eyes were watching her. She lifted her chin a little higher. She was born into this role and would do her mother proud by her actions tonight.

"Lord Perkins. Lady Perkins. It is my pleasure to introduce you to Mrs. Allendale, daughter of the Duke of Diamonte and married to my most honored and trusted aide, Captain Allendale."

Lady Perkins flicked her fan closed and rapped the Duke's arm. "You are bamming us, of course. Lady Allendale is locked in the Tower and your trusted aide is wanted for treason."

The Duke's stern face alerted the countess to the error of her thinking.

Lucy fought not to giggle. She gave a curtsy to them both. "My lord, my lady, it is a delight to meet you. Let me assure you that my husband and I are ardent supporters of the King and Regent and this fabulous country. We would love for Napoleon and those who seek his favor to be conquered once and for all so we may live in peace."

"Well said," countered the Earl. "Welcome. I have a feeling that your attendance tonight will give my wife a jewel in her crown as hostess of the *ton*."

"I am happy to have been of service to you, my lady." Lucy bobbed a curtsy again and was led into the ballroom by the Duke. She stood at the door and took in the colors of all the gowns contrasted with the almost unrelieved black of the men's suits for the evening.

The Duke leaned in. "Does it look familiar?"

She nodded.

"May I lead you in a contra-dance?"

"Oh, no, my lord, the only dance I have ever managed was a waltz with my husband. There were no dancing masters, nor need of them, where I grew up."

"'Tis a shame and one you will have to rectify in the future. Let me procure a glass of punch for you."

"Thank you, my lord." Lucy watched the Duke make his way through the crowd being hailed and welcomed by all. She scanned the room for familiar faces. *Lord, what now? You brought me here, but I have no clue as to why. Who is to appear and how will this free my husband and brother? Oh, please help me!*

She was bumped by the crowd of well-dressed strangers and moved to settle closer to a wall where no chairs had been placed. A large plant provided an interesting hiding place as she glanced about. Who were all these people?

Giddy girls giggled off to one side as they watched a handsome gent walk by. He glanced at them and winked. A rogue to be sure. Some older women were close by, seated and yammering away about this person and that. Names that meant nothing to her. At least Jared's name wasn't on their lips.

Lord Remington, Lord Westcombe, and Lord Harrow entered. They quickly spied where she was and moved to other parts of the room. She smiled at how she had gone from no family to this band of brothers who were now seeking to defend her, Jared, Katrina, and Michael.

She wondered where Katrina was.

A master of disguise, she had told Lucy she would

be there but doubted that any of them would pick her out or discover her. "Only Michael might figure out if he suspected I was here, otherwise I would most likely fool him too," she had said.

Lucy grinned at her adventuresome sister-in-law. Even though she was now a mother she seemed to enjoy partaking in the drama of Lucy's life. Lucy was grateful that they had become more than sisters-in-law, but friends as well. God had provided many blessings when she came to London.

The air was stifling and the tendency of some of the beau monde to eschew bathing provided for an unsavory culmination of fragrances to waft around her. She sneezed. She pulled out her fan and brought it up to partially hide her face but to also prevent some from learning her identity or seeking her out.

Or did that go against the goal of uncovering the Black Diamond? She wished she knew what to do. She shook her head. Sure, as if God would just write on the wall or talk to her through the plant, after setting it on fire, of course.

"What has brought that delightful smile to your face?" Wellington presented her with a glass of punch.

She took a sip. "Silly thoughts and nothing I desire to share."

"I'm shocked the bucks have not flocked to you yet. Are they blind?" The Duke frowned.

"They do not know me and are probably intimidated by you, my lord. You would have to make introductions for them to approach me, and for what? I don't dance and am a married woman."

"How else are you to discover what you need?"

She shrugged. "I do not know. I am waiting for God to show me that step."

"He got you this far, I expect we can trust Him to see you through to the end."

"Whatever that end may be." She frowned and took another sip of her punch.

33

Jared scanned the crowd. He and Michael had made their way in through the garden, bypassing the people queued at the entrance. It meant crawling over a garden gate and interrupting a romantic interlude for one couple. Now they were inside, blending in with the crowd.

"Is the Regent here yet?" Michael asked.

"No. He will probably be fashionably late as is his wont." Jared located his brother, Marcus, in a corner chatting with members of Parliament. The very thought made him want to yawn, but Marcus was animated, and Jared could tell his brother was scanning the crowd.

Michael spotted Theo doing the pretty on the dance floor with a debutante who had little fortune or looks to recommend her.

Phillip was wandering around the room, making small talk with those he met.

"She's here," Jared whispered.

"Who?" Michael responded.

"My wife." Jared took a step forward and a hand grabbed his arm and held him back.

"Slow down. You don't want to get in the way of whatever God showed her."

Jared swallowed. "No. I want to see her. Be near her."

"I wouldn't be surprised if Katrina were here as well," Michael said as a young maid came by with a tray of wine glasses. Michael lifted one off for him and Jared. "I don't see her though, do you?"

"No, but she is petite."

"So is Lucy and you had no trouble spotting her."

"How could anyone not see her? She shimmers with the candlelight on her almost white hair and that lovely neck..." A man moved to allow him to see her better. "...but that dress is indecent! Who brought her here like that?"

Michael's grip grew stronger. "Rein yourself in. She is yours."

"She looks as if she's displaying herself for sale. I've seen prostitutes in Portugal with more modesty than that gown," Jared seethed.

Michael shook his head. "Do you ever listen to yourself? Could you be more buffleheaded than Theo? More than half of the women here have dresses far more scandalous than your wife's. Look at those damped underskirts, leaving nothing to the imagination. Or over there, that prime piece with jewels dripping almost to her waist drawing attention to..."

"Enough." Jared watched as the Duke of Wellington conversed with Lucy and left her side. A dance was coming to an end. He shook off Michael's arm, glared at him, and strode through the crowd to his wife.

Her gaze caught him. Her sparkling blue eyes widened with surprise and her perfect lips formed an 'o'.

He came forward and bowed to her. "Lady Allendale, would you do me the honor of this waltz?"

She curtseyed, placed her hand in his, and gave him a smile. "I would like nothing better, Captain."

He led her to the floor and took her in his arms, careful to keep the prescribed space between them. He longed to crush her to himself but was determined to not add any more scandal to what tonight might have simply by them being here. The music began and he smiled down at her. "I have missed you, sprite." Her smile made promises he hoped he would get a chance to take her up on.

"I have missed you as weel then."

"What is the plan for this evening?"

"I do not know. The Regent is to be here. Perhaps my father will show?"

"You want a confrontation with your father at the Earl of Perkins's home?"

"You told me to draw. I drew several sketches, and this was the one God impressed me with as real."

"And is it?"

She tilted her head and her eyes squinted.

"Real. Is it real?"

"Yes. May we enjoy this moment together?"

He nodded and spun her around the floor, aware that many eyes watched their progress. And why not? He had the most beautiful woman in the room waltzing in his arms. The song came to an end. He released her and bowed.

She curtseyed and put her hand on his arm as he led her off the floor. "Jared?"

"Hmmm?"

"I want you to know, I love you."

He frowned. "This isn't quite the place for endearments."

"Just in case something bad happens tonight, I wanted to tell you."

A shiver ran up his spine. "What do you mean

something bad? Like what?"

"All I know is something will happen."

"With three people here, who are wanted for treason, why would you imagine anything bad could happen?" Jared looked at her as he brought her back by the tree she had staked out earlier.

"Four."

"Excuse me?"

"Four. Katrina is here as weel then."

"Where?"

"She served you drinks a short time ago and collected your empty glass on your way to dance with me."

Jared glanced around. Michael was near the garden doors surveying the crowd. He saw no sign of the elusive servant. "I should have known it was her. Footman are the only ones to serve drinks. I must be losing it if I didn't detect that something was off with her."

"She said you would likely not discover her. I almost didn't except that after she served you, she looked over at me and winked."

"That sounds like her."

"She will have fun teasing Michael about that for a long time to come."

"Wouldn't be the first time."

~*~

Lucy wished she could leave the party with Jared and hide away from the issues at hand. They were not safe. Her only real hope was to plead her case with the Prince Regent.

A disturbance at the door revealed his arrival.

The Duke of Wellington approached him and soon the portly Prince glanced her way.

"I think we are about to have our meeting."

As the prince drew near, her breathing grew heavy and she fanned herself. The room started to spin. Somehow, she managed to execute a low curtsey.

"Well, well, what have we here? Two of my most noble subjects or traitors to the Crown?"

"Your Highness," Lucy whispered, "we are your humble subjects and devoted to England."

"You are from far away."

"Yes, your majesty." The fan kept moving.

"Stop that infernal fan. Put it down and let me look at you. The daughter of Diamonte, eh?"

"Yes, my liege."

"You will honor me with a dance." The prince held out his arm to her.

"I am sorry. I only know how to waltz." Her hand came to cover her mouth. Had she angered the prince by her honesty and refusal to dance? Who turned down the Regent?

He smiled. "Then a waltz it shall be." He snapped his fingers. A footman came to do his bidding and was soon scurrying to the orchestra. "It is my favorite dance of all and likely the only time I will get to hold you in my arms without your husband threatening to murder me."

She smiled and glanced at Jared. "He is devoted to me, but I am sure he will permit one dance."

"As loathe as I am to be apart from my bride, I believe I can survive." Jared bowed with a smile and took a step back.

Lucy put her hand on the Prince's arm. As round as he was, he exuded charm. The music began and so did their dance.

"Wellington tells me that you and your husband, as well as Sir Tidley and his wife, have been set up by your father with these charges of treason."

"We believe that to be true. He threatened to do so if Jared didn't sacrifice his life to prevent it. My husband has been a faithful servant to the Crown for many years at great cost to himself. Your Highness, if you could see the way he suffers as a result of the torture he endured to protect this country that he loves, you would never doubt his faithfulness to you, the King, and for this nation."

"And what of you, my lady? Raised in Scotland and yet profess to love England?"

"I am British by birth and have married a staunch defender of the Crown who retrieved me at great cost to himself to fulfill his duty."

The Regent smiled. "Was it his duty to marry you? I don't ever recall that being something we required of our agents."

"That is a story for another day. I am pleased to be wed to an honorable man."

The Prince was surprisingly spry on his feet in spite of his girth.

"My father, the Duke of Diamonte, is the threat to your reign and the sovereign rule of this nation."

"How so?"

"He has confessed to my brother that he anticipates sitting on the throne of England as Emperor and has partnered with Napoleon."

"Napoleon would never share power with one such as your father. No offense intended, my lady."

"None taken. I believe your life and that of your father, are in imminent danger, and our arrest was an attempt to keep us from warning you."

"But you have foiled him at that. And what will the cost to you be?"

"My life, if that is what it takes to ensure your safety, and win back my husband's, Sir Tidley's and Mrs. Tidley's reputations."

"You would risk your beauty to save me?"

"If it were required of me. Yes."

"I never before needed a woman to protect me but your brave words make me believe you speak truth. I will see you all exonerated of the charges placed against you."

The music wound down. "Thank you, Your Highness."

"It was a most enlightening dance." The Prince raised her hand placed a kiss there.

She smiled.

The Prince led her to the dais where the orchestra was. "I would like to make a proclamation," he declared and waited for the murmuring to subside as the music stopped.

"Lords and ladies, I would like to make it publicly known that the charges of treason against Captain Allendale and his lovely bride here, Lady Allendale, as well as Sir Tidley and his bride, Mrs. Tidley, are false. These people love our nation and have fought to preserve the monarchy. I want to make it clear that anyone who claims otherwise will be imprisoned for treason."

A blur rushed to the stage but was held back by Lord Remington and Lord Westcombe.

Lucy pointed to the man who stood before them. "Your Highness, this man, the Duke of Diamonte, also known as the Black Diamond, is the true traitor."

The Prince stepped down, leaving Lucy behind. He came up to Diamonte's face, darkened with rage, as he struggled against the men who held him.

Lucy was grabbed from behind and dragged off the dais. She struggled against the arms that held her. One covered her mouth and she bit it. One painful crack—

34

Jared watched in horror as Lucy was abducted. He was on the opposite side of the room and had been so proud of her having won the Prince over. Now as the Prince stood face to face with the Black Diamond, his wife was in mortal danger.

As he drew near the Prince he could hear Lord Diamonte bluster about his imminent reign and how if he were not released, Lucy would be tortured and killed.

Jared was out of breath by the time he reached the Prince's side. "Your Highness." Jared bowed. "This man will torture her whether you free him or not. Do not believe a word he says."

The Prince looked at Jared and nodded, his jovial face now marred by a frown. "Take him away gentlemen. To the Tower with double guards."

Jared took off where he had last seen Lucy but there was no sign of her. Then he saw it. Her fan. He picked it up and ran out the back door where Katrina awaited him. "Michael leapt on to the back of the carriage. They turned right out of the alley but beyond that, I do not know."

Marcus, Phillip, and Theo arrived to hear the end of this. No words were exchanged. They took off for the mews to garner some mounts from the Earl's stable.

Katrina followed.

"Stay here and let the Prince and the Duke of

Wellington know what has happened," Michael said.

She bristled.

"Katrina, please. We need to leave knowing that other resources can aid us."

She nodded and ran back to the townhouse.

Jared sprang on his horse. With his friends by his side they soon ascertained the direction of the carriage and began to trail it west.

"Perhaps he is headed to his estate?"

"Too far away," Michael stated.

"He's heading toward Rose Hill," Marcus remarked.

"Or past it. Wasn't Bastian's house out near Stone?" Phillip remarked.

"That must be where he is taking her." Jared pushed his mare harder. They would leave a note at the next inn and continue on in pursuit.

Marcus looked over at his brother. "*De ja vu?*"

Jared remembered the mad dash to rescue Josie from her abduction. It ended with a bloody fight and Marcus almost dying. He nodded to his brother. *Lord, please let us rescue her and get out alive.*

~*~

Lucy was livid. How dare they treat her this way? The men had boasted that she was being held hostage until her father was released. She hoped and prayed that no one would give in to that request. It was a lie. Her father would do anything to gain his freedom and take over the throne.

She awakened, slumped in the seat of a carriage careening down the road. She didn't know what direction they were headed. They had not taken her weapons. This was a hasty kidnapping and not well-planned. She had accomplished her mission with success. They had all been exonerated and the Black Diamond captured. She smiled even through the pounding in her skull. She reached up to touch the area, and in the moonlight could tell there was blood on her glove when she brought her hand back down.

The door was locked. She would not be escaping that way. What could she do? She reclined on the bench and tried to sleep in spite of the bouncing.

~*~

Jared almost slipped from his saddle due to exhaustion. The carriage had changed horses several times but had never let its occupant out. The men had all changed horses too and tried to keep up but as the carriage had various drivers that took turns, they were not stopping for anything else.

Marcus, Theodore, and Phillip were exhausted as well. It was evident with every stop.

By mid-morning they had reached the inn at Didcot, close to Rose Hill.

Theo was to stay there to provide direction to those who would hopefully be following.

The rest stopped in at Rose Hill to apprise the other wives of what was happening and to change horses.

Lady Remington, Jared's sister-in-law, also known as Josie, had a different idea. "You have a good idea where she has gone, and Michael is with her. She is not alone or unprotected. You all need to rest and then continue so you are ready for whatever comes."

Marcus looked at Jared with a frown. "You

haven't slept for two days. Josie is right. Rest and then we resume our journey."

"And pray that God keeps Lucy safe," Jared whispered before he trudged up the stairs with the men to their various rooms.

Marcus placed a hand on his shoulder when they reached the top. "We will all pray that Lucy stays safe."

~*~

Lucy was awakened and dragged from the carriage only to be tossed on the dirt courtyard before a dilapidated country estate. One of the men hauled her to her feet and half carried her up the crumbling steps. The door opened. She was shoved inside and taken to a windowless inner room with one lantern lit. The man dropped her and she collapsed on the floor. She crawled to the settee and pulled herself up. She was thirsty. So thirsty. A tumbler and water were on the table and she helped herself to some. So tired. She stretched out and fell into a woozy sleep.

~*~

Her hair hurt. Without opening her eyes, she reached up to find pins still in her hair. How did she fall asleep like that? She started to pull out pins and a lump under her hair was tender to the touch. When did that happen? She shivered and opened her eyes to blackness. Now she remembered coming to this place. One light had been lit when she had been tossed in here, but they were all out now. Where was that water?

Don't drink it.

What? Really? But I'm so thirsty, Lord.
Trust me.

She sighed. She would wait and trust. Dust pervaded her senses and she sneezed. Her mouth felt as if it was stuffed with cotton. She tried to recall the room when she had entered. At some point her captors would return and she wanted to be ready. But how if she couldn't see anything? How could she find a weapon? Or even hide?

The strike of a match caught her attention and she looked through the darkness at the tiny glow as it moved. It hovered and grew. She guessed a candle had been lit and shivered that someone was there she could not see.

"How nice of you to visit me, my darling."

Her heart pounded at the sound of that voice. How…?

The light came close to the face of the person holding it and her fears were confirmed.

"Father? I thought…"

"That I was locked in the Tower?" A throaty laugh followed. "Obviously, I am not. I am here, with you. I keep my promises."

"You don't make promises, you make threats."

"I make threats to those who keep me from fulfilling my promises. I owe you nothing, but you, my dear, owe me everything. You are my ticket to ruling this country."

"What makes you think you are fit to rule anything? You are nothing but an evil, traitorous…" Lucy shook her head in disgust. Her head throbbed.

"You seem tense, my dear. Would you like more water?"

Lucy shook her head. "No. I will forgo that

pleasure. Would you like a drink? I will pour one for you."

"You are kind, but I will await tea."

"You are civilized enough to enjoy tea?"

"Tea serves a purpose, so I endure it."

"Rather than drink a glass of water right now? That makes no sense."

"I don't expect to make sense to you. A mere woman is insensible on the best of days, and irrational on the worst of them."

"I'm surprised you married and had children."

"I needed an heir, but you were born."

"I'm an accident you didn't want. So why bring me here now?"

"Have you read the story in the Bible about Abraham being required to sacrifice his son?"

"Yes, and God intervened and provided a lamb so the human sacrifice was unnecessary."

"In this case, it is Lucifer that demands your blood be shed. Alas, other women have been selected but have escaped in the past. Make no mistake, there will be no magical rescue by a silly sheep again. We have abducted yours.

"You loved that ridiculous animal. I have no doubt your husband will be joining us soon as well and will meet a similar fate. He will be the key to helping me earn the distinct favor of the Emperor, as well as my god."

"You're twisted." Lucy could only see his face as long as the candle was held in front of him. The flames cast an eerie shadow that flickered over his glowering features. The firmness of the thin line of his lips, as the glint in his eye led her to believe he was serious about what he proposed.

"Rise and come with me. We have no time to lose." He reached for her wrist, grabbed it, and pulled her to her feet. The door opened with a mere shout and he set the candlestick on a small table near it before they exited.

The brightness of the hall blinded her.

She was dragged down a hallway toward a ballroom at the back of the home. A few men were present. A large wooden table, similar to what she imagined knights of yesteryear sat at to dine before going to battle, dominated the center of the room.

Light shone in and dust motes danced in the air. Sconces lit and placed at regular intervals on the wall provided more of a haunted feeling to the room than any real light. What few draperies remained were tattered and moth-eaten. One that was closed had irregular spots of light shining through. The entire room testified to abandonment and decay. The air was musty and chilled her. Her ball gown was thin. She looked down to find it torn and marred with dirt. That was the least of her worries.

Her father brought her to a heavy wooden chair and flung her into it. She rubbed her arm where it had hit the wood. Soon she was tied up. The men moved nearer. Their eyes roamed her body as if she had been stripped. Her soul quivered inside as her courage ran to hide, while fear taunted it.

Do not succumb to fear. He that is in me is greater than he who is in the world. God will rescue me. And as long as Jared is free, death is not a horrible end to be feared. She glanced at the men creeping closer. Death may not be horrible, but the process of getting there might be more than she could bear.

"Do we get to play, my lord?" A gnarled older

man drooled as he came close. His hand moved to touch her, but the crack of a whip elicited a cry from his lips as he fell backward.

"You can watch, but don't touch," the Black Diamond said.

Lucy saw him more clearly now as he cracked his whip around to urge the men to step away from her. Her father was not wearing the same suit he had worn at the ball.

"Father, why are you doing this?"

He laughed, deep and dark. "Power. I was meant to be more than a Duke. Did your mother ever tell you that she'd been sold to me?"

A hole opened up in her heart and threatened to swallow her whole. "What do you mean? Didn't you love my mother? Your wife?"

"Love? What's love? You think that your marriage to your Captain is love? Where is he now? There is no such thing as love. Lust certainly, but love? No. She was a means to an end but when she had you, as much as I was disappointed you were not a boy, I realized you could be something more than an heir."

"How?" She was afraid she wouldn't like the answer.

"That diamond on your shoulder marks you as mine. I have been close on five other occasions to having the key to my power, only to have it snatched from my fingertips by my own son and his 'friends.' But now, my very own daughter, the one destined for this role to begin with, has unwittingly been brought back for me to fulfill my destiny." He touched her chin with one finger and lifted it up. "Ah, beauty incomparable. You far surpass the others. Your mother caught wind of my plan for you which was why she left and hid. I knew where you were all along. With Damon dead, I had hoped they would send Michael after you so I could kill you both, but it is better that you are alive for this. We shall wait for Captain Allendale to arrive before we begin our ceremony."

"C-c-ceremony?" She gritted her teeth to keep them from chattering.

"Yes, you are my ultimate offering to guarantee my success. Eventually I will ensure that your half-brother meets his end, but for now he is harmless. I will save him for another time." He leaned over, ran a finger down the side of her neck, and down along the fabric of her dress as it rested against her chest.

Lucy struggled not to vomit. Surely he wouldn't...

He smiled. "Oh, yes I will. My wife denied me relief as well as my daughter. You shall pay for her sins before you die." He snapped his fingers and left the room with the men following behind him.

Did they look at her knowing her fate and approve? Who were these men anyway? What control did her father have over them? None of this made sense. *Oh, Lord, I don't mind coming home to see You and Momma, but spare me this if You would.*

35

Jared almost collapsed from his horse as he rode up to the inn at Stone where Michael awaited them. "Have you found them?" Jared grabbed his friend's lapels.

Michael nodded but his look was grave. "It's an old estate. I've asked around and they said it used to be owned by some man named Sir Bastion who had been tried and found guilty of treason."

Marcus remained seated. "Jared, you remember Bastion. He's the one who was obsessed with Josie. The one I uncovered by entering that brothel."

Jared nodded. He glanced at his brother and frowned. "You learned far more at that brothel, didn't you?"

"Only of his betrayal and that he liked things rough. Josie would have died shortly after her wedding, I have no doubt."

"Bastion is dead, but now the Black Diamond owns the property. When it had been sold, no one knew the identity of the Black Diamond. With easy access to the ocean from the inlet on the property, it was no wonder Diamonte wanted it. But why Lucy? What is up with his obsession with these women?" Marcus pondered aloud.

Michael cleared his throat. "I know first-hand the brutality of this man. We need to be careful though. Remember Wolton? We thought he had died after Valeria's rescue."

"Do these guys have nine lives?"

"Well, there was that valet of mine who seemed to not want to stay dead," Michael offered.

"Your battle is not against flesh and blood but against the powers and principalities of the air. Isn't that in the Bible somewhere?" Jared asked.

"Yes, and from what I've seen we are fighting a much bigger battle here," Marcus added.

"I suggest we pray," Theo said.

The men headed to the local chapel. Each sat in a pew for private prayers.

Jared swallowed his fear. Lucy was in danger and close. Yet God had not given him leave to rush in and save her. He was a veteran of intrigue, but this spiritual battle was new to him. How did one fight an unseen enemy along with a flesh and blood one?

~*~

The room grew dark and cold. Lucy shivered as the ropes cut into her skin. Every move had rubbed more and more flesh away from her bare arms. She was still so thirsty. She had prayed and tried to sleep. Her attempts to work her bonds loose failed. A gape in the windows showed a storm rolling in. She wondered when Diamonte would make his move.

The door slammed open sometime later and the Duke's scowl doubled the size of her goosebumps. A lackey was with him and he growled to the poor man, "Untie her. We are running out of time. We need the full moon and a clear sky but the storm rolls in. Your swain is nearby, dearest daughter. While I may not be able to fulfill the sacrifice, I want I have an alternate plan."

The Duke was wearing a many-caped great coat and a top hat. A sword was at his side as well as a side arm.

The bonds loosened, and the Duke lunged forward to grab her jaw.

"Ow!"

"Open." He bellowed and proceeded to dump the contents of a metal flask into her mouth. She gagged on the foul substance. Some spilled on her face and burned against her skin. When the flask was empty her father slammed her mouth shut and plugged her nose. She struggled to resist the urge to cast up her accounts and by the second attempt of her stomach's revolt, she drifted into darkness.

~*~

Jared led the group as they approached Sir Bastian's former estate. Marcus was closer to the house. Michael and Jared split off and stuck to the hedges to spy any movement. Theo and Phillip were closer to Marcus. All were armed. Jared spied motion on the west side of the house and waved Michael over.

The Duke of Diamonte appeared to be dragging someone out and through the grass and field towards the cliffs.

"Is that your father?" Jared asked.

"It is. But I thought they arrested him in London."

The two men followed but could no longer stay hidden as brush became nonexistent. They were soaked to the skin. Thunder shook the ground beneath them and lightning tore up the sky around them.

The Duke came to a halt at the edge of the cliff and pulled his sword.

"Halt!" Michael yelled.

Jared stared at the lump on the ground.

Lucy! Her dress was ripped and filthy. Her hair sprawled around her filled with dirt and grass. She was limp and his heart trembled.

Michael directed his focus to the man standing over her. "I thought you were arrested," Michael stated.

The Duke puffed out his chest. "So, you finally met my twin brother. Your uncle. He's under the delusion that I will share my throne with him once we win this war."

The Duke pulled out his long sword and raised it high to the sky. He screamed out words in some unknown tongue and his eyes blazed red when he looked back at Jared. "Say farewell to your wife. She is mine, and always has been."

"Oh, dear God, no," Jared pleaded.

Another flash of lightning connected with the tip of the sword. The Duke dropped Lucy.

She tumbled off the edge.

The Duke's body shook with the bolt as it catapulted him over the side of the cliff.

Jared and Michael raced to look down. Lucy was sprawled on a rocky ledge only a few feet below the ledge.

The Duke's lifeless, broken body was twisted on the rock-strewn shore. He still held his sword and another finger of lightning connected with it, making the body dance. As the tide rose, the dead man was slowly caressed by the waves and dragged into its depths.

"Go get a rope, Michael. I'll be with my wife."

"Go down, and I'll help you get her back up."

Michael undid his cravat in case they needed the length.

Jared lowered down to the rocky ledge, taking care not to step on Lucy. She was close to the edge and he feared that if she awoke she would move and fall over to her death. If she wasn't dead already. He knelt down beside her and felt for her pulse. "She's alive."

He dragged her close to the cliff wall. There was little room to maneuver. He dragged his wife up into his arms and then draped her over his shoulder. Michael wrapped the cravat around his wrist, laid down on the ground above, and tossed him the end.

Jared grabbed for it, wrapped it around his own wrist, and used it to help him climb the rocks with his precious cargo.

Michael backed up and helped pull them both away from the edge.

Jared sat his wife on the ground and checked for broken bones or other injures. Her breathing was faint. "We need to get her out of the rain."

"To the house or the inn?"

"The inn, to be sure." Jared took a deep breath, frowned, and gathered her into his arms again. Her head rolled and came to a rest against his shoulder. A noxious odor came from her.

"I think she was poisoned."

"Why do you say that?" Michael walked by his side as they strode toward their hidden mounts.

"Smell."

Michael leaned in and sniffed. His eyes grew wide. "Put her down. We need to get her to throw up."

"What?"

"We need to get the poison out of her body before it kills her."

Jared dropped to his knees and tipped Lucy's head to the side. "You are sure about this?"

Michael frowned and nodded.

Jared removed his glove and stuck his finger as far back down her throat as he could.

She vomited the wretched smell.

"Again."

"Once isn't enough?"

"Most likely not. Trust me. I'm not doing this to get my jollies."

Jared repeated his action and fought against casting up his own accounts. When they were done, Jared rolled her back into his chest.

Michael helped him rise and they moved quickly to the horses.

Once back at the inn, they entrusted Lucy to the lady of the house to get her cleaned up and in a gown.

The stable hand fetched the doctor.

"I'll retrieve the others," Michael offered. "You stay with Lucy and make sure she survives."

"She has to. Right? God wouldn't bring us this far to take her now, would He?"

Michael gulped. "I wish I could answer that in the way you want. We've both been at war long enough to know that sometimes the best people do not survive." Michael put his hand on his friend's shoulder. "Remember, her sacrifice was not in vain. The Black Diamond is no more. He will never rule England. He will never rape another young girl. He will no longer be responsible for the deaths of thousands of our best men on the battlefield. I want her to live. I know you want that more. We've done all we can and now the rest is up to the true King."

Jared looked at his friend and nodded. "Go. Fetch

the men. The army will be here soon, I suspect, to make sure everyone is rounded up."

Michael left.

The landlady came to take him to his wife's side.

He entered the room and sat on the bed holding Lucy's icy cold hand. Jared bent his head and prayed.

36

Several weeks later

"Close your eyes, Lucy. We are getting close." Jared grinned.

"Aye, aye, Sir Allendale." Her husband had been knighted for his bravery. Lucy grinned at him and placed her fingers over her eyes.

"No. I don't trust you." Jared pulled out a cloth he had brought for just this occasion, placed it over her eyes and tied a loose knot at the back of her head.

"What? I'm your wife. How could you not trust me?" She smiled and reached her hand out until she grabbed his cravat. She pulled him close and whispered, "If you want my eyes to close, all you needed to do was kiss me."

He looked at those tempting lips and took the invitation. He broke off the kiss as the carriage drew to a stop.

"Mmmmm. I could go for more of that kind of medicine," Lucy purred.

"You'll have to wait, sprite."

The door opened and Jared stepped down. He reached a hand for her and lifted her to the ground. "Ready, milady?"

"I hope so."

Jared untied the handkerchief.

Her gaze took in the two level, tudor style manor house.

"Welcome home, Lucy."

Her eyes watered and she looked up at him. "It's beautiful. It's more than I imagined it would be." She threw herself into his arms and hugged him around the neck.

"Ahem."

Jared looked up and grinned as he pried Lucy's arms from around his neck. "Yes, Treadwell?"

Lucy's dazed expression cleared as she looked at the butler and the array of staff that had come out the doors.

"Would you like to introduce your bride to the staff now?"

"Ah, yes. Lady Allendale, please meet our estimable butler, Treadwell."

~*~

An hour later in the drawing room decorated in cream with dark blue accents, Lucy sipped her tea as her husband lounged next to her.

"I'm grateful to finally have you home, Lucy. I don't know if I could have returned here and been happy without you by my side."

"But you purchased the place before you ever met me."

"True, but a certain blue-eyed pixie turned my heart inside out and upside down and after all you have put me through, I don't ever want to let you out of my sight again."

"God worked it out though, didn't he? My uncle was hung for treason with the rest of my father's minions. The Black Diamond is no longer a threat to any of us."

"He almost killed you, Lucy. How can you speak

so calmly of his death?"

"The thing I am saddest about was that he killed Scallywag. I'll miss that little guy."

"Had you been out to see your pet before things blew apart?"

"I had little opportunity to visit him. I feel bad about that."

"Come with me." Jared stood and helped his wife to her feet.

Lucy appreciated his assistance. She had not regained all her strength after the ordeal they had been through. The doctor had told him that had he not emptied her stomach when they did, she would likely have died. She was grateful to Michael for that. Her husband led her to the back of the house, out into the garden, and toward the stable.

She stopped at the sight. There were a dozen sheep there, all with black faces and legs. "Oh, sweetheart. Thank you. I didn't realize you wanted to raise sheep."

Baaaaa. Baaaaaa. A plaintive bleating drew her attention as a lamb separated itself from the group and scampered over to her.

"Scallywag?" The lamb put his hooves up on the first rung of the pen and stretched his head towards her. He wore a brass bell.

"You father lied to you. Your lamb is alive and well. The land here is conducive to sheep. I planned to raise horses, but there's enough room for both here. Do you mind very much being married to a boring farmer instead of an exciting soldier?"

"Not at all. I'm even happier to just be married to you."

"Ah, you only want me for my title," he teased.

Lucy turned from scratching her lamb's head. She wrapped her arms around his waist and leaned her head against his broad chest. "I was willing to marry farmer Jared. Your title doesn't make you the man you are, it only confirms it."

"You deserve better than me," he protested.

Lucy shook her head. "No man could be better. Now come with me back inside. I want to take a nap in our suite and need your assistance with my stays."

"I hired you a lady's maid."

"True, and I am grateful." She grabbed his hand to lead him back inside. "However, there are certain needs only a husband can tend to." They climbed the stairs and entered the suite.

"Really? Well, if there is any way I can be of service to you…"

"You will, dear, you will." She locked the door and turned to untie his cravat.

"Sprite—"

Lucy cut him off with a kiss and did not let him get in another word.

Epilogue

Everyone had reconvened for Christmas at Rose Hill.

Marcus and Josie mingled with Phillip and Beth, Michael and Katrina, Theodore and Valeria, and Lucy. Even Jared's sister, Henrietta, and her husband Charles, the first to encounter the plot of the Black Diamond, were present.

Years ago, he had witnessed Marcus's marriage. All of the rest of them had been single. None of them, besides Marcus, Josie, Henrietta, and her husband Charles, knew the Lord.

So many years later and there were children scampering underfoot. Each man had found a woman to love and a relationship with God. Their nemesis, the Black Diamond, had been vanquished.

Jared walked over to his bride.

Lucy looked up at him with a raised eyebrow. "I have a special gift for you, Jared."

"You do? I'm not sure my heart can take any more surprises."

Lucy handed him a wrapped package. "Open it, please?"

The couples gathered close, watching them.

He would do almost anything to make his pixie bride happy. He untied the ribbon and draped it around her neck. He opened the lid and pulled out a tiny, brass set of booties. He looked up at her as she grinned. It took a few moments for the significance to register and his eyes grew wide. "Really?"

Lucy nodded. "You will be a father in the spring." She whispered those words and turned a becoming shade of pink.

Jared leaned over and kissed his bride. She threw her arms around his neck. He picked her up and spun her around.

Everyone applauded and soon he was separated from his bride as the women pulled her away to offer their words of advice.

The men patted him on the shoulder and one shoved a snifter of brandy into his hand.

"Drink before you pass out. You're white as a sheet, Jared." Michael grinned.

"I'm going to be a father."

"Yes, you are, and you'll be a great one too. Love always blooms at Rose Hill."

Jared nodded, slammed his brandy, and gave the glass back to Michael. "Excuse me, men."

He strode to his wife and took her hand. "Excuse me, ladies." He stopped to loop his arm under her legs. "Come along, sprite. I want to celebrate in private." They left the room to hoots and hollers from the men and titters from the women.

Lucy wrapped her arm round his neck and settled into his chest. He climbed the stairs and slammed the door. They were not seen again until breakfast the next day.

Don't miss the rest of the
Black Diamond Christian Gothic Regency
Suspense Series

Here's a sneak peek at
The Lord Phillip's Folly

Prologue

London

Across the misty sky flew a dark figure with wings flapping silently amidst the noise of the city of London where the elite of the *ton* prepared for this night's entertainments. As the black bird swooped and dipped amongst the chimneys, he found what he searched for. Make that "whom" he searched for. He spied her on the balcony gazing up at the sky awaiting him. He dove from his height only spreading his wings within a few feet to slow descent and land lightly on her outstretched arm.

"Duke," the young woman whispered. "You're back. I've been waiting for you."

His head bobbed but he refrained from speaking. His mistress frowned. He longed to see her smile. He tilted his head to the right, straightened it, and reached his neck forward to put his long dark beak to her cheek and rub gently.

Tears dangled at the edge of her eyelashes. "Tonight is the night, Duke. I cannot go through with what Papa plans. I must escape. All these years... I cannot endure any longer."

Duke was silent, listening. He bobbed his head.

She continued. "Lord Wolton has to be sixty, if not older and has the most nauseating odor. He is creepy and I'm certain he has some evil hold over Papa. But I cannot. I will not allow myself to pay the price for Papa's salvation. He's acted foolishly, and I love him, but I won't..." She glanced up at the sky. "Why would God allow this to happen?" She shivered, although the mid-April evening was warm. "Why couldn't I simply be loved for who I am? Why all this unrelenting…evil?"

Duke ruffled his feathers and shook them, once again rubbing his beak against her cheek.

"Watch over me tonight. I've no clue how I'll escape, but I don't want to lose you when I do. Wait outside in the garden and follow wherever I go. Can you do that, sweetheart?" Her intense golden-green eyes gazed into his.

"I love you," Duke squawked, nodding and making a kissing sound. He'd do anything for her.

"I love you too, Duke. What would I have done this past year without you?"

Movement from the dressing room alerted him to danger. Duke flapped his wings and took off, circling twice above her before settling on a nearby tree. She blew him a kiss.

He bobbed his head in acknowledgment as she turned to step back off the narrow balcony and close the doors to the bedroom behind her.

He would protect his mistress.

1

Spring 1810
Manchester

Despicable town. Infuriating family. Frustrating obligations. In spite of all that Lord Phillip Westcombe had returned to London. He enjoyed hibernating in the North Country the past few months. Peace and solitude had become a comfortable companion since his friend, Lord Marcus Remington, married Miss Josephine Storm at Christmas. Their happiness was something he did not begrudge them, but he found it difficult to be around. It pointed to a gaping hole in his own heart.

Instead, he spent the time studiously applying himself to his estate, and enjoyed managing the property. He was happy for Marcus and Josie, but the process of falling in love tended to be messy and complicated if their path to the altar was any indication. He did not want that in his life.

Yet here he was, back in London for the season.

If it hadn't been for his mother's pleas, his father's command, and his little sister's enthusiastic encouragement, he would still be at Stanton Hall. Avoiding the matchmaking mammas and the cloying attempts of young debutantes trying to trap him into the parson's mousetrap was one of his least favorite pastimes. At five and twenty he had spent the last few years gaining some town polish along with experience in how to avoid the snares of the marriage mart.

It was primarily his adoration for his sister, Penelope, that brought him here. He hoped she would find a man worthy of her hand. As one of her family, he owed her the courtesy of squiring her through the season, keeping a careful watch on the court of admirers she was sure to develop.

As Fenway, his valet, stepped away from tying his cravat into a spectacular waterfall, Phillip looked in the mirror. His blond hair carefully combed off of his face—every hair in its place. His ice-blue eyes scanned the image before him as he attached a ruby pin into the folds of the linen and smiled. Perfect white teeth set in a long face with a strong jaw and aristocratic nose and full lips. His new black coat fit like a glove. Perfection was an art. With the help of his tailor and valet, he was a master.

It was time to do his duty to his sister, please his parents, and dance with the wallflowers. With a final tug to his jacket, he nodded to Fenway. "Don't bother waiting up for me." He left his chambers determined to make the best of the evening.

~*~

The Earl of Manchester and his wife of thirty-two years stood ahead of him in the receiving line. They had asked only that Phillip, their second son, remain by the side of his sister Penelope for her come-out ball. He was the last person to greet people before they entered the ballroom.

Faces swam past him in a blur of color and stench. Why some in the upper ten-thousand refused to bathe perplexed him. He greeted each gentleman with a bow of his head and every woman with a lift of their gloved hands within an inch of his lips. His sister simpered next to him, giddy that this evening was in her honor and likely to be a 'crush,' to propel his mother into rapturous delight.

Waiting for an escape, he discovered an unknown face presented to him.

"I'm Lord Follett." The older man gave him a bow. Phillip could see the balding head, and the odor of alcohol on his breath warned him the man was already in his cups. "This is my daughter, the Honorable Elizabeth Follett."

Phillip sucked in a breath at the vision before him. Her soft red hair was pulled up and held in place by small white flowers. Her dress did not do her coloring justice. But it was the eyes, those green eyes that drew him. They spoke a message to him he couldn't quite decipher. It wasn't one of desire or seduction as he so often saw. More of abject terror.

Because of him?

He held her hand. "Welcome to Manchester Hall, Miss Follett." He allowed his lips to touch the glove and a shock traveled through him as she gasped. He straightened as one corner of his lips rose. *Ah, she'd felt it too.* Instead of terror, there was curiosity, and, as those lashes lowered, he sensed a mystery.

"You are too kind, my lord." Her husky voice whispered as the crowd pushed her forward toward the ballroom. He watched her go, the sway of her hips barely discernable beneath her gown.

"Phillip?" His sister nudged him.

"Yes, Penny?"

"Will you escort me in? Father said he would lead me out for the first dance. Anthony is to dance with me next and then you. You won't forget, will you?" Her brown eyes held an eagerness he knew would someday turn to *ennui* as the years marched on and she was subjected to these now exciting activities over and over again.

"How could I ever forget? You are by far the most beautiful woman in the room and I would be honored to dance with you."

She slapped him with her fan and giggled. "I'm glad you came home, Phillip. I've missed you."

He tapped a finger on her nose and lifted his elbow. She placed her hand on his forearm and he escorted her into the ballroom. Handing her off to his father he skirted the room, periodically shaking hands with people he knew but not stopping to chat. He wasn't in the mood for talk. His eyes scanned the mass of bodies. The Earl of Manchester determined it was late enough to begin the ball.

Phillip hated these events. When he was younger, he didn't mind attending and flirting with the available misses, but now it wore thin. Was he getting old or growing up? Managing the estate left to him by his maternal aunt, Martha, upon her removal to the here-after two years hence had been a better use of his time and energy. He'd encountered success in turning a modest inheritance into profitable investments after Lord Remington took him aside and encouraged him that even as a second son, he could be prosperous and productive.

Phillip failed in his attempt to share his successes with his family. They persisted in the belief he was a ne'er-do-well, frolicking around aimlessly, gambling, and wenching his way through his monthly allowance and inheritance. As if he were still a callow youth fresh on the town.

Before Lord Remington's warnings and direction, that might have been true.

Yet his family considered him to be a wastrel, doomed to destruction if he didn't settle down with a wife soon. His father even suspected he was hiding in the north with a mistress. As if he'd waste money on such as that? He was long over his dalliances with ladies of the night. It irked him that his father would hold such a low opinion of him.

Phillip was fully cognizant that although his family loved him, he was far from the perfection of his older brother. He glanced around the ballroom and spied Anthony, only two years older than himself. Anthony tended towards portliness and while he pretended adoration toward his wife, Phillip knew that Anthony's excesses far surpassed his own when he was younger. He feared his father was misled in the belief that his heir was honorable and trustworthy to inherit the earldom someday. Phillip shrugged. Since Anthony's wife had presented him with two sons already, the title would never pass to Phillip. He found contentment in establishing his own path, and a wife was not integral to his success.

If his mother and sisters were any indication, women usually spent money, which did not help much in increasing wealth. Marcus's bride might be the exception, but it was really too early to tell on that account as they were fairly new to marriage. They had come in earlier and were on the dance floor, besotted with one another.

The orchestra finished playing the first dance. Phillip sought out his mother to lead her into the next one.

~*~

The Honorable Elizabeth Follett escaped the first dance with an excuse to check her hem but now she couldn't avoid the inevitable as she was led to the floor by Lord Wolton.

His face quickly grew red. He started wheezing with the execution of the steps of the dance. At over three times her own age, he was a prosperous landowner and neighbor. He possessed small dark eyes, bushy eyebrows, and very little hair on top of his head, which perspired terribly. His long sideburns only served to emphasize his jowls. His hands were plump and clammy to the touch.

A shiver of distaste overtook Lizzy every time his reached for hers as required by the movements of the dance, and even more at the lascivious look in his eyes as he would scan her body. His smile, crooked with a few darker teeth accompanied by his foul breath, made her fight against the bile threatening to rise inside when they drew close.

The only highlight of the exercise was the sight of the golden god dancing two couples down. Occasionally his eyes met hers in the course of the dance and she only hoped he could read her desperation. Ah, but beautiful sons of earls were not known to rescue the daughters of barons were they?

Led back to her father after the dance, she nodded her head and murmured a soft thanks to Lord Wolton.

Lord Follett had no real repute in the *ton* and felt his position keenly. He nudged his daughter and urged her, "Smile, Lizzy, for heaven's sake. Lord Wolton desires your hand, the least you could do is encourage him a little."

Lizzy once again tried to suppress a cold shiver at the very thought of any more interaction with Lord Wolton. Her father blustered and yelled when she stated her objection to the match. There would be no rescue for her from that quarter. She closed her eyes and took a deep breath, clenching her hands tightly together silently praying to a God she wasn't quite sure even existed, for a way out of the hell destined for her.

Opening her eyes, she glanced across the room to observe Lord Phillip Westcombe leading his sister out in the country dance. She could not take her gaze off of him. His kindly manner as he interacted with his sister was charming. And that smile. Would she even be able to breathe if he ever smiled at her like that? He was the stuff dreams were made of. She felt hope surge through her. Maybe, just maybe...

~*~

The evening dragged on with one dance after another. After supper, Phillip returned his young partner to her chaperone with an elegant bow. He found his attention captivated by the young woman who'd haunted him since her introduction earlier. She was difficult to miss with her red hair, although red was a bit strong to describe its softer hue. Hair that once curled around her face hung straight. She was pale, standing alone near a potted plant by the doors leading to the gardens below, as though she were hiding. She glanced his way and their gaze held. He read a silent plea and began to move in her direction.

He wove through the crowd surrounding the ballroom, stopping for brief handshakes and pats on the back as he maneuvered to that side of the room. He kept an eye on the young woman. She tracked his progress at times furtively searching the crowd. His curiosity was aroused.

"Miss Follett." Lord Phillip bowed over her hand and spoke softly so as not to be overheard in the noise of the ballroom. "May I be of assistance?"

"Lord Westcombe..." Elizabeth sighed. "Yes...I wonder..." Her eyes once again held a silent entreaty.

"Would you perhaps like to stroll in the garden?" Phillip extended his arm, and nodding, she wound her hand around it and walked outside into the fresh, cool evening air. Heat radiated up his arm at her touch. With every step, he was more aware of the woman by his side than any he'd ever known. It puzzled him. They stepped down into the garden lit with lanterns. Her lack of chatter perplexed him. Most women he met attempted to talk their way into a proposal. Few couples were in the gardens this early in the evening although lamps had been lit. He knew all the best places to engage in less than gentlemanly behavior due to his wayward youth. He led her down a path to an area by a small pond. Open and exposed. He would not compromise this young woman.

Phillip assisted Miss Follett to the bench, leaned against the tree next to it, and waited. She clenched her hands in her lap, took a deep breath, and began. "I need to escape. My father is forcing me into a marriage I do not want." Cautiously, she raised her eyes to meet his and he noted the tears at the edges.

He reached for his handkerchief and extended it to her as he came to sit beside her. "Is there no other way out of this marriage? Surely, they cannot force you to the altar. We do live in a civilized society."

"Civilized?" A short bark of laughter escaped the young woman. "My life has never been civilized. You'd be truly horrified if I told you the things I've endured." She turned slightly to look him in the eye and reached forward to put her hand on his arm. "Truly, if I do not escape tonight I have no other hope except—"

Phillip's eyes narrowed as she considered her words. Was she being overly dramatic? Was this a manipulation? Miss Follett wasn't trying to trap him into marriage herself, was she? From what he understood, she came with a healthy dowry, something he certainly didn't need. She was far from unattractive and given time during the season her own court of admirers would vie for her favors. Yet he sensed truth in what she claimed and that before him sat a desperate woman. The knight-errant in him fought its way to the surface disturbing the peaceful waters he tried hard to maintain. "What is it you require?"

"To disappear. Somewhere, anywhere they cannot find me."

"And then what? You re-appear elsewhere? How would that be explained? The scandal-mongers would have a feast that could destroy any hope you would have of making a respectable match. What about your future? Where might you live and how would you marry if you are cut off from your father and your inheritance?"

"You fully understand the complexities of my circumstances, Lord Westcombe. To me this matter is of life and death. My life. My certain death. If I am forced to marry, I guarantee I will be dead within the year. So, my only hope is to escape. Will you assist me?"

Phillip stared at her, considering, as the silence stretched taut between them. He tended to be a good judge of people and this woman told the truth. Finally, he came to a decision and nodded to her. "Can you remain here for a few minutes? Will you be all right?"

"You won't fetch my father?"

"No, merely a discreet friend who might assist. Trust me. I am a man of my word."

"I'll be fine. I'm not alone." Her face relaxed as she looked up past the tree to the stars twinkling in the sky.

Phillip wondered at her odd statement. There were other couples in the garden, but none near here. Giving her a short bow he surreptitiously returned to the ballroom. Once he entered he searched until he spied Lord Marcus Remington finishing up a dance with his bride. Phillip wove his way through the crowd to Marcus's side and whispered in his ear, "I require your assistance."

Marcus raised one eyebrow, nodded, and together all three made their way to the hallway and a private room. Phillip shut the door behind them.

"Well, Phillip, what is it?" Marcus relaxed one hand on his wife's waist as he stood beside her.

"I need shelter for a young woman in desperate need." *Now* who sounded melodramatic?

Marcus and Josie exchanged looks before staring at him.

"Phillip? Why does this woman need immediate shelter?" asked Lady Remington.

"I've done nothing wrong or to be ashamed of. She came to me for help."

"What do you want?" asked Marcus.

His wife nodded her head in agreement.

"I must spirit her away immediately. Could you depart and have your carriage go down to the corner alley? I'll bring her there unnoticed. After we arrive at your home, you can hear her story for yourselves."

Marcus nodded and escorted Josie out of the room.

"Dearest, I'm feeling tired and would like to go home now," Josie simpered as she fanned herself.

"Certainly dear. You look fatigued." Marcus's strong deep voice would suggest they were leaving for that reason alone.

Phillip slipped out the door of the library and wandered back to the garden, avoiding the few partygoers there. He accidentally came upon a few couples engaged in flirtation before he found his way back to Miss Elizabeth Follett. "Come," he whispered as he gave her his hand to help her stand.

"Where...?"

"You ask for my help yet now you resist? Trust me. I shan't harm you."

"I never doubted that for a minute." She rushed alongside him as they slipped through a spot in the hedge and made their way down the alley. Staying in the shadows they waited silently for the Remington coach to pull up. The rise and fall of her chest as she caught her breath was distracting.

He forced himself to focus elsewhere.

The carriage arrived and Lord Phillip assisted Elizabeth inside, entering behind her and closing the door. Marcus tapped on the roof to signal for them to start and they headed for the Remington home.

"Lord and Lady Remington, may I present the Honorable Elizabeth Follett to you?" Lord Westcombe intoned.

"Miss Follett, it is our honor to meet and assist you this evening." Josie reached across the carriage to squeeze the newcomer's hand. "You shall be safe with us."

"Thank you," Miss Follett whispered.

Phillip leaned back against the squabs and willed his pulse to slow. What had he done? He had acted on her behalf but belatedly wondered how this would reflect on him. Where was his neat, orderly life now?

2

Lizzy leaned forward to look out the window as they pulled up to the Remington house. Her awareness of the man sitting next to her caused her stomach to flutter. *Silly girl!* He was a kind soul helping a damsel in distress. Nothing more. Lord Phillip assisted her from the carriage and they followed Marcus and Josie to the entrance of the building. Leading her to the drawing room, Josie requested tea be brought. As Lizzy paced in front of the unlit hearth, Lord Remington moved past her to put the kindling in and strike the match to get a fire started. Phillip had gone to the sideboard for a glass of brandy and brought one for his friend.

Silence hung in the air until the tea tray arrived and the servants departed, closing the door behind them.

"I cannot stay long, my parents will miss me if I am not back before the end of the ball," said Phillip.

Lizzy stopped pacing as her heart raced. "What?"

Lord Remington went to her side to escort her to the settee next to his wife who handed her a cup of tea after quietly inquiring how she preferred hers.

"Phillip, you cannot rescue her and then abandon her here," Lady Remington protested.

"I will return once the ball is finished."

"But what is to become of me?" Lizzy whispered.

Phillip looked at Marcus. "Her father is forcing her to marry Lord Wolton against her will."

Lord Remington's eyebrows rose. He nodded. "You were kind to help her escape such a fate. But why would your father do that?"

A shudder shook Lizzy and she placed her cup and saucer on the table lest she spill it. "Wolton has some kind of hold over my father." She pulled off her gloves revealing red wrists with the marks of fingers on her pale skin.

Phillip growled. "Your father did this to you?"

Lizzy nodded.

Josie reached over to touch her arm gently above the injured area. "I'm eager to hear your story, but in due time. You may spend the night here until we can figure out how to best assist you." She glanced over at her husband who nodded in agreement.

"Phillip, I hope you realize what you're doing. We don't want to be caught interfering between a young woman and her legal guardian."

Lizzy piped up, "I am of age. I possess my own inheritance."

Phillip looked surprised. "Given that, how can your father force you to marry someone you dislike?"

Elizabeth wouldn't meet his gaze, looking down into her teacup as tears started to flow. "Trust me, he will."

Josie looked at Phillip with pleading eyes. "We shall figure this out in due time."

Lizzy pulled his handkerchief out of her reticule and used it to dab her eyes.

Lord Westcombe moved over to stand in front of her and she looked up at him. "I'm sorry I must leave. I promise you, I will return in a few hours. I could leave you in no better hands than Lord and Lady Remington's. You'll be safe here." He bowed to her and with a brief good night, he left the room to return to the Manchester ball.

~*~

Twice in one evening he had abandoned Miss Follett. It went against the grain of gentlemanly behavior. Being seen at the dance, however, would absolve him of any participation in the matter. In the end, it could possibly save her reputation and keep him from the parson's mousetrap.

The dancing was winding down and he took to the floor with another debutante. After the dance concluded he returned her to her chaperone's side and sought out his mother. Lady Manchester was short but retained her youthful figure. In spite of a few grey streaks in her light brown hair, she was still considered a beauty. Phillip tended to take after his father in looks and temperament.

"Oh, Phillip, there you are. I wondered where you had disappeared to." She tapped his arm with her fan. "Found someone you simply couldn't resist, did you? I heard the gardens were busy this evening." She giggled.

Phillip grew warm at the suggestion he'd been carrying on with a guest on his parents' property. It saddened him that she would believe something like that of him. Sometimes a past was a hard thing to live down. "You were searching for me, Mother? What can I do for you?"

"Lord Wolton was agitated earlier as the young woman he was pledged to dance with disappeared.

Lord Follett, the young lady's father, was unable to locate her. We had the withdrawing room checked and surreptitiously asked around but nobody remembers seeing her. It's as if she has vanished into thin air. I do not need to tell you that this is not the kind of notoriety we want associated with your sister's come out." She gave him a coy wink. His mother enjoyed the fact that along with being a squeeze her ball would be remembered for the disappearance of the Follett woman.

"What do you think has happened to her?" he asked, schooling his features to impassiveness.

She leaned toward him and was forced to look up as she whispered. "She is worth a fortune and has sole control of the money as of yesterday when she turned one and twenty. Rumor has it that Lord Wolton intended to marry her by Special License tomorrow." She paused and gave a shiver of disgust. "Personally, Phillip, I think the girl ran away and I couldn't blame her. I'd do the same if Wolton were my intended groom."

"If they were eager for her to wed him, why wait until she gained her majority? She no longer needs his permission for her marriage. I'm praying she is safe from that sorry end. But where would she go? Does she have relatives in town who might shelter and protect her?"

"None that I'm aware of. It troubles me. A young woman alone in this town is destined for only one thing and already her reputation is ruined by this event." Lady Remington shook her head sadly. "It's too bad, really, as she seemed to be a sweet girl and was passably pretty." Of course, she probably thought no one could ever be as beautiful as her own daughter.

Phillip listened to his mother and remained silent as he scanned the room for Lord Follett or Lord Wolton. He failed to locate them. "Where is her father and the potential bridegroom now?"

"I believe they left for the evening in an attempt to keep things quiet so when they find her they can whisk her away to the church and prevent a scandal."

"What if they fail to locate her?"

"I pray for that, Phillip, and I hope she is safe. At some point, however, she will need to access her fortune which will expose her to discovery."

"You are far too wise, Mother. Is there anything you need from me for the rest of this evening? I wouldn't mind calling it a night myself."

"Really? Phillip, you seriously cannot be thinking of going to your club or any of those other places tonight."

"No. However, I do plan to meet a friend."

"Fine. You may leave, Phillip, but remember, I expect you to accompany us to some of the balls this season to help keep an eye on a potential suitor for your sister's hand. I am counting on your support. I will send a list of entertainments I expect you to attend."

"I'll do my best, Mother." Phillip bent and gave her a kiss on the cheek. "Good night." He strode out the door and took a brisk walk to the Remington house. He wondered if Miss Follett was yet awake. He wouldn't mind seeing her again.

~*~

"Come, Elsa will help you change. You are a little taller than me but I'm sure I have a gown that will suit you for sleeping," Josie urged.

Elizabeth sank into the chair by the cheerful fireplace. "It's hopeless. There is no way out of this."

"Miss Follett…"

"Elizabeth please, or Lizzy."

"Elizabeth it is, then. A name that speaks of dignity, determination, and grace."

Lizzy looked up at that, startled. "Thank you."

"You may call me Josie. Now, what is concerning you?"

Elsa began pulling the pins out of Lizzy's hair and letting the heavy locks fall down around her shoulders. "My father has evil friends. He told me I needed to marry Wolton. I had no choice. But I'm tired of being a victim of men's schemes and debauchery."

"What *are* you talking about?"

Lizzy rose as the abigail put the pins on the dressing table and left to get a nightgown. She turned to Josie. "Maybe I can show you. Would you undo my dress?" Elizabeth turned around.

Josie rose to undo the fasteners going down the back of Elizabeth's gown. Letting it fall to the floor she pulled up the back of her chemise to reveal her back.

Josie's gasp echoed around the room.

Elizabeth walked behind a screen and finished dressing. She suspected her face was now the color of her hair.

Josie sat, mouth agape. "I'm so sorry, Elizabeth. I suspect there is much more you are not telling me."

"Yes, m'lady." Lizzy sat across from her with her head bent, awaiting condemnation from the Viscountess.

"Elizabeth, what you have endured was not your fault. It is a crime this can be done to a young woman with no one to protect her. God loves you, and Lord Remington and myself will do all in our power to protect you from further harm."

"You won't force me to leave? I am unworthy of your kindness."

"You are more than worthy. You are a precious young woman who has suffered evil. I suspect your battle will not be only one with your father and disappointed groom, but that a spiritual dimension underlies this."

"I don't understand." Lizzy folded and unfolded the handkerchief she still held, her thumb unconsciously tracing the initials embroidered in the corner.

"You've been subjected to great evil. More I'm sure than you've shared thus far. These things are not normal or in any way condoned by God. Like you, I don't understand what hold Lord Wolton has over your father that would force him to sell you in this manner. If your suspicions are correct you are destined for more of the same. I will need to share some of this with my husband, and possibly Lord Westcombe, so they can make discreet inquiries."

Lizzy panicked. "Must you?"

"I believe it is necessary if we are to protect you and give you freedom from the terror you've experienced." Josie leaned forward, put her arm on Elizabeth's, and looked her in the eye. "I want you to be free of the prison you find yourself in. Free to select a husband of your choice. Free to be all God has created you to be as a woman, a wife, and a mother someday."

"I never dared to dream that far." She hugged herself.

"I understand," said Josie kindly. "I believe it would be good for you to get some rest now. We will talk more in the morning when we can consider this with a fresh perspective as to what's to be done. By then Phillip might be able to give us information on what happened at the ball when they discovered you missing. I'm sure there was an uproar over that and his mother is relishing the notoriety it is giving her daughter's come out."

"Oh, I've ruined it for them, haven't I?"

"No. She will be in alt. Never fear. Phillip won't fail in keeping your secret. He has too much to lose by confessing anything."

"What do you mean?"

"A marriageable man kidnapping a young woman from his parents' ball? The only way he'd ever live that down would be to marry you himself."

Lizzy's heart sank. "I could never dream so high as to seek someone as fine as him for a husband."

"He is quite a figure of manhood is he not? A man of honor, as well. You can trust him. Now get some rest."

"May I keep the fire burning?"

"That's fine. I'll instruct Elsa." She rang the bell and the maid appeared.

"You've been all kindness, m'lady."

"Josie."

"Thank you, Josie."

"It is our pleasure. Sleep well and have pleasant dreams." Josie departed after giving discreet instructions to the maid.

Lizzy blew out the candles and strode to the window. She lifted the pane. Duke came to sit on the sill. "I'm well, Duke. Thank you. I'll see you on the morrow."

Duke nodded and flew off.

The windows were closed and the drapes were drawn. She settled into a chair by the fire, the vision of blue eyes and a strong chin were better dreamt of awake. *I'm in a safe place, I'll be fine.* She'd abandoned everything for safety. But in doing so she courted scandal. There was no way to save face after this. Even under the auspices of the Viscount and his wife, there was little cachet to be had as a runaway daughter of a baron. Even if she could gain her fortune, she'd expose her location. How would she live? Where would she go? Wearily she sought her bed and drifted into an uneasy sleep.

She ran away from one nightmare straight into unknown darkness with few options.

~*~

Duke flew to the top of the tree and settled in to sleep. The noise of the city made that hard. The gas lamps encroached on the darkness he was accustomed to in the country. His mistress was well. He spied the man who brought his mistress here, return. Duke bobbed his head. He'd do. Lizzy went with him willingly. She was safe and the terror he'd seen in her the past few days was momentarily gone. He could rest and wait to find out what would happen next. She wasn't clear of all danger yet. Evil lurked in the darkness and he would do anything to protect her.

Download the rest of Lord Phillip's Folly from your favourite online retailer.

ACKNOWLEDGEMENTS

It would be impossible to thank everyone who has helped me on my journey, so I apologize in advance for those I will miss. It doesn't mean you are any less valuable, and thankfully, God keeps better track of those things than I do, and His "well done, good and faithful servant" has more merit than any thanks written here.

So here it goes. Special thanks to:

Elisabeth Herman – you amaze me. Thanks for all the ways you've invested in me.

Doris Pollard Wichern – I miss you and am sad you didn't get to see this series published. Your encouragement and belief in me is still a blessing even now.

Lisa Lickel – thanks for being such a wonderful mentor, friend, and shoulder to cry on when the publishing process throws me those curve balls. I don't think I would have ever taken that first step in this journey to publication without your gentle push.

Pastor David Mundt – for your support and believing in me and the calling God has on my life.

Sally Shupe – my faithful editor. Thank you for finding all those silly errors!

Nicola Martinez – my beloved Editor-in-Chief, who continually supports my writing while allowing me the joy of helping others on their journey to publication. I'm grateful for our partnership and friendship.

ABOUT THE AUTHOR

Susan M. Baganz chases after three Hobbits, and is a native of Wisconsin. She is an Editor with Pelican Book Group specializing in bringing great romance to publication. Susan writes adventurous historical and contemporary romances with a biblical world-view.

This book is the final full-length novel in the Black Diamond Regency series. *The Baron's Blunder*, Henrietta's story, is a novella and prequel. Prior stories include: *The Virtuous Viscount, Lord Phillip's Folly, Sir Michael's Mayhem*, and *Lord Harrow's Heart*. Each stand alone but are more fun read in order A Christmas Regency, *Gabriel's Gift* released last year but is not part of the series. She is also the author of contemporary romances in the Orchard Hill Romance Series, *Pesto & Potholes, Salsa & Speed Bumps, Feta & Freeways, Root Beer & Roadblocks, Bratwurst & Bridges*, and others coming.

Susan speaks, teaches, and encourages others to follow God in being all He has created them to be. With her seminary degree in counseling psychology, a background in the field of mental health, and years serving in church ministry, she understands the complexities and pain of life as well as its craziness. She serves behind-the-scenes in various capacities at her church and is a member of American Christian Fiction Writers (ACFW), and serves on the board of the southeast chapter. Her favorite pastimes are snuggling with her dog while reading a good book or sitting with a friend chatting over a cup of spiced chai latte. Learn more by following her blog, www.susanbaganz.com, her Twitter feed @susanbaganz or her fan page: facebook.com/susanmbaganz

Thank you

We appreciate you reading this Prism title. For other Christian fiction and clean-and-wholesome stories, please visit our on-line bookstore at www.prismbookgroup.com.

For questions or more information, contact us at customer@pelicanbookgroup.com.

Prism is an imprint of
Pelican Book Group
www.PelicanBookGroup.com

Connect with Us
www.facebook.com/Pelicanbookgroup
www.twitter.com/pelicanbookgrp

To receive news and specials, subscribe to our bulletin
http://pelink.us/bulletin

May God's glory shine through
this inspirational work of fiction.

AMDG

You Can Help!

At Pelican Book Group it is our mission to entertain readers with fiction that uplifts the Gospel. It is our privilege to spend time with you awhile as you read our stories.

We believe you can help us to bring Christ into the lives of people across the globe. And you don't have to open your wallet or even leave your house!

Here are 3 simple things you can do to help us bring illuminating fiction™ to people everywhere.

1) If you enjoyed this book, write a positive review. Post it at online retailers and websites where readers gather. And share your review with us at reviews@pelicanbookgroup.com (this does give us permission to reprint your review in whole or in part.)

2) If you enjoyed this book, recommend it to a friend in person, at a book club or on social media.

3) If you have suggestions on how we can improve or expand our selection, let us know. We value your opinion. Use the contact form on our web site or e-mail us at customer@pelicanbookgroup.com

God Can Help!

Are you in need? The Almighty can do great things for you. Holy is His Name! He has mercy in every generation. He can lift up the lowly and accomplish all things. Reach out today.

Do not fear: I am with you; do not be anxious: I am your God. I will strengthen you, I will help you, I will uphold you with my victorious right hand.

~Isaiah 41:10 (NAB)

We pray daily, and we especially pray for everyone connected to Pelican Book Group—that includes you! If you have a specific need, we welcome the opportunity to pray for you. Share your needs or praise reports at http://pelink.us/pray4us

Free Book Offer

We're looking for booklovers like you to partner with us! Join our team of influencers today and periodically receive free eBooks and exclusive offers.

For more information
Visit http://pelicanbookgroup.com/booklovers

www.ingramcontent.com/pod-product-compliance
Lightning Source LLC
Chambersburg PA
CBHW021132260626
47169CB00005B/1570